Peppermint Grove

MICHELLE JACKSON

POOLBEG

Published 2013
by Poolbeg Press Ltd
123 Grange Hill, Baldoyle
Dublin 13, Ireland
E-mail: poolbeg@poolbeg.com
www.poolbeg.com

1

A catalogue record for this book is available from the British Library.

ISBN 978-1-84223-551-5

Typeset by Patricia Hope in Sabon

Printed and bound by CPI Group (UK) Ltd, Croydon, CR0 4YY

www.poolbeg.com

About the Author

Michelle Jackson is the bestselling Irish author of *One Kiss in Havana*, *Two Days in Biarritz*, *Three Nights in New York* and *4am in Las Vegas*, which have been translated into Dutch, German, Portuguese and Norwegian. In October 2010 her first non-fiction title, *What Women Know*, which she co-wrote with Dr Juliet Bressan, was published. She also contributed to the Irish Epilepsy Society's collection *The Thorn and the Rose* published in 2011. Extracts of her work have been chosen for publication by the *Irish Daily Mail*, the *Irish Independent*, the *Sunday Tribune* and various Irish women's magazines.

She is a native of Howth, County Dublin, where she lives with her husband and two children.

For further details her website is www.michellejackson.ie

Also by Michelle Jackson

One Kiss in Havana
Two Days in Biarritz
Three Nights in New York
4am in Las Vegas

Published by Poolbeg

Acknowledgements

I always say that I will keep these acknowledgements short but there are too many people to thank so here I go again . . .

As always my dedicated and encouraging publisher Paula Campbell and her wonderful team in Poolbeg have been a terrific support so yet again huge gratitude to – Kieran Devlin, Sarah Ormston, Ailbhe Hennigan, David Prendergast and editor extraordinaire Gaye Shortland. Many thanks also to Cormac Kinsella and Conor Hackett who have looked after me so well in the aftermath of publication.

To the booksellers who have been so enthusiastic and supportive of my books in every chain and branch that I have visited – many of you have become dear friends and thank you so much for bringing my books to your readers.

Big thanks to Ros and Helenka and their team at Edwards and Fuglewicz literary agency who have been tremendously supportive of my books and helped to place them around the globe.

I have been very fortunate to have a team of willing readers who coax and cajole me along the path from researching to writing and editing. My longest suffering reader Clodagh Hoey and fellow readers Wendy Buckley, Carla Clery, Tryphavana Cross, Maressa O'Brien Raleigh, Karen Hennessy and Karen Rudd do a tremendous job.

After the devastating news that my dear friends Rachel and John Proctor had decided to emigrate to Australia, I found some consolation and a world of inspiration when my family and I went to visit them in Perth. They introduced us to the most marvellous group of friends who looked after us superbly and showed us all that Perth had to offer and we are lucky now to be able to call them our friends too – thank you, Nicole and Brian, Donna and Declan, Michaela, Brett and Michelle for opening your homes to us, giving us such insights and making us feel so welcome. Many thanks also to Declan's mum Madeline Kelly who gave so much of her time telling me about old Perth. To our Irish friends who have also made Perth their home, Rob and Karen Hennessy – thanks for your company, insights and the bike!

Thank you to Andrea Leivers for contributing her name to a character in this book as part of the fundraising effort 'Authors for Japan'. Huge thanks to the fabulous Melissa Hill who so kindly endorsed *Peppermint Grove* and read it in the midst of her gruelling schedule. It is a huge thrill for me to have her name on the cover of my book.

Thanks to the wonderful writers, readers and friends who are always on Twitter, Facebook and in 3D – at launches and lunches – it's so good to be part of such a vibrant and creative community. And a massive thank-you to the mums in the Burrow National School who arrange play-dates and pickups at certain times of the year when I go around with my head in the clouds in the thick of writing and editing!

My parents Pauline and Jim Walsh are truly amazing and I can't find the words to thank them enough for everything that they have done for me.

My beautiful family Brian, Mark and Nicole made this book the most special as they trekked halfway around the world to help me write it – you keep me grounded and remind me of the things that really matter in life! I am truly blessed.

And finally massive thanks to you, the reader, and to each and every one who has written to me over the years. I couldn't continue on without your support – I hope that *Peppy Grove*, as I have affectionately come to call it, doesn't disappoint!

P.S. Happy Birthday, Richie – hope you like your character ;)

This novel is dedicated to the Irish Diaspora and all who have friends and loved ones living abroad

Prologue

Perth, Western Australia
Autumn 1976

Angela put the last of Kevin's clothes into the small brown suitcase. She clicked the fastener closed and sat down on the bed, feeling a gentle kick from her unborn child. She was not sure if she was doing the right or wrong thing by her children but taking them back to Ireland seemed like her only choice. Fred could follow if he wished. Her husband loved this town and revelled in the new life that they had made here. But for Angela the squawking crows reminded her of a baby crying and she longed for the sweet sharp thrill of the sparrow and the thrush. When she put her nose to the bright pink roses in her garden, they just didn't have the same scent as the ones in her mother's garden back in Dublin. Yet she would leave this place with a stone in her heart and a sickness in her stomach.

Fred entered the room. He stared first at her and then at the small brown suitcase.

"So you are really going then?"

"I told you that I was," she replied, tight-lipped and looking straight ahead at the empty wall.

"Where will you stay?"

She pursed her lips.

"With your mother, I suppose?" he answered for her.

She shrugged. "Or maybe with my sister. I don't care. I have to get out of this place."

"I think you're being very cruel, Angela – I need to be with my son – Kevin needs me."

"He never sees you – if you aren't at work you're at the pub. You don't need your family."

"My family is the very reason why we made the move to this country – a fresh start! It's been good for us, Angela – I've plenty of work – you don't want for anything."

"What would you know?" she sighed. "You're never here."

She stood up and looked her husband hard in the eyes.

"Our plane leaves in three hours."

Chapter One

Ruth just had to tell Julia her news. It was a big step but she was sure that her best friend would be pleased. She was driving back from dinner with her boyfriend and was disappointed with his reaction but she could rely on Julia to always listen and be there for her.

"Julia, it's me!"

Julia was sitting up in bed. She had taken work home and was sorting out her priorities for the Travel Show she would be visiting in London in two weeks' time. But she always liked to take a call from her best friend.

"Hiya, Ruth – how are you?"

"Julia – I've done it – I'm taking the plunge!"

Julia couldn't believe her ears. Had her friend finally seen sense – was she going to finish her disastrous relationship with her villainous boyfriend of ten years?

"Oh, well done, Ruth – I'm so glad to hear that you've made the break – you know that it's the right thing to do."

"I just walked into the office this evening and said it straight out – he was so shocked."

Julia had to think twice. "What was Ian doing in your office?"

"Not *Ian*, silly – Oliver! I told him where he could stick his

3

job! Said I'm sick of working for a brute who expects his staff to work until seven o'clock every day – and work weekends!"

Julia bit the side of her cheek and closed her eyes. It had been too good to be true. The four hours spent with Ruth the night before had all been in vain. She was pleased that her friend was freed finally from her painful employment but this wasn't the news that she wanted to hear. Ruth needed to see real sense and, although Oliver was a slimy creep, at least he wasn't sleeping with her. She felt a lecture coming on but wondered if this was the right time for it.

"I'm pleased that you are out of that place, Ruth, but what are you going to live on? If you walked out you won't get redundancy or the dole, you know!"

Silence at the other end of the line.

"Oh, I hadn't thought of that," Ruth said sheepishly.

Julia had to think quickly. She really needed to give her friend a boost but up to now had put off offering her a job as she didn't want to cross the boundary of their friendship. It would be changed forever and maybe even damaged if Julia became her boss. But Julia was well connected in the travel business and only this morning had heard of a wonderful opportunity with Tourism Ireland, working out of Australia. It was a two-year contract and would suit Ruth to a tee with her marketing experience. She really needed to do something drastic to rescue Ruth – but this job was something that she was reluctant to suggest as it would mean putting such a distance between herself and her best friend. But lately Julia had said goodbye to so many friends who had to move away for work to the far corners of the world. It was becoming a sad fact of life in Ireland that the emigration drum was sounding again as it had done for her parents once upon a time and her eldest brother Michael who now resided in Singapore.

"Ruth, I have just the job for you – you would love it so much – working for Tourism Ireland promoting Ireland abroad."

"Oh Julia, I don't want to be travelling all the time – you know Oliver had me running around and never gave me my correct days off."

"It wouldn't be like that at all – you would be in the one place. The job is in Australia."

Silence and shock from the other end of the line.

Julia spoke gently. "Ruth – you must have thought of it at one time or another – it really wouldn't do you any harm to go abroad for a while."

"B-b-but what about Ian?"

Julia took a deep breath – she didn't want to say what she thought about Ian Hawkins.

"What about your career, Ruth? Think of the great opportunity. I can call my contact in Tourism Ireland and set up a meeting for you next week – it's just what you need."

"I'm not sure, Julia – I mean, what about my mum and dad? I can't leave them."

"Your mum and dad are well. Your mum missed you at first when you moved out but she has got used to it. I bet they would love to come and see you in Australia!"

"B-b-but I can't just go – I'm thirty-four!"

"What's that got to do with it?"

"I'm too old."

Julia was beginning to lose patience. Ruth should realise by now that Julia knew what was best for her.

"I'll call you tomorrow, Ruth. Okay?"

Ruth sniffed down the phone and hung up. She knew her friend well enough by now not to push the point. She got out of her car and turned the key in the door of her apartment in Clontarf. It was nice but she missed the warmth and cosiness of her home in Sutton Park. She had moved out because she needed a place where she and Ian could meet away from the watchful eyes of her mother. But since her younger brother, Niall, had moved out five months ago to get married, her mother had been asking if she would consider coming home again. If it wasn't for Ian she would definitely move back there.

There was a lot that she would have done with her life if it wasn't for Ian. November was the hardest month of the year – all the build-up to Christmas would be upon her in a couple of weeks, reminding her that she would be spending another special time of year without a partner of her own. Her parents wanted her to go with them down to Kerry where her older brother Kevin lived with his wife and two children. Niall would be going to his new wife's family and for the first time she realised that she could possibly be totally on her own with her parents this year.

She turned on the light in the kitchen and the fluorescent bulb flickered. It was on the way out – how would she change it? She'd have to wait until Ian came around – although he probably wouldn't know what to do either. He employed a local DIY man to do all the handiwork around his palatial residence at the end of a cul-de-sac on the south side of the city.

She pulled out the chair from under the kitchen table and sat on it. The seat was cold and even the cushion didn't soften the hardness of the wood. Everything seemed amplified this evening. The coldness, the emptiness and the loneliness. She wondered why Julia never commented on these moods and emotions – surely she felt them every now and then? She never mentioned that she was feeling older or longing for a partner. Ruth felt lucky that at least she had Ian. But Julia never spent an evening completely alone – her kookie granddad and bridge-playing mother were always knocking about her house. The emptiness of the apartment echoed as she breathed out loud, amplifying her seclusion. This was not what she had planned for her future.

It made her consider Julia's offer more carefully. Especially now that she wasn't sure if she would be able to pay next month's rent. Her landlord had the deposit so that would give her a few weeks to work something out. She could go back to Sutton Park.

Suddenly her phone rang. It was Ian.

"Hey there," she smiled into the phone.

"Ruth, I have to go on an overnight tomorrow – I forgot one of the lads asked me to change – and I've Lisa's birthday party on Sunday so we won't be able to go to Johnny Fox's for the afternoon – I'm sorry."

She had only left him half an hour earlier – why hadn't he told her then? He was making even more changes to their plans in recent months and at times she wondered if he was seeing someone else.

"But you promised that you would stay with me – it's been nearly two weeks!"

"I'm sorry, kitten – you know I want to be with you but the airline is really tightening the pilots' belts – they have put me on four Paris runs back to back this Saturday."

Ruth knew well how it felt to be the understanding partner, following whatever Ian's needs were, but right now she was the one traumatised after walking out on her job and for once she wanted him to comfort her. He had finished up in the restaurant without dessert, pretending to be interested when she disclosed all that had happened earlier with Oliver.

"I really wanted to have some time with you this weekend. I know that it's Lisa's birthday, but what about me?"

Ian huffed down the phone. "I am doing the very best that I can, Ruth – you know that I have the children to think about – they are the innocent ones in all of this."

Ruth bit her lip – he had a knack of making her feel bad when in fact *she* was the injured party. Julia had coached her on this matter: *Tell him that the children were not in the equation when you met. Tell him that he was the one who made the decision to have children.* But Ian had wangled his way out of the responsibility for bringing his children into the world. He had blamed a burst condom for the conception of his first child, Lisa, and said that his wife, Ciara, had tricked him into believing that she was on the pill for the birth of the twins.

Julia had rolled her eyes and tut-tutted when she heard his excuses but Ruth had believed him.

Lately, however, Ruth was finding it more difficult to believe the words out of his mouth. He had been promoted to captain two years ago and was now even more cocky and sure of himself than he had been when they'd met.

"Look, do what you've got to do," she sighed. "I'll talk to you after the weekend."

"Good girl, kitten – sweet dreams."

As he hung up the tears started to stream down Ruth's cheeks and she felt a deep desire to do something radical. She really wanted to call Julia again but she would pour herself a glass of wine first and think about what she should do.

Julia was only twenty-four when she first dabbled in matchmaking. It was a resounding success, leading to the marriage of her sister Odette and the gorgeous Craig Fagan, and had led her to believe that she had a natural gift. Ruth was with her at the time. It was regrettably the same evening that Ruth met Ian Hawkins but Julia liked to dismiss the fact that the two matches coincided.

Julia loved to be the life and soul of the party. Her sister Odette was the complete opposite and was naturally reserved – especially in the company of strangers.

It was a dull dank evening in February when Julia had coaxed Odette to join her in Gibneys pub in Malahide where she was meeting a crowd of friends who worked at Dublin airport. Julia had been to school with a couple of the girls who were now flying for the national airline – they had tried to coax Julia to join with them but she was adamant that she wanted to be her own boss.

Julia was very protective of her sister, which was unusual as she was three years younger than Odette. But Odette was recently out of a five-year relationship with an engineer she had met while in college in UCD. Odette had thought they would be getting engaged that Christmas. Instead he announced in the New Year that he was taking a job in Germany and Odette wasn't part of his plans.

Odette was naïve and really only longed for a simple life. Having studied Arts, she was in her third year working for Fingal County Council and longed for the security and safety that a happy marriage would bring. Julia thought that Odette was selling herself short – but that was her choice.

Julia didn't waste time that evening in Gibneys. Craig was an ambitious and steady employee of the national airline and at twenty-nine had been already promoted to a senior position in the finance department. Julia had spent two hours grilling him the week before and all her friends thought that she was interested in him for herself. But that wasn't Julia's intention at all. She organised for her sister to be there with her and, within seconds of arriving, had manoeuvred things so that Odette was sitting next to Craig. Her lack of subtlety hadn't put Craig off and the pretty Odette was instantly attracted to the tall accountant with the strong handsome features.

Eighteen months later Julia was dressed in a cerise-pink cupcake bridesmaid's gown – but she considered it a small price to pay for her sister's happiness.

Ruth's situation, however, was not as easy to remedy. Ian Hawkins was engaged when he met Ruth. And he was married eighteen months later. Her friend of sixteen years was receiving calls from her boyfriend while he was on his honeymoon in Kenya. Ian also worked on the airlines – he was a first officer on a 737 and fancied himself as a smooth operator.

Julia made no apologies for the abrupt way that she always spoke to him. She didn't like his style and she didn't like the way that he used her friend. But, instead of being embarrassed, Ian enjoyed the fact that she was party to his affair with Ruth and was thrilled by Julia's eye-rolls and sharp quips. He had no difficulty organising time away from his bride – filling in several empty roster-sheets with flights that he would never take. His poor beleaguered wife would be none the wiser ten years and three children later.

Julia couldn't understand how her kind and thoughtful friend Ruth was able to shut off her lover's family from her world and run her life as if she was as important in Ian's as he was in hers.

Meanwhile Julia remained single, which wasn't easy as she enthralled men with her soft brunette curls that rested on her shoulders and her dark brown eyes, such a contrast to the aqua blue of her sister's. Of the two, Odette was the more natural beauty but she didn't have the stunning attractiveness of her younger sister whose brown eyes sparkled with mischief and glared with contempt on command.

The only romantic liaisons that Julia would consider were

with foreign men visiting Dublin or if she was away in another country herself. The affairs all had a common pattern which involved a broken heart on the part of the men and Julia delving deeper into her work to distract her from any passion she might have felt. It was much better that way and Julia always came out in control of her emotions and the relationship. She had never had to experience a lover telling her that it was over or that it wasn't working. Instead she remained a mystery.

There was only one boy who had touched her heart, many years before when she was only sixteen. Richard Clery was the heart-throb of the local boys' school – with translucent blue eyes and dark-brown curls. He rode a motor bike to school and every day Julia would walk to Keogh's shop at Sutton Cross and wait for him to pass by and wave. It was at the rugby club disco in the year that she sat her Leaving Certificate that she finally kissed him. He didn't disappoint and their courtship lasted three months. He bought her a bike helmet and took her on trips to Wicklow and Skerries. Then one day out of the blue he announced that he was leaving school and going to work on a cargo ship – he wanted to see the world. Julia never saw him again and sometimes when she allowed her thoughts to run free at night she wondered where he was now.

This was one of those nights.

Julia looked at the alarm clock beside her bed. It was twelve fifteen and she was wide awake. She pulled on her dressing gown and went downstairs to get a cold drink. The tapping of keys on a laptop came from the front room and she peeked in to see her mother engrossed before the screen.

"Hi, Mum – you're up late."

"I'm playing with Omar in Spain and Ellen in Amsterdam – it isn't often that we can co-ordinate to be on at the same time now that Omar is working in a bar."

Julia's mother amazed her. Five years ago she wouldn't have been able to switch on a computer – she was now playing bridge internationally with her new friends from all over the globe.

"Would you like a drink of something? I'm getting some carrot juice."

Without looking up, Carol answered, "Nothing for me, thanks – we're taking a tea break in fifteen minutes and then I'll skype Ellen for a chat."

Julia felt very left out – her mother was available for a chat with a complete stranger in Amsterdam but couldn't say two words to her own daughter who was in the living room in front of her. She went into the kitchen and poured herself a tall glass of juice. She went back to her bedroom and was trying to focus on what she had to do the next day when her phone rang. She knew who would be at the other end of the line.

"Ju-u-lia," the voice babbled at the other end of the line, "I d-d-don't think I can take it any more!"

"Ruth – what's happened now?"

Julia was in her element – straight down to fix-it mode no matter what the hour.

"It's Ian."

Naturally. Who else would have her friend in such a state?

"What's he done?"

"I think he's seeing someone else."

Julia was so close to saying 'Yes, you're right – his wife' but she held back this once. Ruth was too upset.

"Why do you think that?"

"Because he said that he's changed his roster and he only ever does that to see me – I feel like the other woman."

Julia tried hard to be kind but rational thinking was taking over.

"Ruth, I hate seeing you so hurt all of the time and you have been through so much with Oliver who was a complete bully – Ian should have been there for you tonight. Do you think maybe that he just wants you to soothe and comfort *him* but, now that you need help, he isn't there for you?"

Silence at the other end of the line told Julia that she had said enough. She had to be gentle with Ruth who was used to getting knocks from Ian but needed Julia for support.

"Okay," Ruth said reluctantly. "I take your point. So what can I do?"

"You can finish with him."

"I'm too weak – you know that!"

"Ruth, my dear friend – I have known you since you were eight and I can tell you here and now that you can do anything that you want. You must end it with Ian – the relationship has become toxic."

Ruth started to howl on the other end of the line.

"Please, Ruth," Julia begged, "I only want what's best for you. Will I ring Tourism Ireland in the morning? If you aren't strong enough to end it with him in Dublin maybe you should consider getting away – out of sight is out of mind!"

Ruth howled even louder.

"I'm sorry, Ruth – look, come in to my office tomorrow – I'm there all day – we need to get you sorted."

"Okay, Julia, thanks – I'm all over the place."

Everything was falling in on her friend and Julia hated to see it. She would do her best to fix her, now that she was ready to get help.

Julia took a sip from her glass of juice. From downstairs she could hear her mother cackle on Skype to her new friend in Holland. Her mother had found a new lease of life after her husband had died. That was a traumatic time. Julia's father was a builder who would never wear a hard hat and that was to his cost as a JCB digger struck him on the side of his head one day during a routine check of a building development. Julia often cursed the property boom for causing his death but the truth was that she couldn't blame anyone but himself for his carelessness – and, at the end of the day, it was an unfortunate accident and only one of many that happened where buildings were under construction.

Her mother had been a very quiet and demure woman always – totally needy and dependant on her husband to do everything for her. But that was not the case any longer. After his death, Carol had become a marvel in matters of finance and organising the house in the way that she wanted. Her departure into technology was another change and she was now not only playing bridge on the computer but booking flights and accommodation for weekends away with the bridge club. She learnt to drive within weeks of her husband's untimely death and was now also helping the 'old people' on a Friday with Meals on Wheels. Sometimes Julia wondered if her mother would still be an avid fan of *Coronation Street* and afraid to drive if her father was still around.

Carol's father Horatio moved in with the family after the death. Julia enjoyed her grandfather living with them. He appreciated his helpful granddaughter. He had been a watchmaker by trade and spent several hours every day tinkering with the old clocks and timepieces that people brought him to fix.

Julia loved to hear his stories about the old days and what her parents were like when they were younger. She had made it her mission to start a family tree before the year was out. Her grandfather was eighty-seven and, although his brain was sprightly, she worried about his cough and wheezing chest. She was the keeper of the family and would do what was best for every member – her sister and brother, mother and grandfather. She was equally busy taking care of her friends and employees.

As she bit into her dressed cracker, she smiled smugly to herself. Life was good – she had plenty to do and plenty around her to care for. Top of the agenda was fixing Ruth and it was time to move drastically.

Chapter Two

Odette stumbled in through the doors of Perrin Travel laden with shopping bags.

Gillian, the new receptionist, looked up and smiled.

"Hello, can I help you?"

"Yes, I'm Julia's sister and I was wondering if she is here?"

"Oh, of course," the mousy receptionist said, flustered on learning who the visitor was. She put the phone up to her ear and rang for Julia. "Your sister is here." She paused and hung up. "She says go on into her office."

"Thank you," Odette said.

Julia had done well for herself and she was still only thirty-four years old. Her office was in a prime location only a few metres from College Green and, even though it was her father who had bought the lease originally, Julia had taken it over eight years before under her own steam – she was only in her twenties at that time and Odette admired the drive and vision that her younger sister showed and wished that she had a piece of it herself.

Julia rushed to open the door to her sister. She took some bags from her and gave her a kiss on the cheek.

"What a nice surprise! I didn't expect to see you in town."

Odette plopped down on the chair and smiled at her sister. "I don't have to pick the kids up today – they have after-school activities so I thought I'd catch up on a bit of Christmas shopping."

"But it's only November the eighteenth!"

"I know but I want to be organised this year."

Julia watched her frazzled sister peel off her coat and cardigan.

"It's hot in here," Odette sighed.

"I like the clients to be warm and cosy when they're booking their holidays. You look like you could do with a break – is suburbia getting to you?"

"Oh, you sound like Mum – she wants me to go to the Christmas markets in Cologne with her – apparently she has some Dutch friend who she's meeting there in December."

"Oh!" Julia was disappointed that her mother hadn't invited her. She wouldn't have gone of course because someone would have to stay with her granddad but it would have been nice to be asked.

"Don't mind me – Craig is working very long hours – they've whittled his department down to eleven people. How you can just let thirty staff go like that is beyond me. I only get to talk to him on a Friday night these days – then he's off with Jamie and his football team on a Saturday and cycling with his friends in the afternoon. If we go out on a Saturday night it's with friends. After Sunday dinner he sits in front of the fire and then the week starts all over again!"

"But you have your lovely kids!"

Julia wondered what was really up with her sister that she wasn't telling her. She didn't have to wait long to find out.

"I want to have another baby!" Odette blurted out, bursting into tears.

Julia jumped up and went over to console her sister. She handed her a tissue to mop up the tears.

"I don't really know what's wrong with me any more – I should be the happiest woman alive – I've a perfect little son and daughter and Craig is a good husband but I get so frustrated sometimes that I want to scream."

Julia was in new territory.

"And do you think having another baby is going to change that?"

"Jamie is getting so independent and he's only eight – he made his own breakfast and lunch for school yesterday. Charlotte is only five and she told me that she hated me yesterday and that I was the worst mother in the world." Odette sobbed harder. "I wish they were babies again and really needed me."

Julia was knocked for six. She had never seen her sister like this before. She really needed to talk to her in greater detail about how she felt. She wasn't dressed as perkily as she normally would be which made Julia wonder if she was slightly depressed. But what had she to be depressed about? She would find out.

"Put your coat on, we're going for a nice lunch."

Odette blinked back the tears and looked up at her sister. "Thanks, Julia."

Julia felt so loved and needed. She would take her sister to a lovely little deli on Wicklow Street and fix her!

Ruth was the second caller to Julia's office – she arrived just before five o'clock.

"Can I see Julia, Gillian?" she asked the receptionist.

"Yes, I'll call her now."

Gillian spoke with Julia – then told Ruth to go ahead.

Julia was putting the last details of her summer brochure to rest and had recently introduced cruises into the catalogue.

"Hi, Ruth," she said, signing off the last few samples and getting up to give her friend a hug. "Did Tourism Ireland call you?"

Ruth nodded. "Thanks so much, Julia. I can't believe how well connected you are – well, actually, I can believe it – but I have an interview next week."

"Good!" Julia smiled smugly. "And any word from Ian?"

Ruth quickly changed the subject. "And I need help finding something to wear for the interview."

Julia looked at her phone. Almost five – she could go. She had done a good day's work in the office and she had time to spare as this was Carol's bridge night (bridge night *out*, that is) and her grandfather liked to just get a Chinese for himself.

"Right, we're taking a walk around Grafton Street."

"Great – I don't know where to start!"

"River Island – if we don't get fixed up there we can try BT's. Fancy a bite to eat after?"

"Oh yes." Ruth smiled – she felt so much better now that Julia was there to sort her out.

Chapter Three

Seven o'clock in Singapore. Michael turned over in his bed and sighed. He could go to the gym before work or he could think about her! Against his better instinct he closed his eyes and pictured the lovely Lydia. With her straight blonde hair and sparkling blue eyes, people often mistook her for a Swede. But she was very much an Irish girl and one who knew how to light up a room with her presence. She was clever and witty and intelligent and why he had never asked her to marry him baffled him. He would be forty soon and was beginning to wonder what he was doing with his life. He had ridden the Celtic Tiger for the first half of the noughties and split as things went sour in the economy. Coming to Singapore had been a good decision – he now owned his apartment in Sutton and could live there if and when he decided to return to Dublin. But the last two years had felt shallow and were now at the point of becoming monotonous. It wasn't too late to call Julia. She would throw some light on his situation and help him clear his head.

"Hey, sis," he called into the laptop.

Her Skype clicked on.

"Michael!" Julia was surprised. She loved the fact that she could see his face as she spoke with him even though he was on the other side of the world.

"I'm thinking of coming home for a holiday soon."

"But it's so near Christmas – can't you come home for that?"

"It's not easy – not a Christian country over here – you know that."

"But I thought by now you would get the time – Mum would love to see you sooner though . . . ' She paused. "Actually cancel that – Mum doesn't seem to have time for anyone at the moment unless they play bridge!"

Michael laughed. "How's Granddad?"

"Good – he's thinking of taking up painting – there's a course in the local community centre."

"That pair are a hoot – they are well able to look after themselves – why don't you get a place of your own?"

"That's all very well for you to say, Michael, but what if Granddad fell out of the bed or Mum needed something done around the house that she couldn't manage?"

Michael laughed louder. "Mum and Granddad are in their own little world. Anyway, have you any nice friends that would suit me?"

"I'm giving up on you, brother dear – after you blew it with Lydia I've decided not to waste my matchmaking skills. When are you going to settle down and stop messing around with so many women?"

"Oh, don't do that," he sighed. "You haven't heard from Lydia, have you, by any chance?"

"Of course I have. She's doing well and has met a new man according to our last conversation."

Michael sat up in the bed with the shock. "But she only finished with that other guy a couple of months ago!"

"Yes, but she's a pretty girl and she's thirty-five. She's keen to get settled down."

"Oh," said Michael, uttered dejectedly. He was stupid to think that she had any feelings for him any more. "I don't suppose you'll see her again soon?"

"I've no plans – but we'll meet up before Christmas, I'm sure. Why all this sudden interest in Lydia again? You've got quite a history, you two, and the scars are so deep I doubt she's going to go there again!"

Michael realised that his sister was probably right but he didn't want to think that he would never be with Lydia ever again.

"Look," he said, "I was thinking of dropping a line and seeing how she was."

"I wouldn't do that – I mean, she's deleted you from her Facebook friends since the last time."

Michael was well aware of that. "But I can still see her photos when I look her up through your page."

"Don't do this to yourself, Michael – she has moved on and I thought you had too?"

Julia knew her brother too well and she wondered what was making him feel this way.

"I'll see about leave for Christmas then – I'll try to come home as close to it as I can."

"That would be nice for Mum and Granddad, and for me too!"

"How's Odette?"

"She wants another baby and I'm talking to her about it – Craig's working hard and she's feeling neglected and I've a feeling she thinks another baby is going to fill the gap."

"Maybe she just wants another child?"

Julia tut-tutted down the phone. "It's never that simple – there's a reason for everything and I know her too well. I'll keep you posted though. Anyway, I'm really tired – I went shopping with Ruth and got her a nice suit for her interview next week."

"Why is she changing job?"

"Her boss was a bully and a brute – I've suggested a job in Perth."

"Scotland?"

"No, silly – Perth, Australia!"

"Well, she'll have plenty of company there – half of the city is Irish at this stage!"

"I think the change will do her good."

Michael didn't dispute that.

"Okay, sis – I'll let you get to bed. If you've any suggestions about Lydia, though, let me know – I would like to see her again."

"I'm not allowing you to mess her around."

"I wouldn't be – I've changed – I miss her."

"Well, make sure you know how you really do feel – I'm not doing your dirty work to find you've decided you don't want her after all. You can't do that a third time, Michael – it wouldn't be fair!"

"I know that, sis – I'm forty years of age – I'm getting on and don't want to spend the rest of my life alone."

"You will always have some woman at your side."

"I don't want just any woman," Michael sighed. "I want *the* woman!"

"And why have you suddenly decided that Lydia is *the* woman?"

Michael paused, wanting to give the right answer.

"I just know that I have never been happier than when I was with her."

Julia loved her brother madly but she knew what a cad he was when it came to breaking women's hearts – he was a total charmer and unremorseful in most cases. But he was family.

"And what about Nikki? I thought she was *the* one last time you were home?"

"She was too needy, Julia – even you said that!"

"Yes, but that was partly your fault for chatting about your legion of female friends in Singapore!"

Michael paused for a moment and then very quietly said, "You know that I really loved Lydia . . ."

"Leave it with me – let me think about it!"

"You're a star, Julia!" he said with gratitude in his voice. "I knew I could depend on you. Love you to bits."

"Okay then, go before I change my mind – I'll drop you an email later."

"Bye, sis."

"Bye."

Julia made her way over to the fridge and took out some milk for her tea.

Suddenly the front door slammed and her mother appeared in the kitchen. She bounced over in the direction of the kettle and put it on.

"Oh, I could smell Granddad's Chinese from the hall. Is he in bed?"

"Yes, how was bridge?"

"Very good," her mother said lightly. "Are you having tea?"

"Yes – I'll make it!"

Julia took out the tea bags and made them both a brew.

"I've just been on to Michael – he might come over early in December – doesn't think he'll get back for Christmas."

"Oh, that is a shame," her mother said, taking her mug of tea in her hands. "I hope he doesn't come while I'm at the Christmas Market in Germany."

It was Julia's chance to quiz her mother. "Odette told me that you had plans – I didn't know!"

"Did I forget to say it? I'm sorry, Julia – I thought you would probably be busy with work and, well, you might mind Granddad?"

"Of course I can mind Granddad. That sounds like a lovely trip."

"I can't wait! Right, I'm off to bed. Goodnight, love!"

With her mug in hand Carol was gone.

Julia really was happy for her mother but would like to have more interaction with her. Did she realise how addicted she was to bridge? If she wasn't playing it with the bridge club she was playing it virtually or meeting people that played bridge. She would have a word with Granddad the next day and see what his views were on the subject. She took her mug, turned off the lights and made her way up the stairs to bed. Her bedroom was a haven of peace and tranquillity, painted a warm peach with a cream carpet that her feet sank into as she walked. Parked against the wall was a king-size mahogany sleigh bed with cream satin duvet covers. She lit the tea lights on her antique dressing table and they sparkled against the huge oval mirror. It was style from another time but Julia loved vintage furniture – a trait she'd inherited from her father. She missed him sorely and every night before she went to sleep she said a prayer to him. She had been Daddy's little girl and the two used to be the driving force in the family. But, since his passing, the dynamic of the family had changed so much that she felt herself flounder sometimes and wondered how things would be if he was still around. The first thing that came to her mind the day that she heard that he was tragically killed was the realisation that he would not be there to take her down the aisle. Once she realised this, a switch flipped in her consciousness: now that he was gone she wouldn't need to be walked down the aisle. It had been a slim enough chance that she would find someone that would match up to her father but since his passing she had realised that day would never come – she would never meet anyone who could hold a candle to him. And after five years she was pleased that she had saved herself a lot of heartache and could continue her life without a man.

Chapter Four

Michael woke in a sweat. The humidity from outside had seeped through the open window and left him parched. It was six o'clock and sweltering hot – like most mornings in Singapore but especially during this time of year. He hit the switch on his air-con – the room would resemble a freezer in ten minutes. Lydia came into his head again. This was the fourth morning in a row that she had done so. It was six years since he had let her go – so why was she such a hauntingly permanent fixture in his life? Their history had started with a blind date – organised by Julia of course. It was while Julia and Lydia were in college together in UCD and Lydia complained that she wanted a bit of excitement in her life. Lydia being the complete opposite of Michael, Julia felt that he would show her friend how to have a good time but that there would be no love lost. She was surprised at how well the two hit it off and they became besotted with each other for six months – which was something of a record by Michael's standards.

However, Lydia was only twenty-one and Michael twenty-six and the passion that Michael was feeling scared him and he finished with her abruptly. It wasn't until four years later when she was dating a fellow apprentice in KBMD that Michael started to ask about Lydia again. Julia was reluctant this time and grudgingly set up a meeting. The apprentice got the flick and Michael and Lydia settled down to a tempestuous relationship that lasted four years. Everyone thought that they would soon announce their engagement and Michael was on the verge of proposing when he had a moment of weakness with a nurse in Buck Mulligan's at his friend's birthday party. One of his friends told his girlfriend who felt it her duty to spread the wicked news of his deed. If Michael had denied it Lydia would have been happy to believe him. But he told her that he did snog the nurse and that he didn't know her name and that it didn't mean anything. Lydia was distraught and worried that she could never trust him again. No amount of pleading and begging on his part would convince her otherwise. She broke off the relationship and went out that weekend with her friends – when she bumped into Michael at another venue on Lesson Street she saw him do it again and this time with her own eyes. Even Michael couldn't recall what the girl looked like – he was more upset than he would ever admit to a soul about the break-up of his relationship with Lydia and was trying to get comfort wherever. Lydia couldn't get over seeing him in the arms of another woman and insisted that she would never take him back. Over the next few months Michael spent every weekend with a different girl. Julia did whatever she could to take Lydia's mind off her brother but she knew how much she was hurt.

When Michael announced that he was leaving for Singapore, Julia told Lydia very gently one day and was amazed at how she took the news with no emotion or reaction. Lydia had shut him off and, as far as Julia was concerned and even though she knew they had corresponded briefly through Facebook, there was no hope they would ever be an item again. She had made her views perfectly clear to Michael but this only made him think of Lydia all the more.

"You always want what you cannot have!" Julia had berated him.

Michael realised that she was correct but at certain times of the year – especially coming up to Christmas – he thought of her even more.

Although it didn't feel very Christmassy as the beads of sweat fell from his brow in Singapore.

Ruth needed to feel good about the massive move that she might make. She wondered what her mother's opinion might be. Angela had spoken very little about the time she had spent in Perth when her brother Kevin was a little boy. Ruth knew that her father had loved Australia and only came back to Dublin after she was born. It was a chapter in her family's life that she had never been interested in finding out about – until now.

Alone in her apartment on a dark and windy November evening she decided to surf the Internet and see what her new home might look like if she was successful in her interview. Google Images was the best place to start and she typed the word 'Perth' into the search engine. Immediately dozens of images sprang up of a glittering skyline with skyscrapers reflected on the Swan River. An image of a girl and a bicycle parked at the water's edge with a perfect blue sky and the backdrop of the towers made her smile. She used to cycle as a little girl – it made her feel free and like all children she loved it. She could see herself living a healthy lifestyle in the sunshine with great hope for the future. It wasn't as if she would be leaving a lot behind – at the moment there were very few positives in her life. She wondered if Ian would be upset about her leaving but, ultimately, apart from the odd night that he spent at her apartment and the few occasions that they met in discreet locations, his life wouldn't change much. Realising this had had a massive impact on her self-esteem and made her feel like a shadow – an invisible partner in a relationship that was unbalanced and going nowhere.

She could feel a choking sensation in her throat and decided to press on and look at more images to take away these feelings. She came across a postcard image of rocks standing erect on what looked like a massive desert. They were shaped like bishops' mitres, a stark contrast to the vibrant blue of the sky behind. She hovered the cursor over them and found out that they were called 'pinnacle rocks'. She would love to see them. They were unlike any natural phenomenon in Ireland. It made her wonder what other wonderful things she would see in this new continent that was so far away from her home.

She flicked through more images. The beaches were stunning with long stretches of white sand contrasted against the deep blue and aquamarine hues of the Indian Ocean. Cottesloe Beach, whale-watching, zoos filled with marsupials were all things to be explored in Australia and she felt butterflies flit in her stomach. This was the fresh start that she needed. And as the wind howled outside her window she hoped and wished that she would be offered the job in Perth. She was ready to take on a fresh start and an adventure that would bring untold surprises

Chapter Five

Julia was concerned about Odette – she hadn't been herself at all on Friday. At least she would be able to observe her sister later when she went to Sunday lunch in Malahide.

Odette and her husband lived in Seapark – a well-located comfortable family home close to the beautiful suburban village. It was one of the older developments but Odette and Craig had gutted their house and turned it into a haven stylish enough for the pages of a magazine. Craig hadn't gone wild investing in shares during the boom but their refurbishment had put them back to square one with their mortgage and they had bought an investment apartment in Swords that was now difficult to let. At the time Odette felt that they were missing the boat as they watched their friends leaving the estate and moving to fancier new housing developments that cost millions of euros but she was grateful now as their repayments remained hefty each month and he was concerned about losing his job.

Julia jumped into her Audi and put the bottles of wine and chocolates on the passenger seat. She had tried to coax her mother to join her but she was shopping for a new case for her travels to Cologne.

Granddad had turned down her offer of a lift to Odette's. "Your grandmother always made such a fuss on Sundays that now I like to have them to myself!" he assured Julia as she walked out the door.

As she pulled up in front of the house, she saw a Mercedes convertible parked there. It could mean only one thing and she hoped that the owner would not be staying for lunch.

The silhouette of a tall broad figure filled the glass panels. Dylan answered the door. He leaned forward, expecting a peck on his cheek, but an air-kiss was as much as he got.

"Julia, how nice to see you again!" he said in cool low tone.

"I didn't know that you were going to be here!" she exclaimed, taking off her coat and placing it at the end of the banisters.

"That's a lovely welcome for your brother-in-law!"

"You are my sister's brother-in-law but *we*, I am pleased to say, are not related!"

"Better put the smile on before we go in to the Brady Bunch," Dylan quipped. "They're in the front room."

How Craig's brother infuriated Julia! He was always so smart and chirpy in such a condescending manner. Odette assured her that he didn't behave this way normally and it was an effect that Julia had on him.

Odette unloaded the clean cutlery and crockery from the dishwasher. She felt so lonely in the kitchen now. Craig was upstairs putting the children to bed. She would never have believed that it was possible to feel lonely in a house with a husband and two beautiful children – but she did. She wasn't able to speak with Craig about things that mattered any more. He was usually grumpy when he came in from work. The presence of her sister and his brother earlier had diverted the discomfort between them for a while but when they left the peculiar ennui that had settled between husband and wife for the past two years had returned.

She wanted another baby – she was sure that she did. However, she was well aware that she needed to be having sex in order for that to happen. The truth was that Craig hadn't touched her once over the last six months.

It was probably her fault to start – her way of punishing him for not wanting a baby. She would never have believed that she would use sex as a weapon – she had read about women doing it in *Cosmopolitan* and similar magazines and she had laughed, thinking she would never be like that. She tried to think back to when her life had become humdrum. Why couldn't she be happy? She had so much to be thankful for and yet she was miserable. Maybe it was the long hours that Craig worked – maybe it was the competition of the mothers at the school – maybe it was the fact that she had never travelled or had adventure in her life. She had never wanted adventure but now she was feeling unchallenged and stifled by the fact that the only sense of self-worth she got was from her children's spelling-test results and participation in activities. Another baby would keep her busy and happy for now. Julia couldn't understand – she was in a totally different world. Odette wished that she herself was as focused and self-assured.

Carol settled down for her first game of the evening. She liked this time of the day. Several Australian bridge players who were early risers liked an online game after breakfast. The weather sounded divine – especially in comparison to the dark Dublin evenings. Bob was on and so was Helen. It was comforting to have a nice game with players who were like-minded and of similar ability. Suddenly she got a message from Greta in Northern Ireland. Greta was recently widowed so Carol liked to lend her a sympathetic ear – or the online equivalent. Greta lived alone but had a grown-up daughter and two sons who seemed to be in her house often. She and Carol shared a love of crime novels and often compared notes and suggested new titles. She had never actually spoken to Greta but they corresponded while playing bridge and she often made a new table to accommodate Greta.

Julia entered the living room and started to speak but her mother interrupted.

"I'm just playing out this hand, dear – would you put the kettle on and I'll be in to the kitchen when we're finished here."

It was hopeless. Julia had to control her tongue.

Suddenly Carol's phone bleeped.

"Can you check that message for me, Julia, please – I'm expecting word from Treasa – she wants me to make up a table with her."

Julia read the message aloud: "Ready in ten mins – do you have Ita's number? Will she play too?"

"Tell her I have to finish up here first – to give me twenty minutes and then can you business-card Ita's number to Treasa, please?"

Julia watched her mother flip the cards on her screen and suddenly wanted to laugh. She texted the numbers and messages and left without saying a word. Her mother didn't look up from the screen.

She went into the room where her grandfather slept and worked and watched TV. He was dozing in his armchair and the TV was blaring in the background. His work bench was covered with tiny springs and the skeletons of dozens of watches. The fine craft tools were lined up in a row along the edge of the table and the lamp that he used to see the finer details of his work was left on.

Julia took a rug and placed it over his legs. There was no point waking him. She turned off the TV and went back into the kitchen. Dylan was on her mind. He managed to irritate her like nobody else. Today he had touched her Achilles' heel – he had no idea how the travel business worked but insisted on commenting on the direction people were taking with their holiday plans. Odette said that he only wanted to show he was interested in her work but Julia felt as though he was teasing. She couldn't say it to her mother because she wouldn't listen – she couldn't explain to anyone – this was a war she would have to wage on her own with nobody else understanding how much he annoyed her.

It was eleven o'clock and time for bed with a good book.

Carol was elated after trashing the competition around her all night. She said goodbye to Treasa and shut down her laptop.

Her watch read two o'clock in the morning and she realised that she had forgotten to speak with Julia. She would check and see how her daughter was in the morning. If only she could talk to Julia the way that she spoke to Odette – even Michael over in Singapore understood her needs better. But Julia was a good daughter and it was only out of concern that she wanted her mother to behave differently.

The truth was that Carol *had* to change after her husband died. She really had no choice. It was such a shock to find that you couldn't do anything for yourself. Her own father had lived superbly on his own for twenty years and his moving in had been more Julia's idea than anybody's. She was so like her father. It was important that she didn't overwork in the same way that he had.

Chapter Six

Julia liked Mondays. She had a meeting at eleven with her staff and would plan her aims for the upcoming week. She wondered how Dylan was feeling today after the Irish coffees. Hopefully she wouldn't have to tolerate his company again until Christmas. Maybe he would go skiing this year like he had done two years before. She smiled as she considered the prospect and opened her email. There was the usual deluge after the weekend and she scanned through them quickly until one in particular caught her eye. It was from Lydia. Julia read through and smiled at the invitation to have dinner in Salamanca restaurant on Wednesday. She was relieved that she had an excuse to meet her. Julia had an uneasy feeling where Michael and Lydia were concerned but there was a powerful desire to fix Michael that was much stronger than the voice of reason that she used more frequently.

It was strange that Lydia should contact her only the day after Michael had asked about her. Julia was a practical person who didn't believe in mumbo jumbo but she did believe in the power of thought, and positive thinking especially. Telepathy was something else that she found fascinating and after watching the scientist Sheldrake's talk on the internet she was convinced that if you thought about someone enough they would get the signal from your thoughts and eventually contact you. It explained why animals knew when their owners were on their way home – or how the Aborigine men knew to come home from walkabout at the exact time that their wife was about to give birth. All living things were energy wrapped up in matter and that made perfect scientific sense as well as fulfilling her need to believe her gut instinct.

She read on and saw that Lydia was happier than she had been in years. Her boyfriend was not only a policeman but a sergeant and, even better than that, a detective sergeant which meant that he did not have to wear a uniform and drove an unmarked car.

But it was the way that she spoke about his kindness and gentle manner that made Julia's alarm bells ring.

At the moment she would wait and see what transpired during their meeting and she wouldn't mention Michael unless the conditions seemed right.

Ruth brushed down the grey skirt that Julia had picked out for her the previous week. The jacket was stylish and the suit a cut above anything Ruth would usually choose. But this was a job that would take her into a new direction not only in her career but in her life. She wondered if she truly wanted to make the bold move to the other side of the world at all. She entered the stylish lobby of the Westin Hotel where the appointment had been set up by Julia. It was to be a purely informal meeting as the position was not to be filled until January but Julia had assured Ruth that if she got on well they might decide to just give her the job.

Ruth braced herself as she approached a man sitting at a table with a laptop open on the table in front of him. He had a brochure advertising Australia on his lap, leaving Ruth in no doubt that he was Steve Nelson, the director of Tourism Ireland in Australia. He stood up as she proceeded toward him with her hand outstretched.

"Ruth Travers?" he asked, his head cocked.

"Yes – Mr Nelson?" she replied.

He smiled widely. First appearances mattered. "Please call me Steve!"

As Julia would say – you are in there, girl! Ruth knew that the interview could only go in one direction from that moment.

The next forty-five minutes were an informal chat and when Úna, Steve's colleague, arrived the three were giggling and chatting about life in Dublin and how much they all had in common. It was a culture shock for Ruth – she had become accustomed to game-playing with Oliver and taking hammering after hammering on her confidence. Now she felt physically refreshed by such enlightened company. If everyone was like this in Perth she would seriously consider making the move. The only thing blocking her was the thought of being so far away from Ian. She really wasn't sure that she would be able to stand the distance between them. There was no way that Steve or Úna guessed her reservations – as far as they were concerned by the end of the meeting, they had found the girl for the job!

Julia waited with great anticipation to hear how her friend's interview had gone.

Ruth was almost breathless as she called and relayed the details. She liked Steve and the way that he made her feel intelligent, important and competent. Julia listened patiently and as Ruth spoke the realisation truly hit her that Ruth might well get the job. Julia had nothing to complain about. The desire to protect her friend was her motive for organising the interview. She really didn't know how else to help Ruth to see what a hopeless relationship she was embedded in. But now, as the excitement in Ruth's voice resonated with Julia, she felt a pang of loss. Could her friend actually be leaving and starting a new life on the other side of the world? Julia had dealt with emigration before and when Michael first left for Singapore she had cried for three days. But even though he was family, Ruth was different: Ruth was her best friend. She was not sure how she would cope without her and, as she listened to her tell about the interview, all she could focus on was the emptiness that she would feel without her.

"That sounds great!" she said in the most enthusiastic tone that she could muster.

"I know, I have never felt so good after an interview," Ruth chirped. "Except that – please don't hate me, Julia, or think that I am ungrateful – I am worried about moving so far away."

Julia had to dig deep inside herself to remain cheerful. "It's such a great opportunity you'd be mad not to take it, especially the way things are going here in Ireland."

"I realise all that but you know why I don't want to go. Ian and I have been together so long I don't know how to tell him."

"I'm sure he'll understand and if he loves you he'll want what's best for you."

"You always say the right thing, Julia, but Ian is unpredictable and, even though you find it hard to believe, he is sensitive."

Julia had to bite the side of her cheek to keep from saying something that might upset her friend. "Maybe it's best to deal with Ian after you are offered the job."

"Yeah, you're probably right – can't count my chickens until they are hatched!"

And Julia wished that Ruth would be more selfish and think of herself first.

Michael was so tempted to go ahead and send his email to Lydia – time was rushing on and the longer she spent with this ridiculous policeman the more chance she had of falling in love with him. He would first send it to Julia for her seal of approval – he had to be sure that it had the correct tone. He gave it one more look over before pressing 'send' to his sister.

Dear Lydia

I hope that you are keeping well and all is good in your world. You are probably wondering why I am emailing you after you deleted me from your Facebook friends – but you know me – I never was one to take a slap on the face to heart. The truth is that I have been thinking about you and it's not just the approach of Christmas that has me feeling this way – although the best Christmas I ever spent was with you ?

Julia told me that you have met someone and I hope that he is good enough for you – he had better treat you with all the love and respect that you deserve. I am very jealous of him because there aren't any girls like you over here.

Singapore is hot – all year around to be honest – even in the rain. Julia said that it is mild at home this year and no sign of snow. That is good.

I keep up with what is going on by reading the Irish papers every day. I hope to get home for a few days early in December and was wondering if you might be free to meet up? I understand that you might not want to, but if your boyfriend isn't the jealous type he might not mind us meeting for a coffee for old times' sake?

I miss you so much, Lydia, and I really need to see you again.
All my heart
Michael

Julia was sad for her brother when she read his email to Lydia. For all his experience of life and bravado he really was behaving very naively. Just because he was missing Dublin and deciding that he wanted to settle down, it was unfair of him to expect that Lydia understood these changes. He really was asking too much of her. Michael was not around when Julia had to sit and listen to Lydia's sobbing after their last break-up. It was Julia's job then to turn up at her friend's house with tubs of Haagen Dazs ice cream and boxes of handkerchiefs. It went on for weeks and Michael was cold and utterly unconcerned about how much he had hurt Lydia. He couldn't understand why Julia took it all so personally either. Lydia was his affair as far as he was concerned and his sister should be seeing his point of view. But Julia was a good friend to everyone and she longed to see everyone happy and, even though Michael was her brother, she would never take sides. She was pleased that she had kept her integrity and been fair to both of them but she did feel sad for her brother and the lonely situation that he now found himself in.

So she set to reworking the email and making it sound more pleasant and fun – a lighter approach that might give him some chance of getting a response from Lydia. She wanted to get it back to him so that he could send it on to Lydia as soon as possible and she would know how her friend felt before they met in a couple of days' time.

Hi Lydia

I hope that you haven't deleted this email before opening and if you are at line two already that there is a pretty good chance you will read on ?

I was devastated to be knocked from your friend list on Facebook – please tell me what I have to do to get back on it or I'll always have to snoop around by checking your photos through Julia's profile and run the risk of her deleting me too!!

So here I am in Singapore and I don't have to tell you it is hot – all year around to be honest – and even though the ambassador is having parties coming up to the Christmas season I am wishing it was more like Dublin, to get in the party mood.

I hope to get home for a few days early in December and was wondering if you might be free to meet up for a coffee and chat for old times' sake? Phew! Looks like I got you to read through the entire email – look forward to seeing you.

Hope you are having fun

Michael

Julia put 'new version' in as subject and emailed the amended text to Michael – she knew that he would have the good sense to send her revised email.

Suddenly the phone rang and Ruth winced when she recognised Steve Nelson's number. Her hands shook and she took a deep breath before saying hello.

"G'day, Ruth – Úna and I really enjoyed meeting you today and we knew instantly that you were the girl for the job – we don't want to mess around interviewing other people if you feel the same way – so we'd like to offer you the two-year contract with the possibility of something more permanent even sooner."

Ruth squealed with delight. "Thank you, Steve – this is very exciting – I got your email earlier outlining conditions and pay and it is very attractive."

"All you need to say is yes and then we can get rolling right away – how does first week in January sound, to start in Perth? We can get started before that and lay down the ground work sorting out visas etcetera in December?"

"Perfect – I can't tell you how exciting this opportunity is."

"I hope that you'll like it out there – they're a great bunch and you will fit in well. Have a glass of wine tonight to celebrate and I'll call you in a day or two, okay?"

"Thanks again, Steve – talk soon."

Ruth was filled with the excitement of the world of possibilities that had been opened to her. But in the pit of her stomach was a pain. She dreaded telling Ian because she had no idea how he was going to take it.

She would possibly wait until after dinner and see how confident she felt.

The doorbell rang briefly and the door-latch clicked. He always let himself into the apartment but gave a courtesy buzz as he turned the key.

Ruth stirred the Thai curry one more time and wiped her hands in a tea towel.

Ian was in the kitchen before she reached the hall. He raised his brow and gave a wide boyish smile, exposing perfectly straight teeth. His hair was thinning but it suited the shape of his face.

"Something smells good and I'm not talking about the curry!" he said, grabbing Ruth by her waist and kissing her on the nape of her neck.

Ruth shivered. She loved the way he took ownership of her when they were alone. He made her feel so sexy and passionate and even after all this time the thrill of being his woman – even on a part-time basis – was what she wanted more than anything else in the world. There was no way that she could tell him tonight – he was in such buoyant form – maybe her news could wait.

"Don't you want to eat first?" she said wickedly.

"No way!" he said, turning the dial on the hob where the curry rested. "The hot thing that I fancy is standing right in front of me!"

Ruth let Ian take her by the hand and lead her into the bedroom. She fluttered inside at the prospect of her aperitif. This was Ian at his very best – this was what other women only dreamed of having – this is what he would never have with his wife. He had assured her that the humdrum of normal living was left on the other side of the city with Ciara – but what *they* had was special.

Odette listened to a car pull up in the driveway and she presumed that it was Craig – it was a pity that he wasn't a little bit earlier as he could have put the children to bed. They loved it when he kissed them goodnight as they saw so little of him during the week. But when the doorbell rang she was startled. She went out to the hall and recognised Dylan's silhouette through the glass. She opened the hall door and was greeted by the smiling face of her brother-in-law who looked surprisingly unkempt. She had never seen him with stubble before and his clothes were casual to the point of scruffy. Nonetheless she kissed him on his cheek when he leaned forward and asked cheekily where his brother was.

"Where do you think, Dylan! I'm sick of all the work that he is doing lately. Have you noticed how much pressure he is under? He's difficult to live with at the moment and he has no time for me or the kids."

Dylan followed Odette into the kitchen, brushing his fringe back from his brow.

"I know better than anyone what it's like out there in the workforce," he said, "but Craig is luckier than most – he's not going to be made redundant – as long as the national carrier stays flying he's going to be employed – not like the rest of us!"

"Oh dear – is everything okay with you, Dylan? Don't tell me you're in trouble with work."

Dylan sat down at the kitchen table and watched Odette fill the kettle.

"I'm luckier than most – I've been politely asked to hand in my notice but the package they've offered me is difficult to refuse so I've decided to take it."

Odette's mouth dropped. "You've been let go?"

"It's time I moved – I've been with Avaxa too long and I know too much! In fact, it works in my favour and I've had to agree not to work for any competitor for a year so I guess I've been handed an opportunity to do all the things I've longed to do but never had the time."

"But what are you going to live on?"

"The severance package is more than sufficient. Don't worry about me, Odette. I have enough contacts in the energy business to find myself a new position before the end of next year."

"Tea?"

"Thanks, yes, that would be good."

"Wow – that sounds like you have the much-needed time off that Craig needs – and that you are happy about it?"

"Believe me, Odette, I'm ecstatic. I think a change would be good for Craig too though. I don't like hearing about all this late-night work."

Odette put two mugs of tea onto the table and sighed. "It's so depressing hearing of all of these job losses and austerity measures – why has it come to this?"

"It's a cycle – our little country will be okay – it's just like the eighties!"

"I hope you're right."

"Have a bit of faith. So, when are you expecting Craig back?"

"He could be as late as ten but mostly he's home at eight."

Dylan looked at his watch. It was nine.

"Do you mind if I stay until he gets home?"

"Of course not – I'm glad of the company. Come into the living room and we'll stick on the TV."

Dylan envied his brother – Odette was lovely and had given him two beautiful children. His life was mapped out and, although five years ago Dylan would have felt that scene somewhat boring, now he longed for the security and love of a family. His own apartment in Malahide Marina Village was in a prime location but a bachelor pad didn't have the warmth and love that a family home can give. Craig was very foolish and if Dylan's hunch was correct then he was about to make a big mistake.

Ruth rested her strawberry-red hair on Ian's shoulder in post-coital bliss. She couldn't tell him now. This wasn't the moment. But when would be? The truth was that, as she lay like this with Ian, she didn't want to go to Australia. She didn't want to start a new life. All she wanted was to be at his side. She closed her eyes tightly but a tear trickled out and rolled down the side of her cheek.

Ian was almost asleep but he sensed her discomfort and turned to see the tear.

"What's up, kitten – did you not enjoy?"

Ruth gave him a playful thump on his bare, hairless chest. "Don't be silly. It's something else."

Ian rolled his eyes and sighed. "This isn't about Ciara, is it? I told you that I never think of her when I'm with you."

With that Ruth burst into tears. "It's not about bloody Ciara! I'm sick of bloody Ciara – she may be the centre of your world but I have other things that I have to think about and deal with – like – like –"

"Like what?" he brazenly asked.

"Like where I'm going to spend Christmas this year!"

Ian started to chuckle. "Kitten, I'll be over to see you straight after my flight on Christmas Eve."

"That's not it!" she said curtly. "It's where I'm going to be after Christmas – I'm leaving Ireland."

Ian laughed louder. "What are you talking about?"

"I'm emigrating – I've got a job lined up and it's starting at the beginning of January." Her voice was trembling now but Ian's laughter had hurt her. He never took her seriously.

"Good, I'm glad you've got a job – but where are you emigrating to? London?"

She propped herself up on her elbow and looked down at her lover.

"Australia!" she exclaimed boldly.

"You're joking!" he whispered.

"No, I'm not – I've got a job with Tourism Ireland – it's a two-year contract for starters but I'll see how it goes."

"But why Australia?"

"Because that's where the job is!" she said in a very matter-of-fact tone.

"But what about us?"

Ruth fell back from her position of power and onto his shoulder again. She didn't have an answer. She knew what she wanted to say: 'Come with me – leave your wife – get a job with Qantas.' But the truth was she hadn't a clue about their future and from the tone in his voice he hadn't either. He would never leave his children. But sometimes Ruth wondered if the children were just a lame excuse and their relationship only worked on this illicit basis.

"Come on, the curry is waiting," she said as she slipped out from the sheets and pulled her dressing gown over her shoulders. "I'll be in the kitchen."

Ian didn't join her for at least fifteen minutes. He took a shower before dressing and coming to where she sat at the kitchen table.

Ruth had never known him to be so silent. He always had an answer for everything but this time she had done it – she had opened the can and the worms were crawling and wincing their way all over the pair of them.

Craig slammed the front door shut. He rubbed the nape of his neck and put his laptop case onto the ground. He wondered why his brother was calling unannounced. It was not like him and especially this late in the evening.

Odette jumped up when he entered the living room.

"Hey, you're extra late – did you have dinner?"

"Yeah, sorry, I should have told you that I ate in work. How's it going, Dylan? What has you here at this hour?"

"Just dropping by!" he replied, nodding his head and staring at his brother.

"Well, I'm off to bed – goodnight, Dylan," Odette said, giving her brother-in-law a swift kiss on the cheek before she left the room.

Craig sat heavily on the couch and let out a loud sigh. "I've got to get out of this job – it's killing me."

Dylan said nothing. Craig did seem to be under extreme pressure lately but that still didn't explain what he had seen earlier.

"What's up with you?" Craig asked.

Dylan wanted to come out and say why he was there but decided to fish around first and try to draw some information from his brother.

"I saw your car outside the Coachman's Inn earlier – did you go for a pint?"

"You should have rung and you could have joined me."

The casual way that his brother suggested this surprised Dylan. He had expected a different reaction. But Dylan had seen it with his own eyes. There was no doubting that he had been engrossed in a long and lingering kiss with a woman – whoever she was.

"On your own, were you?"

"No, there was a crowd from the office – one of our best is leaving. She's moving to Abu Dhabi – her husband hasn't worked in over a year and they cannot afford to pay their mortgage. They have no children so are hoping to make a fresh start in the Middle East." Craig shook his head. "It's going to get much worse before it gets better, you know – I can feel it. The figures don't add up and when ordinary hardworking decent couples are being forced to leave it makes you wonder who is going to be left in the country!"

Dylan was so relieved that the kiss he had seen was more than likely an over-the-top goodbye and not the seeds of a heated affair – that was providing of course the woman that he was kissing was the woman who was emigrating. Although he wasn't positive, he now had a hunch that that was all it was. He would, however, keep a closer eye on his brother. He had done right not accusing him straight out and would let it lie for the moment.

Chapter Seven

Angela had been here before. She stirred the teabags in the pot and put the lid on.

"And when did you decide to move to Australia?" she asked her daughter.

"Julia told me about the job. I guess I need a change of environment. I was working with Oliver too long."

"He wasn't the worst boss in the world."

"You didn't have to work with him, Mum. That job was getting me down. To be honest, I'm not entirely sure that I want to live in Australia but I've fallen into a rut – surely you can see that?"

Angela didn't argue. "But to move all the way to Australia! Could you not find a job here?"

"It's a good opportunity. Things have slowed down so badly in Dublin I don't know where I would get a job at the moment. I thought you of all people would like the idea of me living in Australia – I mean, you spent time down there."

"And I came home before I had you. There was a reason for that. Australia's very different from Ireland and I'm not sure that you'll like it."

"Well, maybe I should try – I won't know unless I do."

Angela could feel her old self in her daughter's words. But her motives for moving to Australia were not entirely the same.

"I was married to your father and things were bleak in the seventies. We had to commit to staying two years in Australia before we were granted the cheap £10 passage fares but, even so, if it wasn't for your father we would have come back a lot sooner. It's a very chauvinistic society, Ruth – it's not a country for a young girl to go to on her own."

And the more her mother spoke against the move, the more Ruth defended her decision to go. If her mother knew about Ian, she would have her at Dublin airport before she could pack a suitcase. Her mother, however, was seeing the situation from her own experience entirely and couldn't understand what it was like to be out of work and the sense of hopelessness that was sitting on Dublin like a gauze.

Angela wiped her brow and stared at the unpoured pot of tea.

"I suppose I'm just feeling a bit shocked, that's all. I thought that after your younger brother got married I had you all reared and settled. You were the least likely of my children to up and leave and now it looks as if Kevin is going to Canada."

Ruth put her hand up to her mouth. This was news and, although it was difficult for Angela to see her grandchildren in Kerry, at least they were in the same country. Canada might not be as far away as Australia but it could be expensive and difficult to get there.

"I had no idea – when did he decide this?"

Angela took a sharp intake of breath. "He called last night – heaven help me but what more bad news will I get? It always comes in threes."

Ruth put her hand on her mother's and could feel the dread and sorrow. There was no easy way for her to deal with the loss of her children to another country and Kevin had three small children who were likely to become settled beyond the point of return.

"It's like déjà vu, Ruth," Angela said with a shake of her head. "Kevin was doing so well but when they shut that factory in Tralee and he was made redundant I knew it was complete disaster. You see, Kevin invested the profits from the sale of his house in Dublin into three apartments and he used the collateral from his house in Kerry to complete the deals. He's up to his eyes in debt and, without a job or tenants to pay his mortgages, is left with no choice."

Ruth had no idea that her brother had invested in property and felt badly for him. He was a specialised engineer whose skills were so sought after that he earned a good wage but had obviously invested poorly because of the cheap credit and mortgages that were being handed out.

"If only he had kept his house in Dublin and rented in Kerry he would be able to come back and do something here. But he can't get out of paying for those blasted apartments and the bank is giving him hell. I swear I'm so worried about him – the way he's been talking . . ."

Ruth could see that the situation was bleak and her mother was not giving her the entire story.

"So when is he going?"

"As soon as his visa comes through . . ."

"But if he leaves like this he won't be able to come back."

Angela lowered her head and covered her face with the palms of her hands.

Ruth regretted what she had said but knew it to be the truth.

Lydia was shocked when the email arrived. It had been a year since she'd had any contact with Michael and she had managed to stop thinking about him every day, the way that she used to. Anyway, she was very happy with Peter and for the first time since she finished with Michael felt that she had met someone that she could spend the rest of her life with. It was only early days but something felt very right about Peter – he made her feel safe and secure – protected in a way that she had never felt with Michael. At this stage in her life she needed a life partner – she was keen to settle down and start a family. She contemplated deleting the email but curiosity got the better of her and she opened it. Typically he started by joking about her deleting him from Facebook – he sounded in good form.

But the real point of the email was a request to meet and that might just be asking too much. It was strange that he should contact her just before she was meeting Julia. She looked at her diary. In two days she was meeting his sister and she would find out more – she definitely wouldn't answer Michael's mail before speaking with Julia.

Angela returned to the kitchen when her daughter was gone. She put her hand onto her stomach where she felt a pain but she knew that there was nothing she could take to relieve it. Emotional pain was more severe for Angela than any physical ailments. History was repeating itself and there was nothing she could do to stop her son and his family from leaving the hopeless situation they had found themselves in. But the news of Ruth's departure was proving too much to take. She had seen her own brother and sister off at Dublin Port in the 1960s and knew then that at some stage she might well be on the same boat. Angela had tried several positions to ease the burden on the family but when her husband Fred lost his job in 1970 she had agreed to take the £10 fare to Perth. The crossing was bearable and they were fortunate to have calm seas but the sorrow of seeing her heartbroken mother standing at the harbour as she waved goodbye was etched in her memory for the duration of the long trip. Angela felt differently to so many of the other young emigrants who took to their bunks each night with excitement and anticipation of the future and the opportunities that it might bring. All Angela felt was shame and a horrid sense of sadness that yet again a generation of young Irishmen and women would have to leave their homes and their country forever.

The city of Perth was not as she had expected and the streets were most definitely not paved with gold. They were, however, filled with fast cars imported from America and many of the young men coming from Europe found speeding along the freeways irresistible – and paid for it with their lives. It became apparent very quickly that jobs were abundant for young men who were happy to earn a good wage in compensation for being away from their families. Angela found herself alone for several nights each week and clung to the company of other European emigrant women who mostly came from England, Scotland and Wales.

The arrival of Kevin into the world after eighteen months of living in Australia brought Angela the much-needed family that helped fill the hole left by the absence of her mother and siblings. This new bundle of joy offered hope and the possibility of settling in this new land permanently. But as Kevin grew she realised that she missed her mother and Ireland even more and she didn't want her son to grow up speaking with an Australian accent.

Her husband became more settled with his mix of new friends from around the world and he felt a great kinship with the Australian men that he worked and socialised with. For Angela, however, she found the company of some more desirable than others and her marriage was tested in more ways than she could ever have imagined. Australian society was even more conservative and backward than Ireland in the way that men and women were expected to mix. Then there was the secret that every so often came back to haunt her since – usually in sleep.

As she found the four walls of her house close in on her when she discovered that she was pregnant again, she gave her husband an ultimatum. This baby was going to be born on Irish soil and her husband could come home with her or stay in Australia – the choice was his. She set about arranging her passage before her husband could discuss it further and, although she did make the long journey home on her own, he followed six months later and landed a job in the Guinness factory to his wife's joy. They secured a house in Milltown and moved to Sutton when Ruth was eight. Life had been good for Angela since then and she had tried to block out the memory of the time she had spent in Perth.

The irony that her daughter would now be living in the same city that she herself had fled thirty-five years before was too much to take. She made herself a cup of tea and brought it heavy-handedly to bed. She would tell Fred the news in the morning.

Chapter Eight

Lydia arrived first at Salamanca restaurant. She hadn't been before but wasn't surprised that she liked it instantly. Julia had great taste and had told her to try it so Lydia knew that if Julia liked it she would like it too. The waiter led her over to a wooden chair padded with beautiful brocade. She had an excellent view of Trinity Street and the shoppers and workers going about their business. She had only poured a glass of water when Julia came through the door wearing a red wool military-style coat and knee-high riding boots. As usual her hair was shining and her eyes bright with anticipation.

Lydia stood up and kissed her friend's cheek.

"Great to see you, you look fabulous as usual!"

"Ah thank you, Lydia, you're like a breath of fresh air! And I love that colour on you, what is it, electric blue?"

Lydia nodded. "Yes, would you believe Peter bought it for me?"

"A man with good taste in clothes?" Julia pried.

"Yes, and he's a great cook too!"

"Sounds like a keeper? But it is early days."

Lydia's eyes widened and, as she described her new lover, they shone and danced in her head.

"Peter is everything I ever wanted in a man and more. He's thoughtful, considerate and so accomplished. Did I tell you he was in the trials for the Olympics when he was in his twenties – he's a marvellous swimmer."

Julia swallowed hard. Michael had certainly given himself a challenge but Julia had seen many shining halos slip. She would watch and listen but say very little – she knew how to gauge her friend's reactions.

They shared tapas and red wine and updated each other on the health and well-being of their family and mutual friends. Lydia was abuzz with her plans for Christmas and Peter was mentioned in them all.

"And what about you?" Lydia asked. "Is there any nice man on the horizon for you?"

With a roll of her eyes Julia gave her usual answer and explained how busy she was with her work and looking after her mother and grandfather.

"Ah, come on!" Lydia urged. "Don't you want to meet someone nice and maybe have a family?"

Why did friends always want you to want the same things that they did, Julia pondered. She never felt a need – in fact, she always liked to be a little bit outside the trends and doing her own thing. Yet here she was again, listening to a friend falling in love and dreaming of engagement rings and wedding dresses. In Lydia's case she was probably even considering nursery paint!

"I have a family and to be honest at the moment I'm a little concerned about Odette – she seems to have hit a wall. She could do with a distraction or some sort of interest."

"What about exercise? I'm going to boot camp on the nights that I don't meet Peter and I feel great after it."

Julia didn't want to shoot down her friend's suggestion but she didn't think Odette was going to suddenly become sporty at this stage.

"I'll suggest it to her," she said with a smile.

"She could come with me. I go to a great camp in Marino – it's not that far from Malahide."

Lydia was bursting with energy and enthusiasm for life and Julia was wondering if she should forget about bringing Michael up in the conversation.

She decided to give it a go.

"Michael is trying to get leave for Christmas."

"That would be nice for your mum," Lydia chirped. "Actually, he sent me an email only the other day – he sounds in good form!"

Julia was perturbed by Lydia's reaction. She was obviously so engrossed in her life that she didn't care about her old lover contacting her.

"What did he say?"

Lydia took a piece of chorizo on her fork and dipped it into the tomato dressing before slipping it into her mouth.

"Oh, nothing much – mentioned that he was coming home in December – but early December, I think?"

"He's trying to get back for Christmas now – Mum is going away with her bridge club friends early December."

Lydia chuckled. "She's great, Julia – I wish my mum would take a leaf out of her book!"

Julia was keen to steer the conversation back to her brother's email. "Did Michael say anything else?"

"He wants to meet up but I don't think that's a good idea – anyway, I am probably going to be very busy – Peter's family is in Waterford and I'll have to spend time with him down there."

Julia swallowed. This was serious – Peter was making plans for Christmas already.

"That's nice, that he wants you to meet his parents."

"Oh, I met them already – they're just lovely people. I felt like they were my own family." Lydia prodded a lump of goat's cheese with her fork. "I'd like to answer Michael's email but I'm not sure what to say."

"Well, what do you feel like saying?"

Lydia sighed loudly. "I can't deny that I still have feelings for him, Julia – he was the big love of my life. But he hurt me so much that I don't think the love I felt could compensate for the pain that he caused me when we broke up."

"I understand," Julia said sympathetically. "But he seems to have changed and he's even thinking of coming home for good."

Lydia sat up defensively. "But it's a terrible time to settle back here – especially in his line."

"You know Michael – he has a way with him – if anyone can get a job in Dublin he can."

Lydia nodded. "I would like to see him when he does get home. I don't want to upset Peter though. I might just drop Michael an acknowledgement of his email."

"I think he'd like that."

"But I really am not sure that it's a good idea – for the first time since being with Michael I've found someone that I feel I could have a future with."

Julia would have to tell Michael about this development. She felt very sorry for her brother but she was also pleased that her friend was so happy. For now she would enjoy the tapas and Lydia's company.

Michael checked his emails several times daily and was thrilled to see the one from Lydia when he arrived back from lunch. His heart beat in his chest as he opened it.

Hi Michael

Good to hear from you – I spent a lovely evening with Julia yesterday. She was telling me about your plans and I hope things work out for you. It must be difficult being away from home for so long. I do hope you get your leave for Christmas – it really is the best time to be in Dublin.

Work has been busy but I'm trying to get a balance – I'm keeping fit and have joined Boot Camp. I'm dating someone at the moment who is really cool – I think you'd like him.

Give me a call when you get back to Dublin and hopefully we can coordinate a cup of coffee.

All the best

Lydia

Michael read the e-mail over and over but found it difficult to find any true sentiment or feeling in it. She must be in a neutral place, he tried to convince himself. It would be too hurtful to think that she was in love with this guy. He checked his Skype to see if Julia was online but she was away. He looked at his watch

– it was too early in the morning in Ireland and Julia would be furious with him if he called her on her mobile. He would wait an hour or two until she got into the office and try speak to her then.

He opened a report that was awaiting his attention and started to type but his mind was constantly being pulled back to thinking about Lydia. He had to do something and he couldn't wait for Julia's reply. He wanted to answer Lydia's email and he had to do it now.

Dear Lydia

I can't tell you how much it would mean to see you. The thing is, I've been doing a lot of thinking and I really don't want to settle forever in Singapore. I want to come home and spend time with my family – I was only here a couple of months when my father died and I never got a chance to be with the family at a time when they really needed me. The thing is I have always been too selfish and putting myself first. I realise that now and I realise that I was this way with you. You who are the most wonderful, beautiful, intelligent, complete woman that I have ever known. I've never been happier than when we were together. I wish I could turn back the clock and be in that loving relationship with you once again. What happened was all my fault. I want to make it up to you – I want to be with you.

Please, Lydia, let me know if there is any hope at all that you would consider coming back into my life and starting again. What we had was too special – we really can't let our lives be wasted one moment longer. I look forward to that cup of coffee. I know that it is your birthday soon and I have something special for you.

With all my heart

Michael

Then he pressed send.

Chapter Nine

Carol was so excited. She was finally going to meet Ellen and she was sure that they were going to get on famously. She was disappointed that Greta had decided not to join them in Cologne but she would meet Greta another time. She looked at her phone and smiled when she saw the text was from her.

Have a great time. Look forward to hear all when you return. G

Carol smiled. Every time she thought of Greta she seemed to send her a message or an email.

"Are you ready, Mum?" Odette called up the stairs.

"Just coming now!" Carol replied.

She pulled the zip on her small case and checked her look in the mirror. Was she really going to Germany for an adventure on her own? Ellen would be on the road now, making her way to Cologne. They had figured that it would take longer for her to travel by train than it would take Carol to fly from Ireland.

Carol went into the kitchen where Horatio was sitting.

"Will you be okay now, Dad?"

"Well, I just hope Julia doesn't mind about the Brazilian lady coming to look after the house while you're away."

"She knows all about Paola – in fact it was Julia's idea!" Carol assured him.

"Really? Well, you know what she's like – you might come

home to a dead body in the house – the poor Brazilian woman's or mine!"

Carol kissed her father on the forehead. "Just don't do anything silly like falling in love with Paola. I believe she's quite beautiful."

Horatio sat up in the chair. "Well, nobody told me that – I can't be responsible for my actions in that case!"

"Come on, Mum!" Odette urged. "You don't want to miss your flight!"

"I'm coming, I'm coming! Now be good, Daddy."

Carol felt like a small child going on a school trip as she looked out the window of Odette's car. This was so out of character for the person that she used to be. She didn't know Ellen very well but they had been playing bridge online for six months now and the two women had a lot in common. They were both widows, both had an elderly parent living with them and they liked reading the same books and watching the same movies – when they weren't playing bridge of course.

"Have you got all your details – and your passport?" Odette asked.

Carol fumbled in her bag and produced a folder. "Yes, here it is. I'm staying in the Hilton in the Altstadt – that's the old town!"

Odette had to hide a giggle – she wished Julia was here to hear her mother. "Is it really?"

"Yes – and we'll be just beside the cathedral and main train station."

Odette pulled up at Departures.

"Would you like me to come in with you?"

"Not at all, sure you have the small ones to pick up from school."

"Alright then, I'll be here to pick you up on Monday, okay?"

"That's lovely. I really appreciate the lift."

Odette leaned over and kissed her mother on the cheek.

"Thanks again, love, and I'll get something nice for the kids," said Carol.

She pulled her case behind her and walked into the check-in

area. She felt butterflies in her stomach. A part of her grieved about her reluctance to travel in the past and she regretted time wasted that she could have spent travelling with her husband. But it was too late for that now and she had to make the most of her life.

Lydia looked at the e-mail that Michael had sent a few days before. She didn't know how to respond – it was so out of character for Michael to lay his heart on the line in this way. She had spent the most marvellous weekend with Peter in Monart spa retreat. They had lounged around in white fluffy robes. They had walked in the beautiful wooded grounds and she had gone horse-riding with him on Saturday afternoon – Peter was a proficient rider. He was wonderful and gentle and encouraging with her every step of the way. If it wasn't for these emails she would be floating on air. It was cruel of Michael to come back into her life just now – when she had met a man that she felt she could spend the rest of her life with.

But what troubled her more was the fact that she couldn't stop thinking about Michael and, if Peter was so right for her, she shouldn't be thinking of her old lover.

She wished that Julia wasn't his sister. She was the one friend that she would consult on matters of the heart and she would always give a good counsel and advice on what to do – but Michael was her brother and she couldn't be sure that Julia could remain unbiased. However, when he split with her last time Julia most definitely was there for her.

Lydia had to reply to his email and she had to say what she really felt in her heart.

She looked over the text again. She trusted Julia. She wanted to email her right away and see what advice she had. But maybe she should wait until the weekend was over and, if she felt the same, email her early next week – yes, that was the best thing to do.

Carol took a seat at the front of the plane. She had only opened her magazine when a stocky man of medium build asked if the seat beside hers was taken.

"No, I'm travelling on my own," she said and then regretted giving the information. He did seem like a nice decent person, though, and his aftershave was tasteful.

He took out a book and put it on the table top in front of him. It was entitled *How to Play Better Bridge*.

Carol's eyes were fixed on it and she had to pull them away as the man noticed her attention.

The pilot announced ready for take-off and the cabin crew took their seats. As the Boeing 737 careered down the runway Carol noticed the nice man looking at her profile. She felt strangely attractive inside – it had been a long time since she had been noticed by a member of the opposite sex.

"I'm always nervous as we lift off," he said in a soft northern brogue.

Carol giggled like a schoolgirl. "Oh yes, me too." Then she nodded towards his book. "I see you play bridge!"

"I do but I've a lot yet to learn. Do you play yourself?"

"Oh, a little," she smiled.

"It's a great pastime. I don't know what I did with myself before I played."

Carol noticed the glint in the man's eyes. She felt very lucky in her choice of seat.

As the captain turned off the seat-belt sign, the air stewards quickly set about selling refreshments.

"Would you like a cup of tea – or maybe something a little stronger?" the stranger asked. "I have to admit I like to have a brandy when I fly."

"Oh, that's very kind of you – well, maybe I'll have a brandy too then."

"With a mixer? Ginger ale?"

"Oh yes, ginger ale would be lovely."

They clinked their plastic cups together and chatted non-stop over the UK and Holland. When the captain informed the passengers that they were now in German airspace Carol felt giddy but couldn't blame it entirely on the two brandies she had consumed.

"Are you staying in Cologne?"

"Yes, actually – in the old town. I've never been to Germany before."

"Neither have I," he said with a knowing smile.

"Have we met somewhere before?" Carol's tongue had loosened considerably since finishing the second brandy and there was something incredibly familiar about Gerry, with whom she was now on first-name terms.

"I don't want to tease you any more. We have met actually."

"Where?"

"It was online!"

Carol sat up, startled by the revelation. "You know who I am?"

"Yes, and I know Ellen too – Carol, I'm Greta!"

Carol was astounded. She felt slightly nervous. "You're not a woman!"

Gerry laughed. "No, I'm not a woman but Greta is a name I use – I find some of the women players only want to play with other women – they feel more relaxed with them – and I must say I enjoy the chat and sociable aspect of being a woman online. You and Ellen are always so friendly and nice to people when they start playing. I'm not as good a player as you and Ellen but you were both so encouraging I found my game improve after I started to play with you both."

Carol laughed. "I don't know what to say!"

Gerry smiled. "I know I'm taking a big risk by introducing myself this way but I didn't know how else to tell you. I hope you don't mind if I join you for the next couple of days?"

Carol didn't know how to respond.

"In separate rooms, of course," he said. "Ellen told me where you were both staying."

"Does she know that you are a man?"

Gerry shook his head. "I knew that I would be meeting you both at the tournament in the UK so this was as good a time as any to come clean."

He seemed like a kind and gentle man.

"So how much of what you've told me about Greta is true?"

"I am a widower – not a widow. And I'm a retired

schoolteacher. Pretty much everything else that you know about Greta is me!"

Carol chuckled. "I am surprised but, you know, we can have a few cracking games of bridge in Germany – and I hope you like shopping?"

Gerry nodded. "I do. I always seem more relaxed in ladies' company. Thanks for taking it so well, Carol."

Carol was beaming inside. She hadn't had this much adventure going anywhere – ever!

Chapter Ten

Julia was inundated with messages and calls as she co-ordinated the final details of the 2012 Perrin Travel brochure.

The first thing she did was open her emails and there were twenty waiting for her.

She opened the one from Lydia and was startled to see that she had forwarded an email from Michael to her. She was taken aback by the sentiment and the tack that her brother had taken. Why hadn't he sent it to her first before sending it to Lydia? This was not the way to get back to a girl's heart – for a start it was too needy and he was putting himself on a plate to be punished and rejected in any way that Lydia wished to do it. And she, Julia, would have no qualms about sending such a pleading puppy dog on his way after such an email. However, it did say something about the depth of feeling Lydia must still have for Michael that she didn't send him an instant PFO!

She read the email again and considered what to say. In the end she decided to ring Lydia – it was easier than writing it down.

"Julia – am I glad to hear from you!"

"Hi, Lydia – I just got your email – wow, that's certainly spelling it out for you, isn't it?"

"I don't know what to say to him – I've just come back from the best weekend ever with Peter."

"Oh, where did you go?"

"We were in Monart."

"One of my favourite places on earth. Had you been before?"

"No, but Peter had – he brought me horse-riding and we had the most romantic meal in our dressing gowns!"

Julia laughed. "Sounds good but what are you going to do about your other admirer?"

"I was wondering if Michael had said anything to you? He's not playing mind games, do you think? Is he only interested in me now that he knows I've met someone really nice?"

"Relax, Lydia – you know Michael – he's true to his word and if he's saying that he wants you back and loves you then you know that he really means it – he doesn't come out with statements like that easily or often!"

Lydia knew that what Julia was saying was true.

"I'm just perturbed that he is doing this now – now that I am so happy with Peter."

"But if you are so happy with Peter maybe you shouldn't mind being sent this . . . or do you still have feelings for Michael?"

"Of course I do but I've had to put them behind me – I'm just so confused. I don't know how to reply."

"Maybe see how you feel over the next few days. Call me if you need to talk about your reply. He'll be coming home for Christmas now definitely – I'll be picking him up on the twenty-third."

Lydia sighed. "Okay – I've a conference call coming through – I'll ring you back."

Julia got back to work but all the time she was trying to figure out just what was going through her friend's head. She had a gut feeling that Lydia was in love with Peter but still in love with Michael – torn between two lovers, she thought to herself with a little giggle. That was something she would never have to be concerned about – she would always maintain control in her personal life.

Julia dug her head into her paperwork for two hours and was pleased by a well-needed interruption from Ruth when she appeared at her desk unannounced.

"Hi there," Julia smiled. "Boy, am I glad to see you! I've been having the busiest week ever!"

"I'm coming to take you to lunch – I can see that you need it."

"Thanks, Ruth – you're right – I could do with a break." Julia grabbed her coat and followed her friend out onto College Green.

"Right, where to?"

"What about Milano's – fancy a pizza?"

"Okay by me!" Julia walked along beside her friend and could see that she was bursting to tell her something. "So, any news?"

Ruth's eyes danced as she spoke. "Well, maybe – there is a slight chance that Ian is looking for leave from Aer Lingus for a couple of years – he is considering doing some contract work and there's a chance they may let him go."

Julia didn't like the direction this conversation was taking. It would completely defeat the purpose of Ruth's relocation if Ian decided to follow her.

"Go on . . ."

"Well, Emirates are starting up a new route out of Dublin and are offering one-year contracts."

"So . . ."

"If Ian was flying for them he'd only be ten hours from Perth and he could come and stay with me for one weekend a month!"

Julia couldn't believe her ears. She didn't know which of them was more daft. "And what about his family? Surely he'd need to go home any chance he got to see his kids?"

"Well, he would spend the other weekends every month with them."

Julia had to hold back – Ruth was losing all sense of what was right in the world.

She really wanted to shake her friend. This latest notion would cause nothing but heartbreak and be a complete debacle.

"Ruth, I thought your move to Perth was going to be a fresh start."

"It is but it doesn't mean that I have to finish with Ian."

Julia couldn't listen to any more. She really had done her very best for Ruth – if Ian disrupted his family in this way she wouldn't be able to take responsibility for her actions. She had always felt sorry for Ian's wife Ciara but now more than ever.

Julia ate pizza with Ruth, all the time steering the conversation away from Ian.

"You must stay focused on this opportunity that is yours alone – okay, Ruth?"

Ruth nodded but her eyes were saying that she was still thinking of Ian in her heart.

Julia looked at her watch.

"I really have to go back to work now. Only another week and it will be Christmas."

Ruth shook her head. "Mum wants me to go down with them to Kevin in Kerry but I really can't stand the thought of being in the same house as Mum and Orla for an entire night."

"I know what you mean – well, that offer to spend the day with us is still there. Mum and Granddad would love it. Actually, Mum has been a bit odd since she came back from Cologne – I wonder what she got up to?"

Ruth laughed. "She was most likely playing bridge in her hotel room!"

Julia nodded. "You're probably right."

She kissed Ruth goodbye and set off down Dawson Street on her way back to the office. Her head was full of all the tasks that she had to do when she got back. The Christmas season would soon be in full swing.

Chapter Eleven

Julia took the back roads to Dublin airport. It was almost balmy outside – untypical weather for Christmas. All the time Lydia's words were ringing in her head. She wondered if Michael was being too optimistic. She had coaxed and nurtured him as best she could to say and do the right things where Lydia was concerned. She dearly hoped that she had done enough because, even though Lydia was smitten by her policeman, she had made it quite clear that she still had deep feelings for Michael. If Michael were to return to Dublin permanently it really would make a wonderful start to the New Year. She was secretly dreading the drive to Dublin airport that she would be making very soon with Ruth. Although Ruth's circumstances for leaving the country were quite different to so many other emigrants who had to flee from poverty and unemployment, Julia wished there was some other way that Ruth could untangle herself from Ian.

She parked at Terminal Two which she thought resembled the *Starship Enterprise*. It was positioned exactly where the lake and sculpted snowmen used to be on the drive to Terminal One. So much had changed and yet now again people were coming to pick up loved ones who were making the journey home for Christmas like so many of the Irish Diaspora had done for decades.

The vast arrivals hall was airy, with glass up to the sky. Christmas trees and baubles lined the pillars. Behind the barriers anxious families and friends waited to see a glimpse of their loved ones pass through the sliding doors. One chap leaned against the pillar adorned with antlers and a large bunch of roses. Some families had made banners and had come en masse. Others were twitching nervously with one eye on the arrivals screen and another on their watch.

Julia could feel her own heart beat heavily in her chest as she saw that the flight from London Heathrow had landed. After almost two years she would see her brother again. His reasons for leaving Ireland had been for self-promotion and adventure, like so many that left in the mid-noughties. But there was a difference now as those who had left in the last two years were doing so because they felt they had no choice. Her eyes welled up as she saw a man greet his wife and three small children who were wearing Santa hats and making the most of the occasion. It must be so terrible to have to leave your home and family to make a living, she thought.

But her spirits lifted as her brother's tall frame came into view. His hairline had receded a little but his face was fresh and he was fitter than the last time she had seen him. He wrapped his arms around her warmly and kissed her on the cheek. Julia held him close and for a moment felt her father's presence. Michael was becoming more like him with the years and somehow it was a source of comfort now for Julia.

"Hey, sis, thanks for coming to take me home," he grinned.

"I wouldn't expect you to get a taxi!" She smiled back at him. "But depending on what you've bought me you might be getting one back here next week."

Michael ran his fingers through her hair playfully.

"I've missed you and your wit – sounding more like Dad every day!"

"I was just thinking how much you're getting to look like him."

"I'm not sure whether to take that as a compliment or not," he laughed.

They loaded up his bags into the car and waited in line behind dozens of cars anxious to take their cargo of loved ones home for Christmas.

"How's Mum?"

"Probably playing bridge or talking to one of her bridge friends. But there is a slim chance she is cooking the dinner that she said she was preparing for you!"

"What's with all this bridge? She was only learning that a couple of years ago."

"Well, it's taken over her life!" Julia said with a sigh. "In some way it's the best thing ever because it's given her a wonderful lease of life. She's going off to Warwickshire in the new year to play in some bridge festival and she was in Cologne as you know a couple of weeks ago."

Michael shook his head. "Who ever would have thought? I'm sure Dad must be laughing on the other side!"

"It's such a pity that she wouldn't ever travel with him but then he got to do all his travelling before he met her so maybe they've done it the right way round after all."

"Have you heard from Lydia?"

"Not since I emailed you – did she agree to meet you while you are home?"

Michael shrugged. "I haven't heard from her."

Julia said nothing. She worried that her brother was the one who was in for a surprise. Lydia had changed in the last few weeks and was oozing with a confidence that her new boyfriend had instilled in her. But still, Julia wanted her brother home and was going to do everything in her power to bring the two together. If she left it to him, he would make a mess of it and, well, Lydia didn't really know what was best for her either. She would be doing them both a great favour.

Chapter Twelve

It was Christmas Eve. Ruth looked down at the text on her phone.

Flight delayed kitten c u aft xmas xx Ian

Ruth had thought that seeing him would help her get through the next day but it proved too much to take now.

Thank God for Julia, she thought – she was the one constant in her life.

"Ruth, are you sure you won't come down with us to Kerry?" Angela called up the stairs. "You won't see Kevin and the kids before he goes at all now!"

Ruth sighed. She had been through this so many times with her mother. Her main reason for staying had been to see Ian but still she would rather spend the day with her best friend.

"Honestly, Mum, I'm fine!" She called back down. "Are you staying Stephen's Day too?"

"That depends on how we all get on, I suppose – you know how Orla can be!"

Ruth knew how Angela and her daughter-in-law could be together and that the Christmas festivities could go either way!

But she also knew that if Ian managed to pop out of his house on Stephen's Day, she would want to be in Dublin to see him. Since moving back in with her parents it had been difficult to see him but he had been making less effort too. Maybe going to Australia would help her gain a proper perspective on her life.

It was to be the warmest Christmas for thirty years according to the weatherman on the *Nine O'Clock News*. Julia heard the door slam followed by Michael's heavy footsteps on the wooden floor.

"You're home early!" Julia said.

"Yeah, there weren't that many in the Summit. Actually, change that, it was packed – but there weren't that many over twenty-five."

"I thought you'd have liked that!"

"Ha ha, no need to be so sarky, sis. That was in the past – I've changed!"

Julia wondered if a leopard ever did change his spots but Michael was definitely different to the brother that was home two years ago. She wondered what had brought about this epiphany. She would have to find out over the next few days. After all, he wasn't going to be home very long.

"Any word from Lydia?" he asked.

"I told you that she was going down to Waterford to be with Peter's family before Christmas."

"But it's Christmas tomorrow."

"Yes, and she's driving up in the morning to spend the day with her parents."

"Then I suppose Peter will be coming up too?"

"I didn't want to ask. Look, Michael, I told you I would do everything I could – I'll ring her tomorrow like I always do on Christmas Day and maybe even invite her out. So we'll know then, okay?"

Michael sat down in the chair that their father used to always sit in.

Julia could see vulnerability in him that wasn't there before.

"I always feel like I'm doing something I shouldn't when I sit in Dad's chair!"

Julia knew what her brother meant. "Are you okay?"

Michael shook his head. "All of my mates are married and

they can't even go out for a pint without their wives' permission."
He sighed. "I heard in the Summit that Barry Horgan has moved
to Sydney."

"Isn't he married?"

"Yep, and he has twin baby girls. Moved lock, stock and
barrel last October."

"Yeah, well, a lot of people have moved away – if it keeps
going this way I'd be better off starting an emigration service
instead of a travel company."

Just then the front door opened again and Carol walked in,
laden with bags and gifts from her bridge friends.

"Well, that's the end of bridge now until January!" Carol
chirped.

Michael and Julia looked at each other and smiled.

"What's the bet you'll be playing bridge online before the
night is out?" Michael said.

"See," Julia said. "He's only home two days and already he
knows your form!"

Angela hardly spoke all the way down in the car. It reminded her
of a journey to a funeral. In a way it would be her son's wake. Her
beautiful grandchildren were moving to the far end of Canada and
she had no idea when she would see them again. Things would be
tough for Kevin for the first couple of years. No one understood
that better than Angela herself. And then there were the
temptations and new people and friends – people that you weren't
sure if you could trust or not. It wasn't like home where everyone
knows someone belonging to somebody. If her children brought a
boyfriend or girlfriend home she would be able to track down
their family from any part of Ireland and have some idea of what
they were like. New countries held all sorts of secrets. It was in her
interest that those secrets and events from her own past were
tucked far away on the other side of the world and that is why it
didn't sit comfortably with her that Ruth would soon be returning
to the very same city she herself had fled so long ago.

"Penny for your thoughts, Angela," Fred asked gently as they
drove along the M7 in silence.

"Oh, I'm just going to miss the grandchildren."

"It's for the best – it will all sort out."

"And where will we be spending next Christmas then?" she snapped.

"Don't blame me – we still have Niall in Dublin."

"And we can always visit Ruth in Australia, I suppose," she said.

"Ah, it's a long way to be going – she'll only be gone two years."

"Maybe not – she might meet an Australian and settle down."

"Ruth is a home-bird. She'll be back," Fred assured her.

Angela turned and looked out the window. "I do hope that you are right."

Julia basted the turkey for a second time. It was browning nicely and the succulent juices flowed down the side of the bird. The aroma from it wafted through the house along with the scent of her cedar-pine scented candles. She was excited about the stunning feast, and the addition of her brother and Ruth was making the day perfect. Perfect apart from the absence of her father of course, but, as she put the bird onto the granite surface that he had built himself, she felt his spirit with her.

Carol had a glass of wine in her hand and Horatio was settled in front of the fire.

The doorbell rang with the first of the guests to arrive. She wiped her hands in a tea towel and went out to the front door. Ruth's arms were laden with colourful packages tied up with silver string and bows.

Julia reached out and took some from her friend and planted a Christmas kiss on her cheek.

"Merry Christmas, Ruth – I'm so glad you're spending the day with us."

"Me too. I don't think I could stand the tension between my mother and Orla for a full twenty-four hours – especially in Orla's house."

"I'd love to be a fly on the wall in Kerry," Julia giggled.

"I don't know who I feel more sorry for!" said Ruth. "Actually, I do I feel for Mum. It can't be easy for her. First losing her son to Kerry and now her grandchildren to Canada, but maybe this will make her get on the plane and hopefully visit us both during the year."

"I love your mum, Ruth," Julia said, "but I've always wondered how she managed living in Australia. Maybe you'll get some insight now that you'll be living there."

Ruth nodded hopefully. "Where's your mum – in the living room?"

"Yeah, go on in to her – she's with Granddad."

Ruth carried two presents in with her. Horatio was dozing in the armchair and Carol was having a quick sneaky game of bridge on her laptop.

"Merry Christmas, Carol," Ruth said. She kissed her friend's mother on the cheek and handed her a gift, then went over to Julia's grandfather.

"Merry Christmas, Mr Daly."

"Aah, Ruth, lovely to see you – and what's this Julia's been telling me about you going off to the other side of the world?"

"Well, it's all your granddaughter's doing, Mr Daly."

The old man sucked in his cheeks. "Aah, she can't help stickin' her nose into other people's business but she has a good heart."

"I'm looking forward to going now, Mr Daly."

"Is Perth anywhere near Rockingham?" Carol asked. "I've a very good friend who I play with most mornings and she lives there."

"I can't say I know, Carol. I'll find out when I get there. How was your trip to Cologne?"

Carol blushed. "It was very nice, thank you, Ruth."

"Maybe you can get the info out of her, Ruth," said Julia as she came in. "She's been very coy with us – hasn't she, Granddad?"

Horatio looked up. "I can't keep up with the lot of you and all of your travel around the world. Yis are just trying to make me jealous!"

"Come on, Ruth, we'll go back into the kitchen and see how the turkey is doing," Julia prompted.

"Can I help with anything?" Ruth asked.

"You could mash the potatoes if you like – that would be a great help."

"So how many are coming today?"

"It was just meant to be us, Michael and Odette's crew – but Craig asked if we had room for Dylan and much as I wanted I couldn't say no!"

"Is he really that bad? I mean, he's always been very pleasant when I've met him."

"You've only seen him at weddings and such occasions. He can be such a pain. And the tension between Odette and Craig is getting worse – I'm at a loss to know what to do about it."

"But surely it's between Odette and Craig, whatever is going on in their marriage?"

"Odette looks to me for advice and she's not coping very well with anything at the moment."

"What does Dylan say about all this?"

Julia drained the Brussels sprouts and put them back on the hob.

"I'm sure Dylan wouldn't even notice," she said. "He hasn't a serious bone in his body and is too quick to make jokes and be smart about those around him – especially me!"

"Oh, okay." Ruth knew when to stop prying.

Odette was next at the door and her children rushed in past Julia to get into the living room and see what their granny and great-grandfather had waiting for them.

"Happy Christmas, Julia," she said, giving her sister a kiss on the cheek.

"Where's Craig?"

"Oh, he'll be here soon – had to pop into the office for something."

Julia cocked her head in surprise. "On Christmas Day?"

Odette just nodded and went into the living room after her children.

What sort of accountancy nightmare couldn't wait a couple of days, Julia wondered?

Odette's children loved Ruth and called her Aunty Ruthy.

They collected their presents with gusto and sat down at Horatio's feet in front of the fire. Torn paper surrounded each of them in seconds.

"Time to put the laptop away, I think!" Horatio nodded to his daughter who wistfully did as she was told.

Suddenly the doorbell rang again and Julia ran out to get it. At first she thought that it must be Craig but sighed when she realised it was Dylan.

"Happy Christmas, Julia!" he said, handing her a Poinsettia and bottle of expensive Fleurie wine.

"Thank you and Happy Christmas to you too." She smiled politely.

"I love Christmas – it's one of the few days you have to be civil to me."

"Don't push your luck!" she said, kicking the door closed behind her with the heel of her shoe. She nodded in the direction of the living room. "They're inside."

Dylan went over to his sister-in-law first and looked around for his brother.

"Oh, Craig had to go into work for something!" Odette explained.

Dylan was troubled by the news. What on earth could have him in head office on Christmas Day? And it was a Sunday so he shouldn't be in there anyway. He would have to have serious words with his brother after dinner.

"Will you have a glass of sparkling wine or something warmer?" Julia asked Dylan.

Dylan raised his left eyebrow and with a glint in his eye asked, "What would the warmer option be then?"

Julia clicked the roof of her mouth with her tongue. "I've mulled wine in the pot – or you could have a cup of tea!"

"Well, the first option sounds lovely."

Ruth came out from the kitchen with a glass of the mulled wine in her hand.

Dylan smiled warmly. "Nice to see you again, Ruth – Merry Christmas."

"Hi, Dylan, Merry Christmas."

Julia interrupted. "I need to get some wine for Dylan – will you join me in the kitchen, Ruth?" She beckoned to her friend.

"You can have mine – I haven't touched it," Ruth said, handing her glass to Dylan with a gracious nod and following her friend out to the kitchen.

Julia started to clatter around in the big drawer under the hob. "Where is my carving fork? I'm sure I left it in here."

"You never said how dishy Dylan has become – I love the unshaved look – he's so much cooler in those casual clothes."

"Oh, he's retired now – or redundant if that's the way you want to look at it. He's so jammy and such a smoothie that he really makes my skin crawl."

Ruth poured another ladle of mulled wine into a clean glass. "He's fairly dishy-looking to me and it's obvious that he has the hots for you, Julia. Did you see that look he gave you when you suggested he tried something warm? I was watching from the kitchen door and I could see the desire oozing out of him."

"Don't be silly – he just likes to tease me and I have no idea why!"

Ruth wasn't going to argue with Julia and have a pointless debate that she would never win.

It was almost time to serve dinner when Craig finally rang the doorbell. Odette jumped up to let her husband in.

Julia had sensed Odette's tension and the way she had been looking at her watch for the previous half hour. Something was very wrong and she needed to intervene.

"Time to carve the turkey!" she announced.

The juices flowed and Ruth helped by dishing out the plates of meat. Julia had prepared the most perfect table and lit red candles to shine on the baubles and holly in the centre display. Every guest had a goblet and cloth napkin that co-ordinated with the gold serving dishes catering for the roast potatoes, buttered parsnips and curried Brussels sprouts. Christmas burned in the air from the aroma of the scented apple-cinnamon candles dotted along the table. All present, ranging in age from five to eighty-seven, were content and blessed to be sharing this special day, and everything about the mix just worked.

Ruth laughed and chatted happily to Dylan who sat at her side. Julia was pleased that he was distracted and concentrated her energies on ensuring that her sister and brother-in-law were in good form. Their children were most definitely having a good time and Horatio was enthralled by the speed and alacrity with which they demolished their dinner.

Julia produced a Baked Alaska – knowing it was Horatio's favourite and she felt that he deserved the call for dessert. By the time Irish coffees were served she was ready to collapse and sat in the corner of the living room on the recliner with her feet up.

The other guests were still at the table, busy in a debate about the state of the European Union led by Craig who was wholeheartedly sickened by the state of the public and semi-private sector. He had never been so serious and Odette sat mute and noncommittal throughout the conversation.

Dylan took a break and went into the living room where Julia was sitting.

"That was a fine dinner, Julia!"

His tall figure filled the door frame.

"You can't go wrong sticking a turkey in the oven and peeling a few vegetables!"

"Why can't you take a compliment from me?"

"What was wrong with what I just said? Why do you always pick holes in everything I say?"

Dylan laughed out loud. "You are saying exactly what I feel! I think you'll find that it's the other way around, Julia!"

Julia was tired and in no form for a discussion. "Whatever!"

Dylan stood out of the way as Ruth entered the room.

"Thanks, Julia," she said. "That was wonderful."

Julia shook her head. "You're welcome! Sit down and keep me company, Ruth – Dylan was just going – weren't you, Dylan?"

He waved his empty glass in a gesture of concession and left the room.

"He's really interesting," said Ruth. "Did you know that he plans to travel?"

Julia shook her head. "No. Well, I hope that he goes sooner

rather than later. And, the way I feel about his brother, I hope he takes him with him."

"What happened with Craig today?"

"I don't know – he's been acting really strangely and you saw how late he was today. I don't know what's going on but there's some awful strain between Odette and Craig and I hate to see it."

Ruth felt strangely pleased that she didn't have such big problems. Ian was spending this day with his wife and family but for the first time in years she didn't mind – she wasn't pining for him or feeling odd like she usually did when she spent Christmas with her parents.

It was midnight before the last of the guests had left and Julia was ready for bed. Ruth had already disappeared off to the spare room and Carol was sneaking upstairs with her laptop under her arm in an effort to have a final game with some of her friends in another hemisphere or timezone.

"Goodnight, Mum," Julia whispered.

"Goodnight, Julia – I thought that you did everything beautifully – you made us all feel like you father was still here, making the day move so smoothly."

Julia beamed inside. It was those few simple words that completed the day for her. She had kept his memory and Christmas traditions alive in the Perrin household.

Chapter Thirteen

It was coming to the end of Michael's stay and he was well aware that time was running out and he would have to do something radical if he was to see Lydia. Julia had advised him not to contact her again. He had to wait until she responded to his emails.

But he was losing patience and he couldn't get on the plane for Singapore without seeing her.

He looked at his watch and decided to call his sister.

"Hello," Julia said. She was in a changing room in Monsoon on Grafton Street, trying on a beautifully embroidered silk top.

"Julia, it's me. Have you heard from Lydia?"

"I told you that I would call you if I had – she's probably at the sales like me. Give her some time."

"But that's just it – I don't have much time."

"She knows when you're going back and if she wants to see you she will. You have to have a little faith."

Michael listened and protested but finally agreed that it was better not to contact Lydia.

After Julia hung up, he set about calling Odette to kill some time. He was about to drive to see her in Malahide when his phone bleeped with a text message. It was from Lydia.

Can meet in Clontarf Castle at four if suits? L

Michael felt his heart pound. Of course it suited. He would go anywhere to see her and now he only had an hour and a half to wait.

Lydia wasn't completely sure why she had sent the text. She had managed to put Michael out of her mind on Christmas Day and for two days after. Peter had made it a magical festival and she could honestly say that it was the best Christmas she had ever spent. She didn't want to hurt Michael but she was feeling confident that she could face him and not feel in any way attracted. Peter had not produced a ring but she was sure that it was only a matter of time before he would. Meeting Michael would give her complete closure on her past and leave her free to start the future with a clean slate.

She parked close to the foyer and walked in, brushing her palm along the mane of the bronze lion that stood at the entrance. She was totally cool and calm. She had arranged to meet Peter at eight after he finished work and they were going into town to have dinner with his friends. She could do this, she repeated to herself.

Michael had suggested that they meet in the reception but there was no sign of him. She walked around the corner and into the older part of the hotel. Hidden away in a cosy private alcove Michael sat surveying the menu. She took a sharp breath – the repeated mantras were no use to her now. It had been five years since she had seen him and he had changed very little. But he still managed to floor her on first sight. Her insides turned to jelly and she had to hold onto the back of a nearby couch to prevent her knees from giving way. Yes, she was strong and a different woman to the one that had been in a relationship with Michael but she had been naïve to think that she could just meet him without feeling this way.

Michael looked up and smiled as she approached the alcove where he sat. He rushed over to kiss her. She offered only her cheek.

"Lydia – thanks for meeting me – I was afraid I'd be back on the plane without seeing you."

Lydia said nothing. She was feeling too emotional and scared of the words that might slip out if she started.

"Will you have a coffee – or maybe something to eat?"

"A cappuccino is good," she said with a little nod.

"So how was your Christmas?"

"Oh fine!" she said, raising her brows and nodding her head. Feeling silly.

"And work, how is that?"

"Good," she blurted.

Michael could feel the sweat build under his collar – she wasn't making it easy for him and the phrase 'drawing blood from a stone' was coming to mind.

"How are your folks?"

Lydia was finding it difficult to hear what he was saying. The words were there and she could understand them but they made no sense. A waitress came by and took their order but she still sat there feeling like a fragile china doll.

In his nervousness Michael started blurting out everything about his position in Singapore and his desire to move back home. He was wound up like a performing monkey and didn't stop to draw breath.

When the waitress returned with the coffee Lydia picked up the cup gratefully – delighted by the distraction. But her jellylike fingers dropped the cup on the table and the brown liquid spilled all over her boots.

"Lucky they are black and leather!" Michael said, trying to make light of the situation. But the awkwardness wasn't going away for either of them. Michael soaked up the liquid with paper napkins and asked the waitress for another cappuccino. He didn't know how to relieve the tension between them – this reunion was not going as he had expected.

"I'm fine now, thanks." Lydia stood up and shook herself down. "I don't know what's wrong with me!"

Michael stood up beside her and stared deeply into her eyes.

"I still have feelings for you, Lydia – you know that I do – I can't let my life go by without doing something about these feelings. They are gnawing away at me as I try to sleep at night. Is there any way that you could feel the same?"

Lydia was confused. She couldn't deny that she was feeling an incredibly electric passion that she hadn't experienced since she had last been with Michael. She sat down and he sat next to her. They held hands – unable to look away from each other's gaze.

"Lydia, please answer – do you have these feelings too?"

She couldn't stop the words from falling from her lips. She was in a trance now.

"I do."

Michael was sitting patiently at the kitchen table waiting for Julia's return. He was sure that Lydia would consider his feelings and they were on track to reconciliation. When Julia did come through the front door, laden with bags from the Christmas sales, he jumped up and helped her.

"Julia, I met Lydia – it went great!"

Julia was in the middle of unwinding her scarf but Michael's enthusiasm made her smile.

"Hold on – give me a minute – I need to take my coat off. Why don't you put the kettle on and you can tell me all about it?"

He did as she suggested and Julia followed him into the kitchen.

"So when did you hear from her?"

"I couldn't believe it – she sent me a text shortly after I was speaking to you. Then we went to Clontarf Castle and I swear she was in a daze – totally into me – we were right back to the last time that we made up."

Julia didn't want to burst her brother's bubble but she was astonished to hear all of this – especially after Lydia's account of the marvellous Christmas that she had spent with Peter.

"And did she say that she wanted to see you again?"

Michael placed two mugs filled with tea onto the kitchen table and took a seat.

"I told her that she should take a holiday in Singapore in the New Year and that it would be my treat. A week, a month – whatever she felt like. Then we could discuss what we both wanted."

"Did you not scare the living daylights out her, Michael? It's not like you to come on so strong."

"This is Lydia and me we're talking about – we know each other so well, it's different."

"Alright," Julia shrugged as she took a sip from her mug. "I just don't want to see you getting hurt."

Michael was adamant that his feeling were reciprocated.

Julia listened more but didn't comment. She didn't want to see either her friend or her brother mess up again.

Chapter Fourteen

Ruth needed somewhere safe to store her special keepsakes. It was one of the last tasks that she needed to do before packing her suitcase for her journey to Perth in two days' time. Over the years she had kept her love letters and special mementos in a wooden jewellery box that she had bought from a stall in George's Street market. The box was carved in India.

She carried the box downstairs and went into the kitchen where her mother sat at the table reading the newspaper.

"Mum, do you have somewhere safe where I can keep some old bits and pieces?"

Without looking up, her mother said, "Your father put a stairs in the attic – you know, one of those ones that you pull down. There are plenty of nooks and crannies up there."

Ruth turned on her heels and climbed the stairs. She wondered when her father had done that. Was she so consumed by her own life and her affair with Ian that she never even heard about the stairs? She looked up when she reached the landing and sure enough the knobs that used to be on the attic door were now replaced by a flash new handle. She pulled down on it and the stairs were released. She ascended with ease and was surprised to see a new light switch. Her father had done a wonderful clean-up job and all the boxes there were now arranged in order.

She needed to find a spot where nobody would look because there were cards from Ian in the box that she wouldn't want her mother to read. She went over to the corner and spotted a plank sticking up. She tugged at it gently and it came up in her hands. She put it back into place and it slotted back with ease. This was the ideal place to hide her mementos. As she lifted the board again she noticed a large manila envelope squashed in at the back. Curiosity overcame her and she lifted it out. She could feel the weight and shape of what seemed like three or four slim books inside but the envelope was stuck closed by three pieces of Sellotape. She peeled them back and revealed some notebooks with a sealed airmail letter among them. She pulled out the envelope. Scribbled across the front of it in faded, barely legible writing was a name and address: *Charles Walters, 5 Peppermint Grove Road, Peppermint Grove, Perth, Western Australia.* The handwriting was her mother's. She had written this letter and then didn't post it. How odd! Ruth was really tempted to open it but of course that was out of the question.

Her mother had always been the keeper of a diary and, because she had hidden them away with this letter, Ruth presumed that these notebooks were her diaries from her time in Australia. She really wanted to peep inside but controlled the urge. Diaries were sacrosanct and it would not be right or respectful to open them.

It did mean, however, that her mother had claimed that great hiding place and she would have to put her box of mementos somewhere else.

Ruth found a little nook under the insulation in another part of the attic and put her jewellery box in there. Her mind was ringing with a new curiosity and she wondered what her new life would be like in Australia and if it would be like her mother's.

She went back down to the kitchen and joined her mother at the table.

Angela looked up. "Do you want tea?" she asked. "I'm about to make myself a cup."

"I'll make it for you," Ruth said and, as she filled the kettle with water she asked her mother, "Where exactly did you live in Perth?"

"We stayed in South Perth – all the Irish did at that time."

"What was the name of the street you lived on?"

Angela chuckled. "Don't laugh – we lived on Hope Street!"

"Was there ever any *hope* that you would stay in Perth?"

Angela put her palms up to her face and rubbed her eyes. She shook her head and watched as her daughter put the teabags into the china mugs.

"There was a time when I was happy in Perth – a short time, mind you. I had a friend who lived in Cottesloe which was a very beautiful part of the city – you've heard of Cottesloe Beach?"

"Of course," Ruth nodded.

"Well, this friend of mine was Welsh and a great support to me."

Ruth wondered about Charles Walters and was itching to ask about Peppermint Grove but that would betray the fact she had seen the envelope.

"Steve is organising some accommodation close to the Central Business District – but he said I would most likely choose to live out beside the beaches – he would do his best to get somewhere that was near both."

"Yes, I think you'd be happier and cooler beside the sea. Mosman Park is good and City Beach . . ." Angela paused. "And then there's the likes of Peppermint Grove."

Ruth's ears pricked up as she poured boiling water into the mugs.

"Oh, what a lovely name for a place!" she said, prodding her mother to tell more.

"Did any of your friends live there?"

Angela shook her head and wrapped her palms around the china mug as Ruth handed it to her. "Peppermint Grove is an exclusive suburb . . ." She paused as she took a sip from her mug, then added briskly, "On second thoughts I think a young woman like you would be better off in the city centre."

Ruth wished she had more time to talk with her mother and in two days she would be gone. But she knew from her mother's body language that there was only so much she would divulge.

Julia stirred the ratatouille and waited for the doorbell to ring. She intended to really enjoy this meal as it would be their last together before Ruth's departure to Perth.

It would be nice to send her friend off with a meaningful memento. She thought about the best gift that she could give – it would have to be easy to transport and durable. She remembered times they had spent together as little girls. They used to go to tap-dancing classes every Saturday morning and performed in a show. If only she could find something from that time that Ruth could easily transport with her to Australia. She went into the study and took one of the photo albums down from the shelf. Her father had documented so much of her young life with great precision from behind the lens of his camera. There was bound to be a perfect photograph somewhere. The first photograph was of the two standing beside a slide in their friend Clodagh's house. They couldn't have been more than nine years of age. The next page showed a photograph of Julia with her cousins – Michael was standing in the background with a hose in his hands. Julia recalled Michael drenching them all under a cascade of water seconds later. On the next page she saw a photograph that she had never seen before – it was so poignant that it brought a tear to her eye. Two little pairs of silver tap-dancing shoes laced with pink ribbons resting neatly at the end of the stairs beside each other. Her father must have taken it without her knowing and somehow it said more than all the photographs of the other friends and family members. Julia remembered seeing an offer on the internet for business-cards key-rings and other printed items. She would scan this photograph into her computer in work and make the perfect key-ring so that both of them could have a copy.

Suddenly she smelt something burning and dashed back to the kitchen to tend to the ratatouille. At that moment the doorbell rang but Horatio was in the hallway and went to open it first. Horatio loved Ruth – the two friends had spent many evenings in his home when his wife was alive and, although the years had passed and she was now a woman, he still saw her as a little girl.

Horatio smiled. "It's lovely to see you, Ruth. My goodness, 2012 is going to be a wonderful year for you – think of all the adventure you'll have!"

With that, Julia appeared. "What are you saying now, Granddad?" She gave Ruth a kiss on the cheek.

"I'm only telling her what she already knows!" the old man laughed.

Julia led the way back into the kitchen. She went to the oven and opened the door.

"Are you going to have some of this, Granddad?"

"I had a ham sandwich earlier," Horatio said with a smile. "Anyway, I'm sure you girls have lots to talk about that you won't want an old man to hear!"

Julia pretended to take umbrage at his words but he just playfully brushed his palm against the side of her hair and went into his room which was purpose-built for all his needs and backing onto the kitchen.

"You're so lucky to have a granddad," Ruth said. "I never knew either of mine!"

Julia nodded her head. Family were so important to her. Sometimes to the point that she couldn't contemplate ever having children of her own because she would be so concerned about them all of the time.

The two women sat at the kitchen table and Julia dished out the pasta bake and ratatouille.

"I'm going to miss this!" Ruth sighed.

"I'm sure they have ratatouille in Australia," Julia said brightly, even though inside she felt a knot in her stomach.

Ruth giggled and appreciated her friend's attempt to make light of their situation. "I've always been able to pick up the phone and see you in a matter of minutes."

"And now you'll just have to Skype me in the same way as Michael does and all of my other friends who are scattered around the world."

Ruth rubbed her forehead. "I don't know how I'll cope being apart from Ian – he said that he'll try and come visit in February."

Julia rolled her eyes. "You might meet a fantastic hunky Aussie!"

Suddenly the kitchen door swung open and Horatio hobbled over to the kettle.

"I'm sorry, girls – do you mind if I make a cup of tea?"

Julia jumped up and went over to help her grandfather.

"I'm fine, Julia – sit back down there with Ruth." Horatio chuckled. "She'd have me in the knacker's yard, Ruth, stopping me from doing my bits and pieces." He paused. "So why the sad faces?"

"I'm going to miss home, Mr Daly. But Julia was just talking about the opportunities I'll have."

Horatio nodded his head vehemently. "And this is something I have to say she is right about. Travel is the greatest way to broaden the mind. Sure, isn't it my greatest regret that I never left the old sod myself. I've seen generations of young Irish people on the telly and their stories in the newspapers and I've envied every one of them going off to find adventure and a new start in another part of the world."

Julia was aghast. "You never said anything like that before, Granddad. I always thought that you were a home-bird."

"Sure, didn't I try and get your grandmother to move several times and try out different places – but she wasn't happy unless she was a five-minute walk from her mother. It's only when you get to my age that you realise how quickly life passes you by and all of that time – that wonderful time that you think you have plenty of – it just flitters through your fingers like sand in an hourglass. So go and be happy and have adventure and taste all that life has to offer, young Ruth."

"Oh, I'm only going for two years, Mr Daly. It's just a change of scene and, well, it seems to be a positive career move."

Horatio tilted his head and grinned. "You never know what lies waiting for you in Australia. I've read *The Thorn Birds*, you know – watched *The Sullivans* for years – it was one of your grandmother's favourite programmes, Julia. But it's not like long ago – sure, you're only a phone call away on the computer – all of you young people do Skype."

"That's what I was just saying!" Julia agreed.

"And there was a fella on *The Joe Duffy Show* only yesterday, saying that he reads a goodnight story every single evening to his grandchildren who live across the world in Sydney. He does it after his breakfast and sure they are all delighted with the routine."

"Really?" Ruth laughed. "Well, I guess I'm not surprised – plenty of the older generation use the internet."

"And speaking of someone who is always on the internet – where is your mother?" Horatio asked Julia.

"Oh, it's her bridge night tonight."

"I suppose we should be grateful that she's playing with real people at least," the old man said with a roll of his eyes. "Now I'll make my brew and leave you in peace."

"I'll bring it in to you, Granddad," Julia smiled.

"Alright – but remember what I said, Ruth – you won't get this time back. How I'd love to be going off with you and be fifty years younger! There's many the country that was made by the labour and drive of the Irish emigrant. We come into our own when we go off to other countries. It's how we'll get out of this stupid recession the politicians have put us in!"

Horatio shuffled back to his room.

"He's a wise old man," Ruth said with a sigh. "It's not like I'm going away for ever."

"Exactly. It's only a two-year contract – you will be back before you know it."

"Do you think your granddad is right?"

"About coming into our own when we move abroad?"

"Everything he said really – is it in our psyche?"

Julia shook her head. "I think he always felt that Granny held him back. But maybe there's something in what he said – don't forget my father lived in New York for a few years before he married my mum. It certainly made a difference for him and his business skills."

"Did you never consider living abroad, Julia? I mean, we never even took up our J1Visas when we were in college."

"That's because we had it too cushy here!"

Julia giggled. "Because my dad paid us too much to work for him! But I don't regret the time I spent with him – he's gone now and all of the factory jobs in Boston and New York are still there and I've been to the States for work plenty of times with Perrin Travel. So, you see, we'll get to see the world one way or another, Ruth, and I will make sure that I come to Perth to see you as soon as I can."

Ruth stopped eating. "Oh, would you, Julia? I would love that so much!"

"Of course I will – I have a plan already to expand the business with the new route open through the Middle East. It will make such a difference to Irish travellers going to Western Australia and at the moment Perth is the place to be."

"So when are you thinking of coming over?"

"February is a good month for me – so many people book their holidays in January I like to be around and I've the holiday fair to supervise but I could slip away for a week or two in Feb and the business will be fine."

Ruth's eyes started to water. "You've no idea how happy that makes me – I'm not going to know a soul down there."

"It's strange, don't you think, that your mother has no contact with anyone from the time that she spent living in Perth?"

"Very odd!" Ruth agreed. "And I've wondered why my mum is so slow to tell about the time that she spent there. In fact, I was only talking to her about it before coming here."

"Did she tell you anything?"

Ruth shook her head. "But I was putting some keepsakes up in the attic and there was an envelope that she had hidden there with the address of a place in Australia – Peppermint Grove."

"Oh, what a lovely name – I bet it's some romantic little cove filled with wooden cottages with verandas out the front and roses in the gardens."

"It does conjure up all sorts of images – but I Googled it before coming here and the houses are all palatial mansions – it must have been millionaire's row when Mum lived in Perth."

"Wouldn't it be great to find out more?" said Julia.

"I'd love to know what was in the envelope. And she also kept her diaries from that time!"

"Oh, Ruth, you have to ask your mother about it before you go! Did she live there?"

"Apparently not. I'll try to get her to tell me but I've only got a couple of days to do it!"

But still Ruth wondered why Angela disliked Australia so much. When she got to Perth she might have a better understanding why.

Chapter Fifteen

Julia had been dreading this moment. She had never been apart from Ruth for more than a few weeks and, although Ruth's contract was for only two years, things didn't always go to plan and there was always the chance that she would stay longer. Of course if Ruth did meet someone and decide to settle in Perth it would be a wonderful outcome because Ian would finally be out of her friend's life. But it was also a high price for her to pay.

Julia pulled on her coat and grabbed her car keys. She had to have her friend in the Departures lounge no later than 11.20 a.m.

The sky was heavy, with thick grey clouds hanging over Dublin Bay. Sprinkles of rain fell on the windscreen of her Audi. She hoped that she could hold it together for Ruth's sake. It was unlike her to feel so emotional but it wasn't every day that she said goodbye to her best friend.

The front door was open and Angela was dragging a case out to the porch. Julia could feel her sadness as she got to the front door.

"Oh Julia, what are we going to do without her?"

"We won't feel the time passing, Angela," Julia said with a smile. "And maybe you'll pop out to see her soon."

"If I can get her father to make a move I'll definitely be there before the year is out. But I'm glad that you'll be going out soon to check up on her – when exactly are you going?"

"The first week of February. She'll be well settled by then, I'd imagine."

Angela nodded with a tight-lipped smile. "You'd better come on in – she's still putting the last few bits and pieces into her case."

Julia followed Angela up the stairs and into Ruth's bedroom.

Ruth was sitting in the middle of the floor surrounded by bottles of liquid soap and towels.

"They do have soap and towels in Perth from what I hear!" Julia said with a giggle.

"Oh Julia, I don't know what to be taking!"

"I'll be out in three weeks so if there's anything that you feel you need I'll bring it out to you."

Between them they put three suitcases into the car boot.

"Maybe I'll come to the airport after all," Angela said.

"It's okay, Mum, we can say goodbye here – it's probably best."

"Your father is going to do himself an injury up there – maybe you're right – I'll go up to him."

Ruth had already said goodbye to her father. He was upstairs in the bedroom, desperately trying to fix a shelf that had been needing attention for at least two years.

It was no more than a twenty minutes' drive to Dublin airport.

The two were chatting about the practicalities of the journey ahead when Ruth suddenly said, "You know, I'm really intrigued about that airmail letter and Peppermint Grove. I'm almost sorry I didn't have a look at the diaries!"

"Oh, Ruth, you couldn't look at your mother's diaries!"

"I know, I know! I didn't. But wouldn't you love to know who that man Charles Walters was and why Mum was writing to him?"

"You'd wonder alright," Julia agreed. "Hey, maybe we'll check it out when I come over."

"I'm sure that whoever lived there doesn't any more. I suppose it could have been work-related but, if that was the case, then why hide the correspondence? Mum writes a diary but she's not a hoarder and I see her chucking out statements and documents all of the time. Same applies if the letter is something trivial – like, I don't know, a thank-you letter or something."

"Yes, the fact she kept it at all seems to mean it's something significant and special."

Ruth turned and looked at her friend's profile as she drove along the M1. "You know, this is what I'll miss more than anything – having someone to speculate with and talk about anything, no matter how silly."

"Skype me when you get to Dubai, won't you?" Julia asked sadly.

"Yes, I'll do my best."

Ruth hadn't mentioned Ian once, Julia noticed – but *she* certainly wasn't going to bring him up.

Julia drove up to the car park at Terminal Two.

"Where are you going?" Ruth asked.

"I'm coming in with you to Departures."

Ruth shook her head. "No, Julia, please just drop me off. We don't even have time for a cup of coffee and anyway I want to get some duty-free."

"Oh!" Julia was disappointed but would do as her friend wished.

She parked at the set-down bay and got a trolley while Ruth unloaded the bags.

So this was it – Ruth was actually leaving and Julia had a knot in her stomach. She couldn't break down in front of her friend. Instead she hugged her tightly and kissed her on the cheek.

"It's 28° in Perth today and there's talk of a heat wave so enjoy all that sunshine and keep some for my stay. It won't be long before you're picking me up at Perth airport."

Ruth nodded. She was feeling incredibly cool or maybe it was numbness. She watched Julia drive away and pushed her trolley into the airport.

Ian had promised that he would meet her in the Duty Free.

Julia had to fight back the tears as she drove along the M1 on her way in to work. Ruth had had no idea how upset she was and Julia didn't want her friend to be any the wiser. She had to concentrate on her work. The tears filled her eyes but she kept focused. She had a business to keep going and people who needed her here. She was doing what was best for those around her but she felt sad and lonely as she had just sent her best friend off to the other side of the world and it was a very long way away.

She parked in the city centre and touched up her make-up before going into the office.

"Good morning, Julia," Gillian said.

Julia grunted and went into her office, shutting the door tightly. She sat down and put her head into the palms of her hands. She had to pull herself together and get on with her work.

A message came through on Skype from her brother and she was relieved to take his call.

"Hey there, Michael – how are things in Singapore?"

"I'm miserable, Julia, and I've had only one enigmatic email from Lydia – I swear I haven't a clue what she means."

"Send it to me – I'll try and decipher it!"

Michael sighed. "I really thought that she opened up when we met – I was totally honest with her and she was completely into me."

Julia worried for her brother. He could be slightly delusional at times and, even though he had an irresistible attractiveness with most women that he met, sometimes his confidence was askew.

"I've just taken Ruth to the airport, Michael, so I'm feeling a bit fragile myself."

"Ah, she's gone, is she – that's good. When are you going to see her?"

"In February."

"Great, so I guess you'll be calling in to me on the way?"

"No, sorry – I forgot to tell you that I'm flying Emirates through Dubai – it's much quicker – saves flying through London."

Michael put on a sad face. "Not fair. You have to come and see me. I'm hurting bad over Lydia."

"You'll be fine," Julia assured him. "I'm surprised you haven't found some Asian beauty by now to cheer you up."

"I'm a reformed character, Julia – I keep trying to explain – I'm holding out for Lydia. Hey, what about if I come down to Perth for a couple of days while you're there?"

It sounded like a good idea to Julia. "I don't see a problem with that – I'm sure Ruth will have room."

"Cool – maybe you can ask when you speak to her?"

"I'll give her a chance – she's probably only at Duty Free in Dublin airport by now!"

"Okay, I have to get a few bits done here before I finish up for the day – I'll look forward to that little trip."

"Okay, Michael – I'll let you know what I think of that email – give me a day or two though, won't you?"

"Will do."

And then he was gone.

Julia felt very alone again.

Michael's email came through and she braced herself before reading it.

Dear Michael

It was good to meet you at Christmas and I hope that you had a safe trip back to Singapore. Things are extremely busy in work since I've returned with more redundancies on the cards. I'm hoping that things will pick up when we have pared our expenses down.

I'm looking to buy somewhere nearer the city and although I'll lose a bit on my own apartment there is great value at the moment and you know how I've always wanted a place in Sandymount.

I've taken up horse-riding too which I know is a strange departure for me but I really enjoy it. I may be going to New York with work in February which will be a lot of fun and no doubt I'll do some shopping.

As you can see my life is very busy. I hope that things are going well for you.

Thinking of you

Lydia

Julia read it a second time just to make sure that she hadn't missed anything. It seemed like an email that Lydia would have sent to a stranger. She worried about what Michael had been expecting from his ex. It was perfectly clear to Julia as someone from the outside that Lydia was not interested in rekindling the relationship. She did wonder what Michael was confused about. The last three words 'thinking of you' could just be taken as 'take care' but Julia knew her brother well enough to realise that these were the three words that he had focused on and possibly read and re-read to himself, wanting to believe there was more to the email than it was saying. She didn't want to give him any false hope. Yes, Lydia had agreed to meet him and got emotional on seeing him, but from this email Julia deduced that she had fallen back into her comfortable lifestyle with Peter and didn't want to pursue anything more than a friendship from afar with her ex. She would have to consider her reply to Michael carefully.

Ruth put her feet up on the comfortable lounger on the Emirates Airbus. She was finally on her way to her new home. It was kind of Steve to book a business-class seat for her journey. Ruth was thrilled by the upgrade and comforts that accompanied travelling in style. It compensated for Ian's 'no-show' at Duty Free. Instead she'd got a text saying that he had to report for a meeting in Ops and that he would Skype her later. Ruth felt incredibly proud of herself for not getting upset and it seemed to her a clear indication that leaving Ireland and Ian behind was the right move.

She took the glass of champagne handed to her by the beautifully attired air steward. With fresh flowers in a metal bowl hanging from the wall in front of her, Ruth felt like a star. She sipped from her glass and settled down to watch the first new movie on her individual entertainment system. She had read the novel *One Day* and was keen to see the movie.

After three glasses of champagne and several damp tissues the film ended. She imagined Ian and her as the characters Emma and Dexter and was truly miserable until she spotted *Downtown*

Abbey – she'd watched the full series before but it would take her mind off Ian.

The air steward was a charming Aussie – he told her that he was from Western Australia.

"Are you stopping off in Dubai?" he asked her.

"No, I'm travelling on to Perth."

He giggled, showing gleaming white teeth. "You won't have to worry about missing your connection then."

"Why not?"

"The Perth flight is full of Irish people emigrating – it's been known to wait for the connecting passengers if this flight is ever delayed."

"Oh, I'm not emigrating. I'm only staying for two years."

"You're gonna love it – might want to stay a bit longer!"

"Oh, I'm not sure about that but I'm looking forward to spending time there – my mother lived in Australia in the seventies."

"Whereabouts?"

"South Perth – are you from Perth?"

He nodded again. "It's a great city if you like the outdoors life. I grew up in Cottesloe which is a really nice part of the city beside the beach."

"Is that near Peppermint Grove?"

He nodded. "Peppy Grove – yeah, it's only a couple of blocks away. Fancy part of town, Peppy Grove – they have their own shire for a handful of houses – it's the smallest shire in the entire country."

She knew that 'shire' was the word they used for a local government area.

"Mansions, really," he added. "Worth seeing. You should go and check them out."

"I intend to – my mother knew someone who lived there."

"What street?"

"Eh, I'm not sure."

"Well, good luck with that. Now, would you like some more champagne?"

Chapter Sixteen

Julia was feeling truly bereft. On a Friday evening normally she would have called Ruth and made arrangements to hit one of the nicer bars in the Grafton Street area. Now it looked like she would have to settle for a depressing evening in.

Her sister had invited her to a fund-raising quiz in the yacht club the next night and she had quickly declined but Odette had assured her that there would be an eligible bachelor friend of Craig's at it. Dear sweet Odette! Could she not figure out by now that Julia liked the single life and didn't need to be fixed up with one of the sailors from the yacht club? Mind you, if Ruth was here she would probably go along and try and introduce her to new company – the company of anyone that wasn't Ian Hawkins.

Gillian came into the office and disturbed Julia's musings.

"Is there anything else you need me to do?"

"Oh, is it that time already, Gillian?" Julia looked at her watch. "You probably have somewhere to go – it being Friday."

Gillian shook her head. "I'm off home to watch a DVD – nothing exciting lined up for me unfortunately."

Julia didn't know Gillian very well – she had worked for her for seven months and was a reliable and efficient member of staff but Julia had been too busy to pay much attention to her. She didn't even know if Gillian had a boyfriend or had much of a social life.

Julia was desperate to go out and blurted the invitation before she thought about it. "Would you like to go for a drink – if you aren't rushing home, that is?"

Gillian's green eyes widened – she was astonished at the proposal. Julia was somehow out of her league – not just because she was her boss but because of the way she carried herself with such confidence and panache. Gillian was at least eight years younger than Julia but not a sharp dresser.

"Eh, I'd love to but I'm not dressed for going out," she said, shaking her mousy brown hair.

"It's Dublin on a Friday night – lots of people will be dressed in work clothes. I could do with the company."

"Okay. Great!" Gillian said and then felt terrible. How was she going to look standing in a trendy bar next to Julia?

"I'll get things cleared up here and we can pop off in ten minutes." Julia smiled.

When she emerged from her office Gillian was waiting patiently at the door, with the keys in her hand to lock up.

Julia threw her bag over her shoulder and held the door open for Gillian.

"Right, first stop BT's," she said, looking at her watch. "I'll just catch my friend Tony before she clocks off. She touches up my make-up at the end of the day if I decide to stay in town for a drink."

So much for being casual because it was Friday night, thought Gillian. She plodded along a couple of steps behind Julia. She had nothing better waiting for her at home than her cat. Her mother always went out on Friday nights to play bingo.

"This way," Julia said, opening the large swing doors of the department store.

Gillian followed. She had been in Brown Thomas a few times but couldn't honestly say that she had ever bought anything there except an eye liner. She remembered feeling terribly guilty afterwards as it had cost a day's salary.

Julia walked up to the Clinique counter and gave the perfectly primed girl at the counter a warm hug. She turned to Gillian.

"This is Gillian – Gillian meet Tony, my lifesaver!"

Tony held out her hand and at the same time scanned Gillian's face, observing the poorly applied layer of make-up with no colour at all on her eyes or cheeks after her day in the office.

"Lovely to meet you, Gillian – would you like me to touch up your make-up as well?"

Gillian nodded. She had never had her make-up applied professionally.

Tony set to work on Gillian, first fixing her eyebrow line which was scraggy. Then she put some warm brown tones on her eyelids.

Julia sat browsing through the catalogue of new colours while all the time chatting to Tony about where she was going to holiday that year. Julia always gave Tony a special rate when she came to book her holidays – so special that it ensured a make-up artist on tap for the duration of the year.

"I think you should try Egypt – there's nothing like a bit of sun in winter," she chirped on.

Gillian listened attentively, scared to move in case Tony's hand slipped. But of course Tony was a skilled professional and, when she lifted the mirror to eventually show Gillian how she looked, the young girl nearly fell off the stool.

"Is that me?" she exclaimed in amazement.

"It sure is and you have beautiful eyes – don't hide them under that fringe – try keeping your hair back from your face."

'Beautiful' was a word that Gillian would never use when describing herself but she did feel good.

"Tony will look after you if you ever want to be fixed up – just pop in as you pass by!" Julia said.

Tony nodded her head. "Any time, Gillian – just pop in!"

The two girls left BT's with shining faces. It was a mild January evening – almost ten degrees. Julia couldn't help but wonder what the temperature must be in Perth and what it must be like for Ruth. She missed her friend so much. She would treat herself to a cocktail and get to know Gillian better. She needed more girlfriends – life was definitely changing.

As they walked to Dakota on South William Street, they passed a little boutique and stopped to try on some tops – the shop was about to close but Julia was interested in a shirt that was priced 150 euro so the shop assistant was happy to leave the doors open a bit longer.

Gillian fingered through a stack of tops that were perfect for the party season. She winced as she looked at the price-tags. She bought most of her clothes in Penneys.

"That red top is gorgeous – I bet it would look great on you, Gillian," Julia said with a nod.

"Oh, do you think so?" Gillian trusted Julia's taste in clothes – she never came to work looking less than stunning. "Maybe I'll try it on?"

"Go ahead," the shop assistant said enthusiastically.

When Gillian came out of the changing room she was like a new person.

"Gorgeous!" Julia said. "You have to get it."

Gillian looked at the tag. It was seventy-two euros – a fortune! But she was too swept up in the moment to argue. She reached into her purse, pulled out the money that she had put aside to pay her mother for housekeeping and put it on the counter.

When the two left the store Gillian walked with a spring in her step. She watched how Julia held herself and tried to keep up.

The Dakota bar was packed for so early in the evening and people were smoking at the tables outside. When they got to the long bar Julia asked Gillian what she would like to drink.

"Oh, a bottle of Bulmers, please."

Julia clicked the roof of her mouth with her tongue. "It's Friday, Gill, you have to have something more special – what about a Cosmo?"

Gillian just nodded. She was in shock that somebody had called her Gill. She liked it – it sounded cool. Could she actually be looking the way she did and feeling this confident?

Two men walked into the bar wearing tight leather jackets and trendy haircuts. They were tall and handsome and would never normally notice Gillian. But they stopped at the part of the bar where the two girls sat on high stools. One started to chat to Julia but she was having none of it. Gillian copied Julia's snooty expression and sipped on her cocktail glass in the same way as her boss.

"That looks good," the shorter of the two men said to Gillian. "Can I get you another?"

Gillian looked over her shoulder. Was that gorgeous guy really talking to her?

"We are having a quiet drink, thanks, guys!" Julia interrupted.

Gillian turned her head in the direction of the counter but could see the two guys staring intently at them in the reflection in the mirror behind the bar. She felt her heart pound and was gutted when they walked away.

"Honestly!" Julia exclaimed. "What must we do just to have a bit of peace at the end of the day?"

Gillian had often wondered what it felt like to be one of those women who pushed men away like that. Now that she saw Julia in action she understood a little more. She liked the feeling of power. How wonderful to be as confident and in control of your life, she thought. She listened as Julia rambled on about her plans for the business and the trip that she was taking to visit her friend in Perth in February. All the time a terrible mixture of admiration and jealousy rumbled in Gillian's stomach. She had liked being called Gill earlier. She would do everything in her power to learn from Julia and improve herself. This job was turning into a wonderful opportunity.

"Do you fancy another here or would you rather go on somewhere else?" Julia asked.

"Oh, I don't mind!" Gillian's purse was beginning to feel the strain – first from the top that she had bought and secondly from the round of drinks that she had bought. She couldn't remember the last time that she'd had a cocktail.

"It's my round – we'll have one for the road?"

Gillian was feeling a little light-headed but would enjoy one more drink. She nodded graciously.

No sooner had the waiter put the glasses down on the bar than Julia flinched as another handsome man came over to her. Gillian's eyes widened as the gorgeous man put his palm on Julia's upper arm.

"I didn't know this was one of your haunts!" he exclaimed.

How did she know so many men and attract so many others, Gillian wondered. This one was particularly delicious.

"I seldom come in here – but I felt like a change," Julia said, deadpan.

"Aren't you going to introduce me to your lovely friend?" he asked.

"Gillian – this is my sister's brother-in-law – Dylan."

He held out his hand and shook Gillian's.

"Pleased to meet you," she beamed. She looked him up and down and was too much in awe to say anything more.

"Can I get you a drink, ladies?"

"No, thanks, we've just got ours," said Julia.

"I'm going for a bite to eat in the Trocedero with a couple of the lads that I used to work with – would you ladies like to join us?"

"No – this is our last drink and then we're going home, thanks," Julia replied curtly.

Dylan leaned forward and whispered in Gillian's ear, loud enough for Julia to hear.

"She's mad about me really – but my brother got the nice sister in the Perrin family!" He then winked at Julia. "Are you coming to the yacht club tomorrow night?"

Julia shook her head. "There's a holiday-information day on Sunday so I'll be having an early night."

"Ah, why don't you come and bring the lovely Gillian with you?"

Gillian looked from Julia to Dylan and back – she would so much like to go to the yacht club – she had never been – never even dreamed before of entering such a place.

Julia tilted her head. "Would you like to go to the yacht club tomorrow night, Gillian?"

Gillian didn't know what was the best answer to give – if she said yes Dylan would be pleased – if she said no she felt that Julia would be pleased.

"Whatever you think, Julia."

"Don't let her bully you, Gillian – what do you want to do?" said Dylan.

Julia sighed. "Gillian has a mind of her own – if she wants to we'll go to the yacht club tomorrow but I won't be staying late."

Dylan shrugged. "Okay, ladies – I see you want a bit of peace and quiet – I'll see you tomorrow evening then."

He had only left when Julia apologised. "He's always such a pain, Gillian – he is so naughty to put you in that awkward position but he seems to thrive on embarrassing people and putting them into difficult situations."

"I thought he seemed quite nice and polite."

"Just because he's kind of smart-looking he thinks he can get away with saying anything that he wants."

Gillian breathed out loudly. "He's really gorgeous, Julia – is his brother as handsome?"

"Who – Craig? Em, I guess so – he's sort of handsome. Much steadier and more solid than Dylan. I think Dylan likes to think that he's a ladies' man."

"Oh, and is he?"

Julia shrugged again. "I don't see him with many girls actually. He had a girl for about a year when I met him first. He only seems to date girls for a short time, though, over the last couple of years. Why, do you like him?"

"Oh, I'm sure he's way out of my league!"

"Nonsense! If you like him I can fix you guys up together. Leave it with me and I'll wave my magic wand tomorrow night. That is, if you want to go out to Malahide to the yacht club?"

"I'd love to."

"Right then," Julia said, lifting her glass and tapping it off the side of Gillian's. "Cheers – here's to matchmaking!"

Chapter Seventeen

Steve was there personally to meet and greet Ruth on arrival at Perth International Airport. Her visa and passport were checked and she was rushed out into the balmy warmth of the Australian evening and into his spacious Toyota Landcruiser.

Everything seemed so alien yet in an odd way familiar, like America had felt on her first arrival there with Julia for her twenty-first birthday.

"You drive on the same side of the road as we do!" she noticed.

"Yeah, you're gonna find it easy to fit in with most things."

"And the Irish are familiar with Australian wines . . ."

He laughed out loud. He was wearing cream-coloured shorts revealing tanned legs.

"That's so funny. I think you could tell me a thing or two about our wines. But I'm going to make sure that you see the best of Australia while you are here – that's why I've organised a welcome lunch for you at Sandalford Winery for Monday if that's okay."

"That's very kind of you." Ruth felt that there was something different about Steve now that he was on his home ground. He was certainly more casual and familiar in his manner.

"I hope you'll like your new home."

"I'm sure that I will," Ruth replied, wide-eyed and enthusiastic as the rows of eucalyptus tress flitted by along the Great Eastern Highway.

"That's the Swan River," Steve pointed as they came to wooden bridge and an idyllic setting. "You'll see black swans along the river most days."

"It's lovely!"

A little further on Steve said, "We're having a barbie tonight and my wife thought you would like to join us – that okay or are you tired?"

"Oh, that's so kind of you!"

"We live in Mount Lawley which isn't too far from Subiaco. We can drop off your bags and then we can go straight there."

"That's perfect – you're very kind."

Subiaco was a small suburb nestled quite close to the towering skyscrapers of the CBD – the Central Business District. The roads were laid out in neat straight rows with an eclectic mix of homes built in Edwardian style called Federation houses and bungalows.

"This is your new home," Steve said, pulling up at a beautiful bungalow painted a bright sunny yellow. Pink flowers lined the driveway and a lattice fence surrounded the garden.

"It's really beautiful! All of the houses are so nice."

"Subiaco's a good suburb for younger people – there's always something happening and you are near the CBD."

Steve took her cases out of the back and they went into the house.

Ruth didn't want to take too much of Steve's time so she had a very quick shower and changed into a clean dress that she had packed on the top layer of her suitcase. She was amazed at how fresh she felt after the nineteen-hour trek but the business-class seats had made a remarkable difference to how she felt on arrival.

Steve's house was full of the sounds and smells of family. His wife Michelle rushed out to greet Ruth and already at the barbeque were neighbours and a large gang of children jumping in and out of the swimming pool. It struck Ruth for an instant that if her parents had stayed in Perth this would be the lifestyle that she would have grown up with. But she pushed those thoughts aside. She was here now and this was where she was meant to be.

Steve took control of cooking the meat. Like at home in Dublin, Ruth noted that it was very much the man's job but all the hard work and preparation had been done by his wife Michelle. She was a small woman with a big smile and Ruth liked her instantly. Her little boy and girl were aged eight and nine and the picture of health and happiness. She could see already the benefits of raising a family in this healthy lifestyle. One of Steve's neighbours came over and introduced herself.

"I'm Andrea Leivers – Steve told us that you were coming over – hope you like it here."

Her accent was distinctly English.

"Thanks very much – what part of England are you from?"

"The Midlands. We've been here twenty years and we love it – meet my husband John."

Ruth was swamped by friendly faces and stories of how happy and good life was in Perth. She didn't think of Ian once all evening and was looking forward to starting work on Monday. It couldn't have been made easier for her.

Chapter Eighteen

Julia didn't feel as keen as she had been the night before to invest her time in matchmaking. She knew Gillian didn't really suit Dylan – but she couldn't go back on her word and disappoint her. Odette was delighted to hear that she would be coming along for the quiz and she would do her best to make the most of the evening. She had arranged to meet Gillian later at Malahide DART station.

But first she would write a response to Michael's email. She opened her mailbox to find one from him already there.

> Julia, I didn't do as you told me to! I answered the email and put my heart on the line. I asked her to come out to Singapore and said that I would marry her and take care of her and do everything in my power to make her the happiest woman in the world. Anyway she responded to me with this. Hope you are having a good weekend.

With dread and trepidation Julia continued to read.

> Dear Michael
> It was really good to see you at Christmas and I'm sorry if I gave you any impression that there was any future for us. I

needed to see you to be sure of my feelings for Peter. I didn't mean to be cruel but I knew that if Peter wasn't the one for me I would want to be with you again. I'm sorry to hurt your feelings and thanks for the lovely offer but I am happy in Ireland — yes, the job situation stinks and people are under pressure with huge debt and the weather is gloomy but it's where I want to live and stay. It's my home and I want to be with someone who loves and appreciates the things that I do. I'm not interested in running away or dreaming of bright lights in some far-off place — I like the lights here in Dublin.

I also have found in Peter someone that I can trust and depend upon and you have hurt me in the past and I cannot trust that the same will not happen again. I hope you find someone that will make you as happy as I am now. It might be best if we don't keep in touch.

Have a good life

Lydia

"*Eek!*" Julia found herself saying out loud. Michael had asked for that particular bruising and if only he had bided his time the way that she had suggested there might have been a door left open. But he had really blown it this time and given Lydia the much-needed revenge that she obviously needed to wreak!

There was no way to console Michael – he was a big boy now. She would give him a call when she got home from the yacht club.

Chapter Nineteen

Ruth was fading and jet lag was setting in. There were four text messages from Ian on her phone apologising in different ways for standing her up at the Duty Free but she didn't answer them. She was too disoriented and each step she took felt like she was taking it on the surface of the moon.

Steve came over and whispered in her ear.

"I think you might be exhausted but too polite to say – do you want me to take you home?"

Ruth wanted to stay longer – she had met so many lovely people and was enjoying the big welcome but her eyelids were dropping.

"If you wouldn't mind."

"People will be leaving the barbie soon – we don't stay up late – we're all early risers!"

Ruth thanked her hostess and said goodbye.

Steve was already in the Landcruiser with the engine started.

"You'll probably want to get your bearings tomorrow and rest some more. I can pick you up on Monday and show you the office – then we have an intro lunch at Sandalford. I hope you'll be happy here, Ruth."

Ruth smiled. "I think I'm going to love it here."

But when she had said goodnight to Steve and gone into her

new home, her mood changed. She suddenly felt very alone. Julia wasn't just a couple of miles away if she needed to see her for any reason. Her parents were so far away too. She looked at her watch and the realisation that it was only the afternoon in Ireland hit her. She would be operating on a totally different timeframe and there would only be a few hours in the morning and at night when it would be convenient to ring home. She heard a creak from the wooden floorboards and jumped.

The kitchen was devoid of clutter. She opened the fridge and there was a variety of essential foods on the shelves including milk, butter, eggs and even some bacon. She smiled at Steve's thoughtfulness and went over to the bread bin where a sliced pan, some biscuits, coffee and tea were placed beside a box of cereal. She poured herself a glass of water and turned on as many lights in the house as she could. She found herself checking that the back door was locked and looking at the latches on all of the window frames. It was unlike her to be nervous as she was used to sleeping on her own but she was in a completely different world.

Since her second wind had kicked in, she decided to unpack everything that she had brought. As she carefully removed the padding from the picture frames that contained photographs of her family at her younger brother's wedding she felt some tears well up inside. Another frame containing photos of Julia and her in their younger years brought the tears to the surface. How could she be feeling homesick so soon – surely that wasn't natural? Another strange noise – this time from the air-conditioning – made her jump. There would be a lot to get used to. With care she took each parcel and item from the case and tried to find a place for them.

After another hour jet lag had truly set in and she was feeling woolly and clumsier with each move that she made. This must be what it feels like to be an astronaut, she thought as she placed her toilet bag on the dressing table and knocked over the china pig moneybox that Julia had made for her when they were children. Ruth let out a wail and fell onto her knees. She tried to fix the broken pieces of china but it was beyond repair. For years the little pig had rested on her dressing table collecting loose change and now, when she really wanted something familiar from home, it was gone.

It was time to leave the unpacking and try to get some sleep.

She looked at her phone and saw that there was Wi-Fi available. She wished that she had checked that out before. She ran down to the hallway. Beside the phone was a notepad with a code for Wi-Fi connection. She breathed a sigh of relief and set up her phone. That was kind of Steve to organise broadband – she looked to see if Julia was online but she wasn't. It was Saturday in Dublin and Julia could be anywhere. Not so far away and then again a whole half a world away.

She took her glass and went into the bathroom to brush her teeth. The water flowed down the sink in an anti-clockwise direction and she smiled. She was upside down in a topsy-turvy world and she would have to make the most of it.

Chapter Twenty

Gillian was waiting, wearing the top that they had bought in Grafton Street the day before. Her make-up was slightly overdone and her hair straightened to the point where it stuck to her head. Julia would have to diplomatically take her to the ladies' and discreetly fix her!

"Hi, Julia!" Gillian greeted her boss enthusiastically.

"Hi, Gill."

There it was again – being called 'Gill' gave Gillian a thrill that made her buoyant with confidence.

"Do you fancy popping into Gibneys first – we have plenty of time?"

"Whatever you think, Julia!"

Already Julia was regretting her decision to go out with Gillian again. She was irritating her and bounding along at her side like an over-anxious puppy.

This time Julia ordered a bottle of sparkling wine and they sat at the bar and sipped as the heads of all the eligible men turned to look.

"I love this bar – I was in it once before," Gillian said.

Julia's heart went out to Gillian and she felt terrible for being annoyed with her. For some reason she was on a shorter fuse than usual and she couldn't figure out why. Maybe it was because she watched others move on with their lives – getting married – moving country. For the first time in her life she felt stagnant and she didn't like the feeling. Her trip to Australia would be coming at the perfect time.

"It's a nice friendly place," she said. "I told Odette that we were coming here first . . . oh, here she is now."

Gillian was amazed by the stunning blonde woman. She had an even more beautiful smile than Julia's.

"Gillian – nice to see you again – I recognise you from Julia's office – it's very good of you to come to the club and support the fundraiser."

"It's a pleasure! I've never been to a yacht club before."

Julia looked around. "Where's Craig?"

"Oh, he can't come – said he wasn't feeling very well. He's going to mind the kids."

Julia was flabbergasted – she had been monitoring her brother-in-law's strange behaviour since Christmas and this was another first.

"Have a glass," she said, pouring for her sister.

"Thanks, I need it!" Odette sighed.

Julia would find out exactly what was wrong before the night was out.

Ruth woke in the dense heat of the night, her mind reeling with thoughts of Ian and Dublin. She was still upset about the broken moneybox. It was more than a souvenir or memento, it was a part of home and more importantly it was given to her by Julia. Julia had painted it with her own hands – it was the first gift that she had ever given her. It was irreplaceable – in the same way that Julia was irreplaceable and she was beginning to wonder if Ian was irreplaceable too.

Ruth had never known feelings of loneliness like this. When she turned on the TV the news seemed so alien. She didn't know or really think much about people in Indonesia or LA or Japan yet these were the places that mattered to Australians.

She was on the other side of the world and totally alone.

Gillian was in her element – she knew the answer to every

question about celebrities and soaps and even some sports questions about football. There were four members in each team and Dylan had joined the three girls to make a table. She was flattered by his praise and the evening was turning out to be a massive success as far as she was concerned.

Things were not quite so satisfying for Odette who fidgeted and played with her phone through much of the evening. When Julia got a chance to speak with her sister on her own in the ladies', she asked her out straight.

"What's really going on with Craig? I've been noticing changes in him and I'm really worried for you."

Odette took out her blusher and started to touch up her cheeks. "It's all of this pressure in work and he says that I haven't helped by wanting another baby – he's scared that he's going to lose his job."

Julia wasn't believing these lines. "Every person in the country is afraid that they are going to lose their jobs – things are very tight for everyone. Is there something else? I mean, he wouldn't be playing off side?"

Odette stopped what she was doing, shocked, and looked at Julia.

"I don't believe you are saying that, Julia – you *know* Craig!"

"I know that he's just a man and that the way he has been behaving hasn't been normal."

Odette was defending her husband and Julia knew her sister well enough by now to know that she wasn't fooling anyone – least of all herself.

"Okay," she said, "just don't isolate yourself – you need help while he's going through whatever!"

Odette took her sister by the hand. "I'm fine and when things settle down we'll have another baby – when we start having sex again!"

Julia drew a sharp breath. "You still aren't okay in the bedroom?"

Odette shook her head. "I'm going to lose more weight – make myself more attractive – the Boot Camp is working and come the spring things will improve."

Julia wondered how her beautiful sister had let herself come to this. She wanted to slap Craig for undermining Odette's confidence. Maybe she should try and talk to Dylan – much as she didn't want to.

When the two arrived back in the hall Gillian and Dylan were engrossed in conversation.

Julia felt a twinge of discomfort that she couldn't explain. She should be pleased that things were going according to plan for the evening but she was so used to Dylan showering his attentions on her – albeit sometimes scathing or mocking – that it felt strange to watch him chatting so intently with Gillian.

"Gillian is lovely," Odette said before they were within earshot of the table, pleased to speak about something other than her own predicament.

"Yes, she is sweet. I hope that she isn't biting off more than she can chew with Dylan."

Odette threw her head back and laughed. "My goodness, Julia – can't you see that he is just trying to get your attention as always?"

Julia frowned. "He's engrossed in Gillian's conversation from what I can see."

"Julia, Dylan has had a massive crush on you since the first day he saw you – why, when you give him such a hard time, I'll never know."

"Well, he certainly doesn't behave as if he likes me at all!"

"That's because you unnerve him – you unnerve most men. Surely you realise that you have this effect on other people – especially men?"

Julia was aghast. "I really don't know what you're talking about!"

Odette shook her head. "It's only because I'm your sister that I know you're speaking the truth. For someone so accomplished you can be frustratingly naïve at times, Julia!"

"You're imagining things, Odette – I'm going to the bar to get you some more bubbles!"

Julia couldn't see her sister's point of view at all. It really made no sense and anyway she didn't want Dylan to have any feelings for her – of attraction or otherwise. She should have remained at home and concentrated on the brochures that needed completion before she took off for Perth.

Chapter Twenty-one

Sunday morning and Ruth woke in a state of bewilderment. The loneliness had lifted with the daylight and the squawking of the strange bird in the garden. At first she thought that it was a baby crying but then realised it was a bird. She wondered what kind – there were no seagulls or thrushes to wake her like there had been in Clontarf.

Steve had left a map of Perth with bus and train timetables on the kitchen table. She wasn't in the mood for exploring just yet – she needed to get a handle on her jet lag. But she wouldn't mind finding a supermarket to help get her bearings – Steve had been so kind to leave so much food but she wanted to get some other bits and pieces. She could take a chance and stroll out onto the street or Google. She decided on the latter and found a supermarket called Coles that opened at eleven on Sundays. Her body clock was all over the place and she felt as if it was the middle of the night but it was still only nine in the morning. She wondered if Julia was still awake – it was worth a try. She sent her a text and was thrilled to see her come up online. She set up her laptop and only had to wait for three rings to see Julia appear on her screen.

"Hi, there – how are you getting on – arrived safely?"

"Yep – I've Wi-Fi and my house is fab – very little to report yet, just trying to sort out communications."

"How was the flight?"

"Heaven on earth, Ju – business class was a massive thrill for me. Steve invited me around to his house last night – it was great to meet so many Aussies – they are so kind and welcoming."

"Oh good, I'm glad to hear it – better than my night, that's for sure."

"What did you do?"

"I went to the yacht club against my better judgement. Craig was a no-show again – I'm really worried about Odette – something is up there."

Ruth hated to admit it but she thought so too – especially after watching them at Christmas.

"Was Dylan there?"

"Yeah, and he was fawning all over Gillian."

"Gillian?"

"Yeah, my receptionist – you know her?"

"Gosh, I didn't realise that you were pally."

"Oh, I invited her out for a drink – it was because I was missing you so much – that's what happens when all your friends and family leave the country. I feel like some day I'm going to turn around and be the last person left here."

"Ha, ha – you have Horatio!"

"Even he was saying that he'd love to check out Australia – I swear you have started a trend, Ruth. Oh, and by the way, Michael wants to come over and visit us in Perth when I'm there."

"Well, there's plenty of room – the air-conditioning makes funny noises at night but apart from that it's cool!"

"Thank God for Skype – it feels like you're in the next room."

"I'll keep in touch every day!"

"You had better – now I have to go to bed, Ruth – I'm exhausted. Keep me posted on all your exciting news – I'm depending on living vicariously through you!"

"I'll do my best not to disappoint!"

Monday morning couldn't come quickly enough. Having spent the entire day Sunday totally on her own – not speaking with a soul apart from Julia and the lady in the supermarket – she was ready for work. Steve had sent her a message saying that he would pick her up at eight o'clock and she was counting the minutes.

Her stroll through Subiaco the day before had been nice. It was a lively suburb and there would be plenty to do – if she had someone to do it with of course. She hoped that she would make a friend in work but knew she would be very much on her own with the Tourism Ireland remit. Steve had the tenure for promoting several countries and he took a large portion of the responsibility but Ruth presumed that she would be doing the majority of the work.

The timing of her arrival was perfect for the monthly lunch between all of the departments that Steve managed. She was shown into her office and welcomed by beautiful smiling faces – some Asian, others European, and all highly alert and bright.

"This is the team," Steve glowed with pride. "It's a global office and I think you will have fun working here."

He turned on her computer and showed her the passwords needed to work the system.

"We are going out to Sandalford at about eleven thirty – takes about half an hour to drive there." He winked at Ruth. "You'll be coming with me!"

Chapter Twenty-two

Angela was tormented since Ruth had left. Her memories of Perth were returning vividly as each day passed. The tension between her and her husband had also returned. It was compounded by the fact that that he refused point blank to plan a trip to visit Ruth in the summer.

"There's no reason in the world why we can't go out to see her," Angela had said earlier.

"It's the wrong time to go to Australia," Fred said. "Sure the summer is the only chance of a bit of good weather here – we could leave it until Christmas."

"It's alright for you," Angela berated her husband. "You go around half the day with your head stuck in the newspaper following those bloody horses. I am the one that's going to miss my only daughter."

"Next you'll be wanting to go to Canada and visit Kevin."

Angela bit the side of her lip. She was more anxious about travelling across the Atlantic Ocean as she didn't feel she would be getting a warm welcome from her daughter-in-law, Orla. The Kerrywoman still hadn't forgiven her for asking her to stay out of the family photograph when Niall was married last year. Such a silly thing to fall out about. She should respect Angela's way of doing things and this was after all a portrait of her family with her younger son's new bride. Tensions had always been there since Kevin had moved to Kerry. Angela couldn't understand why Orla was perfectly happy to come to Dublin to find a husband but then insisted on dragging him to the wilds of Kerry with his young family as soon as she got her claws into him. And now as if that wasn't enough she was taking him further away to the other side of the world.

"Don't be silly, Fred, Orla will never have us in her house again."

"After the fiasco at Christmas I can't say I blame her," Fred said with a nod of his head and a rustle of his newspaper.

Angela regretted the little outburst that she had on Christmas Day. She shouldn't have blamed her daughter-in-law for her son's financial difficulties and what was ultimately a national problem. But it was Orla's idea to invest in all those properties and put her husband under pressure to feel that their only alternative was emigration. She would probably not have lashed out were she not feeling so low after Niall's marriage earlier in the year. She was suffering from empty-nest syndrome and it was becoming more and more difficult to fill her days. In the evenings she would write in her diary as she always had but lately it had been filled with little news of activity and more wallowing in self-pity and emotion. It was the one habit that remained constant in her life, before she left for Australia and since she returned. She didn't need to re-read the diaries to recall the exact emotions she felt while living there. But she did need to keep writing. It was the only way she could try and make sense of what happened around her.

Angela had left Fred engrossed in the line-up for the two-thirty at Haydock. He was a simple man who had settled with ease into his slippers after retirement from the Guinness Brewery. He didn't seem to hanker for the life that he had left in Australia and apart from his pint in the Elphin pub a couple of nights a week he made very few demands on Angela or their marriage.

Angela had always said she would never return to Australia and Fred had never shown any interest in going back either. But the pull of her daughter was too much for her and she desperately needed to know when she would see her again.

Chapter Twenty-three

Steve seemed to like showing off the best of Perth as they drove through the suburbs. "We're lucky that our office is so central – you may not need a car but if you want to hire one we can fix you up until you decide to buy or not."

"Oh, I think I would like to have my own car – maybe if there is a website or garage that you recommend I could have a browse?"

"Cars aren't cheap in Perth and you have probably noticed that most people drive Jap cars because they are so reliable."

"I thought everyone would be going around in convertibles in this climate."

"Nah, it's too hot for that – air con is what you need in your car – most important! Get a Rav 4 or something trendy that would suit a young girl like yourself."

"I might just do that," she said with a smile.

They crossed the Swan River and came to a massive white building set amongst lush green gardens.

"That's Burswood – Perth's casino and entertainment centre – sometimes we use the convention centre for work but it's mostly for concerts and shows."

They continued driving and passed the airport along the Great Eastern Highway before coming to a remarkably quaint town.

"This is Guilford – we used to live here."

They drove past the crumbling remains of the Guildford Hotel. "Some say that place was haunted – it burnt down a couple of years back but there's a big push on to save it – it's over 120 years old." He laughed out loud. "You probably know guys with undies older than that in Ireland but here in Perth we haven't got many old places!"

Ruth giggled. Steve was remarkably frank and she liked the familiar way that he addressed her. It was a world away from the type of relationship that she had shared with her old boss Oliver.

"That pub is gorgeous!" She pointed over at a wooden building.

"That's the Rose and Crown." He slowed the car down. "One of my personal favourite spots – hey, why don't we come back here another day – it's one of the oldest . . . but there I go again talking to an Irishwoman about old places!"

They drove over a quaint wooden bridge that reminded Ruth of a setting from a movie.

"That bridge looks just like the one in the *The Bridges of Madison County*."

"That weepy movie with Clint Eastwood – wrecked his reputation as far as I was concerned!" he joked.

"I loved that movie – read the book too. I'm a bit of a hopeless romantic."

"Ah, I'm sure there are plenty of guys with broken hearts all over Ireland since you left."

Ruth took his comments as a compliment and smiled shyly but hated herself for dedicating so many years of love and affection to a man who seemed not to have cared for her after all. She wondered if Ian was pleased in a way that she had disappeared out of the country.

As they turned onto West Swan Road rows of vines – neatly planted in their hundreds – lined up only metres from the burnt-sienna earth at the side of the road. Overhead cables drew a long line of perspective that ended at a point far ahead in the distance. Every few metres a house or gate lodge sprang up amidst the bushes and vines. A blue van that looked like a cross between a racing car and pick-up truck overtook them at break-neck speed.

"What was that?" Ruth asked.

"That's a Ute – very popular with the boy racers over here."

"There's so much to get used to – it feels like America but it's very different, isn't it?"

"We like America – have you noticed all the American TV programmes?"

"Yes – I have to admit that I was up at five o'clock this morning – still not quite on Australian time yet!"

"You'll get there – and here we are now."

They came to the large and imposing entrance to Sandalford Winery, the emblem of a stag emblazoned across the top of the pillars at either side. Sandalford Winery was written along the wall on the left-hand side and Caversham across the other.

"This is where they have concerts in the summer – Michael Bublé played last year."

"I like him!" Ruth said as her eyes scanned all around.

"The others are probably already here."

He parked and a wall of heat hit them as they opened the car doors and stepped out of their air-conditioned protection. The sun baked down on top of them and they quickened their steps to take shelter in the winery.

A couple were eating *al fresco* under a pergola of vines and Ruth watched with amazement as fine water-jets sprayed out to cool them down.

"What a cool idea!" Ruth said.

"My wife doesn't like to sit outside because she says it ruins her hair!" he laughed. "So I always book a table indoors when there are girls in our party – which I am pleased to say there usually are!"

Inside the foyer walls were lined with posters for all of the concerts and performances that the winery had hosted. The main hallway led to a shop and wine-tasting area. Steve rested his hand on Ruth's lower back and gently guided her in towards the counter and the bottles on display.

"I think you should pick our wines for lunch as this is your first time joining us."

Steve had a way of making Ruth feel so special that she

wondered how she had put up with Ian's treatment for so long. Steve was gentle yet firm and manly in a way that Ian had never been with her.

She tasted a sweet red and didn't like it – then tried a few others and settled on a Merlot. The whites were harder to choose because they were all nice but she went for the Verdelho which was a grape variety that originated in Portugal according to Steve. The rest of the crew were all seated when Ruth and Steve finally came into the restaurant to eat.

A huge fireplace made of granite was the centre piece in the cool stone-clad restaurant. Upon it rested numerous cups and medals that the fine wines had been awarded over the years. The furniture was carved from a mahogany wood. A grand candle-stand with dozens of candles rested beside the mantel and more trophies and accolades hung proudly on the shelves.

There were ten altogether sitting for lunch. Ruth had met six already and Steve introduced her to the Japanese tourist board who were made up of Ikuko and Kai. She couldn't recall the names of all the people that she had met earlier but would make a huge effort over lunch to talk to everyone. That was if she got the chance – Steve was hogging her attention and she wasn't minding it one little bit.

The lunch was almost noveau cuisine with minute but tasty portions that resembled amuse-bouches rather than full courses. But the wine was exquisite and Steve poured it copiously into her glass.

"How am I going to go back to work if I have another glass?"

"Don't worry about that," Steve said with a smug grin. "We don't work after these lunches."

The rest of her colleagues were engrossed in conversation but she was sure that it hadn't gone unnoticed that Steve was devoting all his attention to her. She would have liked to speak with the others and mingle more but Steve was certainly making it difficult to do so. When the beautiful Italian Marni came over just before dessert and started to ask her about Dublin and a guy that she had met in Sydney years ago who hailed from Mayo, she felt a little relieved.

Steve went out to pay the bill as peals of relaxed laughter rang out around the table. This was a very different business lunch to any of the ones that she had been a part of in Dublin. Life was different in Australia but, from what Marni was saying, the Aussies were just like the Irish – casual and worked to live – rather than the other way around!

Steve came back to the table and bid his farewells. He looked over at Ruth. "I can drop you home if you like?"

A cackle came from Ikuko at the end of the table and all eyes were on what Ruth would do and say next. A creepy feeling ran up Ruth's back – as if all those at the table were in cahoots or had an inside track on Steve's style and habits.

Damned if she went with him and damned if she didn't, she stood up.

"See you in the morning, Ruth," Helenka from Poland said.

The smiling faces looked up at her and she felt as if she was under a spotlight.

"Very nice to meet you all," she said and waved as she followed Steve.

"They are a good crew and will be there for you if you need any help but you will probably be working mostly on your own," Steve said as he took a left onto the Tonkin Highway, following a different route home. He was very much the polite tour guide and Ruth could understand why he had found his career in the travel industry.

By the time they reached Subiaco it was three thirty and Ruth didn't relish the prospect of spending the next sixteen and a half hours totally on her own until she went into work the next morning.

She felt a smidgen of relief as Steve left her off at the door with a friendly wave goodbye. For a moment back in the winery she'd felt as if he was flirting with her but that was obviously her own insecurities lurking in her head.

She entered her sweet little bungalow and went into the kitchen. Her feet made hollow thuds on the wooden floorboards. This was living alone but it was different – she was living alone in a foreign country. She had to think of something to do to fill her evening but, without a car to explore or somebody to explore with, she didn't know what to do.

She decided to make a cup of tea – it was a start and something Angela would have insisted upon if she were there. She missed her mother and felt terribly far away from her. Was this how it felt for her when she arrived in Perth, she wondered? She might even post a Shout Out on Facebook to see if there was anyone wanting to go out on a Monday night in Perth.

She turned on her laptop after she'd made her tea and browsed. She went onto Skype but even Julia wasn't online. However, Michael in Singapore was. She wondered if he had moments of loneliness like this – it was not an emotion that she had expected to feel so soon.

She pressed call beside Michael's picture and waited as it rang out.

Suddenly a video picture popped up and Julia's brother, attired in a blue shirt unbuttoned at the top, appeared.

"Hey, Ruth – how are you doing?"

"Hi, Michael – I'm in Perth now."

Michael smiled. "I can see that from the sunshine streaming behind you. Is it hot?"

"Boiling – 34 degrees today and they say that this is nice – it can get up to forty regularly in February."

"It's funny, isn't it, when you live at home all you can think of is being in a sunnier place and then when you live somewhere hot you realise that all you want is to be in air-conditioned buildings!"

Ruth giggled. "I'm still excited about the sunshine to be honest but I can see how difficult it must be to work in this heat."

"You get used to it! So when is Julia coming over?"

"The second of February. She said that you might come down while she's here – you're very welcome. I've got a three-bedroomed house."

"Wow, lucky you – I thought they'd have put you up in an apartment?"

"I'm very lucky. Sorry that I didn't get to say goodbye before you went back. Christmas Day was lovely, wasn't it?"

"Julia always puts on a good show. She holds everything together in Dublin."

Michael spoke with such admiration for his sister that Ruth felt a twinge of sadness – she couldn't imagine Niall or Kevin saying that about her.

"I miss her terribly and it's only been a couple of days," she said.

"I'll look into flights – see what comes up as best value – I think I'll probably only get about four days off but that will be enough – I don't want to take up too much of your time with Julia!"

"Actually it would be nice for Julia if you could be here while I'm at work – I don't know what she'll be doing while I'm in the office."

"I'll have to come on a Saturday but I'll make it late! Then you ladies can take me on the town – help me find an Aussie girl to heal my broken heart!"

"Julia told me about Lydia – I hope that you don't mind she did?"

"Hell, not at this stage!"

"So what do you miss most about home?"

"Tayto crisps, Superquinn sausages and of course my family!"

Ruth laughed. She hadn't worked out yet how it truly felt to be an emigrant but she wondered if she too would be hankering after a bar of Cadbury's Golden Crisp after a week or two?

"I think Julia's impending visit has me feeling good," she said. "It's when she goes that I'll feel alone!"

Michael grinned sadly. "I think you always feel alone in a small way when you leave your homeland. It's only natural. A part of you wants to shout out to the world about the fabulous decision you made and how much better life is in your new country than it ever was in Ireland but the truth is that there's no place like home."

"Hey there, Michael – or should I say Dorothy – don't get all sentimental on me now!"

"I guess that's why I wanted to have Lydia back – I was never happier than when I lived with her and we had such a great social life in Dublin. I think that's something you really miss when you go away – there is always something to do in Dublin – even on a rainy November night there's a gig on in Whelan's or a buzz on Grafton Street. Things that you take for granted that just aren't available in every other city in the world."

"Oh God, you're going to depress me now – I was going to shout out on Facebook to see if there was anyone in Perth who wanted to go out. Mind you, I've had a long lunch and a few glasses of wine so I'd probably be better sleeping it off!"

"Hey, don't listen to me! I've just had my heart flung back in my face – I'm looking forward to hooking up with you girls – going to book the flights now!"

"You go and do that – I'll go out and work on my tan in the garden!"

"See you soon, Ruth, and call me any time – thank God for Skype!"

"Take care, Michael."

Ruth closed the screen and felt better having spoken with someone familiar. She had never felt close to Michael in all the years that she was friends with Julia but now, by virtue of the fact that they were only a five-hour flight away from each other and two Irish people living abroad, he was as close as family.

She smiled as she took out her suntan lotion and a towel and set off for the small but welcoming garden. The crow was still cawing in the uncomfortable tone that he had been using that morning but she was getting used to it!

Chapter Twenty-four

Julia was anxious but not sure why before going into the office on Monday. She had left Gillian to take a lift home from Dylan on Saturday night while she had taken a taxi with Odette earlier.

Gillian was bright-eyed and bushy-tailed when Julia walked into the office.

"Good morning, Julia – can I get you a coffee?" she gushed, jumping up to take Julia's coat from her.

"Thanks, Gillian – yes, that would be lovely."

"I had such a great night on Saturday – thank you so much for including me. I can't believe we won the table quiz."

Julia couldn't believe they had won either. And it was on the strength of all the useless knowledge that Gillian carried around. She kicked herself for having such unpleasant thoughts – Gillian had done nothing wrong. She felt unsettled after the evening but it wasn't Gillian's fault.

Julia managed to get through the morning without answering any awkward questions about Dylan but it was clear Gillian was smitten and in the afternoon asked Julia if she had plans for the following weekend.

"None this weekend, Gillian."

Julia had reverted to calling her Gillian but she could take it as long as she knew that there was a chance of seeing Dylan again.

"I don't suppose you'll be seeing Dylan next weekend?"

Julia shook her head. "I certainly hope not!" she said, then realising that she sounded a bit too abrupt she changed her tone and said lightly, "I'm hoping to get the last few bits for the holiday fair out of the way – you know how it is."

"Where does Dylan usually drink at weekends?"

Julia shrugged. "I suppose Gibneys or Gilbert and Wrights – he lives in Malahide – or he could be in town and that could mean anywhere."

"Oh, right – I just thought you might know . . ."

Julia felt bad for being unhelpful – after all, she didn't want Dylan or any part of him so why shouldn't she help Gillian? After all, it was what she had proposed to do last weekend.

"If you like I can give him your number?"

"Could you? He's gorgeous," Gillian giggled.

"Alright!" Julia shrugged. "I'll text it to him!"

She would be in Perth soon and the days couldn't go quickly enough.

Ruth was settling well into her new work and she certainly could not complain about Steve's efforts to make her feel welcome. Her Shout Out on Facebook had been successful and on the rare occasion that Steve was not taking her off to show her some new beauty spot, she would take a trip to Rosie O'Grady's in the city centre and fulfil her need to chat to someone with an Irish *blas*.

She was creating a new page for the website when Steve came over to her desk.

"Eh, Ruth, would you be available after work today?"

Ruth looked up. He did look well – his shirt collar was open and his cheeky grin reminded her of Ian at times.

"Of course."

"Great. I'm meeting some Japanese visitors and Ikuko can't make it. We'll leave in about an hour – okay?"

Ruth went back to her work and the time flew by as she put the finishing touches to her page. She had managed to fit in an email to Julia before Steve reappeared from his office wearing a fresh shirt and smelling of expensive aftershave.

He was chivalrous as always but the short walk to meet the visitors felt different – he was walking slowly and very closely to Ruth. She didn't mind.

"Where are we going to eat?" Ruth asked.

"The C."

"The Sea?"

"The letter C! It's got a great view – you'll see!" he said and they both laughed.

They took the lift to the top of one of the tall buildings on George's Terrace and Ruth was impressed. As the maitre d' showed them over to a table for two, Ruth realised that there was something different about this meeting.

"Are we not expecting visitors?" Ruth asked.

Steve seemed a little anxious and didn't respond as they sat down. He waited until the maitre d' had left before he reached out and put his hand on hers.

"I was hoping that we might have some time on our own together, Ruth – I know that I'd like that – am I being presumptuous or not?"

Ruth was shaking inside. She was flattered but anxious about this new development in her relationship with her boss. Instead of answering she gave him a smile and he in turn leaned forward and kissed her firmly on the lips.

Chapter Twenty-five

Ruth looked at her watch. Julia should be through Arrivals in a few moments. Her heart pounded at the prospect of seeing her friend. She had so much to tell her about her new life – so much needed to be said that couldn't be explained on Skype. She took a second look at the screen and suddenly Julia's fine silhouetted legs appeared from behind the arrival doors.

Ruth waved frantically and rushed over to her friend. The two hugged tightly for a few moments before making their way to the car park.

"It's so good to see you – how was your flight?"

"Good – I can't tell you how glad I am to be here." Julia turned to her friend and, fixing her doe-like eyes on her, said, "Dublin is awful without you."

Ruth comforted her friend with a half-hug.

"It's beautiful here – we're going to have a great time – I've so many things lined up and Steve is just fantastic. Wait until you meet him. We do so many interesting projects – work is fantastic. This town is great."

Julia was pleased to see how well Ruth had settled in.

Ruth proudly showed off her new home to her friend and helped her put her luggage into her bedroom for the next two weeks.

"I can't believe they gave you this accommodation!" Julia remarked.

"I know," Ruth nodded. "It's been a dream settling in here. Steve is just the best person to work for. We think the same – sometimes we don't have to finish each other's sentences."

Julia noted her friend's glowing complexion. Her skin was sun-kissed and her strawberry-tinted hair was shining. The healthy lifestyle suited her well and she was relieved that she hadn't heard Ian mentioned once all the way from the airport.

"So where do you hang out when you aren't at work?"

"Most people barbie over here and everyone is so welcoming and friendly. Steve always includes me in his plans too."

Julia noticed a pattern in the way Ruth talked and she had a terrible feeling that her friend was obsessed with her new boss.

Ruth went over to the fridge and took out a box of white wine. "Would you like a glass – or maybe a beer?"

"Ruth Travers drinking beer – I can't believe it!"

"I don't actually drink it but I like to have it in the fridge – most guys drink it over here. There's a great gang of Irish people – I've met tons in Rosie O'Grady's – most of them are country lads in football shirts and work on building sites but they are great fun!" She giggled and added, "But I am kept busy with Steve."

Julia was already disliking Steve intensely – his name had already been mentioned an unnatural number of times.

"So any word from Ian?"

Ruth threw her head back and laughed. "I haven't had a chance to think about him. He won't Skype me – I mean, he doesn't even have an iPhone. Steve says that anyone who isn't up to date with technology really should be back in the twentieth century and I have to agree with him. Ian thinks he's some sort of superman but he really is limited in many ways."

"Wow – well, I'm glad that you've seen the light – does this mean Ian has been blown out?"

"I haven't told him yet but when he comes out I intend to – of course I should say *if* he comes out."

Julia found it difficult to believe that her friend was actually finished with the dread Ian, but she was willing to give her the benefit of the doubt. Suddenly she heard a noise at the front door and heavy footsteps on the wooden floorboards in the hall.

"Hello?" a deep voice came bellowing into the kitchen.

"Steve – we're in here!" Ruth called. "Steve is taking us out tonight – I told him that you were coming over."

Steve walked over to Julia and held out his hand. "Lovely to meet you at last, Julia – Ruth's told me loads of good things about you."

His handshake was firm and his smile warm but Julia felt a heaviness in her heart like a stone. She didn't need to see much more – in five short weeks her ditsy friend had managed to go straight from the frying pan into the fire!

Chapter Twenty-six

The next morning Julia didn't feel any more comfortable about her friend's relationship with Steve.

"Take my car if you like, after you drop me to work," Ruth suggested. "The zoo is cool – you should go there – and then I can meet you for lunch. Unless you feel too jet-lagged and just want to relax?"

"That's probably the best idea."

Julia was extra quiet and Ruth was acting as if nothing was wrong. Should she ask her friend straight out or should she just go along with the charade? Julia usually knew what to do in awkward situations but she felt so cross with herself.

She had watched Ruth and Steve carry on a double act of the mutual-appreciation society the night before. The smart Chinese restaurant was idyllically set at the heart of the CBD. They had looked out over the river and the lights of the skyscrapers lit up the city behind them but didn't shine as brightly as the chemistry between her two dinner companions.

Julia went over to the fridge and took out a carton of orange juice. She lifted a glass down from the shelf and started to pour. Her mouth was dry but the words that were choking her throat had to be said.

"Ruth, are you sleeping with Steve?"

Ruth looked blankly at Julia – her mouth agape. "Why do you say that?"

"Because he was fawning over you all through dinner last night. And I've never known you to be cross with Ian and he has done some dreadful things that you've happily let him away with."

Ruth sat down at the table and put her head into her hands. She sighed heavily. "I'm not but it's getting dangerously close. Steve makes me feel so good – he treats me so well. He has helped me to see what a fool I have been with Ian for all these years."

Julia sat down beside her friend and took her hand in hers.

"But Ruth – Steve is a married man as well!"

Ruth pursed her lips and shook her head. "Why do married men like me?"

"I don't know, Ruth, but you need to distance yourself from him – you've got too much to lose – I mean, you are working with him. Why don't you use me as an excuse – we could take time out this weekend away from here – you mentioned we could go to Margaret River?"

Ruth nodded. Julia was too kind to reprimand her but Ruth knew that she had to do something. "I think we should go somewhere. I'd like to see Rotto – we can catch a ferry – I'll look up accommodation and book the ferry today."

"What's Rotto?"

"Rottnest Island – it's not far from Perth – twenty minutes on the ferry. Steve says . . ." She paused and grinned. "It's meant to be really beautiful out there. I'm so glad that you came out to see me – what am I like?"

Julia hugged her friend tightly. "You're my pal, Ruth, and that's the most important person in the world. Now, when are we going to check out your mother's secret person?"

Ruth grinned. "You know, I'd almost forgotten about Charles Walters! I haven't even been to Peppermint Grove yet!"

"Well, I must admit I'm dying to see if we can find anything out about this mystery man!"

"I tell you what, you just take it easy for the morning and I'll come back here at lunchtime – I can take a long lunch and we can go somewhere to eat and then check out Peppermint Grove. Okay?"

"Perfect!"

"Right. See you then."

"Take care of you!" Julia called as her friend went out the door. She wished that she could stay longer – two weeks wasn't going to be enough and she could never have imagined this new scenario that Ruth had got herself into.

Ruth was back at one thirty and Julia was having one of her floppy jet-lag moments lying in a half-sleep on the living-room couch.

"I'm not going back to work today," said Ruth. "I can make up for the time after you have gone home. And I've booked us accommodation for Friday night on Rotto – what time is Michael coming in on Saturday?"

Julia was trying to decipher what Ruth was saying – she felt like a little child under the haze of jet lag. "Oh, I think it's about eight o'clock in the evening or something like that."

"Great. I've booked the ferry for two fifteen so we can go to the Fremantle Markets on the way back.

"All sounds cool!"

"Are you too tired to go out to lunch? And check out Peppy Grove?"

"Why do you call it that?"

Ruth laughed. "Everyone shortens words for places or things in Australia."

Julia shook her head and stood up before falling down again.

"Hey, I've got a better idea," said Ruth. "Let's just have a sandwich or something here and we can drive to Peppy Grove when you feel better."

Julia nodded and let Ruth make a salad for lunch. They drank apple juice and ate in the garden with crisp chunks of white cob bread on the side. Julia was refreshed in less than an hour and with her map and Ruth's iPhone in hand as a GPS they went out to Ruth's lovely car – which at three years old was new by Australian standards.

"How much was it?" Julia asked.

"I'd hate to tell you – I'm sure I could have bought one in Dublin and imported it for half the price but it's my treat to myself and I was feeling so lonely during the first week I went mad and bought it on a weekly payment scheme."

"It suits you," Julia said, sitting in.

"I love it and you know what – Ian hates these which makes it sweeter!"

"Why have you turned so much against him? You're beginning to sound like me!"

"I suppose because he's made so little effort to stay in touch and I'm sure all those plans that he said he was making were complete lies. He'll probably replace me with the next available stewardess who feeds his ego the way that I used to."

Julia felt gutted for Ruth but she was pleased that there was a real severance at last in what had been a very unhealthy and unfulfilling relationship.

"Okay, directions please!" Ruth commanded.

"I'm looking at Railway Road – you need to get onto Stirling Highway and that leads you straight there. Just take a left at the end of the road and drive straight until I shout out at Claremont – wherever that is!"

"The roads are great here – even I can find my way around without getting lost. It's so funny at rush hour – they have these helicopters hovering over the freeways and they shout out on the radio stations warning drivers of hot spots – well, I swear, Ju, none of them would last ten minutes in a Dublin traffic jam. They say things like – there's heavy traffic on the Mitchell Freeway for six kilometres and it's more like the middle of the night on the M50 in comparison. There might be a few cars on it but the traffic is always moving – I was in stitches the first time I was warned about avoiding rush-hour traffic – even George's Terrace at five o'clock on a weekday wouldn't have the same amount of cars as Pearse Street at two in the morning!"

"Oh, I'd love that complaint. I'm bringing my car into town less now, even with my parking spot – I can't stick the delays . . . oh, hang on, we're almost there – that was quick. Slow down and take a left onto Stirling now in a couple of turns."

"When?" Ruth yelled, fiddling with the indicators.

"I'm not exactly sure – okay, turn now!"

The car seamlessly took the road onto Richardson Avenue and swept around in a curve onto Bindarring Parade and the beautiful blue of the bay came into view. As they drove along the waterfront, exquisitely manicured houses flitted by on the other side of the road.

"I wonder are those peppermint trees on the esplanade?" Julia asked.

Ruth giggled and watched the wide childlike wonder in her friend's eyes.

"I think you're more besotted by my mother's story than I am!"

"Just keep driving, Ruth – we're having an adventure! I've come halfway around the world to see you – so I'm entitled to one!"

As they continued along the serpentine road the view became more beautiful and each house that they passed was more audacious and spectacular than the one before. The masts and hulls of yachts from the floating moorings flitted by through the trees.

Upturned Optimist dinghies and sail-training boats for children lined the esplanade next to a short jetty. The boathouses marked the marina area and heralded the border of the yacht club.

"Wow, I would love to have seen what this place was like in the seventies when your mum was here."

"Yeah – a lot of the houses are new builds though – I wonder did they just tear down the old ones?"

Julia shrugged. "Let's find Peppermint Grove Road. I'm really impressed by this place."

They drove up along Lille Street and past the entrance to the Royal Freshwater Bay Yacht Club.

"Oh, come on, let's check it out," Julia urged.

"I thought you wanted to see the house?"

"Okay, but on the way back we have to take a peek."

They didn't have to go much further to find their street. And as they drove they really didn't think that the houses could get much bigger or more ostentatious but they did.

143

"Check that out – it's like a Moroccan hotel!" said Julia.

"These are unbelievable," Ruth agreed.

"Number 11, Number 9, hey, I think we're nearly there! Number 5!"

But Number 5 wasn't there – the gates were in place with '5' painted on the pillar but where the house had stood was now an empty site.

Ruth parked and they sat staring at the site, not sure what to say or do.

"What now?" Ruth shrugged.

"Let's get out and take a look around – that little park over there looks nice." Julia opened the door and yelped as the heat from the day hit her like a wall. "Wow, how do you get used to this heat?"

They made their way to a little green.

Julia looked back at the empty site. "I think there's a JCB inside – do you fancy taking a look at what used to be Number 5?"

"I guess we've come this far and it looks like Mum's secret is safely cleared away. What have we got to lose?"

They wandered past the pillars and up the driveway which was more of a dirt track with the grass and all flora cleared away, apart from two mature fruit trees to their left.

"It's a massive site – I'd love to have seen the original house, wouldn't you? I wonder if it was one of those Federation-style bungalows?"

"I guess we'll never know," Ruth replied.

Suddenly a huge jeep careered into the driveway and the two girls had to jump out of the way not to get knocked down. The driver pulled up abruptly and rolled down his window. He wore a hard hat and a crisp white shirt. His skin was tanned a smooth brown and when he spoke he revealed perfect straight porcelain-white teeth.

"Can I help you, ladies?"

Ruth felt like a rabbit in front of a double-barrel shotgun in hunting season.

"Eh, I'm terribly sorry. We were just looking around."

"Is that an Irish accent? I love Irish ladies but what are you doing trespassing on my building site?"

"I, we, I mean . . ." Ruth mumbled, more from the shock of being addressed by such an Adonis than any other reason.

"What my friend is trying to say," Julia interrupted, "is that we were wondering if the owner was here as we think we may know somebody who might like to get in touch with them. But as the house has been cleared away lock, stock and barrel, I guess we can forget that."

"Hey, another lovely Irish lady! This job keeps getting better. Who was it you were looking for?"

"Somebody called Charles Walters?" said Julia.

"Nah, nobody by that name here – the people who own this plot are called Arthurs," he replied in rich Aussie tones. "But I could tell you a thing or two about Peppy Grove – my company have been involved in plenty of the new builds around here. I'm sure I could ask a few of them about Charles Walters. Do you have a business card?"

Julia whipped one out of her purse and handed it to him.

"I'll keep that in mind," he said with a wink.

Suddenly Julia wondered if he was asking for their contact details for some ulterior motive.

"Have a good stay here – are you girls living or holidaying?"

"Both," Ruth said, trying to be more approachable now that Julia had decided to adopt more defensive body language. "I'm working in the CBD and Julia is visiting for a couple of weeks."

The driver took out his card and handed it to Ruth. "Give me a call if you want any work done – we have very reasonable rates," he said, winking again.

"Okay, thank you very much," Julia said with a smile and the two girls teetered down the driveway as quickly as they could.

"Oh my, what a dish, Julia! He seemed to like you too."

Julia threw her head back with a laugh. "I'm not interested in a holiday fling – I'm here to spend quality time with you! Anyway he looks like a bit of a chauvinistic beast – 'I love Irish ladies',", she mimicked naughtily and the two friends fell into the car in convulsions.

This was what they missed about being apart – they weren't able to be themselves with anybody else in the same way.

Chapter Twenty-seven

The next day was spent on Scarborough Beach, languidly basking in the sun.

"It's not what I expected really – those waves are enormous!" Julia propped herself up on her elbows.

Ruth was sitting under a parasol and reading a book. She looked out from under her sunglasses. "What were you expecting?"

"I guess I thought the sea would be calmer."

"It is, further south – down past Fremantle – but this is where the talent and the action is. I thought you might see someone that would tempt you to have a holiday romance and I am determined to be open-minded about meeting someone who is single."

Julia giggled and lay back down. "What did Steve say when you left work early?"

"He was very understanding – which makes me think that it might not be a bad thing to be bonking the boss!"

Julia sat up abruptly.

"Only joking!" Ruth chided. "But we do get on so well – it's a treat for me. And you will never guess but I got a text from Ian today."

"What did he say?"

"He says that he misses me and hopes to get to Perth next month for a short visit. I know that he has no intention of visiting me – I've been let down too many times by him. How could I have wasted all those years?"

Ruth frowned and Julia smiled a tight smile. Ten years was a long time to devote to a relationship that she suddenly realised was never going to go anywhere.

"You know, relationships don't all have to have a sad ending – sometimes couples get married and have babies and live happily ever after," Julia said.

"Like Craig and Odette? How are they, by the way?"

Julia shook her head. "Oh dear – I'm not sure what's going on there. I hope and pray they get over this bad patch. I just want everyone to be happy."

"And what about you, Julia?"

Julia sat up straighter. "What do you mean?" she asked defensively.

"Do you never get sick of thinking about everyone else's happiness and wonder how you can improve your own?"

"I'm perfectly happy – you should know that better than anyone. I'd be a terrible mother and an even worse wife – I love my career and freedom and independence. I'm not going to squander them for some man who will have me popping out sprogs and tied to the kitchen sink."

Ruth laughed hard. "I'd like to see any man try!"

"I have a full and happy life and have never met a man who has tempted me in any way to change!"

As the sun lowered the two girls packed up and bought some fish and chips before returning to Subiaco. They sat in the back garden and drank a bottle of sparkling wine as the crow cawed and the midges appeared from the bushes and the trees.

"I'm beginning to feel quite giddy – can we go for a drink?" Julia asked.

Ruth looked at her watch. "It's seven o'clock. If we don't go out soon they'll all be going home to bed."

"On a Thursday night?"

"Any night!" Ruth joked. "Although if we go to Rosie

O'Grady's there will be a good crowd – they usually have music on a Thursday. It's in Northbridge. We can catch a train, it's not far."

Julia touched up her make-up and Ruth ran a brush through her hair.

"Am I dressed alright?" Julia asked.

"Julia, you could go to this place in your shorts and thongs!"

"Thongs?"

Ruth giggled. "Yeah, that's what they call flip-flops over here – sorry, I must have given you a shock!"

"Too right! I'm not going anywhere wearing only my skimpy string underwear!"

"I don't know how you wear thongs!" Ruth winced. "I'm not built the same as you. I find them excruciatingly uncomfortable."

"You have a fab slim figure so clothes just hang off you – when you're overweight like me you need all the help that you can get!"

"Overweight! Julia, are you losing your eyesight in old age – you are slimmer and trimmer than Odette and that's saying something."

The two laughed and chatted about all the different things that Ruth had learned since moving and in a way it seemed as if she had been in Australia for a lot longer than four short weeks.

They hopped on a train and were in the city in minutes. The façade of Rosie's was definitely colonial but inside resembled pubs seen all over rural Ireland in their heyday. The sign in the window advertised 'Backpacker Night'.

The smell from the carpet was pungent, documenting years of spilled beer and a distinct aroma of curry sauce wafted from behind the bar. The dark-wood counter was covered from view by girls with scaldy suntans and tall Irishmen in hi-vis tops covering their GAA football shirts, steel-capped boots and shorts. The sound of the house band, Blue Jeans, echoed from the next room.

"Where have you brought me, Ruth?"

Ruth giggled. "Believe me, it's the liveliest spot in town and I've come here on my own when I was feeling really lonely during the first couple of weeks. People are friendly and welcoming because we're all in the same boat and missing home!"

Julia felt bad for making assumptions about the bar. She didn't know what it was like to be living so far from home and she could see by Ruth that the sense of the familiar was very important.

"Come on and I'll get you a Guinness!"

Ruth shook her head. "Too hot for that, Julia – get a Night Nurse!"

"A *what*?" Julia thought she was hearing things – that was medicine she had been given by Carol as a child.

"It's cider – really nice. Try it!"

"Okay," Julia agreed and they went up to the counter.

The barman at the other side was tiny. He stood up on a crate before asking Julia what she would like.

"I'll have two glasses of Night Nurse, please."

"No problem," he said and busily poured. "Would you like a pie?"

Ruth interrupted. "It's Backpacker Night so you get a pint and pie for fifteen dollars." She turned to the barman and smiled. "No, thanks, we've eaten."

Julia was fascinated by the smiling faces all around. Everyone seemed to know each other and they were talking happily about their day's work or the football results in the Premiership.

"And you've come here on your own?" Julia asked.

"It was in the first week and one of the girls on the Facebook page 'Irish Families in Perth' said that there was a crowd coming in. They were really nice girls and they play GAA football two nights a week. It's just so good to speak to someone with the same sense of humour. The crowd in the office are lovely but they are from all over the world and it's not the same. I suppose that's why I've agreed to see Steve more and we've had a few dinners mid-week . . . but we were talking about work!"

Julia's heart sank for her friend. Maybe going away wasn't the best suggestion after all and she wondered if she had interfered unnecessarily.

"Do you regret coming out here?" she asked cautiously.

Ruth paused. "No – Steve has helped me but he really is just a distraction and he's so much nicer to me than Ian ever was. I do like the work and it's good for me to have a change of scene like this. This is my life for the next two years and I'm happy about that. By the way, I might not be able to come home this year – do you know it's 1,600 dollars to fly to Dublin?"

"Oh, I didn't realise!" Julia's head switched into business mode. She wondered was there something she could do to help the Irish get home more often. Maybe a discussion with an airline and a special package could be arranged. There were always business opportunities waiting to be tapped.

"Julia, are you okay – you seem in a daze?"

Julia shook her head. "Sorry, I was just wondering if there was scope to set up a link for emigrants coming home or family visiting – it might be worth my while discussing specials with some of the airlines." She pointed over at the unusual tables shaped from old wooden wine barrels. "Come on, let's sit over here at one of these barrels."

The two sat on high stools and put their glasses on Guinness beer-mats.

"You are always working, aren't you?" Ruth giggled.

"I can't help it – it's what makes me happy."

"I just want to find a Mister Right who isn't somebody else's!" Ruth sighed. "And I'm starting to feel my biological clock ticking frantically."

"Ruth Travers, I never thought you'd ever say that!"

Ruth picked up her glass of Night Nurse and took a sip. "Neither did I! I guess I didn't want to admit it but when Niall got married it hurt to think of my younger brother having a child and me in the middle with none. It was different when Kevin had kids – he was always going to have them before me!"

"I know I'm not the typical youngest child – I was always so much my daddy's girl and I wanted to make him proud. It's difficult now that he's gone but I feel he's looking down on me saying 'good move' or 'invest there'! I could never find a man that I loved as much as him." Julia looked sadly into her glass of cider and took a large gulp.

"We are two of the most dysfunctional people we know, Julia!"

Julia smiled. "I never would have agreed with you before but I think I know what you mean!"

A crowd of young Irishmen filtered in through the door.

"Howaya, girls – are yis backpackers?" asked a scruffy man who was wearing a Dublin jersey and beaming smile.

"No, she's on holiday and I'm working in the CBD," said Ruth.

"Arya?" he beamed. "So am I – I'm a lecky!"

"A what?" Julia asked.

"He's an electrician," Ruth interpreted.

"It's a great town, isn't it?" he said to Julia.

"It's cool!" she smiled.

"Can I get yis a drink?" he offered.

"No, thanks, we're fine," said Ruth.

"Good luck!" he said and went off to chat to one of the scaldy girls.

"I told you people were friendly in here," Ruth laughed. "And when you are feeling homesick, two hours chatting to *Lecky* there is heaven!"

"I suppose we are so used to hearing how wonderful it is for everyone who has left our little country as it sinks further into debt, that we don't think about what it feels like to be so far away."

Ruth took another drink. "I never gave it a thought before. And I'm lucky – I'm here through choice not necessity. I could always move back in with Mum and Dad."

"But you are glad you came?"

Ruth nodded vehemently. "I swear I'd never have left Ian's clutches otherwise. I guess I'm missing him too so it's twice as difficult but now I'm on my own I realise that I never really had him. God, it's so annoying to realise that you've been deluding yourself for ten years. I wonder what opportunities I missed out on while I was entangled in his web. Maybe there's a lovely *lecky* out there that I'd be happily making the dinner for right now and feeding his sprogs!"

Julia stood up abruptly. "Stop all this morose talk. I'm getting another drink. We are – well, I am – on my holidays and we are going to have fun!"

For the next two hours they had fun with *Lecky* and his mates. They drank more cider than they should and jumped into a taxi before Julia's jet lag saw her asleep in the corner of the bar. The *craic* was good.

Chapter Twenty-eight

The next morning Ruth came into Julia's bedroom with a mug of tea and some buttered toast.

"How's the head?" she asked.

"I remember now why I don't drink cider – and we'd already had a bottle of bubbles earlier that I'd forgotten about!"

"Drink up. I've got to go into work for a couple of hours but we'll be getting the ferry at three so make sure that you have your bag packed."

"I will – or maybe I'll just take it easy till you get back."

Ruth smiled at her friend. She had been the Julia of old last night – the one she had been with in New York when they were young adults. It helped Ruth to realise that they were at a new stage in their lives, a fresh start of sorts, and she hoped that Julia would find what she was looking for because since moving to Perth Ruth was feeling very much like a new person.

Ruth took her bag and called goodbye as she closed the front door.

Julia sat up in the bed and flopped back down again. The mix of time, alcohol and sunshine were proving to be a lethal cocktail and she would have to take it easy when she got to Rottnest Island. She took her phone and switched it to Wi-Fi to check her emails. It was still Thursday night in Dublin and she was anxious to see how business had been at home.

Gillian had promised to email a report at the end of every day so Julia went straight to her email first.

It started off describing the business in the office before going on to the post. But it was the last paragraph of the email that rattled Julia.

I'm going for a drink to the Shelbourne with Dylan tomorrow night. Thank you so much, Julia, for introducing me to your brother-in-law. He really is so lovely and I never dreamed that I would be taken out to such a nice place. I hope that you're having a brilliant time in Australia.

Julia felt her stomach churn and hoped that it was the Night Nurse from Rosie's making her nauseous. The Shelbourne was her favourite spot in Dublin and Dylan knew that. And why was Gillian signing herself Gill? That was way too familiar for her liking! It worried Julia that she was feeling this way about a man she not only disliked but despised. He had irritated her for ten years so why was she cross about him seeing Gillian? Who was she to judge who either of them should go out with? After all, she had instigated the match in the first place. But it didn't sit right with her because she didn't think that they suited. In fact, Gillian should be down here in Perth and Ruth should be in Dublin going to the Shelbourne with Julia!

It was midnight in Dublin but Julia decided she had better check in and see how her mother and Horatio were doing. She went onto Skype on her iPad and didn't have to wait long.

"Julia, is that you?"

"Hi, Mum, yes, it's me!"

Her mother was sitting in the living room and Julia could tell that she had either been playing bridge or was about to start a game.

"How are things in Dublin?"

"All good here – you are missing nothing, love. Oh, apart from the massive row that I had with the credit-card people this morning. I couldn't understand a word that the girl from the NGB bank was saying. She wouldn't let me cancel Granddad's card – you know how he keeps losing things – he probably left it in one of those cowboy shirts that he wears. I bet it's in one of them but he swears he can't find it. So they wouldn't let me cancel just his – they said I had to cancel mine too because they are on the same account!"

"It's probably a security procedure, Mum!"

"But wait, I'm not finished – I want to book a flight over to Warwickshire to play in a bridge tournament and I'll need to have the card this week – so the cheeky girl tells me that I'll have to wait. I was furious so I told her that I was cutting up my credit card and I went and got a pair of scissors and did it right there on the phone and she was yelling loudly at me, telling me *'Madam, you still owe two hundred euros on the account!'*. I asked to speak to someone who could speak English! I swear, Julia, I think the girl was in Cairo or somewhere mad like that – why can't they have Irish people to talk to Irish customers? That would stop some of the emigration!"

Julia tried hard not to laugh and wished that there was no video on her iPad. She could see by her mother's expression that she was totally wound up about the matter. This was exactly the sort of thing that Julia would have been able to sort out for her if she was there – it made her feel good that she was missed and needed for all sorts of little tasks!

"So how is Granddad?"

"He's in great form – the weather's nice and mild and he's taking his walks on the beach every morning. I think he should get a little dog but he won't hear of it. How is Ruth getting on in Australia?"

"Her house is lovely and her job's going really well. It's a gorgeous city but everything is so expensive!"

"Really?" Carol was surprised. "I thought Australia was meant to be cheap. Where is she staying?"

"Ruth's house is in Subiaco – it's a lovely little suburb – almost in the centre of the city!"

"How was your flight?"

"Good – really comfortable."

"Well, have a good time because you are missing nothing here

– I think Granddad has fallen in love with that Brazilian girl that you sent to do the housework. He's fixing a watch for her! Is Michael going out to you?"

"Yes, he's due here on Saturday evening. I'll get him to call you on Sunday."

Carol frowned uncomfortably. 'Oh, there's no need for that – eh, I'll be busy on Sunday."

"Really? Where will you be?"

Carol went red in the face. "Oh nothing, I'll just be playing a bit of bridge with the girls – you know, Treasa and Ita!"

Julia was curious – she always knew when her mother was trying to hide something. There was no point in prying as she was too far away to find out more

"Okay, well, have fun and we'll call you on Monday."

"Oh yes, Monday is much better!" Carol looked relieved which made Julia even more curious.

The world had turned upside down and she was on the other side of it and could do absolutely nothing about it! First Gillian and Dylan surprise her and now her mother! Julia had never felt so out of control of her life and everyone else's!

Chapter Twenty-nine

Julia and Ruth cruised along like Thelma and Louise and parked at Eshed Markets on Fremantle harbour. The quayside was awash with travellers. The captain was accepting people for boarding. The massive cruiser *The World* cast a shadow on the water.

"Come on, we've only got ten minutes!" said Julia.

This trip was a wonderful opportunity for them to catch up without any distractions, thought Ruth. Have some good heart-to-hearts. Julia had made it obvious that she was not keen on Steve. She really had thought that she had hidden her feelings from Julia but her best friend knew her better than she knew herself.

The captain was charming and flirtatious, wearing a gleaming white shirt and four golden bars on his lapels.

"Hey there, girls, going to Rotto today, are ya?"

They nodded and ran on board the ship.

"This reminds me of Irish college – remember when we took that trip to the Aran islands?" Ruth said.

"Only it wasn't thirty-five degrees in Galway," Julia chirped.

They watched the Fremantle port authority building disappear as they motored through the harbour mouth. A large red peppermill lighthouse stood to their right and a green one to their left. A TV screen ran a video information trailer about Rottnest and it was announced over the tannoy that the bar was now open.

"Come on, now we are both on holidays – what would you like? Cider?" Ruth asked with a cheeky grin.

"Never ever again!" Julia laughed. "I'll have a coke and maybe we can go outside?"

"It's hot today – but at least it will be cooler on Rotto with the sea breeze."

The thirty-minute journey flew by and, as the picturesque jetty at Thomson Bay came into view, Julia gasped. "I had no idea that it would be this beautiful!"

"Neither had I!"

The two gazed as the sandy shoreline drew closer and the sun glistened on the bright turquoise Indian Ocean. Tall pine trees were dotted sporadically behind the dense clumps of the indigenous trees. One large building resembling a hotel and a beach-front restaurant filled the shore-front to the left and a mix of yachts and motor boats were moored in front. A selection of holiday villas jutted out in the distance along the right side of the island and a tall white lighthouse perched high on the hill.

After landing on terra firma, Ruth assured Julia that she knew exactly how to get to their accommodation. Steve had suggested the Rottnest Lodge as a good base and the location was perfect. After a short stroll past the general store and Rottnest Bakery they were at the front of a brightly painted orange building.

"Look out for the quokkas!" Ruth said.

"For what?"

"Quokkas – they're like tiny kangaroos – Steve said they are everywhere!"

Julia dragged her bag behind as they entered the reception of the Rottnest Lodge. The shimmering pool just outside the main entrance beckoned.

"Oh, I think that's our first port of call!" Julia said.

The male receptionist was tall with jet-black curly hair and translucent blue eyes like the azure shades they had seen on the water in Thomson Bay.

"Hello, are you staying with us today?" he asked with a warm smile.

Ruth gave him their details and took the key.

"Breakfast is at seven in the morning and runs till ten."

The girls thanked him and didn't have to go far to find Room 26. The buildings and pathways were quaint and distinctly colonial.

"It feels like we are going back in time on this island," Julia remarked.

"It does have a certain feel – reminds me a bit of Martha's Vineyard."

"Yeah, that's it," Julia agreed as she opened the door to the basic but clean accommodation. "I thought this was a deluxe room!"

"Yeah, pretty basic – but at least the pool looks nice."

They changed into their bikinis and poured on some factor 30 sun lotion.

"It's hot out there today." Ruth said.

Julia nodded. "I can't wait to get into the pool."

The loungers were covered with fresh towels for guests to use and the palm trees gave natural shade from the sun. Ruth jumped straight in and Julia quickly followed. Like most Australian pools it was deep and so refreshing the girls stayed in it for half an hour.

Ruth got out first and sat on the sun-lounger that she had reserved with her wrap. She put on her sunglasses and lay in tranquillity.

When Julia got out she decided to dry off and apply more lotion. She reached down beside Ruth's bed and let out a yelp.

Ruth jumped up. "What's the matter?"

Fear and trepidation were written all over Julia's face. She pointed to a spot beside the large palm tree that was offering them shade.

"There – don't move – there's a massive rat!"

Ruth looked over to where Julia was pointing and started to laugh.

"That's not a rat – that's a quokka!"

"It's a rat – I know a rat when I see one!"

"Julia, I swear – I saw them in the zoo – that's what they look like."

"What are they doing here by the swimming pool?"

"He's probably just looking for a bit of shade!"

With that the quokka turned on his paws and hobbled off through the gaps in the metal gate, to find another place to rest.

"I can't believe that thing!"

"It's a marsupial – Steve told me about them – the first visitor to the island thought they were rats too and that's why they call it '*rottnest*' – he was Dutch apparently and that's 'rat nest' in Dutch."

"Well, Steve is a mine of information – I'm so glad we were warned or I'd have been straight up to reception to check out."

"Lie down and relax – you're on holidays."

Julia did as she was told and the girls basked in the sunshine for an hour before hunger prompted them to find somewhere to eat. They returned to their room and changed into cool sundresses – not too out of place for the laid-back island but enough to make them feel and look good.

"Did Steve suggest anywhere to eat?"

"Aristos apparently is good but there is usually a session of some type in the Hotel Rottnest so we'll go there after."

"Sounds good to me."

They dined on scampi and fries with salad and drank white wine as the sun slowly set. The cool breeze had left and a still calm fell on the island as night drew in.

The clumps of trees that were a dense green mass when seen from the sea were now lit up with fairy lights forming a magical path to the Hotel Rottnest. There were no private vehicles allowed on the island. Apart from the old colonial train that was really a novelty for sightseers, only one little bus did a circuit of the island. Holiday-makers were expected to walk or hire a bike. And there were plenty of families and young backpackers breezing along the pathways on bikes at all hours of the day and night.

The Hotel Rottnest, painted a bright white, beckoned them

with the strains of a guitar and singing. Crowds of Aussie college students and international backpackers filled the tables, drinking from the necks of beer bottles.

"It's certainly buzzy," said Ruth. "Looks like all the tables are taken but we can squeeze in somewhere."

The midges were out but the girls had sprayed themselves before leaving the hotel room. Ruth got three massive bites on the first night at Steve's barbie and made sure that never happened again.

They walked over to the bar and ordered a bottle of chilled white Sauvingnon Blanc. They took the bottle in a bucket over to the quietest table where only one couple sat. The music was good and with the stars twinkling so brightly above in the sky it was difficult to see where the fairy lights in the trees stopped and the real stars began.

"Oh, I've got the nibbles – can't believe it after that gorgeous dinner – will I get us some nuts?" Julia asked.

Ruth nodded.

Julia went up to the long white bar counter which had filled considerably in the few moments since they had bought their wine. A stag party had arrived and the bar staff were working frantically to serve the crowd. She was considering whether to go back to Ruth or wait patiently for her turn when she felt a tap on her shoulder.

"Hey there – Miss Peppermint Grove!"

She turned around and didn't recognise the speaker for a moment.

He wasn't wearing his yellow helmet but his white smile gave his identity away.

"Hello – you're the guy from the building site, aren't you?"

"Yeah, that's right – Brian!" He held out his hand. "And your name is?"

"I'm Julia – my friend Ruth is with me too. Are you with all these guys on the stag night?"

"Stag night? Oh, you mean buck's party! Yeah, my mate Ross is getting hitched in a couple of weeks. Rotto's a great spot to go on tour! Where are you staying?"

"We're at the Rottnest Lodge."

"Oh, we're staying in the Quad."

"What's that?"

"It's the round building – right by the pool. Used to be an Abo prison."

Julia was horrified. She wasn't sure if she more disgusted that he called the indigenous people Abos or that he was staying in what used to be a prison. "What? I didn't know that – am I staying in a prison?"

"Whereabouts are ya?" Brian asked.

"I'm to the left of the entrance."

"Oh, then you're probably in the boys' reformatory."

"Boys' reformatory!"

"You don't like the sound of that?"

"No! And it's not nice to hear the aborigine people being called Abos either!"

"Hey, I hate the way they were treated and still are, to be honest. But us Aussies always make words shorter. And as for the prison, I agree that it is kinda creepy. I think us Aussies are the only race on earth that would turn a prison into a hotel."

He laughed out loud and took a bottle of beer from a tall blonde unshaven guy wearing a sleeveless T-shirt. "Hey, Marty, meet Miss Irish here – she has a cute mate too!"

"Hello, sweetheart," Marty said, winking. "Don't ya just love Rotto!"

"It's very quaint." Julia was taken aback.

"Can I get you a beer?" Marty asked.

"No, thanks, I was looking for . . ." she hesitated, "some crisps – eh, chips – or something to nibble."

"There are plenty of blokes here that would love a nibble later!" Marty laughed cheekily. He spoke with the bartender and gave her some assorted packets of cashew nuts and crisps.

"Eh, thanks very much." Julia was a bit disconcerted by the forcefulness of the Aussie guys – she couldn't find her usual retorts that came naturally when she was out in Dublin. It wasn't that her confidence was shaken but she had to admit she did feel like a fish out of water around Australian men

"Sorry if Marty is a bit brash – he can't help it – and he has a heart of gold."

"Oh, he's grand. Eh, I think I'd better go back to Ruth."

"Maybe I can join you later?"

Julia looked up into his big blue eyes. There was something different about Brian. He was gentler in his manner than Marty and the other Aussies that were dotted around the bar. And it had been a while since she'd had her last holiday fling. She weighed up the options – she had nothing to lose.

"Sure – come over to us – we're sitting at the beach front over there at the last table."

He smiled. "See you in a bit. By the way, I've found out a little about the people who lived in that house."

"Oh! What?"

"I'll tell you later."

Julia was elated when she returned to Ruth. "You won't believe who I met at the bar?"

"Who?"

"The builder from Peppermint Grove. Isn't it a small world?"

"Oh, he was gorgeous!"

"And he's found out something about the house! He'll come over and tell us later."

"Fantastic!"

"He's with a stag party – a 'buck's party' as they say here. I hope he brings a nice friend!"

Ruth smiled. It was like old times when the girls used to be on the hunt and she missed this in being with Julia in recent years, where she turned away every guy who approached her with a smart retort.

"I'm glad to hear that you'll give Brian the benefit of the doubt! He is cute."

Julia nodded. "He has lovely teeth and it has been a while since I've had a holiday romance."

Ruth thought that Brian was gorgeous but she was so pleased that Julia was interested in him she wouldn't get in her way.

They had barely finished their first glass of wine when Brian came over with Marty in tow. The two men sat down at the table beside them and Brian launched into chat with Ruth about the owners of the house in Peppermint Grove. He had looked up the papers belonging to the site and discovered that the house he had demolished at Number 5 was owned by an Emily Walters who was second-generation English. She had been a widow for many years and it was her nephew who was commissioning the new build.

"The nephew's surname is Arthurs so I was thrown a bit but that seems to have been the old dear's maiden name."

"You're very kind to find out for me," Ruth smiled. She was a little uneasy – she didn't want to be the centre of Brian's attention after Julia had expressed an interest in him. "But, you know, I think Julia is even more intrigued to find out about the house than I am – aren't you, Ju?"

Julia was delighted to be brought into the conversation as Marty was heading straight in for the kill and she had no interest in continuing a conversation with a guy who insisted on calling her 'sweetheart' all the time. She didn't want to land Ruth with him either but Ruth seemed happy to talk to Marty and moved seats to be nearer to him so that Julia was now beside Brian.

"Yes, I'm intrigued to find out about Ruth's mother's connection with that house." Julia explained. "She wrote a letter to a man called Charles Walters who lived there and didn't post it."

"Hey, he must have been Emily Walter's husband?" Brian suggested.

"Exactly what I was thinking," Ruth agreed.

Brian turned to Ruth. "And would you not just ask your mum about it?"

Julia and Ruth looked at each other, not sure what to answer.

"Eh, Ruth's mum doesn't like to talk about her time in Australia for some reason and we can't figure out why."

"Ah – sounds like a skeleton in the cupboard – I think this calls for more drinks. Would you like another bottle of wine, ladies?"

"Oh, that would be lovely, thanks – I'll come up to the bar and help you!" Julia said with a wide smile. It was a good opportunity to see if Brian was interested in her and let Marty switch his attentions to Ruth.

"Do you come over here much?" Julia asked Brian.

"To Rotto? Nah, only if there's a reason like the buck's night. There are plenty of people from Perth who have only been on Rotto once or twice – some have never been. I used to come as a kid when I was a scout and we'd camp over at the Abo graveyard and tell ghost stories all night."

"That sounds a bit creepy."

"Yeah, it felt weird. I think there are plenty of old ghosts stomping the island at night – it was bad the way the Abos were treated here and nobody ever put up a headstone for them."

Brian was smart and intelligent in a non-intellectual way, thought Julia. She waited with him while he paid for the drinks and they walked back to the table.

When they arrived poor Ruth was trying to balance a cashew nut on the side of a beer mat to appease Marty. She was an incredible friend!

Two bottles of wine later and Ruth was singing with the bucks, arm in arm, at the bar. Brian had taken it easier than the rest.

Julia hoped that it was because he was interested in spending some time with her so she happily got involved in the singing but kept an eye on Brian. She looked at her watch. It was long past midnight and she fancied an opportunity to be on her own with Brian.

Ruth had finally given in to Marty and was snogging him now at a corner of the bar.

Brian looked over and noticed what his friend was doing. He seemed a bit startled and then turned to Julia.

"Do you fancy taking a walk over by the beach? Or we could go to the salt lake behind our hotel?"

Julia jumped at the offer and followed Brian who had started strolling slowly along the promenade.

"Those guys are going to get too drunk and fall down!" he said and Julia laughed.

The quokkas were out in their thousands, hopping along the path in front of them.

"They are so like rats – I got the fright of my life by the pool earlier when I saw my first one," Julia said.

"Yeah, and they really take over Rotto at night, don't they?"

They came to the wide open green at the harbour front where Julia and Ruth had eaten earlier and the space was covered with quokkas bounding about everywhere.

"Come on, follow me – they know where to scavenge – there won't be so many at the lighthouse."

He put his arm loosely around her shoulder and the stars shone brighter with each step they took along the meandering path.

Julia could smell his skin and it was very different to the way that most of her lovers had smelt. She usually liked her men to smell of cologne. But she definitely preferred dark-haired men like him and he also had the strong features that she liked.

"Are you interested in astronomy?" he asked, leaning his head back and looking straight up at the stars.

"Oh, that's more Ruth's sort of thing – I'm a practical girl. There's enough going on for me on Planet Earth." She giggled.

"It's a great sky in Rotto – good as the outback. Look up there – that's Orion."

The stars were brighter than they had been at home but she didn't know what Brian was talking about. She had been with an Italian called Maurizio once who talked all night about constellations while they lay on their backs in the hill town of Taormina on the island of Sicily but that had not mattered as his English was broken and she loved the tone of his voice. Brian talking about the stars somehow didn't have the same ring to it. A part of her longed for him to snog her. She had made up her mind that she wanted some romance but the build-up all evening had been different to what she had expected. Now he was talking about stars which was another twist in this butch man's bow.

"Are you the project manager on the site at Peppermint Grove?"

Brian shook his head. "No, I'm the architect but it's my business partner who's building the house."

That explained his artistic side and fascination with the stars to some extent, Julia figured.

All the time Brian's grip remained loose but constant along her shoulder. She wondered if he was going to make a move and part of her longed to do something dramatic like throw her arms around him. As they walked further up the hill the crickets started to click and the quokkas were more difficult to spot in the darkness. Only the odd ray from the full moon above them fell on the path they were treading.

"Almost there," Brian whispered.

When they got to the lighthouse the view was spectacular, the moonlight creating glistening jewels in the water and casting ribbons of white along the coast as the gentle waves lapped the shore.

"It's stunning." Julia stared out at the ocean. She felt a very long way from home suddenly. Strange when it resembled the beautiful Burrow strand that ran along the back of her home in Howth. Suddenly Dylan came into her head – this was around the time that he would be meeting Gillian. Why should she care? She was on the other side of the world standing next to the gorgeous Brian? She asked herself the question but couldn't find the answer.

"I've seen this view plenty of times but it always makes me shiver," Brian said.

"Why?"

"Not sure, just a feeling!"

"I live beside the sea in Ireland – I love it. Where do you live in Perth?"

"I live in Karrinyup – it's near the beach – north of the river. How long are you staying in Perth?"

"Two weeks."

"That's a pity – there's plenty you won't see. You should stay longer."

"I've a business at home – I feel bad taking two weeks."

"That's right, you're in the travel business. Where is Ruth working while she's here?"

"She is working for the Irish Tourist Board. She is adamant that it's a change of scene for two years only and then she is returning home. I miss her terribly."

"You two are really good mates then."

Julia nodded. "Friends since we were eight."

"Wow, that's a lot of history!"

Brian's arm slipped down from Julia's shoulder. He turned so that they were facing each other.

"We'd better go back!" he said suddenly.

Julia was deflated. She had expected him at that moment to kiss her. If Gillian was going to be getting it on and Ruth was already in action back at the hotel then she really needed to feel loved, or desired at the very least. She desperately wanted to be taken in his arms and fall down on the sand and have passionate sex – or, at that moment, a snog would suffice. But Brian had already started the walk back to the hotel.

It was seven o'clock and time to meet Dylan at last. Gillian had bided her time in work as there was no point travelling home to change and then come back into the city.

The porter stood wearing a top hat and long coat and he bid Gillian good evening as she walked through the swing doors of the Shelbourne Hotel. The warmth and opulence hit her and she felt butterflies flit inside her stomach. A large display of pungent lilies to her left wafted their scent through the air, their beauty doubled by the massive mirror that rested behind them. She didn't know which way to turn until suddenly someone came up behind her and touched her on the arm.

"Hi there – hope you haven't been waiting long – Craig and Odette picked me up from home and they were a bit late."

Gillian was completely taken aback to see Odette by his side.

"Eh no, I just got here," she said.

"Hi, Gillian, nice to see you again!" Odette said and placed a kiss on her cheek.

"Hi, Odette."

They walked into the large bar and took the settee which was just then conveniently vacated

"Have you had any word from Julia?" Odette asked.

"Yes – well, an email. She seems to have had a good journey and is getting on really well."

"Oh good – I haven't had a chance to ring Mum for news. I'm

sure Julia's worried about the business. Her work is so important to her."

Craig arrived and said hello to Gillian, nodding at her briskly. He went over to the bar and was instantly in deep conversation with Dylan. She wondered why Dylan had brought along his brother and wife – it was strange but maybe a good thing. She would like to be welcomed into the family – so maybe this was a sign!

"What is this about, Dylan?" Craig asked roughly, leaning on the bar. "I hope you aren't trying to play happy families – you should have sorted this evening out with me first instead of going to Odette."

"Why, Craig? Did you have other plans by any chance?"

Craig frowned. "I don't understand why you have such an interest in what I do? Or is it because you're bored now you have no job to go to?"

"See this as a celebration of my retirement."

"Well, get your nose out of my family's private affairs, okay?"

"I don't know why you're being so defensive!" Dylan said with a wry smile.

Craig took the bucket of Prosecco while Dylan took the four glasses, and they carried them over to the table.

"There you go, ladies – in honour of my brother's celebration." Craig looked at Dylan and darted a killing glance.

Julia and Brian didn't talk much as they briskly walked down the path and the Quad came into view. The sound of laughter from the open grass centre of the quadrangle made them change tack and find Ruth with some of the bucks and a group of three other women who had been picked up by them at the Rottnest Hotel.

Ruth's eyes shone when she saw the two coming through the arch in the Quad.

Julia went over to her friend who immediately dragged her to the side. "Oh my God, Marty is Hands Almighty – he wanted to get straight down to it at the bar – until he passed out!" she giggled. "How did you get on with Brian? You've been gone absolutely ages."

Julia shook her head. "Very strange – I thought we were getting on and then he suddenly said we had to get back."

"Maybe Aussie men are a dead loss – although Steve's a great snog!" she giggled.

"Hey, I thought you were giving up married men!"

"Yeah, but Marty was like a washing machine – he really needs a couple of lessons!"

The two fell around laughing.

"Come on, let's go to bed."

Brian waved goodnight, then helped one of the bucks up off his knees and over to his bedroom while the girls slipped away.

They passed a couple of quokkas outside their bedroom and with help from the moonlight found the lock and opened the door.

"This place gives me the creeps!" Ruth said suddenly.

"What does? Rotto?"

"This room!"

Ruth shivered and went over to the bed. "Do you want to take the double bed – I can sleep in the single over here."

"I don't mind – whatever suits you!"

Above their heads the fan swirled noisily but they were glad of the relief from the dense heat.

"What's that smell?" Ruth asked as she pulled the light blanket over her legs.

"I don't smell anything!" Julia said. "Will I turn the light out?"

"Okay, but do you mind if we leave the bathroom light on?"

"No problem – I'll be asleep in a couple of minutes," Julia yawned.

Ruth shivered again and a powerful headache came over her – it could be the start of a hangover or the effects of the sunshine from the day. It had been particularly hot. As she closed her eyes she thought that she heard a hiss but put it down to her imagination. From the corner of her eye she saw something dark move along the wall and as her eyes became accustomed to the darkness she could make out the silhouette of a cockroach. Her mind started to play tricks and she imagined what it must have been like when it was a boys' reformatory. She had read the notice outside telling how young European boys had been transported to the island in the early parts of the twentieth century for truancy and bad behaviour. The legacy reminded her of the anguish that must have been suffered by so many young Irish boys and girls in places just like this in Dublin and all over rural Ireland. How cruel the world was and how awful to be so very far away from home! She sank into a sleep and twisted and turned in the heat of the night.

It was only a few minutes later when she was woken by a cold presence travelling along her body. She opened her eyes and felt the salty taste of blood in her mouth. She licked the back of her hand and could see that fresh blood had left a mark. Suddenly her phone bleeped with a message. She cleared her throat and felt more blood rise as she licked her other hand to see if the blood was still there. It was. She walked over to the bathroom, picking up her phone on the way. It was a message from her mother – she would read it later.

She looked at her reflection in the bathroom mirror and blood seeped from her lips. She spat into the sink and washed her hands. Cupping some water in her clean palms, she rinsed her mouth out and looked at her teeth and lips. No sign of blood. Her hands were clean and her headache had lifted. She looked around but there were no more strange feelings like there had been when she had gone to bed. A peace and calm had descended on the room but Ruth couldn't figure out what had just happened. Something supernatural was behind it. That was all that she knew.

Before getting back into bed, Ruth opened her text message.

Hope you are having a good time with Julia. Mind yourself mum xx.

It was strange that her mother had contacted her at that instant – sometimes mothers have a sixth sense. Ruth returned to bed and lay on her back. Something had brought her to this island and she didn't know what it could be.

Gillian was delighted with the way the evening was going – this was the most plush bar she had ever been in. The decor made her feel like she was a character in *Downtown Abbey*. All the fine paintings and heavenly drapes were luxurious beyond her wildest dreams. She had enjoyed the Prosecco and the wonderful sandwiches Dylan had ordered. It was good that Craig and Odette were there after all as it took the pressure off her. As the night was drawing to a close she waited expectantly for her chance with Dylan.

Dylan stood up and helped Gillian on with her coat.

"Where do you live, Gillian?" Odette asked.

"Beside Cabra," she said with a shy smile.

"We'll drop you home," Odette said.

Gillian was upset by the 'we'. Surely she was going to have some time with Dylan on her own?

"Odette and Craig are keen to get home to the baby-sitter," Dylan explained.

"Of course," she said politely. "I can always get a taxi – it's not on your way to Malahide."

"It's a Friday night – best to be safe."

Gillian was dreadfully disappointed and wanted to be as far away from the group as possible as she could feel tears threaten to well up in her eyes.

"No, honestly – I'll get a taxi."

Dylan insisted and the four walked to the car park.

Odette took the car keys and drove out of the city. Gillian directed her and made sure that the car was parked outside one of the large houses around the corner from where she lived. She had done this before, on the night after the quiz when Dylan drove her home. She didn't want him to know that she came from a small corporation house.

Odette brought the car to the kerb and waited until Gillian went up to the gate.

Gillian stood at the closed gate and waved goodbye.

"She's grand, drive on," Craig said.

"No, I want to be sure that she's safe," Odette insisted.

But thirty seconds later she was still fiddling around with the latch. A dog barked loudly and Gillian began to be concerned that she had picked the wrong house.

"Go and help her!" Odette insisted.

Gillian waved them on frantically. But Dylan got out and went over. He released the latch easily and bid her goodnight again. Gillian walked up the drive nervously and the beast at the rear of the house kept barking hysterically. She managed to slip down behind a hedge at the front door and prayed that they hadn't seen her and would drive away. A light came on in the house where she was hiding and she had to run behind another hedge before the owners came to check who or what was disturbing their animal.

To her relief she heard the car starting up and driving away. She came out of her hiding place and fled down the drive, getting to the gate before the front door opened. She ran as if her life depended on it. She had bit off more than she could chew by accepting Dylan's invitation. She could cry and she wondered what sort of a fool Julia would think her when Odette told her all about the night.

Chapter Thirty

The next morning Julia rose bright and early.

"Are you awake, Ruth? That must have been the best night's sleep I've ever had."

Ruth sat up in the bed. "Good, I'm glad I didn't wake you. Julia. I had a crazy experience last night."

"What – with Marty?"

"No – here in the room – I think I felt a ghost or something."

Julia laughed. "You should have gone for the walk with Brian – he was going on about ghosts and funny feelings too!"

"I'll be glad when we get back to Perth."

"Well, it's a lovely morning – do you want to hire a bike and take a look around after breakfast?"

Ruth nodded. "We can't leave without cycling around the island and we must snorkel too, Marty was telling me. I wonder what state he's in this morning?" She giggled.

"I'm mortified by the way Brian took me for that walk and then dumped me," said Julia. "What was that about?"

Ruth shook her head. It was strange – Julia usually picked and chose men at her command. But then again Brian wasn't just any man!

Breakfast was laid out across two counters and there was a good selection of fresh fruit and pastries as well as the hot dishes.

Julia ordered a pot of tea for two and took some freshly made toast and fruit.

"It's a nice breakfast, isn't it?"

"Brekkie!" Ruth giggled. "You're in Australia now!"

"Must remember that!"

"You know, it's great here but I can't help wondering what it must have been like when it was a prison."

"Honestly, Ruth – what's got into you? I'm glad we're going back to Perth later. Actually I can't wait to see Michael too."

"Yeah, that will be good." Ruth leaned forward. "Don't look now but the bucks are on their way over."

"Hey, sweetheart, where did you run off to?" Marty came bounding over to the table.

"I didn't run off anywhere – I think it was you who passed out, Marty! It was good fun, wasn't it?" Ruth grinned.

Marty nodded. "Brian's gone back to the mainland – caught the first ferry – asked me to say goodbye to you girls."

Julia felt disappointed. "We're going back this afternoon but going for a cycle first."

"Hey, yeah, go to Parker Point – it's great. Take your snorkels."

With that Marty went off to pile layers of bacons and sausages on to his plate.

The girls packed their bags and left them in the holding room at reception. They went out into the bright sunshine and passed the smiling faces of young families and backpackers all going in the direction of the bike-hire shop.

Rotto was very different in daylight. Still feeling unsettled by her experience the night before, Ruth tried not to dwell on it. She took a purple mountain bike and followed Julia along the path.

"It's a shame that Brian went home early," Julia said. "I would like to see him again."

"We have his business card – remember?"

"I know but we can't really call him, can we?"

"He said he would help us find out more information about Number 5. Maybe he's shy. I think we should call him when we get back to Perth. You do like him, don't you?"

Julia shrugged. "I suppose I'm not used to getting dumped at the final hurdle by a guy but, yes, I liked him. I did wonder if he really liked me though. He's quite a thoughtful bloke and into the stars. Did I tell you that he's not a builder, he's an architect?"

"No, I don't remember you saying that. Marty is a postie but seems to spend most of his time surfing and swimming at Scarborough."

"A postie?"

"Yep – a postman!"

Julia threw her head back, laughing. "I can't get used these abbreviations!"

The signposts were clear and the two headed for Parker Point. Clouds were scattered against the cerulean blue sky which helped to take away some of the heat from the day before. They came to their first small hill and passed a dried salt lake which was so arid the trees were pushed up by the roots and falling over on their sides – parched for some water. In the distance a bell tinkled and a small single-carriage train chugged along the old iron rails that ran in front of them. The girls stopped and watched it pass slowly.

"I really feel like I'm in Australia now – this is what I imagined the outback would be like."

"It is, sort of – Steve brought me up to the Pinnacles the week after I got here and the drive was amazing – so much vast desert. I noticed a lot of the trees were parched along the way. I think water is an issue here and the summers are very dry."

Julia grinned. "We could give them some of our rain from Ireland – although January in Dublin wasn't as bad as usual – much milder than everyone expected."

They cycled on to a crossroads and kept left on the path for Parker Point. They came to the first scenic stop where 'Henrietta Rocks' was printed on a signpost. The view was breathtaking and in the distance a sheltered cover and beach beckoned. They continued along the meandering road where they met gentle hills followed by long runs taking them quickly to a hidden glade with bare carcasses of trees that seemed to be hissing loudly with noise, the tap-tap of birds against some of them almost drowned out by a shaking sound that resembled a shaman's rattle.

"What is this place? It gives me the creeps!" Ruth shouted out.

"Come on! Hurry up in case there are any snakes!" Julia cried and the two raced on until they came to another stop where many people had dumped their bicycles and the bus waited for passengers.

"This is Porpoise Bay – let's stop here – I'm dying for a swim," Ruth begged.

Julia was just as keen to dive into the beautiful clear azure sea. They had to negotiate many decked steps before they reached the beach. A welcoming party of two quokkas waited at the bottom of them. The girls found a private spot to strip off but already the daytrippers had arrived and the beach was getting crowded. Some small yachts bobbed a short distance away on their anchors.

"It's idyllic, isn't it?" Julia said, wading up to her thighs in the warm clear water.

Ruth followed with snorkels in hand. Tiny colourful fish flitted by in massive shoals.

"Here, Ju – put this on!"

Julia put on the snorkel and the two dived into the crystal-clear water. It was freedom and beauty at its best and the girls were swimming in unison – so happy to be together again.

After a while they took a rest on a couple of boulders at the edge of the reef.

Ruth lifted her snorkel and shook out her wet hair.

"I forgot to tell you that an American fellow was eaten by a shark here last year!" she said.

Julia shrieked. "You're not serious?"

Ruth nodded. "I know, hard to imagine but it happened. He was diving alone."

"You'd better not tell Angela."

"Oh, Angela was the one telling me about the sharks – *don't go into the water*!" Ruth mimicked her mother's concerned tone. "It's another of the things that used to unnerve her about Australia."

"Oh, Ruth you have to find out more about that letter. I wonder why she never posted it? You're sure it was in her hand?"

Ruth nodded. "Most definitely. It's hard to remember life without email, isn't it? Letters are so much more romantic – waiting for them to be delivered by a postman."

"Like Marty!" Julia said with a giggle.

Ruth put her snorkel on again. "Eh, yeah, just like Marty!"

"I'm not sure I'd like Marty handling my post after what you said!" Julia giggled and followed her friend as she dived back into the water.

They swam to shore and went over to a sheltered rock where they had left their belongings. It was coming up to lunchtime and they were aware that the boat would be leaving in three hours for Fremantle.

As they dressed, Julia's phone bleeped. She read the message. It was from Odette. She wondered why Odette was up at four o'clock in the morning.

Hope u r having a gr8 time. miss u x O

It was worrying for Julia to get a text like that. She didn't like this feeling of distance from her sister while she was going through a difficult time. She wanted to chat with her but Odette didn't do Skype or technology very well. So Julia simply texted her back.

All good here. Hope mum and granddad are well. Gillian told me she had a date with Dylan! Any news?

She received a quick response.

Not a date really! Craig and I were with them! She's nice. Don't think Dylan that keen on her!

Julia read the text again. What were Odette and Craig doing with them? It was very strange. What was Dylan playing at?

"Everything okay in Dublin?" Ruth asked, seeing the concern on Julia's face.

"Yeah, I just can't figure out why Odette and Craig would have gone out with Dylan and Gillian."

"Julia, you are a control freak – you are on your holidays – let them be until you get home at least."

Julia nodded. "You're right. Okay, race you back to the bike shop!"

But as Julia pushed up the hills and flew down the other sides she couldn't shake the thought of her sister and the others all going out for drinks together.

Marty was at the bike shop when the girls arrived.

"How ya going, girls?" he beamed. "I'm on my way to the Hotel to meet some of the guys. Care to join me?"

"Hi, Marty," Ruth said politely. "Julia and I are going to have a bite to eat at the bakery, thanks."

"Ah, yeah, good grub. Pity you're rushing off Rotto so soon."

"Well, as I told you, Julia's brother is flying in from Singapore tonight so we're going to pick him up."

"Maybe I'll see you when we get back to Perth. I could give you my number?"

Ruth didn't want to see Marty again and Julia knew it by the way she was being so diplomatic.

She took out her phone. "Give it to me now and then I can text you?"

Marty had a massive grin on his face as he called out the ten-digit number.

Ruth put it in her phone but didn't press save. She courteously smiled and waved goodbye and, after getting their deposit back from the teller in the hire shop, the two ran laughing in the direction of the Rottnest Bakery.

"I don't know what to pick – everything is too yummy!" Julia said, eyeing a pie and some delicious Rocky Road cake. "Eh – I'll go for the pasty."

"I'll get these, you get a table – what do you want to drink?"

"A latte, please." Julia took a table under a parasol and watched the quokkas pick the squashed figs up from the pathway and eat them with gusto. She looked up at the trees that lined the open area that was now a playground for the children of visitors to the island. They were all abundant with figs.

When Ruth returned to the table she pointed at the trees.

"Look, I never noticed these are all fig trees."

"Yes, I found that out when I was asking the receptionist about the boys' reformatory – they planted lots of trees here –"

"Ruth, you're becoming obsessed about that reformatory."

"Sorry!" she said and shared out the lunch. "I'm fascinated by this island. It's strange but I feel drawn to the poor boys that lived here – I'm trying to get a handle on this country."

"Good and that means that you aren't thinking about Ian."

"I haven't thought about him once since you arrived, Julia – I must be getting better. I suppose out of sight is out of mind in some circumstances."

Julia nodded. But that wasn't what she was thinking. She was wondering why absence made her more curious about what she was missing at home!

The ferry ride back to Fremantle felt like half the journey it had been on the way out. It was a pet day for the crossing, like the one they had on the previous day. The captain had told them that it could get choppy on this route and they were particularly lucky.

The port of Fremantle was alive with hundreds of people sitting out on the decking at the Eshed Markets. A woman was singing country music, accompanied by a man on an electric guitar.

"Let's leave our bags in the car and go and explore," Ruth suggested.

They took the walk through the busy dockland and walked over the rail-tracks to Market Street.

"Thank God for Google maps!" Ruth said. "I think it's not too far."

They passed the town hall – a pepper-cannister-shaped colonial building with a cast sculpture of one of the countries prime ministers who hailed from the town. Once they got on to Market Street they were almost at South Terrace and the famous Cappuccino Strip. Every restaurant that they passed was packed. Happy customers sat on the verandahs and under the parasols that lined the way to the markets.

A street performer held the gaze of a big crowd as he beckoned to one of the visitors from England to throw up a lit torch to him while he balanced on a rolling tray. The crowd cheered as he defied injury by his great skill and tenacity. A gang of bucks masquerading as pirates cheered noisily from The Sail and Anchor pub and the girls were tempted to stop for a drink as the heat of the day was reaching a climax.

"Come on, only a few more steps and we'll be under the shade of the markets and then it will be much cooler."

Julia followed her friend into the air-conditioned main building. Little stalls filled the sides – art and crafts and plenty of stands for food and snacks.

One of the ice-cream stalls proved too tempting for the pair and they each ordered a pistachio and rum-and-raisin cone. The coldness was a great relief and gave them a second wind to take in the mishmash of trinkets on offer in the markets.

"Look, there's a palm-reader!" Julia said, pointing at a woman who was dressed in a rainbow-coloured kaftan.

"I'm too spooked after last night to go there!" Ruth said with a shake of her head and a lick of her ice cream.

"Okay, let's go into this craft shop."

It was a small area covered from top to toe with hand-painted aboriginal art pieces. The small stones started at five bucks and the didgeridoos went up as high as two hundred bucks. In between were hand-painted boomerangs and kangaroo skins.

"I love the patterns and designs so much. It really is a magical style of art," Ruth said, running her fingers over the stones.

"Hey, why don't I get you a stone and you pick one out for me and we can have them when I go home to remind us of our time here?" Julia suggested.

"Okay – you pick first for me then!" Ruth said.

There were ten different motifs ranging from kangaroos to dolphins and various other animals of the outback. They were then painted on different-coloured backgrounds, making up a variety of combinations.

Ruth went up to the owner of the stall and bought her stone for Julia and when Julia had done the same they exchanged the good-luck stones.

Ruth looked down to see a Prussian blue turtle in her palm. It was the very same stone that she had picked out for Julia.

Julia laughed loudly as she opened the bag with her gift.

"I can't believe we picked the same stone for each other. It's just as well that we never picked the same men!"

Ruth agreed. But maybe with time their tastes were becoming similar. Ruth had liked Brian but wasn't going to say that to Julia the night before. As she had sat listening to Marty she had one eye on Brian and couldn't help listening to what he was saying. She felt bad and wondered if she liked him because Julia did. She had to question why she constantly liked men that were already attached and this one man who wasn't suddenly became more interesting when she saw him with her friend. It was for the best that she was thousands of miles away from home. If only she could control her desires with Steve – it was easy now that Julia was here but how would she be when Julia went home?

Chapter Thirty-one

Michael was elated to see the two girls at Perth airport. He hugged his sister tightly and gave Ruth a warm kiss on the cheek. He was chattier than usual as they walked out to Ruth's jeep in the car park.

"How was your flight?" Julia asked.

"I can't believe that I slept most of the way – I'm ready for you girls to take me on the razz in Perth tonight!" he said excitedly.

"We were going to take it easy tonight as we were on Rotto last night!" said Julia.

"Ju, you are not going to do that to me – I've been with every decent single ex-pat girl in Singapore – I want some passion after coming all this way."

The two girls looked at each other. Another night on the tiles was called for!

The three sat in the plush surroundings of the Red Sea Club in Subiaco.

It was Julia who caved in first.

"I have to go home to bed – sorry, guys. We were up very late last night."

"It's okay, sis – Ruth, give her the keys and we can stay here."

Ruth looked at him with raised brows. "Oh Michael, I'm exhausted too – do you mind if we go home?"

Michael shrugged. "Okay, I get the hint – I'm too old to be out with you two hot young women!"

Ruth punched him affectionately on the arm. "Don't be silly – we really are tired. All that fresh air and we were cycling on Rotto at all hours this morning!"

Michael shook his head in mock wonder. "I know! My little sister cycling! I'd love to have been there – she hasn't been on a bike since she was six!"

It was Julia's turn to punch her brother.

"Okay, I give in, we'll go home," he said with a sigh. "How many thousand miles did I fly for this – remind me again?"

The three hadn't far to walk home and when they got back to Ruth's little bungalow she opened a bottle of wine.

"I know I'll regret this in the morning!" she exclaimed as she began to pour.

"None for me!" said Julia. "I'm for bed!"

Julia kissed Michael on the cheek and went to her room.

"So what did you two get up to last night?" Michael asked. "Julia seems very unsettled about something."

Ruth shrugged. "I'm not sure – she's upset about Odette and Craig – I think they're having a rough time."

"Yeah, I noticed that at Christmas – I think he's got problems at work. I'm amazed at the stress people are under in Ireland. There's a blanket of debt hanging on everyone's head. Doom and gloom like I don't even remember in the late eighties!"

Ruth nodded. "It's so different here – there are things that you forget when you move away and then again things that you miss terribly that you took totally for granted when you were at home."

"It takes a full year to get used to living in any place. I was only in Singapore a couple of months when Dad died. I'll never forget it – it was so awful to be so far away and hear that terrible news. You have to experience it to understand it. The flight home was the worst I've ever travelled."

Ruth took a gulp – she had never thought about that before. She was so fond of Michael's father – he used to call her his third daughter.

"They forgot to tell me then when the dog died – he was my dog! I know it sounds a bit silly but things like that really make you realise how difficult it is to be far from home. My Uncle Paddy, my mum's brother, died a year later and they didn't tell me in time to make the funeral – they didn't want to upset me. I was so mad but Julia calmed me down – they couldn't have waited for me and I wouldn't have made it on time. But it was the fact that it was hidden from me until it was absolutely too late for me to even try to get home that really upset me."

Ruth felt so sad for Michael. She raised her glass and clinked it off his. "Well, I'm one of the Diaspora now so I guess I'll get to know pretty quickly the pitfalls and difficulties." She took a gulp of her wine and it made her feel instantly better.

"You shouldn't listen to me too much, Ruth – I think I'm at the end of my time abroad. I really want to go home and settle down – but I'm concerned about finding work. I read the *Irish Times* every day and every second article is about people leaving the country because they can't find work."

Ruth agreed but was optimistic about Michael's situation. "A lot of the people leaving are doing so because of all the debt they have accumulated. You don't have that problem, Michael – you could return and live frugally until you find something, couldn't you? On the plus side things have got cheaper at home – although they are loading on new taxes with each budget."

"Okay, enough of the morose talk – what's the story with your love life?"

Ruth laughed. "You probably know about my friend Ian?"

"The married man? Yeah, Julia hates him. Did you blow him out?"

Ruth took another sip from her glass of wine before answering. "We got blown out naturally, I think – it's strange but I was only saying to Julia today that out of sight is out of mind as far as he is concerned."

"Lucky you – I've been driving myself mad thinking about Lydia. Julia said I've messed up for good there. The awful thing is I don't think I'll ever find anyone like her again."

Ruth put her hand on his comfortingly. "I'm sure you will."

"Thanks, Ruth, but I know I only have myself to blame for the mess that I've created with my life."

"Michael – you are forty – give yourself a break. And a fella at forty is like a woman at twenty-five – believe me. I've been having serious biological-clock-ticking issues for the last few months."

Michael laughed and held up his glass. "Hey, if we can't find anyone ourselves in a year we can hook up together and make a go of it – I've always thought you were cute, Ruth!"

Ruth lifted her glass to his. "Deal!" she said and finished the contents. "But now I have to go to sleep before I pass out on the spot."

Michael sat back on his chair. "Okay but I'll hold you to it!"

"Come on and I'll show you to your room!"

They didn't have to walk far and Ruth pushed open the door and switched on the light.

"The bathroom is next door," she said, pointing.

Michael stopped and looked at the bed. He then looked at Ruth.

"You know, I can't remember the last time that I shared my bed with another body – all night long!"

"Don't forget the 'all night long' bit, Michael. Knowing you, there was someone in it for a couple of hours last night!"

Michael paused. "I'm lonely, Ruth – can we have a sleepover in your bed?"

Ruth was thrown. "What – like six-year-olds?"

Michael nodded.

This was the strangest request. She knew him well but this was too weird. But she wanted to be gentle with her reply.

"Michael, I think you're losing it a bit – it's not a good idea with Julia next door. You know what she's like! She'll only get carried away and start ordering a hat for our wedding!"

Michael grinned. "It was worth a try!" He kissed Ruth on the forehead. "Sleep well."

Ruth shut the door behind him. She felt very strange as she walked to her room. It was true that while you lived away you did things that you wouldn't do at home but she would never have imagined Michael making such a request. How could he still be homesick after so many years? She didn't want to end up like this. Then she wondered if this was the reason why her mother had packed up and returned to Dublin. She could always quiz her mother but she wasn't the sort of mother that you could sit down and have a real heart-to-heart with. It suited Ruth having a mother this way while she was living the life of a mistress and her mother's lack of interest was a relief. Now that she was so many miles away she wished that she had spoken with her heart open when she lived around the corner from her.

Chapter Thirty-two

The next morning was as bright and sunny as the one before.

"It's going to be very hot today!" Ruth said to Julia as she came into her room with a cup of tea in hand. "What do you want to do?"

Julia rose up onto her elbows. "Morning, Ju – I don't know, you tell me?"

"There's lots that we could do. Go up to Hillary's – nice shops up there. Try the beach?"

"We better see what Michael wants to do too."

"Of course," Ruth said. How could she forget? "Maybe he'd like the beach – we'd better go early."

"Ruth, this early rising thing is killing me – can we not go later?"

Ruth shook her head. "It'll be too hot – unless we go much later this afternoon?"

Julia put one foot out of the bed and then the other. "Okay, early start it is. I'll go in and wake Michael."

Ruth went into the kitchen and started to mix pancakes. She was a little apprehensive about seeing Michael in the light of day after the words that had passed between them the night before, but she needn't have worried.

"Morning, Ruth," Michael said, bounding into the kitchen.

He went straight over to the fridge and poured himself some orange juice. "Sleep well?"

"Yes, thanks, and you?"

"Yeah, great – could have been better though!" he said with a naughty wink aimed at her.

Julia didn't notice and proceeded to fill the kettle with water.

"Ruth says we have to get an early start if we want to go to the beach."

"Beach sounds good to me," Michael agreed.

Ruth stalled for a second. "Hey, if you don't mind the drive, we could go to an inland lake that Steve told me about. He said it's really beautiful – it's called Lake Leschenaultia and about an hour along the Great Eastern Highway."

"Sounds like a bit of an adventure – let's do it!" Julia said.

Michael shrugged. "Fine by me."

Ruth packed up some salad and crackers and picnic food. Then she went to the fridge and took out the ice packs. "Pass me the Esky there, please, Julia."

"The what?" Julia was confused.

"The Esky – short for Eskimo – the cooler bag over on the shelf."

Julia did as Ruth asked and took out some bottles of cold water and beer from the fridge.

The Great Eastern Highway took Ruth's car through John Forrest National Park and the town of Mundarring.

"I texted Steve before we left and he said we should stop off at the Mundarring Weir Hotel on the way back – it's off the road a bit."

"I'm dying for a swim, Ruth, I'll happily go anywhere after that!"

Ruth drove on and took a left at Chidlow, a small outback town with an old-world pub and a couple of stores. The car slowed, making its way now through the meandering roads and the peace of the national park.

"Almost here, I think, if my GPS is working right."

They took a right into a car park and the sparkling waters of the lake became visible.

"Oh, this is a good call!" Michael said sticking his head between the girls' seats in the front of the car.

Lush vegetation surrounded the lake, with types of trees that none of the group had ever seen before. An abundance of unusual birds flapped through the trees and onto the water. Herons, geese and swamp-hens cawed and quacked amid the cacophony of screaming children as they jumped from the pontoon into the water. A warm sienna hue laced with gold flowed along at the water's edge where little children tried to catch the tantalisingly visible fish.

"We should have brought a barbie!" Ruth exclaimed.

"Hey, a picnic is just grand," Michael and Julia said together and then laughed.

"You are becoming very Aussie, Ruth, with your Eskys and barbies!" Julia joked as she removed the bags from the boot of the jeep.

"Come on, let's get a nice sheltered spot over by the trees," Ruth said – she was fitting into the lifestyle well but wasn't there yet.

The girls had put their bikinis on under their clothes and Michael wasn't long changing into his shorts. The three waded out into the bath-like water but didn't have to go far before they could swim out of their depth.

"Come on over to the pontoon – we can dive in!" Michael called.

"My hair is a frizzy mess already!" Julia called back. "You'll have to go on your own."

"Yep, it's all yours, I'm afraid!" Ruth shouted.

The girls went back to their towels and the deck chairs.

"It's a gorgeous spot – good call," Julia said while drying off her arms and legs.

She saw something jump in the distance but wasn't sure if she was seeing things.

"Ruth, is that what I think it is over there?" She stood very still and pointed to the right-hand side of the trees just behind them.

"Oh yeah – it is – your first wild kangaroo. I had no idea that you could see them up here." Ruth was agog.

"Don't move or he'll jump away."

Skippy eyed them cautiously. He was hiding behind a tree and licking his paws.

"I guess they scavenge for the leftovers from the picnics," Julia said.

"He's cute but so skinny. I hope he's okay."

"Ruth – he's a wild animal. I swear between them and the quokkas you'll end up adopting something before you go home."

"I know! I was never clucky like this before, was I, Julia? I don't know what's got into me."

Julia didn't know what was going on for Ruth either but she was definitely changing.

Michael and the girls stopped off at the Mundarring Weir Hotel on their way back to Subiaco. It was off their direct route back to the city but was such a picturesque winding road that they enjoyed the scenery and unusual landscape.

The hotel had been built over a hundred years before. A red British telephone kiosk nestled against the trees in the car park and the lush landscaped gardens catered for outdoor concerts that were held in the summer. The building was made with red bricks that had been transported from England. It was lovingly restored in the Victorian style and the three went into the old bar and sat up at the counter. The light from the stained-glass windows shone in sparkles against the rows of spirits behind the bar, giving the old colonial building a magical feel.

"I wonder if they have ghosts in this building?" Ruth said, scanning her surroundings.

"Ruth, don't start," Julia said, turning to explain her reaction to Michael. "Ruth is convinced that she had a supernatural experience on Rottnest Island."

"Was it those blokes you were telling me about?" he said with a laugh.

"Seriously," said Ruth, "I swear something weird happened in the bedroom. Of course Julia was sound asleep in the bed!"

The barmaid was pulling a pint of cider for Michael.

"Are you guys here to see Paddy?" she asked.

"Who's Paddy?" Ruth asked.

"He's our ghost – worked on the weir when they built it – he breaks beer glasses and makes tools disappear."

"Sounds like Horatio!" Michael laughed. "What do you think, Julia?"

Ruth was intensely interested. "Do you know anything about ghosts on Rottnest Island?" she asked the girl.

The girl laughed. "That place is crawling with them. There's a story of a housemaid who killed herself – a scorned lover. She was pregnant too – or maybe they just added that to the story to be more dramatic. We have to make our history up in Australia!"

She put the pint of cider in front of Michael and started to chat to him, asking if he was enjoying Australia.

Julia turned to Ruth. "I think you're more interested in these ghosts than finding out about your mother's history," she said. "When are we going to check out Peppermint Grove again?"

Ruth was in a daze. "Yeah – I don't know. Maybe we can call around that way tomorrow – there's a nice restaurant called Mosmans that I've been dying to try. It's on the river and we can have dinner there if you like?"

"Sounds good," said Julia.

It was agreed.

Chapter Thirty-three

Dylan woke up to pleasant sunshine in Malahide. He could pop out to Howth and sail in the Brass Monkey series. He was at leisure to do as he pleased until it was time for Sunday lunch in Craig and Odette's house. It was such a difficult time for his brother and sister-in-law and he could feel the strain that they were living under.

He decided to check the weather first – he didn't want to race if there was no wind.

His phone bleeped and he looked at the message. It was from Gillian.

Hi Dylan do u want to do something today? I was thinking of going into town later? Gill

Dylan wondered if he had been cruel inviting her out for drinks the night before. It wasn't his intention to lead her on – he had hoped that they could be friends and he was meeting the others early so he knew that she would still be in town after work. Obviously she didn't see it in the same casual way that he did. He certainly didn't want to hurt the poor girl. He had organised the drinks to see if Craig was available to go out on a Friday night, and watch him in public with his wife. He was still concerned that Craig might be having an affair – there had to be some explanation for his strange behaviour. But maybe he shouldn't have involved a third party – he had just thought, wrongly as it turned out, that it would make for a more relaxed atmosphere.

But that wasn't his only motive if he was to be honest. He knew that he had got a reaction from Julia when he had given Gillian attention at the quiz. He couldn't help his fixation on the beautiful brunette and the way that she treated him so terribly made him like her even more. He felt such chemistry with Julia that he wondered what she'd be like, if only he could scratch beneath the surface and get to know the real woman.

He wasn't going to play with Gillian's emotions any more. How could he let her down gently?

He started to text.

Have plans for 2day. Hope u r well. D

There, that was brief and to the point – she should get the message if she read between the lines.

"Why is Dylan coming to lunch again?" Craig asked, banging his fist on the kitchen table. "He's a big boy and should get a life of his own."

"Why are you so cross with your brother?"

"It's easy for him to come around here gloating, with his massive redundancy and no worries or commitments."

It was Odette's turn to slam her fist on the table. "Oh, so is that what your family is to you now – a worry and a commitment? Well, thanks for telling me!"

Craig lifted his hands and put them to his head. Sometimes Odette infuriated him more than she could imagine.

"For Christ's sake, woman, stop turning everything around and being so defensive."

Odette's jaw dropped. "You have never called me that in all the years that we have been together!"

She burst into tears, ran out of the room and up to their bedroom. She threw herself on the covers and sobbed into her pillow. What was going on with her life? She was so miserable – she couldn't understand these deep sad feelings that were bubbling inside or why she found it so difficult to talk to her husband.

She needed to speak with Julia but it was pointless as she was so far away. Her mother was the only other option. She lifted the phone beside her bed and dialled.

But it was Horatio who answered.

"Hello?"

He always sounded like it was the very first time that he had spoken into a telephone.

"Hi, Granddad, how are you?"

"Oh, I'm here working on a clock for Mrs Dunne – you know, Anna Dunne who moved into the Kanes' old house. How are things in Australia?"

"It's not Julia, Granddad – it's Odette."

"Oh, Odette, sorry – how are you and the kids?"

"We are grand, thanks. I'm glad to see that you are busy – not pining for Julia?"

"She's left me with a lovely girl – Paola – have you met her?"

Odette chuckled. "No but Mum told me about her – she's a real gem. I'm looking for Mum – is she there?"

"I don't know what's got into her since Julia left. She's been going out for long spells during the day, although she's stuck in front of that computer all night. She won't tell me where she's going either. I think we need Julia back here to put manners on her."

"I wonder if Julia will be able?"

"So do I – but Julia is marvellous at sussing people out – look how she chose that smashing Brazilian girl to look after me – I don't mind telling you they have to be the nicest race of people on this earth."

Odette laughed – she could just imagine her grandfather's wicked thoughts. "Behave yourself, Granddad!"

"Ah sure, as your grandmother used to say about Mrs Reilly's dog that used to chase after every car on our road – *if he caught up with one he wouldn't be able to drive it!*"

"Granddad, you're a scream! Will you get Mum to ring me later?"

"I will indeed but, as I said, Odette – she's lost the run of herself – I blame that bridge myself."

"Would you like to come out to us for a bit of lunch later?"

"Not at all – thanks for the offer but I want to get this clock fixed for Mrs Dunne. Time waits for no man, Odette. Take care and give my love to the little ones."

Odette chuckled as she said her goodbyes and put down the phone. Her grandfather's voice had cheered her up no end. She went into her bathroom and washed her eyes, feeling much better in herself. She heard her husband in the distance going out the front door and pulling it closed behind him.

Never mind. Julia would be home soon and she would help her to see sense.

By the time Dylan arrived, Craig had already returned home without informing Odette of where he had been.

For a while the lunch was a mumble of politeness interrupted only by correction of the children. They were keen to go outside and play – sitting up at the table was more of a punishment than a pleasure.

"Were you sailing today, Dylan?" Odette asked cheerily.

"Yes – it was a lovely morning for it. I might pop out to the club later and see if there are any of the lads left – sometimes they have a bit of a session on a Sunday."

"It's alright for the idle," Craig snapped. "What are you going to do with yourself, Dylan – apart from rubbing it in for those of us who have to work to keep this miserable economy afloat?"

Odette glared at Craig. There was no need for this kind of rudeness.

"I'm thinking of going away for a while so maybe you won't have to see that much of me soon!"

Odette was taken aback. "Where? Why?"

"I'm checking out opportunities abroad. I'm too young to retire and I have contacts in London who are keen to start a new project."

Odette breathed a sigh of relief. "At least London isn't that far away."

"Not far enough," Craig muttered under his breath.

Odette got up and started to clear the plates away. She thought it best to leave the brothers alone to work out their issues. She felt so alone. It was just as well that Julia wasn't the one emigrating. She would be counting the days until she returned.

Chapter Thirty-four

The next day was glorious but a misty haze seemed to indicate that it would not be as hot as the day before. Ruth arrived home from work at three and told Julia and Michael that she would have to do full hours the following day.

"That misty haze is smoke moving up from the bush fires down south – that's why it's not so hot today," she informed the other two.

"It was hot enough for me," Julia said. "Michael and I took a walk in King's Park this morning – it was gorgeous."

"Right." Ruth poured herself a cold drink from the fridge. "I'll just take a quick shower and then we can set off for Peppy Grove. I wonder if Brian is working today?"

"Well, you have his business card so why don't you give him a ring?" Julia suggested.

"Julia Perrin! You want me to call him?" Ruth was amazed. Julia never went after a man – ever!

"Why not? It would be a bit of fun."

Ruth wasn't sure if this was a good idea – it might give Marty an idea that she wanted to hook up and make a foursome – she would have to make it clear that was not her intention. "Okay then."

Ruth rummaged through her bag and found the card that Brian had given her on the day they had first visited Peppermint Grove.

She dialled his number and waited. She was through to the voicemail of Brian Nugent. If she left her name and number he would call her back. She turned off the phone.

"He's not answering. Let's just pop down there and we can go for a walk along the Esplanade. We never went into the yacht club either."

"Okay then, let's go," Julia agreed.

The three hopped into Ruth's car.

"Where exactly are we going?" Michael asked.

"Peppermint Grove is where Ruth's mother's friend lived and we are trying to find out about him."

"Girls, you are mad in the head! I thought we were going to some snazzy restaurant!"

"We won't be long there," Ruth assured him.

Michael was observing the houses that flitted by.

"Wow, these are massive!" he exclaimed. "I'd love to plonk one of these on Howth Hill at home!"

"Most expensive suburb in Perth!" Ruth informed him.

They wound around the same roads as they travelled a few days before until they came to Number 5, Peppermint Grove Road. There were lots of cars parked outside today and Ruth was feeling anxious about calling into the site. She recognised Brian's jeep parked at the front beside the pillars. Her heart beat rapidly – she felt bad but must not let Julia have an inkling of her feelings.

Just as they stepped out of their car, Brian appeared at the gate.

"Hey there!" he said.

"Hi, Brian! You jumped off Rotto pretty early next morning!" Julia said, stating the obvious, and couldn't believe that she hadn't come up with a better line.

"Yeah, I had to come on site. We're working seven-day shifts on this project and I need to do checks." Brian looked Michael up and down and then held out his hand. "Brian Nugent."

"I'm Julia's brother, Michael."

"Good to meet you."

They shook hands firmly.

Brian turned to Ruth. "I was talking to another neighbour yesterday and she was able to tell me more about the Walters family – it was really interesting!"

"Oh, I'd love to hear!" Ruth beamed.

"We're going for something to eat," Julia interrupted. "We're thinking of trying Mosmans for dinner if you're free to join us."

"Eh, not tonight, sorry – have to go in to the office – but I could meet you tomorrow? I usually go to the Lucky Shag after a day in the CBD. I'll be there about six. I can tell you what I found out then, Ruth."

"Sounds good," Julia answered. "We'll see you there."

He strode off to his Jeep and they jumped into the car and took the short drive along the esplanade until they came to the nicest restaurant on the river.

The entrance was along a boarded jetty – it felt like embarking a ship or yacht. A lone guitarist played to the small gathering of mostly couples at scattered tables along the window. It was a bright building and the large windows maximised the capacity for the punters to take in the exceptional view. A plethora of sailing ships raced about a kilometre away out on the water. It was only five o'clock but these were the early business-sailors who liked to mix work and pleasure. There were plenty of opportunities to do so, as Ruth was beginning to discover the longer she lived in Perth.

The restaurant was starting to fill up and Ruth assured them that they were fortunate to get a table. It would be heaving by the time they started their main course.

The tables were minimalist with starched white linen napkins and solid jarrah wood surfaces. They sat on beige mock-suede uprights and had an unspoilt view of the marina and boats in the bay.

"This place reminds me a little of Aqua in Howth," Julia said, scanning the menu. "Some nice fish dishes on the menu too."

"Yes, it does have a feel of Aqua alright – without the fishing boats," Michael agreed. "So what do you want to order?" Ruth asked.

"Scallops for me." Julia had made her mind up quickly.

"I think I'll go for them too," Michael said.

"I'll have the crab and parmesan aranchini!" Ruth declared.

The waitress filled all of their glasses with iced water and Michael suggested a bottle of white wine that they all agreed upon.

"So this Brian chap seems to have certainly clicked with you two girls?" said Michael after the wine arrived and was poured. "Which one of you fancies him?"

Ruth was shaken by the question. She looked at Julia who smiled coyly. Ruth had tried to get him out of her head but after seeing him again she realised that she was attracted to him. But Julia was on holiday and she didn't often find a man that she was attracted to.

"Eh, Julia likes him."

"I guess we'll be going to the Lucky Shag then – what's that place like?" Michael asked Ruth.

"It's a bar down at Barrack Street Jetty – lots of people go there after work. Sometimes there are musicians – Steve brought the office crew there on the first Friday after I arrived and they had a DJ."

"Eat up!" Michael said as the food arrived. It was beautifully displayed on white china.

They hadn't much room for dessert but shared a selection of house-made ice-creams and sorbets.

"What do you want to do tomorrow, Michael, while Ruth is at work?" Julia asked her brother.

He shrugged. "It's just so good being here, I don't mind."

"You should take a trip out to Fremantle prison," Ruth suggested. "You can't go home without visiting it."

"Have you been?" Julia asked her.

Ruth shook her head. "No, but I will go – I'm not in a hurry and I've been told that the tour is really good."

"Okay, that's it sorted," Michael agreed.

"You can take my car. Actually, leave it in Subiaco before you come back in to meet me and we can all have a few drinks in the Lucky Shag tomorrow night."

"That sounds like a plan," Michael said, raising his glass of wine. "So we're off to prison tomorrow, little sister!"

Chapter Thirty-five

Carol rose early as she had done since Julia had left for Australia. She was so excited and having the most wonderful few days with her new male friend. He was staying in the Marine Hotel at Sutton Cross so she would slip into something casual and go and meet him before breakfast. She didn't want her father knowing about her friend or he would surely have words to say about him.

This was no fling either. She had found in Gerry a man that fed her mind. She relished the lack of complications that an affair with a man who was in the autumn of his life had to offer. She was no spring chicken herself but with her maturity came a sense of confidence and security that she was relishing.

The day was cold but bright and she looked forward to taking Gerry into Dublin to show him her home town. He had come down from the North on the train and so far they had only been around Howth and taken a trip to Malahide. It was a day for the open-top bus and the Guinness Hopstore. She had lived in Dublin all of her life and had never done either. She might be playing less bridge since Gerry arrived but she was seeing a whole new world on her doorstep with endless possibilities.

After breakfast they hopped on the DART and went into O'Connell Street where the Dublin Bus Tour started.

Carol and Gerry laughed like schoolchildren on top of the

open-deck-bus. The driver informed them about all the buildings that they were passing. The grounds of Trinity College flitted by and, although it was cold, the sun shone on Carol and her friend who was falling more and more in love with her each day.

"And to your left is the old Finn's Hotel," the driver continued, "where Nora Barnacle used to work and James Joyce met her there for their first date on the 16th June 1904 – this was the date that Joyce chose for his novel *Ulysses*, which we now celebrate as Bloomsday."

"I love Dublin," Gerry said out loud.

"I never really appreciated it before – but I feel like I am looking at it with new eyes now." Carol smiled.

"And I feel like I am seeing the world with new eyes since I met you," he said coyly.

Carol blushed. It had been so many years since she had felt desired. She couldn't recall the first flushes of romance with her husband any more. It was like she was feeling this way for the very first time.

"I know what you mean," she said. "Everything has changed since we met, hasn't it?"

"I never thought I would ever meet anyone again – after Alma died I thought that was it for me – thank you, Carol, for bringing me out of myself like this."

"I feel like a teenager again in your company, Gerry. We have a lot to be thankful for." She paused, thinking of Julia's single state. "I just wish my daughter would meet someone," she sighed. "Julia is so controlled. She works too hard and she really needs to let herself go. I don't know what to do."

"You have to let them be the way that they are. I think it's one of the most difficult things about having children."

The bus swung around the corner and they were on Merrion Square.

"To your left is Number 1, the birthplace and home of another great Irish writer, Oscar Wilde," the driver continued.

"Ah now, this man I can agree with," Gerry whispered Carol's ear. "*We are all in the gutter, but some of us are looking at the stars!*"

Carol turned her head and gazed into Gerry's eyes. He was so romantic and thoughtful. She was falling in love with Gerry and her hometown all at once.

After a stroll in Stephen's Green they had a long and leisurely lunch in the James Joyce Room in Bewley's restaurant and Carol told Gerry her innermost thoughts and dreams that she had never shared with another soul. They enjoyed a little window-shopping and finished off the excursion with a visit to the National Gallery and the Jack B Yeats' paintings which Gerry had heard were beautifully displayed.

They then took the DART back to the Northside and Carol was sad to be saying goodbye to Gerry at the end of such a perfect day together. But she knew that her father would be asking questions if she didn't come home and, besides, she didn't want to leave him alone.

"Please, can you stay with me – in the hotel – for just one night?" Gerry pleaded. "I'll be going back north tomorrow."

Carol sighed. Her heart was tugging at her to stay.

"Let me go home and get a few bits and have a word with Dad. I'll make up an excuse."

Gerry hugged her tightly. "Hurry back!"

Carol's heart was beating. But now she knew, after the last four days, how she really felt about Gerry and she was ready for a relationship.

Carol drove quickly home.

Horatio was sitting looking at the snooker on TV in his room when she arrived.

"Dad – I might stay over in my friend Treasa's tonight after bridge – is that okay?"

Horatio raised his left brow and looked at his daughter from the corner of his eye.

"If you say so – that's fine by me. I'm glad to have the house to myself for a bit of peace. I have to tidy it up before Paola gets here tomorrow morning. She's the best company we've had in this place since I can remember."

"All right, Dad. I know you're her biggest fan."

"The Brazilians are such lovely people – great respect for their elders they have too – that's something that young Irish people could do with a lesson in."

Carol nodded. "Yes, Dad. See you in the morning."

"Not too early now," he said with a wink.

It made Carol wonder just what her father really thought. At times he was doddery and then again at other times he was the most alert member of the house.

Chapter Thirty-six

Michael pulled up at the designated parking area and Julia got out of the car. The imposing façade of Fremantle Prison loomed at the top of a mound with shallow steps leading up to it.

It was a hot day and Julia drank from a bottle of water as they climbed up to the two-towered Gatehouse which was built of white stone, with its massive arch and clock-face.

Inside the Gatehouse was information about the various guided tours and an office where Michael purchased two tickets for the next session which would start in fifteen minutes.

"You can take a look in the art gallery while you're waiting," the girl in the ticket office suggested.

A special exhibition was on display in the gallery. It contained the work of inmates who were currently residing in prisons in Perth.

"Come on," Julia said, linking her brother's arm.

They strolled into the first section of the gallery and large glass doors opened electronically. The paintings were impressive from the beginning. The colourful dot paintings by the Aboriginal prisoners stood out particularly.

Michael was reading a brochure. "It says here that none of the artists can be named as they are all currently serving sentences but they will receive payment for the work."

Julia was transfixed by a beautiful study of three turtles painted delicately in shades of grey and white, resembling a constellation of stars. The composition was divided up symmetrically in all directions and it was a remarkable blend of mathematical division and mastery of the paint, the patterns created from tiny dots and the contrast of yellow and orange against the grey making the complete work perfect.

"I don't normally take such a liking to pictures but I would love to hang that in my office," said Julia. "It's number six. How much is it?"

Michael looked at the brochure. "It says here two hundred dollars."

Julia was impressed by the price.

"Come and look around the rest of the gallery," Michael beckoned as he stood at another automatic door.

The paintings varied in theme and style, some reflective, others offensive, but all painted with a remarkable level of skill.

"I'm getting that one of the turtles!" she decided.

"It's nice, I guess," Michael said with a nod.

Suddenly her phone bleeped. It was from Odette.

Hope u are having a good time. Michael arrived? xxO

"Oh, poor Odette, I think she's missing us."

"Missing *you*, Julia."

"I don't know how to help her. Craig is impossible at the moment and she's feeling isolated. I don't know why she can't call Mum – though she hasn't been herself either."

Michael had to agree. There were big changes, he felt, last time that he was home. Big changes with his friends and with Ireland. But still he was desperate to be there.

"Have you heard from Lydia at all?" he asked candidly.

"Oh Michael, you have to forget about her. She's crazy about Peter and if he doesn't propose soon I think that she is going to do it on the 29th February!"

Michael was in shock. "She wouldn't?" he gasped. That was so out of character with the girl that he had once loved so deeply.

Julia nodded. "She sent me an in-depth email a few days ago – I read it on the plane coming over. I'm sorry to have to say it but that last email that you sent was the nail in the coffin for you guys."

Michael felt awfully uncomfortable all of a sudden.

"Come on, let's get that painting," he urged. "The tour is starting soon."

Julia went into the gift shop and paid for the piece. She was disappointed that she couldn't take it with her as the exhibition was running until March but she would ask Ruth to collect it on the designated day when the exhibition was over.

The guide was a chirpy woman who was quick to tell them that her son had been a warden in the prison before the facility was closed back in 1991. She was dressed in warden's clothes and Julia and Michael were on her shift along with the rest of the tourists for the next hour and a quarter.

Julia and Michael were gasping for a drink by the end of the tour. The cells were abysmal and tales of rats crawling over inmates through the night and the stench that took a year to leave the building after the last inmate had been moved had made Julia's stomach churn.

"We need to get something to eat," Michael said. "Do you know anywhere near?"

"Let's go to one of the spots along the Cappuccino Strip – we passed some lovely restaurants the other day after we got back from Rotto."

Michael drove and parked on South Terrace. The first Italian restaurant at the corner was called Gino's and it looked inviting.

"I think we have to order inside," Julia said.

Michael followed his sister and the two chose a panini and fries to be washed down with Coke and water.

"Hey, they have free Wi-Fi here," Michael commented as he looked at his watch. "I might give them a call at home."

"Oh do – I'd love to talk to Granddad."

"Is it too early?"

Julia looked at her watch. "Nah – eight o'clock – Horatio will be up."

They went down to the corner and sat at a quiet table with

the number stand for their order in hand. Michael dialled and put his phone on speaker.

Horatio answered the phone. "Hello?"

"Granddad, it's me, Michael."

"Ah how are you – what's the weather like in Singapore?"

"I'm sure it's extremely hot and humid but I'm in Australia."

Horatio chuckled. "Julia's in Australia too, you know!"

"Yes, Granddad, she's right here with me."

Horatio seemed confused. "I thought she was going out to see Ruth!"

Michael was now laughing. "She is – I mean, we're both here staying with Ruth."

"Oh, that's very good. We're getting very multi-cultural, aren't we? Paola will be here in a couple of hours – I could sit and watch her hoover all day!"

"Granddad!" Julia said.

"Hello there, Julia. Odette rang last night and I thought it was you."

Julia bit her lip. "How is Odette doing?"

Horatio sighed. "She sounded a bit flustered. She was looking for your mother who I have to say has been acting very strangely since you left."

"What do you mean, Granddad?"

"Well, I think she has a man!"

Julia and Michael burst out laughing.

"Why do you think that?" they said together.

"Because she didn't come home last night – made up some cock-and-bull story about staying with Treasa. I could tell by the look on her face that she was up to something!"

Julia was speechless. Horatio never said things unless he was certain that they were true.

"Is everything okay there?" she asked when she got her voice back.

"Of course it is!" the old man scoffed. "I just wish she'd come clean about him and then buzz off and leave me in peace for a few days – *you'll* be back ordering us all about before we know it!"

"Granddad, you're cruel!" Julia said.

"Oh, tell your sister to stop being so sensitive, will you, Michael?" The old man chuckled. "Anyway, you two should be out there having a good time dancing and not worrying about us old codgers."

"We are having a good time," Julia said defensively.

"What are you like, the pair of you? Not a husband or wife between you! Would you ever go and fall in love?"

Julia and Michael could only laugh.

"All right then," said Horatio, "I'll be wanting to hear a full report of the fun you've had when you get back, Julia. Don't wait until you are too old like me – I'm glad your mother's gone and got a bit of life in her."

"Okay, Granddad, so I'll see you soon," Julia said.

"Goodbye now and remember all that I've said – have a good time."

When he was gone Julia looked at Michael. "You don't think he's right, do you?"

"About Mum having a man?"

Julia nodded. "I'm knocked for six."

Michael shrugged. "I don't see why she couldn't but then it would be very out of character."

Julia rested her chin on her palm in contemplation. She had been so concerned about Odette and her troubles with Craig that she hadn't been paying that much attention to her mother's behaviour.

"Come to think of it, she has been extra-secretive since she returned from that trip to Germany. Did you notice anything exceptional when you were home at Christmas?"

"Apart from the fact that she was on the computer, she seemed pretty much the same as usual. Mind you, she was on it for most of the time," Michael said with a grin.

Their food arrived and they tucked in. The portions were huge and they wished they had only ordered one panini to share.

"By the time we finish up here and take the car back to Subiaco it'll be time to meet Ruth," Michael said.

Julia took a chip and dipped it in mayonnaise. The world was changing dramatically around her and she wondered what other surprises were in store for her when she returned home.

Ruth wasn't on her own when the others arrived at the Lucky Shag. She was sitting on a high stool next to Steve and draining a glass of cider. Already the long rows of tables were filling up and Michael and Julia had to move some stools around and squeeze up next to where Ruth and Steve were sitting.

"Hi, Michael – this is Steve. Steve – Michael. And of course you know Julia!"

Julia held out her hand. "Nice to see you again, Steve."

Steve nodded his head. "Of course – Julia. Ruth has really settled in great!" he said with a beaming smile. "She's a super addition to our team."

"Well, I think this lifestyle suits me," Ruth said, not pleased at being spoken about as if she wasn't present.

"Would you guys like a drink?" Steve asked Michael and Julia.

"I'll have a glass of white wine, please," Julia said.

"Thanks, yeah. A beer for me – Corona," Michael said with a nod.

"And another cider for you, Ruth?" Steve said with a familiarity that concerned Julia.

"Yes, please," she replied.

Julia looked around but there was no sign of Brian yet. The sun was going down on the other side of the Swan River and they had a spectacular view of the waterfront and the herons and long-billed birds that glided gracefully across from shore to shore.

Steve left at seven and just after that Brian arrived. The bar was heaving now with after-work clientele who were keen to enjoy the warm summer evening in such a salubrious setting. The sky was now a dark velvet navy, the stars and waning moon beaming down on the revellers.

Brian was smiling although it was obvious to Ruth that he was tired at the end of his day's work.

Julia, however, was ready for action and she immediately

launched into making him fee welcome and beckoned to him to sit next to her.

"Have you been enjoying your stay?" he asked Julia and Michael as he sat down.

"Yes, we went to Fremantle Prison today," Michael replied.

"Gruesome place!" Brian said with a nod.

"I bought a painting – oops, I forgot to check if it's okay with you, Ruth – I can't have it until the exhibition ends in March so can you collect it then and post it over to me?"

"No problem," Ruth said. "And speaking of post, what news do you have, Brian? I'm dying to know what you heard from that neighbour about the Walters."

Michael interrupted. "Let me get you a beer, Brian – what would you like?"

"Eh, a bottle of something German would be good, thanks," said Brian and then turned his attention back to Ruth. "Yeah, it was lucky, I guess. An old lady was just walking by and she wanted to know if I could fix the window in her pool house. I said I'd send one of the guys around and we got talking about the lady who had lived in Number 5. She was a great friend of hers and she said that she missed her. They used to play tennis together when they were younger and in later years played bowls. This old dear was about ninety. She said that her son was friends with Mrs Emily Walters' son and the whole family was devastated when he died. Mrs Walters' husband died soon after his son, leaving the old lady on her own for years in the house that we pulled down."

Ruth was trying to figure out which of the Walters men had known her mother.

"Did this lady give you the names of the men?"

"They were both called Charles – the son was Charlie. I remembered that was the name you mentioned."

"Did she say what had happened to the son?"

"It was a car crash on the highway," Brian said.

"I wonder which Charles Ruth's mum was writing to," said Julia. "Was the son married?"

"Nah, he was the golden boy – his parents adored him. He

was driving a sports car when he sped along the freeway and hit another car."

"What did the Walters do – were they business people?" Ruth asked.

"They were merchants – freight ships and that kind of thing. A booming business in Perth – always is! When the husband and son died, the nephew took over and kept the old lady sweet in her house until she died."

"I would love to know how my mother knew them. She wasn't working when she lived here as far as I know."

"You'll really have to ask her," Brian said with a shrug of his shoulders.

"Well . . . I found the letter when I was in my mother's attic. Then she would know that I had been snooping in her private stuff!"

Michael returned with a fresh round of drinks.

"This is a great spot," he said. His eyes scanned the beautiful people who had all descended on the bar to watch the sunset over the river and mingle with the other beautiful people of Perth.

"There's a nice enough restaurant beside us here if you fancy some dinner?" Brian said, pointing to a wooden-clad building which opened up onto the decked jetty.

"What's it called?" Ruth asked.

"Halo. It's a bit pricey but a nice setting. Is anyone hungry?"

"I'm starving," Ruth admitted. "I had an apple at my desk at twelve and can hear my stomach rumble."

"Okay, let's finish these drinks and go over there," Brian said.

As they drank, Brian told them stories about growing up in Perth and Julia was amazed that Michael was happy to let another man take the limelight – but she realised that he was doing it for her.

They finished up their drinks and walked the short few steps over to the entrance of Halo restaurant. It was very contemporary inside with beautiful jarrah wood on the floors and in the bar area there was unobstructed viewing of the Swan River and the boats sailing by.

This was another minimalist restaurant and the food was artistically displayed as well as appetising, as the waiters strutted by with the plates held high.

Ruth took the seat beside Brian and Michael sat opposite her.

Julia was delighted to be facing Brian. She would work this meal to her advantage. Since meeting in the Lucky Shag she was more certain than ever that she wanted to be with him.

A snooty maitre d' sauntered over to them with large flat menus. Golden hair swept down her back in a ponytail – her black dress reached down to the ground and covered her five-inch heels.

"The specials today are . . ." and she recited the list in the plummy tones of an English governess.

"She's not Australian, is she?" Ruth whispered into Brian's ear.

"Unfortunately she is, but she's so stuck up her own ass she's in danger of disappearing up it – don't let that put you off the food here though – just ignore the snobs!"

Brian was right and the food was delicious. The four chatted about life and the different things that Dublin and Perth had to offer. They were the last people in the restaurant at ten o'clock, being asked if they would like another coffee or if they were ready for the bill.

"I'm getting this," Michael said, taking the black leather folder from the maitre d'.

"No, we're going Dutch!" Ruth insisted.

"No way." Michael got up and went over to the bar, credit card in hand.

Brian was embarrassed that he hadn't got to the bill first. "Let me get the drinks then after – unless you are too tired?"

"I've got a better idea," said Ruth. "Let's grab a cab and go back to my place."

Julia's eyes lit up at the suggestion.

"Okay," Brian shrugged but looked down at his watch.

Ruth turned on the air-conditioning when they arrived at her house.

"Julia, can you get drinks, please? I have to go to the loo."
Ruth ran off to her own bathroom and had to sit on the toilet to
get her head together. She had to control her feelings. She was so
into Brian and couldn't let Julia know. The way that Michael
was becoming so chummy in the back of the taxi was also
beginning to cause her concern. They were naturally forming a
cosy foursome that she did not want to be part of.

She looked at herself in the mirror and brushed down her
clothes. She touched up her lip gloss and decided to go out and
face the music.

It was worse than she had imagined.

Julia was draped over Brian on the couch in the living room
and showing no restraint. Waiting for Ruth in the kitchen with
a freshly poured glass of white wine was a sultry-eyed Michael.

Against her better judgment she went over to him but he
lurched forward and planted his lips on top of hers.

"I've been wanting to do that all night!" he said, grinning
cheekily.

Ruth had to stop it right there. She had to say no. But
Michael didn't give her a chance. He put down his glass,
wrapped his arms tightly around her waist and then kissed her
again. She was snogging him back now and it was nice, so
against her better judgement she continued. She didn't hear
footsteps entering the kitchen.

"Oh sorry, I didn't . . ."

Ruth stopped abruptly and looked around to see a shocked
Brian staring at her.

"Don't tell Julia!" Michael said quickly.

"I-I-I won't – I'll leave you two in peace," he said as he turned
on his heel, pulling the kitchen door behind him.

Ruth's heart sank. What must Brian think of her? She had
snogged Marty a couple of days ago and now she was kissing
Michael. All he needed to be told now was that she had a
married man back in Ireland and at work and he would see her
as the ultimate scarlet woman! She hoped and prayed that Julia
would keep her mouth shut.

"So, are you coming to bed?" Michael said with a wink.

"Yep – my own bed on my own." She shook her head, took a glass of water and left.

Julia was making great progress with Brian. For ambiance she had turned off the main light and switched on a corner lamp when he went out to the kitchen to get a drink of water. He was sitting comfortably next to her on the couch.

"I love hearing about your work – tell me more about the projects that you are working on," she said, taking a sip from her glass.

"Oh, you don't want to hear about buildings and work – I think your job sounds more interesting!"

Julia was winding a strand of hair around the index finger of her left hand. "But I do – I'd really like to get to know you better," she replied, this time batting her eyelids.

Brian was feeling decidedly uncomfortable. He was an old-fashioned type of guy and here she was, making the first move.

Julia leaned forward and put her face so close to his that she could smell his skin.

"I like you," she said. It was a line that she felt was a sure-fire winner. Usually by this stage in the chase she would be peeling off her top but Brian didn't seem like the strong macho man she had first seen on the building site. He resembled a sheep about to be sheared.

And then it struck her!

"You're not gay, are you?" she blurted out.

Brian was perturbed. He shook his head vehemently.

"Good!" she grinned and moved snakelike even closer until she could touch the side of his rough unshaven cheek with hers.

Brian couldn't escape and, after seeing Ruth earlier in the kitchen, he wondered what he had to lose. Julia was pretty and smart but it was the wild Irish looks of Ruth that really attracted him. It was a shame that she was so wild that she seemed to hook up with any man. To tell Julia now that he didn't want to get intimate would be an insult – she had clearly made up her mind what she wanted.

She moved her head so that her lips were almost touching his.

It was a taut anxious moment before they met but when they did it felt good and warm. She gently parted her lips and their tongues rolled together. The taste was new and inviting and Julia was sure that she had chosen well for her holiday romance.

Brian couldn't blank out the image of Ruth in the kitchen kissing Michael, but it helped to turn him on and he continued with the kiss.

Julia wanted action. It had been several months since she had slept with another body. She took his hand and put it up to her right breast.

He cupped it gently but didn't move.

Julia was desperate for more and quickly. With her left hand she started to undo the buttons on her shirt and pushed it to the side so that he could feel the satin and lace of her lingerie. She peeled her shirt off. She had never been with such a passive lover. She decided to straddle him and lift both hands up to her breasts. She was aching for more and at last Brian was becoming more animated. He undid the clasp at the back of her bra and removed it.

Julia was emancipated at last and she started to move slowly against his crotch. She felt him stir and was becoming more excited with each move that she made. It was time to unbutton his shirt and he helped her take it off, revealing a smooth bronzed chest.

She wanted him more now. Reaching for the buckle of his belt, she tugged and released it as she unzipped his fly with her other hand.

She slid off him and he helped her to push down his trousers until they rolled down to his knees. Her skirt was superfluous to requirements and she danced out of it and her underwear in the one action. She straddled him again and could hardly breathe with excitement and desire.

Suddenly Brian moaned – he couldn't understand what was happening. It had never happened before. There was no explanation for it. Even as a teenager it had never happened. But now he was helpless to prevent it. He had ejaculated and what had been cocked and prepared a few seconds earlier now lay limply to the side.

Julia was speechless. She had never had a sex disaster before.

Brian was embarrassed. He didn't know what to say or do. It must have been the thought of Ruth that had disturbed his concentration.

"I-I-eh . . ."

"It's okay," Julia said, making light of the situation. The whole moment went from anticipation to awkward so quickly that she winced in her nakedness and started to dress. "It happens all the time – it's very common."

Brian wanted to say that it didn't happen all the time and it had never happened to him but he didn't want to make the situation worse. He stood up and pulled on his trousers.

"I'd better go home – I have to be on site at six." He stuffed his shirt inside his waistband and patted down his hair. "Say thanks to Ruth – she must be gone to bed and eh – say goodbye to your brother too."

Julia followed him out to the hall door and, without a peck on the cheek or a mention of meeting another time, he was gone.

Julia stood with her back to the closed front door. It was awkward and awful and not something that she ever wanted to experience again. She was getting sick of relying on random men on holidays to fulfil her. She wondered what it must be like to be in a relationship with someone that you made love to day-in day-out. To have that security. But then what it must be like to have that taken away from you. That was possibly the main reason why she had been slow to try commitment before.

Chapter Thirty-seven

Gillian was frantically checking her phone every few minutes. She had become obsessed by Dylan. She had heard nothing from him and she desperately wanted to know if there was a chance of meeting up with him again. She decided to take a chance and send him a text.

Hi Dylan would you like to go to the pictures tonight? Gill ?

She thought that the smiley face was non-confrontational and she didn't want to be too forward. She waited until noon to send it but when there was no reply by four thirty she was feeling agitated. An email might be a better option but she didn't have his address. She could always call him. But she was afraid of becoming tongue-tied and sounding foolish.

She looked at her watch – it was night in Australia. Julia's request of an email at the end of every day had to be completed.

Gillian wondered if Julia had any idea how lucky she was. If only she had some of her boss's confidence. But if her experience at the Shelbourne had taught her anything it was that it wasn't easy to just swan in and be the *femme fatale*.

Carol was moping around the house after Gerry had gone back home.

Horatio didn't want to upset her but he did want to know what was going on.

"Will I make you a cup of tea?" he asked her when he came upon her at the kitchen sink.

"No, it's okay, I'll make it for us both."

He sat at the table and watched her. She was in a daze putting the teabags into the pot.

"So when are you going to tell me about your new man?"

Carol almost spilled the water as she poured from the kettle. "My new what?"

"Your new man – don't tell me that you slept over in Treasa's – you aren't ten!"

Carol was horrified. She babbled madly. "I've been playing bridge all week like I always do –"

"If you don't tell me I'll ring Julia in Australia and tell her that you're holding out on me.'

Carol sighed. "Okay – but don't say anything to the kids. His name is Gerry and he lives up in the North – I met him playing bridge online and . . . well, we are close friends."

Horatio laughed. "And where was he staying for the last few days?"

"In the Marine Hotel."

"For God's sake, woman, you are old enough to bring a man back to your bed! And Julia is going to have to deal with him whether she likes it or not!"

Carol shook her head. "You know how she adored her father – it would break her heart and I don't want her to think that he has been replaced for me either."

"Look, if I'd met a woman that I liked after your mother died I'd have got married again. But I was just pleased with the peace and tranquillity to fix my clocks at two in the morning if I wanted without anyone complaining!"

Carol poured the tea. "I wasn't expecting to ever feel this way again but it is more awkward bringing a boyfriend home to your children than your parents. I had never realised it but the pressure is enormous."

Horatio chuckled. "And then you become the child . . . now you know how I feel. I know Julia has a good heart but when she fusses over me, telling me that I might fall and hurt myself or do something stupid, I find it infuriating."

Carol put his tea down in front of him and went to get the milk from the fridge. "I'm sorry – I've been known to do that to you too. Mea culpa."

"Carol, we only have one crack at this life," Horatio said, in a more serious tone now. "Please don't let happiness pass you by. How I wish I had travelled more and been a bit more of a rebel but your mother had such tight reins on me I . . . ah, maybe it was for my own good! But go and be happy and let the young people sort themselves out!"

Carol smiled and planted a kiss on her father's forehead. "Thanks, Dad. I know I don't say it often enough but I love you."

"Ah, don't be getting all soppy on me now – I'm off to fix a clock!" He stood up, lifted his cup and gave his daughter a wink as he went out to his room at the back of the kitchen.

Carol sat down at the table and stared into space. She would take on board what her father had said but she was still dreading telling her children – especially Julia – about Gerry.

Chapter Thirty-eight

Ruth was awake early. She had heard Brian leaving the night before and was keen to find out what had happened. She didn't want to wake Julia but the suspense was killing her. She slipped on her dressing gown and went into her friend's room.

"Morning! I have to go to work soon."

Julia lifted her head, slowly realising that she wasn't in her own room at home, and the memories of the night before started to flood back.

"Ruth, I'm so glad to see you – what a disaster!" Julia shook her bed-head and rubbed her eyes.

"What happened?" Ruth asked, dying to know.

"Well, I hope Brian isn't like other Aussie men because he was no performer!"

"Oh! Tell me."

"The whole experience was like a damp squib – he then came in his pants before I even got a chance to get going properly."

Ruth didn't know whether to laugh or cry. "You're joking!"

Julia shook her head. "Nah – I don't know, Ruth – I'm seriously thinking of setting up a booty call back home – getting sick of taking my chances on holidays!"

"Julia, you sound like a guy – what about settling down and

finding someone nice to have a proper relationship with – like you are trying to get me to do?"

"I don't know where he is or if he exists. Actually, that's probably it – he doesn't exist. My mother got the last good man on the planet."

"Julia, you could give guys a chance when you get home. What about Dylan? He's lovely and he's single."

Julia was horrified. "Not a good idea and he will probably turn out like his brother . . . speaking of which, I need to call Odette and see how she is – what time is it in Dublin?"

"After midnight."

"Sugar! That's too late." Julia shook her head.

"If you don't ring now you'll have to wait eight hours and the chances are that then she'll be getting the kids up for school."

"Okay, I'll try her now. Do you have to work all day?"

"Yes, sorry, I've used up my quota. Besides, it's Michael's last day so I'm sure you want to do something together."

Julia nodded. "Will we meet you back here at five?"

"Perfect – have a good day and we can both bring Michael somewhere nice tonight – maybe we can go to Cicerello's in Fremantle – it's a chip shop with a difference."

"Sounds good!" Julia said as she lifted her phone and rang her sister.

Odette was quick to answer.

"I can't tell you how good it is to hear your voice," she said.

"Hi, Odette, I'm missing you and missing work – Gillian didn't send me an email yesterday. How are things with you?"

"Good, thanks . . . well, you know – the same. Dylan came around for dinner on Sunday – I don't know how he puts up with Craig – I don't know how I put up with him either."

Julia hated to hear her sweet sister sound so sullen.

"Odette, Michael's going back tomorrow – it's been great seeing him again so soon."

"I'm glad – I thought he wasn't himself at Christmas – is he still lonely?"

"Yes – a lot of his friends in Singapore are transient, moving from country to country for two years here, two years there. I can see his point of view and I think turning forty last year has had a massive effect on him."

Odette sighed. "Well, sometimes married life isn't all that it's cracked up to be either."

"Don't worry – things will turn around for you two." Julia bit her lip. She hoped that she was right. "How are the kids?"

"Great – busy and in good form. I'm careful not to let them see the tension between me and Craig."

Julia's heart sank. "What about Mum and Granddad?"

"Mum has been out a lot and Granddad is delighted with the Brazilian girl. I think he wants to take a trip to Brazil!"

"Well, I'll be home towards the end of next week – time just flies by here, now that I've got over the jet lag."

"What is the weather like?"

"Always sunny – not as hot as Ruth predicted thankfully so we've been able to do a good bit of sightseeing."

"Well, make the most of it – it's been mild here but it's certainly not bikini weather."

"Right. I'm going to get Michael up now – see you next week."

"See you next week and thanks for the call . . . miss you."

"So where are we going today?" Michael asked his sister who was flipping pancakes at the hob.

"I think we should just go to the beach – City Beach is close and then tonight Ruth suggested we try some special chipper in Fremantle."

Michael nodded. "Sounds perfect. What about your man Brian – are you seeing him again?"

Julia giggled as she flipped the pancake and slid it onto a plate.

"I don't think so – shame really, I thought we had something. I think he told us all that he knew about the house anyway – really, Ruth should just ask her mother the story."

Michael took the pancake from Julia gratefully and laced it with lemon and sugar.

"That's if there is a story." He shrugged and stuffed a piece of pancake into his mouth.

"That's what's wrong with you – no romance! No wonder Lydia doesn't want anything to do with you!"

"Ouch, that hurt, Ju!"

"Well, maybe if you had been more considerate and not played around – I nearly forgot that – then you would be married to her!"

"Don't rub it in. I still think about her, you know." He looked down at his already-empty plate and Julia felt sorry for him.

He might be all bravado to most but she knew the real Michael and he was a loving, good and kind brother. Even as a child he protected her from the hair-pulling arguments with Odette and always took her side. When her father died she realised how like him he was in many ways and she knew that he longed for the steadiness and security that a happy relationship would bring. She flipped another pancake and tossed it onto his plate.

"Okay – enough morbid talk, brother. We are going to have fun on the beach and then enjoy your last night in Perth."

Steve was in bounding good form at work and Ruth realised that she had to keep him at a distance. She had noticed when he joined them at the Lucky Shag the night before that he had expected her to follow him as he left and was disappointed not to have a kiss. He was standing inside her office now and enquiring about her plans for later.

"Julia and Michael are still with me so I think we're going to Fremantle for supper and then he has a flight to catch in the morning."

Steve shut the door behind him so that the others couldn't hear and sat down at Ruth's desk.

"I'll be glad when your friends are gone – maybe we can spend more time together?" His wide grin unnerved Ruth. She had found him attractive and in a way she still did but if she were to have a relationship with him it would mean that she was playing out an old pattern. She really needed to start off with a clean slate. Now that she realised she could like someone who was available, she felt a sense of hope for her future. But she had to be careful how she played it with Steve. He was, after all, her boss and she did want to give Perth a chance. It was the best job opportunity open to her and she wouldn't be able to stay if she didn't have the work permit that Steve had organised. Besides she really liked her job. She decided to call his bluff.

She stood up, walked around her desk and propped herself on the edge of it.

"I'm so glad that you feel the same way as I do," she said. "When do you think we should tell Michelle?"

Steve cocked his head to the side. "Tell her what?"

"Tell her about us – I am so looking forward to sleeping with you and we only have to wait until the divorce comes through – you see, I've kept my virginity for my husband and when we are engaged we can sleep together."

Steve was speechless. "You'r-r-re a virgin?"

"Yes, and I'm so pleased that I waited for you. It won't be long now – when do you think the proceedings can be started?"

Steve shook his head. "Eh, I didn't realise you felt this way, Ruth – I don't want to hurt Michelle and I have to think of the kids – I mean, they need a father. I wasn't going to divorce my wife – I thought you were looking for the same thing as me."

He rolled the seat backwards with his feet and started to get up. Sheer terror in his face now. Was this girl for real?

"But, Steve, you know that you're irresistible – I couldn't just settle for a little piece of you – not when I've waited all these years."

"Ruth, I like you but I think it might be better to keep our relationship professional. You see, Michelle might go crazy and I wouldn't want to hurt her – you know what I mean."

Ruth feigned a hurt expression. "Oh, Steve, don't reject me – I'm not sure if I can take it."

Steve was now at the door.

"Eh, Ruth, you're doing a terrific job and I have to go out now for the afternoon so I'll see you tomorrow – keep up the good work."

Ruth felt a sense of smug satisfaction as he disappeared. A new strength had taken over her since moving to Australia. She had said goodbye to one of her demons and would only consider single men in future.

Ruth drove to Fremantle. It was a short journey and they wanted to catch the sun going down over the ocean. Michael and Julia giggled as they listened to her relay the tale of Steve in her office earlier.

"I can't believe that he believed you were a virgin!" Michael said.

"I don't know whether to take that as an insult or a compliment," Ruth said into the rear-view mirror at Michael's reflection.

"A compliment most definitely," Julia said with a big grin. "So does this mean that you're on the hunt for Mr Right?"

"Yep! I am only taking single men on."

"We've made a deal, Julia, that if we don't find someone in a couple of years we'll get married!" Michael chirped from the back.

Julia was fascinated by the prospect. "Seriously? I'd like that – my best friend would be my sister – cool!"

Ruth was more reserved about the arrangement. "Hold on and see what happens with Lydia."

"Ah, I hate to admit defeat but she's the one that got away, Michael," Julia quipped.

The sun was low in the sky as they approached the harbour at Fremantle but a lovely orange-and-red-hued light cast shadows on the boats moored at the marina. The large wooden chip shop was painted a nautical blue and a lovely white-and-blue canopy covered the entrance. A large sign in orange-and-blue neon flashed brightly, announcing that they were at their destination.

"*Cicerello's – established 1908 – WA's No 1 Fish 'n' Chips –* Cash Only!" Michael read the sign out aloud on their way in the door. "Hope you have cash, Julia."

"Absolutely, it's my spin tonight."

"No way! Let me," said Ruth. "It's been lovely having the company – after my first few days I was counting down to your visit. You have no idea how lovely it is to see people from home when you are away."

"Look at that!" Michael said, pointing up at a canoe that a

shark had taken a big bite out of. It hung from the rafters and on the wall was a newspaper article about the shark involved.

Ruth and Michael waited for the orders for cod and scampi with chips while Julia went to search out a table outside from where they could watch the sunset.

"Wow!" Julia said as she emerged onto a decked area dotted with white parasols and sturdy wooden benches and tables. They were in the perfect position to take in the complete view of the boats bobbing in the harbour. She found a nice table at the water's edge.

Ruth and Michael came out carrying trays laden with delicious seafood and drinks.

"This place is packed," Ruth said.

"Yes, and look at all the families," Julia commented.

They were halfway through their dinner when Julia decided that she needed more tartar sauce. She got up and went into the counter. The queue had shortened and she was beside a man and his wife who were staring at the menu. He looked vaguely familiar but Julia couldn't place him.

"I think I'll get the chilli mussels," he said with a distinctly Dublin accent.

Julia tried not to stare but it was difficult not to. His hair was peppered with grey strands but he was still quite dark. His eyes were the blue of Paul Newman or David Essex . . . that was it . . . but it couldn't be!

"Nah, Richie, they were too spicy for you last time – remember!" the woman said. She was most definitely Australian but she looked Italian.

"I'll play it safe then and get the scampi," he said.

Julia wanted to burst – it was Richie Clery. She hadn't seen him in almost twenty years. What were the odds on meeting him here? She had often wondered where he had ended up. She had to say something.

"Excuse me but you wouldn't be Richie Clery from Sutton, would you?"

He looked at Julia for a few seconds and squinted. He tilted his head and suddenly the penny dropped. "Julia?"

Julia nodded. "Yes – it's me. I can't believe it. How are you?"

"Good – good, thanks! My, it's been a long time! I haven't been back to Ireland for almost twenty years."

"I was thinking it had to be that long. Are you living here?"

"Yeah, I live in Peppermint Grove."

Julia's mouth dropped. "Wow! Fabulous houses there."

"It's a nice place to live – Julia, this is my wife Donna."

"Pleased to meet you," Julia smiled and the woman shook her hand warmly. "When did you come out here, Richie?"

"Shortly after I left Dublin. The boat that I took brought me from Southampton to Fremantle and I liked it here and they needed someone to work at the port for a while. I didn't go back to sea after that – started my own shipping company after a couple of years and never looked back. Perth's far from everywhere so we'll always need to ship stuff."

"That's amazing. I'm with my brother Michael – do you remember him?"

"Sure I do!" Richie said. "Hey, do you mind if we join you after we get our food?"

He looked at Donna and she nodded enthusiastically.

"I was just getting some tartar sauce," Julia said.

Richie handed her over a tub that was on the counter. "There! I'll put it on my tab."

Julia went back to the others who were almost finished their chips.

"You'll never guess who I met up there – Richie Clery!"

"The Richie Clery with the motorbike?" Ruth asked.

"Yep – unbelievable, isn't it! You go halfway around the world and then meet someone who lived down the road from where you grew up!"

"What's he look like?" Ruth asked. "God, you were mad about him!"

"I know – yeah, he looks good and he's also happily married by the looks of it. And you'll never guess where he lives!"

"Where?" Ruth urged. She hated the way Julia drew a story out.

"Peppermint Grove!"

"*What?*" Ruth gasped.

Michael shook his head. "That's an amazing coincidence."

"There's something about that place," Ruth giggled.

"Well, he must have plenty of cash to afford a house there!" Julia said.

They didn't have to wait long until he arrived.

"Hi, everyone! This is Donna my wife." Richie's manner as he introduced his wife showed the love and high regard he had for her.

"Pleased to meet you – I'm Ruth." Ruth shook hands with Donna.

"And my brother, Michael – you remember Richie..." Julia added.

"Of course I do," Michael said and shook hands with them both.

"So what has you all in Perth?" Richie asked once they had set up their food on the table and settled down.

"We're visiting Ruth – she works here now," Julia explained.

"I'm on a contract for two years," Ruth said.

"Ah, you might stay – most people do." Richie chuckled.

Richie had a story for every year that he had been there and each was more colourful than the last. He offered to help Ruth in any way that he could and told her that she should call him if she felt homesick. Donna was a lovely woman – she described herself as a homemaker but Richie was quick to boast about all of her philanthropic work.

"Maybe you would like to come to some of our fundraisers – they're good fun," Donna said to Ruth. "We're a friendly bunch."

Ruth had to agree and said how easy she found settling into life in Australia.

Julia was in her own world while the others spoke. Life went on around the world for everyone and she had a profound thought that in a funny sort of way no matter where we all were – we would all end up in the same place eventually.

Chapter Thirty-nine

Julia took Ruth's car after she dropped her at the office, to drive Michael to the airport. Ruth had hugged Michael warmly as she wished him a safe flight home and Julia dreaded her own departure in a few days' time.

"You know, I'll be glad when you do come home for good," Julia said as she drove.

"I'm going to actively seek a position in Dublin when I go back," Michael promised.

She kissed him on the cheek and hugged him tightly before he got out of the car.

"I hate goodbyes, Ju. Drive off quickly, please."

Julia nodded and did as her brother asked. Tears filled her eyes. It had been a bonus seeing him so soon after Christmas but it could realistically be a year or more before she saw him again. It was so hard to be parted from people that you loved. She wondered how so many people watched their loved ones every day take a flight to a new part of the world and sometimes never saw them again.

Richie Clery didn't seem to miss anybody or anything since he had left. He was etched very firmly on her mind after meeting him the night before. Back in the nineties he had been such a rebel but now seemed so settled and happy. Of all the people that she had ever known, she would never have imagined him to be the picture of domestic bliss that he had turned out to be. He didn't go on about his three children that much but on the couple of occasions when he had mentioned them he spoke with such pride and care that it made Julia question what she had been doing with her time. Okay, she had a successful business of which she was proud but that was really only ever going to fulfil one part of her – what about all the rest of the stuff that Richie and Donna had spoken about? Richie was an only child who lived with his estranged father when he lived in Dublin. It was no wonder that he had settled down and family had become so important to him once he had found the right woman. And did she, Julia, think that she could have been that woman? Definitely not. She wasn't sure that there was a perfect partner for her but she would like to have someone that made her smile the way that Richie had smiled all the night before.

Back at Ruth's house in Subiaco, she went out to the back garden. She would be home in six days and wanted to have a golden tan of sorts before she arrived back to the cold of Dublin. She decided to pour herself a glass of the Sandalford Verdehlo and read a book in the back garden. She was looking forward to a lovely evening with her friend, chilling and discussing life the way that they always did.

The loud whirr of helicopter blades startled Horatio as he stood in the kitchen making an early-morning cuppa. Curiosity sent him out into the garden to take a closer look. The coast guard often carried out reconnaissance trips along the Burrow Beach and over Howth Harbour – even at night he had often watched a pillar of white light shining down onto the water or speeding along the strand.

It was becoming a more familiar occurrence and only last week the Garda divers had found the body of a woman who had hurled herself off the cliff at Balscaden. Horatio felt a chill at a thought of the poor souls who felt so lonely and helpless that they thought the only option was to end it all. How must it feel to be in that state of depression and despair? He was fortunate to have never felt that way in his eighty-plus years. Even after his beloved wife died he always felt that there was something to live for – his children and now his grandchildren who were the greatest achievements of his life. Sure, he could have travelled more and perhaps been more ambitious in his career but he was happy and as he grew older he realised that a content life was more than most could ever hope for.

It was too mild for February. The birds were not in their nests yet but the crocuses and daffodils had all sprouted early. He had seen a cherry tree yesterday with blossoms bursting out. There was so much to love about this journey on earth, he concluded, and went back inside the house to drink his tea.

Julia had at last come in from the garden and was about to have a shower when her mobile phone rang. It was her mother.

"Julia – how are you?"

Julia thought she sounded grave and hoarse.

"Hi, Mum – great, thanks – I hadn't expected to hear from you – how is everything at home?"

Carol sobbed into the speaker. "Julia, something terrible has happened."

Julia's brain jumped into overdrive. "It's Granddad, isn't it? Oh my God, is he all right?"

"Yes, your grandfather is fine. But there has been a terrible tragedy and it's Craig."

Carol could hardly speak – the weight of what she had to say was choking her. "He didn't come home from work last night and then they found his car parked at the east pier this morning. His mobile phone was left on and sitting on the dash. They found his body a short while ago – he'd jumped off the cliff."

Julia was speechless. She couldn't take this information in. She wished that Michael was still here – that Ruth was home.

"Are they sure?"

"Yes, very sure. I have Odette here with me – she's sedated and Granddad is looking after her. Dylan has the kids – they don't know yet."

Julia couldn't digest everything that her mother was saying. She had to get home and quickly.

"I'll get a flight home today. Oh my God, poor Odette! I wonder what made him do such a thing – oh, good God, this is a nightmare."

"The body won't be released from post mortem for a few days so there will be plenty of time for the funeral – just take it easy down there."

"But what about the rest of you? I have to be there!" Julia sobbed.

"We are all able to manage, Julia – we'll see you when you arrive. There is nothing anybody can do for now."

"Can I speak to Odette?"

"She's not in a condition to speak with anyone – she's distraught. Apparently she had put off speaking to him about the tension that had built up and she sat at home all last night waiting for him to come home so that they could have the talk that they needed. I'll get her to ring you if and when she needs to. Take care of yourself, love."

Julia put the phone down and sobbed loudly into the palms of her hands – she didn't think that she was coherent enough to book a flight for herself at the moment. She called Ruth.

When Ruth heard what had happened she jumped onto a train and came home.

Julia was sitting in the same position as she had been since hearing the news from her mother. Her tearstained face was red and blotchy and all Ruth could do was rush over and hold her dear friend in her arms.

Ruth felt in her pocket and took out a tissue to wipe the tears and dribbles away from Julia's hair.

"You need a cup of tea and a lie-down, Julia. I'll book a flight after you drink it."

Julia nodded and went over to the couch and lay down. It was the most horrendous news to hear while so far away. If she had been at home could she have done anything? She hadn't been very close to her brother-in-law but she always took him as part and parcel of her family. He was the father of her beloved niece and nephew. How could he do this to them and to her sister? She cried out with anger at him for leaving his family this way.

Ruth handed her a mug of strong tea with sugar added. It tasted strange and uninviting but she drank it nevertheless.

"What happened exactly?" Ruth asked.

"I don't know any more than I told you. Mum just said that he didn't come home from work –" She sobbed before starting again. "And then they found his car at the pier in Howth and the coast guard picked up his body a while ago."

Ruth was shaking now. Suddenly Australia didn't feel like a couple of flights from home – it felt very far away. This was an example of just how far. She would get down to seeing what flights were available straight away because the only place Julia wanted to be right now was back in Dublin with her family.

The Malaysian Airways flight was leaving in four hours. Julia insisted that she wanted to go for it and she didn't care how much it cost. It was the quickest option. She would have two stops but a short transfer in Kuala Lumpur. Ruth was in shock herself and feeling very bad that she selfishly didn't want her friend to leave so soon. The drive to the airport was quiet and Ruth had a lump in her throat – holding back so many things that she wanted to say. How could she help her friend while she was in so much pain? She had never felt so helpless in her life.

At the airport Ruth made sure that Julia's luggage was checked in properly and waited with her until it was time to board.

Julia hugged Ruth tighter than she had ever held her before.

"I really wish you weren't living here – I wish I'd never told you about this job but, you know, it's probably the best thing I have ever done for anyone. If I hadn't meddled in matchmaking all those years ago my beautiful sister wouldn't be going through so much pain right now. I feel like it's all my fault."

Ruth had to calm her friend down to see sense.

"Julia – Odette and Craig would have probably met with or without you – they both drank in Gibneys and it was inevitable. You must not blame yourself in any way. Odette loved him."

"But she was miserably unhappy for the last couple of years and now it's clear he was too. It really is my fault."

236

Ruth looked her hard in the eyes.

"Julia – don't let me ever hear you say anything like that ever again – you always try to help people – if it doesn't work out it is not your fault." She paused. "Besides, Odette has her beautiful children and she did have good times with Craig. You have to get a perspective on this – we don't know the full story yet."

Julia nodded. That was true – it could have been an accident. But people didn't go out on their own and ditch their car the way that Craig had without a motive.

"Call me as soon as you get home," Ruth said. "I'd love to say I'll be back in a couple of weeks but that's not going to happen."

Julia shook her head. "I know that and I wouldn't expect you to either. You have been sweetness itself looking after me and Michael and I was having such a lovely time – apart from the disaster with Brian – nice guy but so not for me. You know, one thing I've learned from seeing Richie again – there is someone for everyone and maybe I should not create obstacles any longer. I might even consider a relationship with an Irishman!"

This made Ruth laugh and broke the tension.

Even Julia was smiling now. "Yes, can you imagine – Julia Perrin and an Irishman? It might happen yet!"

As she drove back alone along the Great Eastern Highway she felt as if she was going to burst into tears but that was not going to help her friend or herself. She had to be strong and focus on her life in Australia – no matter how hard the next few days would be.

Angela was torn as she heard her daughter crying down the phone, the pause between her replies emphasising the terrible distance between them. She was a strong woman in her own way – there had been pivotal times in her life where she had made her decisions and stuck to them. This was one of those times. She didn't need her husband's permission to travel to Australia – she had taken the trip before without him and she would do it again!

"I'm coming out to see you, Ruth. I'll be with you before this month is out if I can."

"Mum that's very kind of you but really there is no need – I'll be fine."

"I know what that place is like better than anyone and how lonely and isolated you must be feeling – I'm going to the travel agent's tomorrow."

"I'm not lonely or isolated – honestly, Mum, I'm having a good time – it's just that this sad news has shaken me a little."

"I know that, Ruth – that's why you need me to come and visit. Everything may have been fine but you will be feeling sad after that shock and that's why I need to be with you."

Ruth let her mother rant on because she really did want to see someone from home and soon.

Chapter Forty

Julia held Odette by the crook of her arm as they walked down the aisle behind her husband's coffin. Her sister was a composed widow and determined not to shed a tear. Julia wondered how she was strong enough to hold it all together but the frightened faces of little Jamie and Charlotte showed that Odette had more to think of than her own grief.

Horatio was taking it badly and for the first time ever needed a walking stick to help him make the short journey from the car to the church. The tragic death of someone with such small children had a terrible effect on the congregation and the fact that he had taken his own life brought dreadful bitterness and regret.

Dylan was at the forefront of the church ceremony. His speech was touching and wonderfully supportive. Without dwelling on the terrible end of his brother's life, he focused on his great achievements and the wonderful legacy that he had left behind in his children. There wasn't a dry eye left in the congregation afterwards.

Julia went to commend him on it as they got into the cars outside the church, but he didn't seem to take much notice of her – it was clear his concerns were focused largely on Odette and his aunts and uncles who were visibly disturbed by the whole scenario. Dylan was totally on his own now – no parents or siblings.

Julia regretted desperately how offhand and rude she had been to him over the years – her prejudice and pride had prevented her from giving him a chance. Odette had said that he was thinking of moving to London and Julia wished and hoped that he wouldn't go, because she didn't feel like superwoman at the moment and she knew that Odette would need all the support she could get.

The cortège drove to Fingal cemetery and Julia was reminded of the last time that she had been there. In a strange way she felt her father with her now, helping and supporting her spiritually in the way that he done since his own death.

And the big question that hung in the air and on everyone's lips was one that no one was willing to ask – why? Why would Craig do such a thing?

The funeral lunch was held at the yacht club and Dylan had organised every detail to perfection. He must have been in a terrible state of shock but Julia had to admire the way that he held everything together. His care and thoughtfulness towards Odette and her small children made Julia almost desire him. It wasn't the first time that she had felt this way. When she had been in Australia and heard that he took Gillian out for drinks with his family it had touched a chord with her that didn't make sense. But now, as he swept around the room seeing to every detail of the lunch and ordering drinks for everyone, she felt a shiver as she again thought of her father. That was who he was behaving like and the realisation made her think of Dylan even more fondly.

Julia looked over at her mother who was sipping a cup of tea in the corner of the room next to Horatio. Carol was very worried for her daughter and, for the first time since her husband's death, Julia could see traces of the old Carol return. She wasn't so self-assured nor had she turned on the computer since the terrible news.

It was an awful way to return to Dublin and Julia hadn't had a chance to review what was happening to her business. Remarkably, Gillian appeared to be handling everything well and her team were managing without her. But a time like this makes people reconsider their priorities and what really matters in life. While Julia was in Australia she had time to consider what mattered and now with Craig's death she really had to ask herself what life was all about – what did she want to leave as her legacy?

Julia stood up to go over to her mother but just then a stocky man who was about the same age as her mother walked through the door and made a beeline for Carol who stood up as she saw him. The man went over and hugged Carol tightly and she put her head on his shoulder and cried.

Julia had never seen him before but guessed that this was the man Horatio had spoken about while she was in Australia. Carol took the man's hand and led him out to the balcony. Julia was desperate to follow them but Horatio noticed what was going on and gave her a firm nod which told her to stay where she was.

Julia was torn and walked over to Odette but found her flanked by friends and neighbours. She felt so alone and decided to leave the room to compose her thoughts and take stock of the situation. Everything was changing around her and she wasn't sure where she fitted in with anyone in her life any more or if she indeed fitted anywhere.

Chapter Forty-one

Michael was frustrated in Singapore. Even a proposed party later couldn't distract him from the anguish he felt. He was concerned about his sister and his entire family. He was angry with Craig for doing what he had done. He couldn't see any other point of view. And he was angry at himself for being so far displaced from his family. He had been away for too long but it would be foolish just to walk out – he had earned shares in his company and he wanted to go home with a nest-egg. However, at times like this money wasn't very important. His family needed him and he needed them. It was the Catch 22 situation of the emigrant and his home.

He decided to call Julia – the funeral would be in motion now and he wanted to be connected in some way.

Julia was outside on the balcony of the yacht club. She had avoided her mother and her new friend but realised that it would only be a few moments before they would be introduced and she dreaded the thought of speaking to the man who had replaced her father. When her phone rang she felt relieved.

"Julia, it's me."

"Michael, it's so good to hear you. It's been the most awful day. I don't know how Odette has managed to keep it all together so well. Dylan has been wonderful."

"I told you he was alright, Ju. I wish I could be there."

"Don't worry – really you are better off there. Nothing can make this situation any easier."

"Well, I'm more determined than ever to come home now. Especially for the kids."

"It would be nice for Jamie to have you around – and Charlotte too – they are going to miss out so much not having a daddy." And then Julia's eyes welled up again like they had done so often during the day.

"Has anyone any idea why he did it?"

"We just don't know. He had been acting very strangely but Odette thought that it was work pressure and Dylan thought that he was having an affair. There really is no glaringly obvious reason – the police said that people can be depressed and those that live with them don't realise it until something like this happens. It turns out that he was doing a huge amount of extra work and there was a terrible atmosphere in his office. But there must be people living with that every day up and down the country."

"I don't suppose we'll ever know."

Julia sighed. "Well, we can't ask him now and that is going to be the difficulty for Odette. And in time we'll have to tell the children the truth too."

"It really is a mess. How's Mum?"

"Well, it looks like Granddad was right – a man has just arrived and swept her off – she never mentioned him to me. I guess I'll meet him in a few minutes."

"Go easy on him, Ju – you know how harsh you can be on some men!"

"Hey, that was the old Julia Perrin – so much has happened these last few weeks I don't know who or what I am any more!"

"Call me later if you need to – I can't sleep here at the moment – it's so damn hot and all the stuff going through my head is really getting to me!"

"Hurry home, Michael!"

Suddenly Lydia arrived on the balcony and walked in Julia's direction.

"I have to go here – bye." Julia hung up, aware she was

leaving Michael confused at the other end of the line. "Lydia, you are so good to come!"

They hugged warmly.

"I'm so sorry that I couldn't make the church. I couldn't get out of today's meeting but I wanted to see how you were."

"It hasn't been easy. It's all a bit of a haze at the moment. Come inside and have a drink. Tell me all about your happy life – I need to hear good news!"

Lydia followed her into the lounge and they took a seat by themselves.

"I've been looking at houses in Sandymount," Lydia said. "I think I told you that – oh, and how was Australia, I forgot to ask?"

"It was really lovely – cut short by six days of course – but Michael came down to us for the weekend and we had a really lovely time."

"And how does Ruth like it?"

"She's enjoying it – not too homesick so far."

Lydia took one of the cups of tea that were being passed around by the waiters.

"Before I forget, you must thank Peter for us," said Julia. "He was really wonderful about Craig. It helped hugely to know that someone we knew, even indirectly, was handling the case. He has been so comforting with Odette and made all the questioning so easy. He even brought out a lovely Ban Garda who was wonderful with the kids."

"He has his good points," Lydia smiled proudly. "Howth wouldn't normally be in his jurisdiction but there are so many suicides at the moment that there is a fear it is becoming endemic – the guards are trying to keep them all as quiet as possible and, knowing that you were a friend of mine, he jumped in to get involved immediately. It won't make the papers, he assured me before I came out. I know it's not much but I hope that that's some help."

"You've no idea how much that helps. I could never in my wildest nightmares have imagined how awful something like this is for a family."

Lydia recognised the start of tears in her friend's eyes and gave her a warm hug.

"Thanks, Lydia," Julia said as she pulled away. "And what about you – how are things?"

"Well, no rings yet if that's what you mean! And Peter doesn't seem that keen to go house-hunting with me. He says he loves where he is. Sometimes I think all men are the same!"

This was the first time Julia had heard a cool word said about Peter. She wondered if his halo had slipped for some reason. As far as the Perrin and Fagan family were concerned, however, Peter was some sort of superman.

"Are you still considering asking him to marry you on the 29th?"

"Well, when I emailed you it was a bit of a joke because I honestly thought that he had the ring bought and all – it was something his sister had said at Christmas – but now I'm beginning to think that I may well have to do it myself. Men change when you move in with them, don't they?"

"Well, I wouldn't know – I've never lived with anyone else except Ruth! And that was only for a summer!"

Lydia backtracked. "Don't get me wrong – he's really good to live with – and now that I'm in his apartment I thought that he would be territorial but he's not at all – I can do what I want with the place. But I'm the one selling my apartment and he isn't interested in finding a dream house like I am."

"Is his apartment nice?"

"It's lovely – you must come over some night – actually, we must do that next week. I'm sorry that I've been so caught up in my relationship with Peter – I've been a terrible friend."

"You have not! You're a wonderful friend and I can always rely on you at any time!"

Lydia smiled. Then she noticed something unusual over Julia's shoulder. "Who is that with your mother?"

Gerry had walked into the lounge holding Carol by the arm. Now he was shaking hands with Horatio and sitting down beside him.

"Oh, that's her new fella that she hasn't told me about – I can't believe that he has showed up!"

"Where did she meet him?"

"Playing bridge online."

Lydia laughed out loud.

"I know, it's hilarious, isn't it?" said Julia. "Even my mother can meet a man – I'm beginning to think that there's something wrong with me."

"Julia, you were never looking for one – all the men around are looking at you and you could have your pick of any of them – don't you realise that?"

Julia was amazed by Lydia's remark. What was she saying? That to the rest of the world she was some sort of Ice Queen? That made her feel bad.

"So what do you think of my mum having a new man?"

Lydia shrugged. "It's great – everyone has a right to happiness. I can see that it must be hard for you when you miss your dad so much – but you have to ask yourself: would your dad have minded?"

Julia shook her head.

"So, if he wouldn't mind, then why should you?"

That was very true. Her father hadn't a jealous bone in his body – it was his 'live and let live' nature that she had admired but she hadn't followed his lead. Instead she had tried to control everything and everyone around her. But there was time to change and maybe she shouldn't be so offensive with her opinions. Her mother was upset and it was sad that she couldn't confide in her daughter that she had met someone. She suddenly vowed she would make this man welcome – because if he made her mother happy then that was all that mattered.

"Thanks for coming, Lydia – you have helped more than you will ever know! And please thank Peter again – from all of us."

Lydia smiled at her friend as they got up to go over and meet Gerry.

Carol was on her own in the kitchen when Julia came down to get a glass of water.

"Thanks so much for today, Julia – you've been so nice to Gerry. I didn't know how you would react."

"Oh, Mum!" Julia could have cried. "Have I been that awful to live with?"

"Well, you do have your opinion on things and I know how you felt about your father. I didn't want to upset you."

Julia felt terrible. "I'm so sorry if I am a pain at times. My whole world – our whole world has been shook up. This thing that has happened to Odette is awful – I really can't make any sense of it."

Carol nodded. "Peter tried to explain to me after he had spoken with Odette the other day – it is a fine line between sanity and insanity. People are in a state of despair all over the country with debt and worries . . . but taking your life is so final – so unjust."

Julia sat down at the table beside her mother and put her hand on top of hers.

"We'll get through this, all of us," she assured her. "Gerry is a lovely man and I'm glad that you have someone nice like him to help you at this time."

"I told him not to come down for the funeral but he wouldn't stay away and I have to say, when I saw him coming in through the bar in the yacht club, my heart lifted with relief. I may look like I am busy in my own world since your father died but, you see, when he was alive he was my entire world. I loved him so much but maybe too much if it is possible to do such a thing. Playing bridge and driving and all the other things that I do since he passed away are the new me – they are all things I need to do in order to cope. I realise now that nobody should love anyone too much. Odette will be fine – she can't see it now, I know, but there will come a time when she will realise that this is how it is meant to be."

Julia had never known her mother to be so philosophical or profound. She was so proud of her that she just wrapped her arms spontaneously around her neck and cried. The two women stayed in an embrace for what must have been only a couple of minutes but felt like an hour. The comfort and love they were receiving from each other brought a peace between them that hadn't existed since before Julia's father died and, for the first time since hearing the news of Craig's untimely death, she felt as if something good had come out of it all.

Chapter Forty-two

It was seven days since Julia had left and Ruth was feeling very lonely. She was not long in the door from work and the street was quiet outside. She couldn't bring herself to watch the American programmes on TV so she picked up a book and turned on her iPod in the dock. Pink Floyd's 'Wish You Were Here' came on and she wanted to cry. Who did she want to be here? Ian? She would love his familiar loving arms around her now but his silence over the last few weeks made her realise what a small part of his life she must have been. And she didn't miss the guilt. So being apart from him brought relief and this was the first time she realised it.

Then there was Steve. Did she miss Steve's attentions? Probably not. She missed his company, though, and she didn't blame him for stopping all form of contact outside of work hours since her little performance the week before.

Julia? Definitely she would love to sit and have a laugh and share a bottle of wine with her best friend. And, yes, she would even like to be by her side as she consoled Odette.

She opened the pages of her novel and tried to concentrate on the words but it was difficult. Suddenly she heard a ring at the door. Nobody really called to the door in Australia – it wasn't like Sutton or Clontarf where there was often a plethora of school kids looking for sponsorship for this or that – or window cleaners asking if you needed their services. People generally didn't arrive unannounced – well, not to a single girl in Subiaco anyway. She got up and went into the hall.

The silhouette of a man stood at the other side of the door. He was tall and at first she thought it might be Steve. As she got closer the outline became more familiar and she was surprised when she opened the door to see that it was Brian.

"How are you going, Ruth – I hope I haven't called at a bad time?"

He stood tall and handsome. He had changed out of his work clothes and looked like he had recently washed his hair.

Ruth was speechless at first. She directed him to come in before she spoke, presuming that he had come to see Julia.

"Hi, Brian – gosh, Julia left for Dublin a week ago."

"Oh, I thought that she was going home yesterday?"

Ruth wondered why he had purposely called, knowing that Julia had left. "She had to go home early."

"Is everything okay with Julia?"

Ruth shook her head solemnly. "She had some bad news unfortunately – her brother-in-law died tragically a few days ago."

"I'm sorry to hear that." Brian was genuinely concerned.

"Would you like a drink? A beer?"

"I'm driving but I'll have a Coke if you have some?"

"Come on into the kitchen – to be honest, I'm happy to have some company – I've been feeling very sorry for myself since Julia went home."

"I'll bet. She was telling me what good mates you are."

Ruth put ice in his glass and poured Coke on top. She then poured a glass for herself.

"So what happened to the brother-in-law?"

Ruth felt strange talking about something so delicate to Brian but she was pleased to be able to process it with someone. "He took his own life. Tragically."

"Gruesome."

"He jumped off a cliff. It must be the most horrible way to die. Sometimes the coast guards have problems finding the bodies but Craig's washed up with the tide at a beach nearby. I can't imagine what must have brought him to do such a thing. He had a beautiful home – his wife Odette is even more gorgeous than Julia and his kids are little pets."

Brian took a sip from his Coke. He was slouched at the kitchen table and seemed to be pondering each word that Ruth was saying.

"I had a mate that killed himself. Hung himself in the garage of his home. No reason that anyone could figure out – a beautiful wife, home and little baby boy. I don't think anyone can really know what's going on inside the head of someone that does that."

Ruth felt her eyes well up.

"What do you say we cheer you up?" he said.

"Huh?"

"I don't know if you have any plans but maybe you'd like to come for a walk with me along Cottesloe? I know it's getting late but we should squeeze a couple of hours out of the sunset."

Ruth had never been so delighted at a suggestion in her life.

"I'm in a bit of a mess!" she said, looking down at her shorts and T-shirt. "Let me put on something else – I'll only be a minute."

Brian sat waiting while she frantically tore through the heaps of unsuitable clothes that had gathered on her bedroom floor. She pulled out the drawer and chucked top after top on to the bed. Finally she settled on a black top with beads around the cleavage and a pair of white three-quarter-length pants – she was relieved that she had showered when she got in from work. She ran a brush through her hair and touched up her eyeliner and mascara. She looked at herself in the mirror – the sunkissed freckles were joining up around her nose and she looked healthier than she had in months. Something was going right then and although Brian had never said why he had called she was truly delighted that he had.

Brian stood up as she entered the kitchen.

"You look good," he said with a wide grin.

"Thanks." Ruth grabbed her phone and keys and slipped them into a tiny bag. "Okay – ready.

Brian parked up under some massive pine trees where hundreds of crows dived and soared from tree to tree. They stepped out of his jeep and walked in the direction of the seafront. The rooftop of the famous Indiana Tearooms peeped up behind a creeper-covered pergola – two beautifully carved baby elephants sat at the inviting entrance.

"Have you been to Cott Beach before?" Brian asked.

Ruth laughed, amused by the Aussie's imperative shortening of words. "I drove by but I haven't actually had a chance to inspect the Tearooms – I'm really curious after reading about Heath Ledger's memorial service. That was held there, wasn't it?"

"Yeah, that was tragic. It really put Cott on the map though. The beach is nice for a walk and the doctor is here tonight."

Ruth stopped walking for an instant and turned her head inquisitively. "What doctor?"

Brian laughed. "The Freo Doctor – the Fremantle Doctor. That's what we call the southerly wind that comes in on warm summer evenings. When I was a kid we didn't have air-con and my mum would open all the windows and doors in the house and the Freo Doctor would work his magic and cool us down."

"Oh, that's so cute! Does everyone call the wind 'The Doctor'?"

"Sure – there's even a beer named after him – they serve it in the Tearooms!"

He nodded over at the Edwardian-style building that was in their clear view now. It was quintessentially English in design and wouldn't have looked out of place in Brighton or Eastbourne. It was made of a warm ochre stone with long windows and tall arched walkways down at the beach level. Ruth wondered what wonderful tales the walls could tell of the millions of holidaymakers who had passed through it since the start of the twentieth century.

They walked in synch along the green promenade until they came to steps that brought them down on to the beach.

"Look out there – kite-surfers!" Brian pointed.

"They are making good use of the Freo Doctor. And there are so many ships on the horizon – what are they? Tankers?"

"Yeah, all going to Freo."

"Actually, when Julia and Michael were here we bumped into a friend of hers from Dublin that she hadn't seen for twenty years and he has a shipping company. He lives here now in Peppermint Grove."

"He has plenty of money then!"

"How expensive are the houses there?"

"They average out about three million dollars but can go up to anything – I saw one advertised for twenty-seven million a few days ago but that is mental money. I can't complain because it's all good for me and my business. You must have noticed all the rebuilds in Peppy Grove and in the nice parts of the city."

"Yes, and it reminds me of what Ireland was like in the boom – I hope that it doesn't go the same way here."

"Nah, we've got the mines – and China and India will keep us busy supplying them for the next ten years at least."

They were walking on the sand now and Ruth decided to take off her shoes and feel the sand between her toes. The waves were beating heavily against the shore and the swimmers were battling with the tide. There was so much activity with young families having picnics and after-work people taking exercise that Ruth appreciated the good healthy lifestyle that she had on offer in her new home.

"This beach is lovely," she said.

"You should come here in March when they have the Sculpture by the Sea exhibition," Brian said, pointing along the strand.

"What's that?"

"It's an exhibition of pieces of art and you can touch it and climb around it – it's great."

"You must like art, having studied architecture?"

"Sure – I wanted to go to art college but my mother wanted

me to get a real job!" He laughed as he spoke. "I'm not really a hard-hat type of guy – I like to look at the stars and wonder what the hell it's all about."

Ruth was melting with each word he spoke. He really was the perfect guy. It was too good to be true that he was single too and obviously available or he wouldn't be here with her. She felt thrilled inside.

"Yes, I wonder what life is all about," she said. "Where do we go when we die? Is there a heaven? Is there a God?"

"I'm not sure if there is one but there is definitely some spiritual presence that lives on after we die. I've always been fascinated by ghosts."

Ruth laughed. "Me too – I'm not really sure what it is but I do get strange feelings about places – like when we were in Rotto."

Brian's face lit up. "Rotto is crawling with ghosts and spirits. Did you know that the antipodal point to Rotto on the Earth's surface is the Bermuda Triangle? I'm sure there's something to that. You can draw a triangle out into the Indian Ocean from Rotto and that whole area is full of shipwrecks, just like at Bermuda."

Ruth wasn't sure what antipodal meant but figured it was the completely opposite point on the other side of the Earth.

"What other antipodal points are there that are interesting?"

"Well, Easter Island is antipodal to the Indus valley and they both have a strange type of hieroglyphics that are only found in those two places. And wait for it, the writing is all related to the constellations of the night sky – isn't that crazy?"

Ruth was seeing a different Brian to the one she had seen before. He was so animated when talking about the stars and how crazy coincidences around the world fascinated him.

"It's all probably just a coincidence!" she said.

"But don't you think it's maybe more than a coincidence that you came to the exact house on Peppermint Grove where I was working and then you were on the same island as I was a couple of days later?"

Ruth could see where this was going and his passion and

belief in what he was saying was striking a chord inside her. She'd had strange feelings of her own on Rotto and since arriving in Australia. She'd had thoughts that she would never have considered before. How closed her life had been while she was in Ireland hankering after a married man who had kept her in a state of stagnation! Watching Brian explain about stars and ancient writings gave her a fresh outlook. He was even more handsome as he smiled and the sun started to slowly turn an orangey red and slip further down the sky.

"I don't suppose you're hungry?" Brian said suddenly.

"Well, I am a bit actually."

"Come on," he said, taking her hand. "I'm taking you for dinner."

They ran up the steps beside the Indian Tearooms and through the welcoming pergola and porch.

Brian bounded up to the maitre d' who was looking though her list.

"Hi there, I was wondering if you have a table for two?"

She smiled courteously. "I'm sorry, sir, we're fully booked tonight." Suddenly her phone rang. "Excuse me," she said, lifting it up. "I see . . . well, thank you for letting us know." She wrote something into her book and looked up at Brian. "Well, you came at the right time – I've just had a cancellation."

Brian grinned at Ruth. "Coincidence?"

"Come this way, please," The maitre d' led them over to the best table in the restaurant. They had an uninterrupted view of the Indian Ocean and the last of the beachgoers who were packing up for the night.

"It's absolutely gorgeous," Ruth sighed.

It was easily the most picturesque place she had been. The interior décor tastefully echoed the nautical theme with whitewashed cladding around the walls and blue-glass tea-lights on the tables. The furniture was a rich mahogany and the floors a lovely stained jarrah wood. In the corner was a seating area with dark leather couches and a glass table resting on the trunk of a tree. Books lined the shelves behind this space and wonderful maritime knick-knacks dotted the walls. But it was the long windows that looked out onto the Indian Ocean that captured Ruth's gaze.

She felt giddy and excited as the maitre d' handed her the menu.

"So what will you have?" Brian asked.

The menu was bistro style with a selection of pizzas and seafood thrown in for good measure.

"I don't mind – what do you recommend?"

"Oysters?" he suggested with an eyebrow raised.

"Yum – yes, I would like that and maybe a pizza?"

"Don't forget to try the 'Doctor'! The beer I told you about!"

And Ruth smiled – he had already arrived. Brian was her doctor.

Ruth wiped her lips with her white linen napkin.

"That was delicious and I have to say that 'The Doctor' did the trick!" she said.

"Nice beer then?"

She nodded. "It's been a lovely evening. You called at the perfect time – I was feeling very sorry for myself."

Brian beamed. "I'm glad that I called around too." He looked at his watch. "I guess we'd better go – we both have work early tomorrow."

Ruth nodded. She didn't want to go even though they had been among the first to arrive and they were definitely among the last to leave.

Brian paid the bill and they stepped out into the balmy night air. The sky was filled with millions of brightly shining stars.

"There are your stars now!" Ruth said.

"Yep, and I like Orion best!"

"Which one is that?"

Brian pointed up to a diagonal line of three stars and explained they were Orion's belt – he then showed where his hands, feet and head were. They were in no hurry to get back into the car as neither wanted to ruin the mood but it was time to end the evening.

As he pulled up outside her house she longed for him to come in and even spend the night but it would be too soon and she remembered how badly she had behaved all the times that she had met him before.

"Maybe we can do this again sometime?" he said. "Or something different?"

"Sure, I'd like that very much. You know, I've never had a picnic in King's Park and it's only around the corner."

"Hey, that's a good idea – how about Friday? Actually, Thursday would be even better – it's sooner!"

Ruth nodded her head. "Yes, I'd like that – what time?"

"Will I drop by shortly after five?"

"Okay and, hey, I'll do the food because you paid for dinner tonight!"

He bid her goodnight with a friendly kiss on the cheek. She didn't know whether to be flattered by his restraint or offended but she got out of his jeep and waved as he drove down the road.

Her step was light as she went into the house. There was something so genuine and lovely about the way he treated her that she felt she had met someone very special. Maybe there was something to the way the world worked and all the coincidences were pointing to this moment.

She was in her house five minutes when her phone rang and it was Ian.

"Hey, kitten – are you missing me as much as I'm missing you?" Ian purred down the phone.

Ruth felt sick. Her heart thumped heavily in her chest. She had loved this man for ten long years and, after no word at all for weeks, here he was calling her out of the blue.

"What are you calling for?"

"That's no way to talk to Iansie! Hey, baby, I've organised time off! I'm coming over on Friday!"

Ruth was filled with fear and dread at his words. "Coming where?"

"To Perth! And I can stay a whole week!"

This was unprecedented behaviour for Ian – did he finally realise what a devoted girlfriend she had been for all these years?

But she'd had it with married men. She wasn't going to share anyone ever again. If she wasn't sure before, the lovely evening that she had just spent with Brian, talking from her heart and looking at the stars, had fixed her.

"Well, I'm sorry, Ian, but you will have to change your plans – I don't want to see you and anyway I've met someone else."

Ian chuckled. "Hey, kitten, I don't want to share you but if I have to I will – I mean, I really need to see you and have –"

"Ian, don't call me again," Ruth cut him off, "or I'll have to change my number. I am through with you – now have a nice life!" And with that she switched off her phone. She felt liberated. From now on she was only going to have relationships that were honest and where there was no third party involved.

Chapter Forty-three

Michael read the email and then re-read it.

The job was too perfect. It was a permanent position in the Irish Financial Services Centre at a time when most companies in the complex were letting people go. But they would like to meet him to discuss what sort of package they could put in place.

How was he going to tell his boss that he needed more time off? He decided to ring Julia and see what her thoughts were.

Luckily she was online.

"Hey, Julia, how are things there?"

Julia watched her brother's face appear on the screen and smiled. It was always wonderful to see him and especially at the moment when her family was in such a state of disarray.

"Michael, it's been the most awful week – right up there with Dad's funeral but this was even worse."

"I spoke with Odette last night. She sounds numb."

"She's still on sedatives. It's too difficult to cope with. I think that she has been remarkable."

"I should have come home . . ."

"No, we told you not to, and although we'd have loved to see you things were so dreadful it really wouldn't have made much difference."

"Well, there's a job opportunity in the IFSC and I've a good chance of getting it – I'm not sure of the full package but they want to meet me – should I come back and take my chances?"

"How badly do you want to come home? This has been going on for months. If they offer you crap money would you take it just to be here?"

Michael stopped to think for a minute. His life was passing him by and he knew where he wanted to be.

"I definitely would come home for less money – I couldn't give a damn about the shares any more."

"There's your answer then."

"And I know you are going to snap at me but have you had any word from Lydia?"

"She was at the funeral – actually her boyfriend Peter handled the investigation and was wonderful with Odette and the kids. He couldn't have been more sensitive."

"That's good!" Michael huffed at the computer.

"Honestly – he's really nice."

"So is she engaged yet?"

"Remarkably not but don't hold out."

"What do you mean?"

"Well, she seems all set to propose on the 29th of February."

"I really thought you were joking when you said she was doing that."

"Well, apparently not – and that's only next Wednesday so you'll be put out of your misery by then!"

"The best man won, I guess. But I may find my Miss Right when I return – unless you've got anyone in mind for me – what's this Gillian like that's working for you?"

Julia shook her head. "She's a good worker but I don't fancy having her for a sister-in-law." She was glad she had been able to give Gillian her newfound confidence but she certainly didn't want her as part of the family. "There are half a million women in Dublin. I'm sure we can find you *one*."

"I'll be depending on you, Julia! So – will I chuck it all in here and come home?"

Julia would normally have her sensible head on, thinking through all of the options and considering what would be best, but since Craig died she knew what she wanted – she needed those that she loved around her.

"Yes, Michael – come home."

Julia called around to Odette after work. Home was the only place that Odette wanted to be and the children needed some sort of routine in their day. She was keen to tell her Michael's news – Odette needed to hear positive things now.

Julia didn't want to see her sister upset about anything after all that she had been through. She was very concerned about how she was going to cope on her own over the coming weeks and months. But Odette wasn't on her own. When Julia pulled up outside her house there was a car already in the drive. Dylan's Mercedes neatly fitted into the spot where Craig's always used to be. Odette had asked that her husband's car be sold or taken away at the very least – she couldn't stand to look at it.

Julia hesitated for a moment – wondering if she should go in or not. The last thing that she wanted to do was to crowd her sister. Odette had turned down her offer to stay after the first couple of nights. It had only been a week and Julia didn't like the idea of Odette staying on her own at night with the children.

Dylan answered the door and greeted Julia kindly but courteously. Too courteously. She wanted to tell him how much she appreciated his care and concern for her sister but there was never a correct moment or place for her to do so. It certainly was not appropriate in front of Odette who appeared as she entered the hall.

"Hi, Ju," Odette said, walking like a zombie and falling into her sister's arms.

"I've got my bag in the boot and I've come for a sleepover if you want me to stay?" Julia said.

Odette didn't comment. She went into the kitchen and put on the kettle. So many people had called since Craig's death that she did it as automatically as breathing.

"Where are the kids?" Julia asked.

"In bed," Dylan answered. "They've asked to go to school and see their friends."

"And will you let them?" she asked Odette.

Odette shrugged.

"I've told her that I can get them ready and take them in the morning," Dylan answered once again.

Julia could see that her sister's brother-in-law was by all appearances taking on the role of chief caretaker and, as he had no employment to go to, it did seem to make sense. Julia wanted to do more – but it didn't really matter who did what because everything was a haze for poor Odette and Julia would do whatever to keep things on an even keel – if at all possible.

Dylan attended to the tea-making and they sat and drank it at the kitchen table.

It was more than awkward. Julia didn't want to upset Odette by talking about the painful facts but neither could she ignore the realities of the situation. She tried to ask about how the kids were taking it but tears welled up in Odette's eyes and Dylan shook his head slightly at Julia, telling her not to go there.

"I'm going up to check on the children," Odette said eventually, standing and putting her mug in the sink. "I think I'll lie down myself then and see if I can sleep for a while. Thanks for everything."

As Odette left the kitchen and retreated up the stairs, Julia started to follow but her sister turned and stood with her hand on the banisters.

Julia halted.

"There's no need to stay – honestly, Julia," said Odette. "Dylan said that he would, as that way it would be easier to get the kids out to school in the morning."

Julia was astounded but Odette seemed to think that what she had said was normal.

"Okay," said Julia and retreated back to the kitchen where she sat down again, finding it hard to conceal her feelings from Dylan.

"I was talking to that policeman Peter earlier," he said. "Apparently there will be no need to ask Odette any further questions so that's a relief."

"Yes, I'd heard. Have you been here all day?"

He nodded.

"You must be exhausted."

Dylan shook his head. "I'm fine – you know, sometimes you wonder about the timing of things and I wondered why I was made redundant at the time but I can see now why and it's good to be available for Odette."

He was so calm and composed that she wanted to find solace in his company but she remained uncomfortable – possibly because she had been so wrong about him all along. She lifted her handbag as a signal that she was leaving and stood up.

He saw her to the door and she left for home with troubled thoughts flying through her head. What would the neighbours say about Odette's brother-in-law staying at the house? But then again what did it matter what the neighbours thought? Craig's death was a big enough scandal to keep those that were not friends quiet for a while and those that were friends would understand.

And then there was her own mother who had hooked up with a widower and was making a new life of her own.

She parked in the drive of her own lovely home and went into the kitchen where Horatio sat reading a newspaper.

"Hi, Granddad."

"Ah, love, were you with Odette?"

"Yes, but Dylan's staying with her tonight – it looks like the kids might go to school tomorrow."

"He's a good lad, that Dylan fellow – I have to say I did think he was a bit flash when I met him first but he is one nice guy and so good to Odette and those kids. It looks like Odette married the wrong brother."

Julia was astonished at her grandfather's appraisal of Dylan. He would never usually comment on someone in this way. It grieved her that she was so wrong about Dylan all along. It upset her even more the way that she had treated him over the years. There was no longer any doubt in her mind: she was stuck up and difficult to please. Maybe she was no longer attractive to men – after all, she had tried to seduce Brian but he was left cold by her advances.

"Julia, you're in a world of your own there – tell me."

Julia sat down beside her grandfather. "I don't know what's wrong with me. I never seem to meet someone. I never really wanted a committed relationship to be honest but now that I see how devastated Odette is it makes me wonder if we all need to have a mate?"

"I loved being married to your grandmother. Don't get me wrong – it wasn't all wine and roses – there were times when she would drive me to drink. Literally! I would go down to the Fairview Inn and stay there for hours until I was sure that she was gone to bed. But that is what being married is all about – tolerance and security. I always knew that she would be there for me and she always was."

Julia nodded. She remembered her grandmother vividly and she was the sort of woman who fussed around the house all day but always made sure that everything was just right and that you always had a cup of tea in your hand or a ham sandwich.

"I loved her carrot cake," Julia sighed.

"Ah yes, that recipe went with her to the grave – what a cook! And her tea-brack was even better."

They giggled, fondly remembering the past.

"But the greatest gift she ever gave me was your mother," Horatio continued. "There is nothing better than to have your own flesh and blood around you. I can see that you are the same, Julia, and you would be a great little mother."

"Me!" Julia was very surprised by her grandfather's commendation.

"Yes, you – you're always fussing around trying to help others – you are just like your grandmother. That's why you should find yourself a good man and do what is the most natural thing in the world."

"But what about all that you said before to Ruth and me about travel and all that?"

"Arragh, Ruth needed to move to get away from that Ian fella."

Julia was stunned. "You know about Ian?"

"Of course I do – your father never soundproofed the back

room when he was building it and I heard you pair rabbit on about that terrible fella on so many occasions that I don't know how I ever managed to keep my mouth shut about it!"

Julia laughed. Her grandfather was a scream but he was also a wise old man.

"Okay – I take on board all that you say."

"Mind that you do now, Julia. And give that Dylan lad a chance."

Julia didn't know if she could take any more bombshells from her grandfather.

"What?"

Horatio stood up. "You know it – the way he looks at you – he couldn't take his eyes off you at dinner this Christmas. I've said enough for one night." He leaned forward and kissed his granddaughter on the forehead. "Nighty-night, love."

Julia was left sitting speechless on the kitchen chair – he had certainly given her plenty to think about tonight.

Chapter Forty-four

Brian called on time to Ruth's delight. She had been counting the minutes all day until she would see him again.

A misty haze had settled over the city, taking a few degrees off the temperature. They loaded up the car with a picnic basket containing the goodies that Ruth had purchased in Coles supermarket – plus a few nice fresh salads she had made herself and some Anzac biscuits that were too good to pass. They also had an Esky, containing among other things a bottle of sparkling wine.

They had only to drive a couple of blocks before they were at the entrance to King's Park.

The view was peeking through the high trees as they parked in one of the bays beside Fraser's restaurant. Brian took the picnic basket and the Esky from the back of the Jeep and handed Ruth a tartan rug to carry. Then he led her along a pathway with the vast skyscrapers of the CBD to their left.

The view of the beautiful Swan River, broad at that point, was becoming clearer and she quickened her step – eager to see more of the water.

The landscape was a perfectly manicured blanket of neat grass. Around the circumference giant trees and palms lined the borders. Sailing ships dotted the river and the ferry from South Perth chugged its way into Barrack Street Dock.

Children ran barefoot in front of them, giggling.

They walked on and perched high in a corner of the park was a towering monument overlooking the river and the city beyond.

"What's that?" she asked.

"That's the State War Memorial – in a crypt underneath is a roll of honour listing the names of all Australians lost in wars abroad, beginning with the Boer War. We call the memorial 'The Anzac' because we visit it on Anzac Day, our national day of remembrance."

"Where does the name 'Anzac' come from exactly?"

"The initials for the Australian and New Zealand Army Corps who fought at Gallipoli in the First World War."

They had reached a semi-circular granite wall with a stone bench running along its inner side. A different place name was etched into the wall every couple of metres, each commemorating a battle from wars around the world where Australians had fought.

"This is the Court of Contemplation," Brian said and pointed to the burning flame in its middle. "And that is the Eternal Flame burning so that we never forget. But I prefer to call it the Whispering Wall!"

Brian rested the picnic basket on the ground, took her hand and put her sitting at one end of the semi-circle under the name Gallipoli. He then walked to the other end about twenty metres away and sat down.

He put his lips to the smooth surface of the stone wall – still warm from the heat of the sun and whispered. It was as if he was sitting beside her and speaking directly into her ear. At first she thought it was some kind of trick but then he said it again and this time it was louder and clearer.

"You are beautiful."

It sounded better the second time but she giggled. Then she winced, wondering if anyone else could hear, but the joggers running by didn't flinch or grin.

"I'm not being funny!" he whispered. "It's true."

"Thank you," she said quietly.

To which he replied, "You're welcome."

She had never come across such a phenomenon.

Brian stood up and walked back to her. She felt the moment was almost upon them when he beckoned to her playfully to join him at what looked like a gazebo. It was another viewing point and this time the landscape below moved like a magic picture. She could clearly see all the boats on the river and cars on the freeway in detail now.

"How about here for our picnic?" he asked.

It was a beautiful spot and the sky was now tinged with pink wispy clouds that floated across the bay like torn candyfloss.

Brian shook out the tartan blanket and placed it on the grass outside the gazebo.

Ruth set about cutting the chicken and putting the salads onto the plastic plates.

"Will I open this?" he asked, lifting the bottle of bubbles from the Esky.

"Yes, please," Ruth nodded.

It wasn't that the food was extra-delicious but eating *alfresco* in this way made it taste sweeter.

The setting sun was shining on Brian. His tanned skin and sparkling blue eyes were so attractive to Ruth that she found it difficult to concentrate on what he was saying.

"I have to tell you something that you probably know already," he suddenly said. "Just to come clean."

Ruth's heart pounded. What bombshell was he about to drop?

"I did fool around with Julia that night when we went back to your house after the Lucky Shag and . . ." he half-smiled, "let's just say it wasn't a lucky shag – more of a complete disaster!"

Ruth giggled. She admired him for telling her. She didn't want to paint a dreadful picture of Julia either by telling that she already knew, so she just smiled. "That's okay. For a moment there I thought you were going to say that you were married and I was about to get up and go!"

Brian laughed anxiously.

Ruth was taken aback by his reaction. "Don't laugh – you

aren't married – are you? Because I've been there in the past and now I wouldn't contemplate a relationship with a married man – period!"

Brian paused. "Of course I'm not . . . Do you believe in love at first sight?"

"Eh – I think first impressions matter but sometimes it takes a while to get the timing right."

Brian nodded. "Timing is important. I'm glad Julia is gone back to Ireland too. You see, I fancied you from the first time I saw you in Peppy Grove."

Ruth was startled. She'd had no idea.

He continued. "When I saw Julia on Rotto I was keen to see if you were there too but then good old Marty butted in – like he does!"

"I'm flattered. It doesn't matter what happened before – Julia won't mind either."

"Good!" Brian said. "Because I'd really like to spend more time with you, Ruth, and get to know you better. I feel you see things the same way as I do."

Ruth was blushing. Brian took her plate and placed it down beside the rug. Then he took Ruth's chin gently in his hand. Neither spoke – they just stared into each other's eyes. The setting was perfect for the prelude to their first kiss.

When their lips touched, gently at first, neither wanted to close their eyes but it happened naturally and they sank onto the rug in a close embrace.

Ruth felt her arm crunch the Anzac biscuits into crumbs but couldn't care less – she never wanted the kiss to end.

The birds sang in the trees and the balmy warmth of summer enveloped them. Ruth pulled back first and for several moments they stared into each other's eyes. The silence between them was heavy with desire and passion and they kissed some more before they returned to eating – but this time fed each other grapes and other titbits.

The sun was gone from the sky before they packed up and strolled back to his car. They almost walked over a couple who were entwined in rapture next to an empty pizza box and four empty bottles of beer. Ruth turned to Brian and smiled. It was good to see others feeling the love on this special night.

The first stars of evening were shining in the sky. Brian took the picnic basket and Esky out of the boot and didn't wait to be asked inside. It was a given that he was going to spend the night there. Flushed with anticipation and desire for each other they went into the kitchen and Ruth took a bottle of sparkling wine out of the fridge.

"Shall I open?"

"Looks good."

She fumbled with the wire and foil at the top of the bottle and he came over and helped her. The cork went pop and flew out, hitting the ceiling.

"Oh, I hope we haven't marked it!" she giggled.

"No worries, I've a team of painters that can fix that!"

They clinked their glasses together and went out into the back garden where a couple of crickets and small birds croaked and tweeted.

It occurred to Ruth that Brian had never mentioned who he lived with. She didn't want to pry but if she was going to get into a relationship with him she would like to know more.

"Do you live on your own?"

He paused and she saw a hesitation in his eyes.

"Nah – I'm sharing! But not for long. I'm looking for somewhere else."

"So you rent?"

"Eh – no, I'm looking for somewhere new to buy – houses prices keep jumping – that's what's taking me so long to find a new place."

But Ruth didn't want to talk about house prices and neither did Brian. He put his glass down on the table and walked over to her. He kissed her more forcefully now and put his hands under her soft strawberry hair until he cupped her head perfectly.

She was out of control. Melting inside and longing to feel his tongue in her mouth again. This was how she wanted to be kissed. It was passion so different to what she had felt with Ian. He picked her up in his strong arms and carried her through the kitchen and into the hallway.

"First on the right," she said.

Inside, he gently placed her down onto the bed and started kissing her again.

Ruth arched her back – she was in agony and ecstasy, longing for more. Brian didn't disappoint. He lifted her top, revealing the lacy lingerie that she had specially picked out for the evening, hoping that this would be the night. He peeled the straps down from her shoulders and kissed her breasts. She was aching for him now and urgently kicked off her jeans as he undid his shirt.

He slipped out of his trousers and fell onto the bed beside her where they kissed with such desire that Ruth thought she would pass out. His breathing was becoming heavier as she reached inside his underwear – longing for what was coming next.

She groaned in ecstasy as he entered her. He was a slow and passionate lover – moving in a rhythm that suited her needs perfectly. She wanted to come several times but didn't want the moment to end. They released together amid a torrent of pleasurable sighs.

Ruth was speechless. Brian continued kissing and hugging her gently, stroking the side of her cheek and telling her how beautiful she was. She had never felt so loved – ever!

Ruth was walking on air the next morning and couldn't conceal the grin on her face as she entered the office. Kai and Helenka stood at the water cooler trying to draw information from her about what had her in a buoyant mood. But she was keen to keep her private life separate from work and instead told them that her mother was coming to visit and that was why she was in such good form. But she knew that they didn't believe her!

Later at lunchtime she slipped out to meet Brian who had come into the CBD to enjoy a sandwich with her at the Dome Café.

She told him that her mother was coming over to visit in a couple of weeks and was startled by his response.

"Oh, that's great – I'd love to meet your mum – is she as beautiful as her daughter?"

Ruth blushed and rolled her eyes.

"Hey, why don't you ask her about the house in Peppermint Grove then? We haven't got any more leads or info and I'm sure there's a story."

"Wouldn't it be funny if there was no big story and it was just some sort of courtesy or business letter about the rent?" Ruth said.

"Well, I think it was fate that we met and we have Number 5 to thank for that."

Ruth smiled and let him hold her hand gently. They were getting closer as each day passed and she was loving every moment that they spent together.

"Fancy coming for a sleepover in Subiaco tonight?"

"Yes, please – and I have a treat planned for tomorrow night if you're free."

"Oh, what is it?"

"Just going to bring you somewhere nice so you can dress up and let me spoil you."

Ruth beamed. She had been so used to going only to places where Ian wouldn't be spotted by his wife or her friends and now she was with a man who clearly wanted to show her off and, to top it all, he even wanted to meet her mother. Was she actually sitting with the love of her life?

Chapter Forty-five

Coco's restaurant had without comparison the best vantage point of the CBD and city skyscrapers at night. Brian had arranged a taxi to pick them up at Ruth's and they took the last ferry crossing over from Barrack Street Jetty to the south side of the river. The sun was still in the sky but only just. It was the most romantic form of transport for a date.

Brian held out his hand and helped her onto the jetty when they arrived on the southside. The Bellhouse restaurant at the quayside was filling up and picnickers were lining the promenade along the river.

He didn't let go of her hand for the short walk across the road and up the steps to Coco's restaurant. It was a huge glass-fronted building with an *alfresco* veranda accommodating large round tables and some smaller more intimate ones. Each had a square parasol overhead.

Ruth looked back at where they had come from – the skyscrapers formed a beautifully symmetric pattern on the pond-still water. Twinkling lights added to the magic that surrounded them.

The maitre d' was friendly and took them to their table which had a perfect view.

Brian was wearing a pale blue shirt and cream jeans. Ruth was pleased that she had an opportunity to wear her special white embroidered cocktail dress that she had only worn once before. It had been at Dromoland Castle on the only weekend away that she'd had with Ian over the last three years. She felt confident that she would have plenty more opportunities to wear the dress, now that she was with Brian.

They scanned the menu and Brian ordered a bottle of champagne.

Ruth's heart danced as he held her hand and kissed her fingertips. This was possibly going to be the best night of her life.

They started the meal with some Bloody Mary Oyster Shooters and Ruth managed to keep any juice from splashing on her dress.

Brian recommended the Angus scotch beef and Ruth ordered it also.

"That was delicious!" she said when they'd finished. "Is this the best restaurant in Perth?"

"Maybe – but it certainly has one of the nicest settings."

"I'm so happy to be here. Selfish of me, maybe, considering what Julia is going through right now."

"So how are things in Dublin – how are they all after the terrible tragedy?"

"Oh, I don't know what it must be like over there. Horrific, I would imagine. I do miss Julia though – we did so much together."

"I'd say. But Julia's loss is my gain. When is your mum coming over?"

"I'm expecting her next weekend."

Brian sat upright. "Must be on my best behaviour then. What does she like to do?"

Ruth shrugged. "What a great question! I'm ashamed to say I don't know. Now Julia's mother likes to play bridge and go shopping – but my mum – that's difficult. She does keep a diary and I've often told her that she should write."

"Maybe she'll be inspired when she comes here."

Ruth wasn't so sure. "If you knew how she felt about Perth in the seventies you certainly wouldn't say that but then again you never know. I think there is something about telling your story and all Irish families have plenty of emigration stories."

"My mum told me that I had Irish ancestors but I never looked up my family tree – I guess I should."

"There are websites now apparently that can make it easy for you. Especially if you have English ancestors."

"I must look into that. You can help me." He clinked his glass against hers.

The way that he spoke, making plans and including her in his, made her heart dance.

"Does your mum live in Perth?"

Brian lowered his head put his glass down solemnly. "My mum passed away a couple of years back."

"Oh, I'm sorry to hear that."

"Thanks," Brian said with sad nod. "I miss her so much. You see, I never met my father."

"Is he still alive?"

"No, he passed away when I was six – he was . . . let's just say he was no good for my mother. She was relieved when she heard that he had died because he used to bash her around. She was always afraid that he would come looking for me when I was little."

"Oh, that's so sad. I'm sorry. Have you any brothers or sisters?"

"No – my mum and I lived with my granny and grandpa when I was a kid. I'm an only child!"

Ruth felt her heart fill with emotion. She wanted to wrap her arms around Brian and love him forever.

Brian paid the bill and left a handsome tip. Ruth was utterly satisfied and feeling slightly merry after sharing a bottle of champagne and some beautiful Australian white wine.

"Would you like to go for a walk along the esplanade?"

"Sounds divine," Ruth smiled. She felt a thrill as he took her hand in his and squeezed it tightly.

They ran across the road but settled into a stroll on reaching the esplanade.

"That was a fabulous meal!" she said.

"Come here early on a Friday and you'll see all the local TV and media people having a long lunch."

"There's a restaurant in Dublin like that – it's called the Unicorn."

"I'd like to go to Dublin some day."

"Well, why don't you come with me when I go home? I don't have any plans to go at the moment but maybe next year?"

"Great idea!"

Ruth was thrilled that he didn't seem to flinch when she mentioned 'next year'.

How different it was being with a man that you could make plans with – someone who regarded you as important! She didn't think of Ian but she did think about all the time that she had wasted being second fiddle and she would never play that role again.

Brian wrapped his arm around her gently and they kissed now and then as they meandered along the water's edge.

"I must come up to Karrinyup sometime and see your house. Are you near the beach?"

Brian stopped walking. "Eh, that's kinda awkward at the moment."

Ruth was puzzled – it had never occurred that it would be an issue. Surely if he was willing to meet her mother he could bring her to his home?

"Why is it awkward?"

Brian sighed deeply and turned to face Ruth, the lights from the CBD the only source helping her to see his expression and it was pained.

"Ruth, I've been putting off telling you this because I wanted to see where we were going and then you said something in King's Park that worried me . . ."

Horror struck at Ruth's core – what could he possibly be hiding from her? She felt numb but said nothing as she waited to hear.

"I share the house like I told you before but it's a complicated house-share – you see, the person I'm sharing with is my wife."

Ruth heard the word *wife* in slow motion – his lips moved and she heard the word like it was bellowed from a loudspeaker. Her head started to spin and she felt her flesh turn to jelly.

"But you told me that you weren't married – I asked you!"

"Look, I know it sounds bad but we don't get on – it's been a terrible relationship for years . . ."

But Ruth was jogging away from him. He stood there stunned and then set off in pursuit. She was almost back at Coco's before he caught up with her but this prompted her to run faster and she darted on to Mends Street barely able to see through her tear-filled eyes. A taxi almost ran her over but she hardly noticed. She pulled at its door frantically and jumped in.

"Where to, sweetheart?"

"Subiaco – as quickly as you can."

Brian was left standing at the side of the road watching in despair as Ruth was driven away. He dialled her number frantically – he had to explain the situation.

Ruth sat in the back of the cab, utterly deflated. Brian's call came through but she fumbled with the buttons and switched her phone off. Her tears were choking her. The concerned taxi driver offered her a handkerchief which she took gratefully.

Brian had been too good to be true – and she had to ask herself why did she always attract married men? But Brian was worse than Ian or Steve because he had lied – she felt like the most gullible stupid woman on earth.

Chapter Forty-six

Julia was almost sorry that she hadn't agreed to go out with Gillian that Saturday evening. She had been on more familiar terms with her since she'd given her more responsibility in the company and Gillian had risen to the challenges that came with them. But Julia felt her employee was overstepping her boundaries. Her obsession with Dylan was more than irritating and Julia did not feel right discussing her sister's brother-in-law with a woman that wasn't part of her family.

When Gillian had suggested earlier that week that they go out on Saturday night, Julia was quick to respond.

"I'm not in form for socialising yet – it's been too soon since Craig passed away." Julia felt that she was being generous but Gillian found it difficult to conceal her disappointment.

"Has Dylan got a girlfriend, do you know?" Gillian had pried further.

"It really is none of my business what he does with his private life," Julia snapped, "but at the moment I think he's in too much grief to be thinking of such things – much the same way as myself!"

Then she felt terrible as Gillian winced and skulked out of the office.

Julia was too emotional right now to deal with such stress and couldn't understand her own emotions either. She was confused and all around her had changed dramatically since Christmas which – it was hard to believe – was only two short months ago!

But now a long lonely evening stretched ahead. She decided to call Ruth – it had been a ridiculously long time since they had spoken and she needed to be cheered up.

Ruth was online so Julia quickly Skyped her and waited to see her friend's lovely face.

When Ruth came into view Julia was concerned. Her friend's red puffy eyes and running nose were not what she'd expected to be greeted with. Despite the fact that they were thousands of miles apart, Julia could feel her friend's pain.

"Oh Ruth, what's happened?"

"Julia, you must be fucking psychic – I've never needed a call so badly in my life. I've had it with bloody men – they are all the same – fucking bastards!"

Julia was startled to hear so many crude words in one sentence from her friend who never cursed.

"Ruth, you look like you've been crying forever – what is it – is it Ian?"

Ruth threw her head back and rolled her eyes indignantly. "Another fucking bastard – boy, do I pick 'em!"

"Who – what is going on?"

"You were right about Brian – he is a dead loss and wait for it – he's married!"

"*Brian the architect?*"

"Yep – I've had a couple of dates with him and I put off telling you because I was so damn happy. That's my fucking problem – what a dope I am! Do I have '*Come screw me, all ye married men!*' tattooed across my forehead?"

"He's married?" said Julia, stupefied with amazement.

"Yep, and living with his lovely wife while he was screwing me and trying to screw you! What do I have to do to get a decent man, Julia?"

Julia was so shocked that she was glad of the time delay in their conversation. She really didn't know how to console her friend.

"I think the world has gone crazy over the last couple of days. If you want to know how to get a man maybe you should take up bridge!"

"Huh?" Ruth squinted in to the screen to see if Julia was joking. "What's bridge got to do with men?"

"Carol has gone and met herself a man – I swear, Ruth, we are hopeless cases – my mother has Gerry from Northern Ireland running up and down the country after her."

Ruth wondered how Julia was coping with such a dramatic change in her mother.

"Are you okay about it?"

Julia smiled and nodded. "You know, after all that has happened to us since Christmas I feel like just saying 'Bring it on!' – I mean, what can happen next?"

Ruth shrugged. "I can't say but I do know that I'm a disaster when it comes to men."

"Looks like we both are. And, by the way, Dylan has practically moved in with Odette."

"Are you serious?"

"Yep!"

"And what about Gillian – I thought he was dating her?"

"Well, I don't know about her. There's something in the water in Dublin at the moment – everyone is acting so strangely. Horatio is in love with the Brazilian housekeeper and she's easily fifty years younger than him – as long as he doesn't frighten her away – the last thing I need to cope with now is housework on top of everything else!"

Ruth couldn't help but laugh. A call from Julia was just what she needed after what she had been through tonight.

"Oh but, Ju, you don't really think that Dylan has the hots for Odette – I mean seriously?"

"It's been so bizarre since Craig died. Odette is not herself naturally but she doesn't confide in me the way that she used to – she seems to need Dylan more than anyone. And I was in shock when I met Gerry first –"

"Wait, I can't keep up – tell me more about Gerry!"

"Would you believe they have already been away together –

away as in Germany! And they are off to the UK soon. I swear this whole bridge scene is a cover-up for some sort of online dating system. They are sending each other music and stories and e-cards and all sorts. It's a virtual community that has spilled over into the real world."

"What does your granddad think of it all?"

"I think Mum finding love has made Horatio frisky – he was very shook at the funeral but seems to have bounced back remarkably quickly – he keeps saying that life is short."

"Well, it can be bloody long when you keep jumping from one disastrous relationship to the next!" Ruth declared.

"Ruth, don't be so harsh – how were you to know that he was married?"

"Well, obviously I should have asked – what sort of a feckin' eejit am I?"

"Ruth, you have to stop cursing for a start!"

"I can't help it – I've been deranged here for the last two hours – it's two in the morning."

"Gosh – I'm sorry – I had no idea that it was so late there – I'm all over the place!"

"I'm just pleased that you did."

"So how long has Brian been married?"

"I don't know the details."

"So what did he tell you about it?"

"Nothing."

"Nothing? Why?" Julia scrunched up her face.

"Because I just ran."

"You ran?"

"Yeah, I ran away – we were walking along the Esplanade SOR and I just ran away from him!"

"And did he not run after you?"

"Oh yeah, but I was quicker – I don't know where I got the speed from – I just couldn't look at him. I jumped into a taxi and came straight home."

"Did he try to call you?"

"Yeah, but I wouldn't answer. He came around to the house but I wouldn't let him in. He kept saying 'Let me explain' – so I just said that I would call the police if he didn't fuck off and after that I've been cursing at the cushions and the wall until you rang."

Julia nodded her head. "Okay, so now I can see where the cursing comes in. And do you like him?"

"I hate him – fucking bastard!"

"Before you knew that he was married, did you like him?"

"Julia, I'd fallen in love with him – why do you think I'm so bloody angry? We even did *it* – twice!"

"Oh boy, Ruth – you do need to talk to him."

"I can't – I swore after you were here that I would never *ever* sleep with a married man again – then the first guy that comes my way is *voilà* – another married man!"

Ruth started to sob again and Julia wished desperately that she could hug her friend. It felt so difficult to be apart at times like this.

"I wish I was there, Ruth."

"I wish you were here too, Ju – oh God – I'm so sorry for ranting on – how selfish am I? We should be talking about you and how you're coping after Craig's terrible death and dealing with a new man in your mum's life."

"And now Michael is coming home for good."

"For good? Has he got a job?"

"No – he's returning on the 1st March for an interview. Oh I do hope that he gets it!"

"Wow, I never thought that he would just pack up and drop everything like that!"

"Ruth – I told you everyone has gone crazy! So I've changed. I am going to be philosophical in future – no more sorting people out or giving advice – it's live and let live for me from now on!"

Ruth wished that she felt the same way but all she felt was a rock in her heart and disappointment with herself and the world.

Chapter Forty-seven

Lydia had planned what she would do. She had booked a table in the Unicorn restaurant where Peter had taken her on their first date. He would wonder why they were going somewhere so nice on a Wednesday evening but she would make up an excuse – it could be a present from the Perrin family for all the help he had given them with Craig's case. All she had to do was get him there and then she would order a bottle of champagne and pop the question. This was just a little shove in the right direction.

Carol was nervous about driving all the way up to the North of Ireland on her own. She had been slow to agree to the trip as she wanted to be there for her daughter to help with the children and talk things through. But Odette didn't want her around at all and that saddened her. Her daughter had made it quite clear that she wanted only Dylan to be around her house. Carol worried that Odette might be trying to fill the gap left by her husband with his brother. But she had to respect her daughter's wishes and while she was annoying her so much the only thing to do was to disappear. Besides, Gerry had been trying to get her to come up to his part of the world for months and she was now ready. Life was short.

She would never have imagined that her son-in-law would do

such a thing but she herself had suffered from bouts of depression throughout her life that she now regretted terribly. All that loss of energy that should have been spent doing things that she enjoyed and helping others.

The road signs were good and she knew from Gerry's clear directions that she hadn't far to go now. Going to his home and seeing his life would be as much an eye-opener as she was sure it had been for him when he came to Dublin. At least now she needn't be clandestine. Julia and Horatio liked Gerry very much and, although Odette was in no position to see what was going on around her at the funeral, she did notice Gerry and even said that he seemed nice. Carol shivered as she thought of her poor daughter and her little children. Why did things like that have to happen?

She took the next right which she saw was the entrance to Hawthorn Way and counted six houses until she saw Gerry's Ford Mondeo in the driveway. She turned into the drive and stopped. She was excited and thrilled that she had completed the odyssey on her own. Life was to be savoured and she hoped that if her children were to learn anything from Craig's unfortunate departure that it was to embrace life. It was too late to wonder why he did it – time couldn't be turned back and he was gone forever – but those that remained behind had a duty to live their lives to their fullest.

And as Gerry stepped out onto his front porch with a beaming smile, beckoning her to come further up the drive, that was something that she intended to do.

It was brave and adventurous and something that Lydia would never have imagined doing before she met Peter. He was coming to meet her in the Unicorn straight from work. His broad dark figure sauntered into the restaurant – he was wearing a smart pinstriped suit and she loved that dishevelled coolness that he had at the end of the day. Like a character from *CSI New York*.

He spotted her quickly and went over to the window where she sat sipping on a glass of table water.

"I hope I'm not late," he said, looking at his watch before leaning forward to kiss her.

"No, I was early. Did you have a good day?"

He sat and took his napkin and put it on his lap. "Hectic – most days are hectic but they just seem to be getting worse!"

Lydia was so proud of him.

"So what's on the menu tonight?" he asked, his eyes scanning the card.

"Peter, I've been so looking forward to tonight."

Peter looked up from the menu. "Every night is good for us – we have a great life, Lydia – when I see what so many poor souls have to go through every day I thank God for my life."

"I don't know how you remain so positive – I really only got a glimpse into the awful things that you have to deal with on Craig's case. The Perrin family are so grateful for all that you did for them."

"Believe me, Lydia, that wasn't the hardest – not by a long shot. I had to call around to a couple tonight whose son went missing . . ." He stopped. "I'm not going to talk about work tonight – it's too nice being out like this."

Lydia smiled. "You can say anything to me, Peter – we've done so much these last six months and living together has been wonderful."

He agreed with a nod and poured himself a glass of the water.

Lydia was desperate to just blurt it out and see what he thought of her proposal but she had planned to wait until after the main course. She was nervous inside but wanted the moment to be right.

Chapter Forty-eight

Julia drove as close to the front door as she could – the boot of the car was full of Michael's luggage – he'd had to leave a lot of his furniture and ornaments behind.

He stood on the driveway and pounded the ground with his foot.

"I'm home! You know, Ju, even if I don't get this job I'm just glad to be back. Call me a young fogey if you like but that's what I am!"

"Give you a year or two and you'll be called an old fogey!"

"Hey!" Michael couldn't get cross with his sister. He was so thrilled to be home.

Horatio came to the front door. He had been so looking forward to seeing his grandson. He held out his arms.

"It will be nice to have another man in the house," he said, hugging his grandson tightly.

"I won't be staying more than a week or two, Granddad – the apartment is available soon – the tenants are moving out so the timing has been perfect."

"Ah, you won't want to leave here once you've met Paola – she's a beauty. But hands off, she's mine!"

"Granddad," Julia chastised with the crossest voice she could muster.

But the mood was too jovial among the three for crossness to last.

"Where's Mum?" Michael asked.

"She's popped up to the North to Gerry. He came down here last week – they've been seldom apart since Craig's funeral."

"And he stays over?" Michael quizzed.

"Yep!" Julia said with a roll of her eyes.

"Julia doesn't think us old folk are up to much – she's got a lot to learn!" Horatio said with a shake of his head.

"Come in and have a cup of tea and sit down," Julia ordered them both.

They were laughing and dipping Rich Tea biscuits into their mugs when Julia's phone rang. She saw Lydia's name flash up and considered leaving it to ring. The call would be more than Michael needed after the long flight from Singapore. Lydia's engagement would not help him to settle any better and for now she was just pleased to have him home.

"Are you not going to answer that?" Horatio asked.

Julia shook her head. "Nah – I'll call them back."

Julia called Lydia when she was sure that Michael was asleep in bed. It was one o'clock in the afternoon and she was anxious to hear how she had got on in the Unicorn restaurant on her big night.

"Hello?"

"Lydia, it's me – Julia – come on, spill the beans, I'm dying to hear how you got on!"

Lydia paused at the end of the line. Then she started to sob.

Julia had expected to hear wonderful news – not sobbing.

"Julia, I've made a terrible mistake – we were having a lovely meal and he was kind and considerate and attentive like he always is but then I told him that it was the 29th of February and I proposed. He thought it was a joke at first and then he got really angry. I've never seen him like it. He told me that I was crazy – what did I expect from him so soon? He had moved in with me quickly and he was happy with that but now I wanted to go and ruin everything by rushing into marriage when we didn't know each other well enough."

"Lydia, I don't know what to say – I thought he was saying all sorts of things about commitment and settling down?"

"Yes, he was, but he said he was in no rush to get married. And what really upsets me is the fact that he wouldn't consider kids if he wasn't already married. His last relationship lasted ten years. I don't want us to be together ten years and then he decides he doesn't want to get married!"

Julia was tempted to put on her rational and reasonable hat and offer some sound advice but that was not what her friend needed. For now she was just going to listen.

"I'm so sorry, Lydia – maybe he felt his manhood was threatened or something and that proposing was something that he should do? He has something of a superhero aura about him!"

"He's like that in public but he's really sensitive when we're on our own – that's why I can t understand his reaction."

"How old is he?"

"He's thirty-nine."

"How long did you say he went out with his last girlfriend?"

"Ten years – and he was eight years with his previous girlfriend."

"Maybe he's a serial monogamist?"

Lydia sighed heavily down the phone. "Julia, I don't want to lose him but I feel like life is passing me by – my job isn't as important to me as yours is for you. I want a family more than anything."

Julia had to bite her tongue – she didn't want to say what she was really thinking.

"Look, why don't you come out with me tonight?" she said. "I could do with a bit of fun."

Lydia sniffed into the phone. "Okay," she said reluctantly. "I'll see you after work?"

"Yeah, that would be great – I'm only heading into the office now and I have to visit Odette on the way so the later the better."

"That's the nice part about being your own boss, I guess!" Lydia was envious.

"I collected Michael from the airport today – he's come home for good."

"Oh!"

"Don't worry, I won't tell him that we're meeting." Clearly Lydia was shaken at the mention of her brother – that was interesting, thought Julia.

"Thanks, Julia – I couldn't take a head-melting situation with him at the moment."

"I know and he's very vulnerable too so I don't think seeing you would help."

"Okay. Talk later – and thanks."

Julia turned off her phone. She would swing by Odette's on the way into work. There was something in the air that she couldn't put her finger upon – a sense of everything just falling apart for those around her. Ruth and Lydia were broken-hearted. She had to watch Odette and her children in pain. Carol was the only woman who had found happiness and she hoped that everything was going well there or she wouldn't be able to cope.

Dylan's car was in the driveway and it was almost two o'clock in the afternoon. Julia parked and rang on the door.

Odette opened it quickly on seeing that it was Julia.

"Come in," she smiled brightly. "I'm so glad it's you – I couldn't stand another do-gooder offering to help. I'm seriously thinking of booking a trip to the country for a few days and just taking the kids away from all this."

Julia followed her sister into the kitchen and looked around.

"Is Dylan here?"

"No, he left his car here last night to make it look like he was here – just for security – he's been so good, Julia."

"He has alright – and where was he?"

"On a date with Gillian, I think – she is so weird – I seriously think she is stalking him!"

Gillian had said nothing when in work the day before. But her sister was the person that Julia had come to see and she had more pressing needs.

"Sit down and let me make the cuppa!" Julia said.

Odette practically had to fight to get the kettle from her sister. "No, I need to be doing things – Julia, my mind is going crazy and has been for months. I need to get back to some sense of normality – life has changed and I am on my own now so I just have to get used to it."

Julia surrendered the kettle. "Odette . . . do you have any idea what was going on inside Craig's head? I'm sure you need to process it."

"I know he felt the tension between us but I really don't know what else could have made him do something so drastic." She shrugged as she filled the kettle. "Dylan has looked at our finances and they are not as healthy as I would have imagined. Also he had taken out a large insurance policy on himself a year ago which makes me think that he was planning this in some way."

"But then he wouldn't have committed suicide because the insurance won't pay."

Odette suddenly became defensive. "It hasn't been proven that is what he did – but yes, I know it doesn't make sense. Life doesn't make sense at the moment."

Julia reached out and held her sister in her arms. There was nothing she could do to help relieve her pain.

"Will I come back later – tonight?" she asked.

Odette nodded. "Yes, and please stay, Ju."

"I will," Julia assured her sister. "Michael is going to come out to see you later too – he took a nap for the afternoon. Actually, I'll get him to come here when he wakes up – I just remembered that I have to meet Lydia for a little while after work but I'll come back here later."

"Okay. You'd better go into work – I've taken up enough of your time."

Dear sweet Odette, Julia thought fondly as she got into her car and battled through the city traffic into her work. She wasn't sure how she could help her – but she would do everything that she could.

Her thoughts jumped to Gillian. She really wasn't sure what that girl was doing but, one thing for certain, Dylan was entertaining her and she couldn't figure out why. Julia would have liked to believe what Horatio had said now – that Dylan had feelings for her – but he hadn't shown any signs of it since she'd returned from Australia. There was always the possibility that he did like Gillian a lot – why did it seem so incredible?

The curiosity was stinging her by the time she got to work.

Gillian had a beaming smile on her face when she saw Julia.

"Hi, Julia – how are you doing?"

"Good, Gillian – any urgent messages?"

Gillian shook her head. "I spoke with Cruise Holidays today and they would like to discuss their brochure with you – also that domain name you enquired about is available so I bought it."

"Great."

Gillian had come on so much in the last few months. It made Julia wonder just what exactly the girl was capable of.

"How are things with you?" she asked.

"Oh fine! You know me."

But that was just it – Julia felt that she really didn't know Gillian at all.

"Is it okay if I go a few minutes early this evening? " Gillian asked. "I have to see someone."

"Of course. You've been doing hours of overtime with the funeral and all the time that I've been away. Thanks for everything."

"That's okay!" she said with a smile and a swagger that Julia hadn't noticed before. She was radiating confidence and it made Julia uneasy and curious – she wondered was she meeting Dylan again by any chance.

Julia focused on her emails and the day's tasks to take her mind off the thoughts that were running through her head.

Three hours had passed and she hadn't answered all of her emails or made all of her calls but she could hear Lydia's footsteps coming through reception. Her work could wait – she turned off her computer and braced herself. Lydia would need a lot of support.

"Hi, Ju, thanks so much for meeting me – I know you are up to your eyes."

Julia kissed her friend on the cheek and grabbed her coat and bag.

"I told you I am always here for you, Lydia. Where do you want to go?"

Lydia shrugged. They walked out onto Wicklow Street and found their way naturally onto Grafton Street.

"Let's try the Bailey?" Lydia suggested.

They found two high stools in the corner of the bar and ordered a glass of wine each from the barman. Once he was out of earshot Julia listened as Lydia told her the story of the disastrous proposal in detail.

"I can't believe that he said he didn't want to get married," Julia said.

Lydia shook her head incredulously. "That's the crazy bit – he's all smiles as if nothing has happened. I mean when we came back from the Unicorn that night he just went into the bathroom and then got into bed in silence. Then he said to me today that he was talking to friends who had bought extra tickets for the Madonna gig in the summer and did we want to go?"

"Well, at least you know that he's planning on being with you – I mean, he didn't want to move out or anything like that."

"Oh no, he's normal as anything and that bit I find weird. I mean, if we can't have an argument and work it out afterwards how are we going to be able to survive a marriage together? I swear he's just brushed it under the carpet as if nothing happened and we are expected to move swiftly along – on his terms, mind you – and play the perfect couple again."

"Maybe there's no such thing as perfect." Julia had to say it – she had never believed in perfect. It was possibly another reason why she had never been keen to enter into a committed long-term relationship.

"I don't know what to do, Julia. The sheen has been tarnished – don't you hate it when that happens in a relationship?"

"It happens at some stage with every relationship – it's how you both handle the aftershocks that will determine whether you have a future together or not."

"What made you so wise, Julia Perrin? I mean, for someone

who doesn't get caught up in relationships you have plenty of wise words."

Julia threw her head back and laughed. "I'm a know-all, Lydia – you should have figured that out by now. But I'll say something that I probably shouldn't when you are feeling this way. I think Michael really loved you and for all his bad qualities he has bucket-loads of good ones."

Lydia looked down at her fingers and fiddled with them nervously. "I know I was cruel to shoot him down after I met him at Christmas," she sighed. "But I would have kept him on ice if he hadn't sent me that whingy needy email a couple of weeks later. He was putting pressure on me and I thought that he was just jealous because I had met Peter. I also thought that it was only a matter of weeks before a proposal." Lydia rolled her eyes and sighed again. "What am I like?"

Julia smiled. "Lydia, you were in the throes of the honeymoon period. This is just another stage. You have to decide now if you want to move forward with Peter on his terms and see how the next six months go or if maybe he isn't the one for you."

Lydia knew that Julia was right. She would have to see how she really felt but she was aware that doubt had already set in.

Chapter Forty-nine

Julia drove out of the city and headed for the northside. It was seven o'clock and although it put pressure on her time-wise she was glad that she had made the effort to see Lydia. She had almost forgotten about Michael who would definitely be up by now. She dialled home and Horatio answered the phone.

"Michael and I are having a great time here – so don't rush home!"

"I thought Michael was coming with me to see Odette?"

"Give the lad a chance – he's very jet-lagged and anyway I'm after opening a couple of cans of Guinness and we might pop up to the village for a pint in the Abbey Tavern later. It's not often I get my grandson to myself and if you stay with Odette tonight we'll have no one bothering us!"

Horatio did have a point and Michael would be suffering from jet lag. Tomorrow would be a better day for Michael to call and see Odette. Besides, Julia really wanted to spend the night with her sister and it was good that Horatio had company now.

"Okay, Granddad, tell Michael to come to my office in the morning and we can go out to Odette's for lunch – mind you, she could be in a daze herself – I never know how she will be from hour to hour let alone day to day.

She called to tell Odette that she would be there soon and to ask if she would like her to bring anything. Odette fancied some crispy duck pancakes from the Chinese takeaway and Julia picked some up along with a bottle of red wine from the off-licence. She had bought enough for three just in case Dylan was joining them. Secretly she hoped that he would be there – Gillian had been so secretive in work and she wanted to ask him about her and see what was going on.

When his Mercedes came into view, she smiled. Then a terrible thought came into her head – maybe his concern for Odette was too great and he was in love with her. Could he be seeing Gillian in case Odette or anyone would suspect his true feelings? That would explain why he wanted to go out for drinks as a foursome when she was in Australia. Could that be why Craig did what he did? Julia's mind was playing tricks and she felt guilty for having such awful thoughts.

She lifted the brown package with the duck and slid the bottle of wine under her arm. She would get her overnight bag later – she might not need it after all!

Dylan answered the door and Charlotte stood like a little fairy at his side.

Julia groaned inside – she bent down to kiss her niece and Dylan took her bags from her so that she could sweep Charlotte into her arms.

"Are you staying for a sleepover, Aunty Julia?" the little girl pleaded.

"Maybe – if your mummy wants me to."

"I want you to and Uncle Dylan can stay too – it's lonely 'cos Daddy's not here."

Dylan looked at Julia and both were unable to answer, their hearts heavy in their chests at the little girl's words. She was too young to understand that she would never see her father again.

"Let's go in and see what Mummy is doing."

Julia bounced her niece on her hip and went into the lounge where Odette was sitting on the couch, looking listless and depressed.

"I've got the pancakes and duck," said Julia. "How about I take Charlotte to bed and you two get started?"

"Thanks, Ju," Odette said, glancing up at her sister but making no move to greet her.

"Where's Jamie?"

"He's in the playroom on the computer game," said Dylan. "I'll take him up to bed too and afterwards we can get going on the food."

Julia and Dylan gave each other a knowing look that spoke a multitude. Odette had fallen into the abyss again as they had both seen on several occasions since Craig's death. Julia was pleased now that Michael wasn't seeing his sister tonight.

She went into the kitchen and put the food into the oven to keep it warm, then went upstairs to help Dylan put the children to bed.

Ten minutes later she and Dylan were in the kitchen making preparations for the meal.

"Is she still taking those tablets?" Julia whispered to him as he took out the dinner plates.

"I think so – they make her go like this – I think she'd be better off with a glass of wine and a good cry," Dylan said.

"So do I!" Julia agreed as she struggled with the unfamiliar corkscrew.

"Here, let me help you with that cork," Dylan said, taking the bottle from her.

Julia put knives and forks on the table, then went into the lounge where Odette still sat immobile.

"Will we all eat together in the kitchen?" she suggested to her sister.

Odette nodded and stood up trancelike as if she was sleepwalking.

Dylan started the conversation off lightly, discussing the upcoming St Patrick's Day festivities and announcing that he had bought tickets for himself and the kids to see the parade from the grandstand.

"They'll enjoy that," Odette said gratefully.

"I got one for you too, Odette," he said.

Odette put plum sauce on her duck and started to wrap the pancake around the meat. "Why don't you go, Julia – I don't think I'll be up to the parade this year."

Dylan looked at Julia. "It might be nice for the kids to have their aunt and uncle take them out – what do you think?"

Julia nodded. For a terrible minute she had been picturing Gillian next to Dylan in the stands with her niece and nephew.

"Yes – that would be great – lovely!" she said vehemently. Oh God, she thought, I'm getting crazy like Gillian. What the hell has come over me!

Dylan was bowled over by her reaction and just tucked into the pancake he had assembled. He wondered how a woman who couldn't stand the sight of him a couple of months ago now was really keen to go to the St Patrick's Day Parade with him. Yet he wasn't complaining – maybe she was learning a little compassion. The entire family on both sides had been through so much since Craig's death that he should not be surprised by the change.

The Abbey Tavern's stone-clad walls had housed many great evenings of drinking and chat. Michael and Horatio sat up at the solid mahogany bar – an open turf fire blazed in the hearth.

"I dreamt of this place while I was in Singapore. There's nowhere like it!" Michael said, lifting a creamy pint of Guinness to his lips.

"Ah, it's great to have you back, son. But don't regret the adventure – never ever regret time spent having an adventure."

Michael laughed and licked his Guinness moustache from his lips. "I wouldn't call my five years an adventure but I certainly had a chance to think about life and what I wanted. It's funny how you need to go away sometimes to sort out your perspective on home."

"Ah, I'm glad you decided to come home – and it's only a pity you didn't bring a lovely girl back with you!"

Michael took another slug from his pint. "The girl that I want to settle down with is here but it looks like she's going steady with that policeman who handled Craig's case."

"Really? Who would that be?"

"Do you remember Lydia?"

"Julia's friend – of course I do. You courted her for some time, didn't you?"

"Yes, many years ago."

Horatio nodded his head. "It's a terrible thing to let a woman slip away from you like that – I always say women are a bit like the Number 31 – you'd be waiting for ages and then three come along together."

"Well, when you get on a bit it's harder to get one that likes you at all!"

Horatio threw his head back and cackled. "Wait till you get to my age – you might as well be waiting for the Hill of Howth tram to come back into service – unless you take up bridge by the looks of things."

"What do you make of this Gerry fella that Mum has hooked up with?"

"He seems like a nice little chap. Very different to your father, mind, but that's no harm. Carol is more independent now than she ever was in her life – I mean, she went straight from our house after marriage to her own with her husband. It was different years ago – none of this living together. You don't know how lucky you young folk are!"

"Granddad, you never cease to amaze me!"

"I amaze myself – all I need now is your mother to go up to the North for good and Julia to go and get herself a fella and then I could get myself a lovely Brazilian girl – one of about forty-six, let's say – what do ya think, Michael?" He gave his grandson a naughty wink.

"Horatio Daly, I don't know where we got you from at all!"

"But I'll tell you this: if you like a young one then you have to go after her – get her any way that you can. I had to follow your grandmother to Dun Laoghaire and drag her back on the 46a. It was very romantic and it was the best day's work that I ever did. Ah now, drink up, lad – there's a hole in this glass – I need a refill!"

Michael was elated to be home. He would take his grandfather's advice on board – he was a wise old coot. It was precious moments like this that he had missed while he was living away – there was nowhere like home and nowhere like Ireland.

Julia got up and looked at her watch. It was two o'clock in the morning. After Odette had gone to bed Dylan decided that he would too and he took the spare room. Charlotte had been sleeping with her mother since her father's death so that meant that Julia was sleeping in a haven of pink with a white net canopy above her bed and a wooden crown headrest against the wall. It was an awkward sleep and she had forgotten to bring a glass of water to bed.

The bathroom light was left on for the children in case they needed to go to the toilet in the middle of the night. It was things like that Julia never thought about – having children was a fulltime occupation and it would be extra difficult for Odette now with the full burden of responsibility as mother and father.

It was kind of Dylan to be so hands-on – of course, if he had a family of his own he wouldn't be in this position to help. Julia stepped into the hall and tiptoed into the kitchen. She was startled when she opened the door and saw a large figure beside the fridge.

Dylan was drinking the end of a carton of orange juice by the neck. The old Julia would have chastised him but in light of all that had happened in this house over the past few days, Julia's perspective on what did and didn't matter had changed utterly.

"Can't sleep either?" Dylan asked.

Julia shook her head.

"I could make some tea if you fancy a mug?"

"If you are having one, then yeah, thanks."

Dylan hit the switch on the kettle and went to take out the milk from the fridge.

"I lie awake at night and wonder why – why the hell did he do such a thing?" he said. "It gets under my skin and crawls around like an alien. Can you figure it out?"

Julia shrugged. "I can't. I guess he could have been clinically depressed but never told anyone and couldn't get out of it."

"I thought that he was having an affair at first. I spoke to one of his colleagues though after the funeral and he was shocked when I said it – he said that Craig wouldn't have had the time – he was always working. He took responsibility seriously and longed for more security. It was difficult for those who had been in the company so long to cope with the changes. I know he was jealous of my situation and I didn't blame him. It's good to be out of the shackles of a permanent pensionable job. I'll start my own business up when I get back."

Julia turned her head in surprise. "'Get back'? Where are you going?"

"Well, I was offered a job in London that I was going to take until this happened but now I'm going to do something that I have been thinking about for years – I'm going to do a round-the-world trip."

"Wow – for how long?" Julia was taken aback by the disappointment she felt at this revelation.

"A year at least. I've seen a lot of the States already so I'm starting off in South America and going around to Australia the long way. Then I'm going to do Asia, India, Africa and any part of Europe that I haven't seen."

"Sounds like it will be quite an experience."

Dylan nodded. "I hope so. That's why I want to spend as much time as I can with the kids now."

"When are you planning on going?"

"In about a month."

This was a good opportunity for her to quiz him about Gillian.

"And what about your girlfriend? She hasn't put in for any extra leave so she won't be going, will she? Unless of course she's going to resign."

"My girlfriend?" Dylan seemed amused. "If I have a girlfriend that's news to me!"

"Gillian," Julia said. "You've been seeing a lot of each other – according to a little bird?"

Dylan shook his head. "Gillian is a lovely girl but we never dated. I asked her to come out with me one night with Craig and Odette because I was trying to suss them out – I knew something was up with Craig but couldn't figure it out. I should have just asked him, huh?"

"Don't blame yourself – I'm sure there was nothing any of us could have done – Craig was on the edge and that is the unfortunate thing about suicide – sometimes family are last to know."

Dylan nodded and put on his stiff upper lip. "But as regards Gillian there was nothing romantic between us ever."

"Oh I see!" that was definitely news for Julia. She wondered then why he had been out with her the night before but didn't dare to ask.

Chapter Fifty

Ruth had received eleven text messages and three voicemails from Brian since the night they had spent in Coco's. She hadn't answered any of them. She was relieved that he hadn't called around to her house again and was scared at night in case he did. She was feeling weak and lonely and would be tempted to let him in. His messages said that he and his wife were in the process of separating. But she didn't care. The fact that he hadn't come clean with her at the beginning was enough to blight the relationship for good. She couldn't bear the thought of a long discussion over his marital status – it would bring back too many bad memories. She wanted to cry often and hard and, only for her mother's impending visit, she would be considering chucking in her Australian adventure and returning home to Julia and her family. But it would be a shame – work had settled down well and she loved the banter in the office with the gang – she had become very friendly with Helenka and had been out with her to a sophisticated bar in the city the night before. She tried to be pleasant and fun but every so often needed to go to the bathroom to pull herself together and drag her thoughts away from Brian.

His persistent messaging didn't make it any easier.

Julia had suggested that she heard him out but Julia didn't

understand that it was more than just the way that he kept the facts of his marriage hidden – she did not want to be in a relationship with someone who was married before. It was a bad-luck omen as far as she was concerned and nothing could convince her otherwise.

But now she really had to pull herself together: her mother was about to arrive.

Angela felt her stomach flutter wildly as the plane descended into Perth airport. The lights of the runway came into view and she felt a dread that she had managed to keep hidden in her darkest memories for over thirty years. Nineteen hours on her own had given her plenty of time to think. She had slept intermittently after she boarded the second leg in Dubai but exhaustion was hitting hard now.

Filling out the landing card felt surreal – she had sworn that she would never return here. Time could not heal the memories or the hurt or betrayal.

But there was consolation after she stepped through Immigration. Ruth stood with her eyes shining behind the barrier at Arrivals, bright highlighted tints now in her strawberry-blonde hair.

Angela was so pleased to see how much the sunshine had enhanced her daughter's natural colouring.

"You are the picture of health, love!" she said, pushing her trolley aside so that she could embrace her daughter tightly.

"It's so good to see you, Mum!"

"It was a much easier trip than the one I took when I was pregnant with you all those years ago."

"Ah, I'm glad it was good."

"You'll never guess but I got an upgrade to Dubai and lay there like Lady Muck for most of the flight. I even drank champagne!"

"Fantastic – how did that happen?"

"They double-booked my seat and when they discovered their mistake Economy was full – the other person was really cross with them so they gave him the seat and they told me that I was going up to business class."

Ruth laughed. "I'm pleased for you – that was a nice treat."

"So tell me all – oh, it is hot here!" she gasped as they stepped out into the warm Perth sunshine.

"I don't know where to start – give me the trolley and I'll put the cases in the boot – my car is just over here."

The two women beamed with the joy of each other's company as Ruth's Jeep booted along the highway.

"Slow down a bit – these roads are treacherous – always accidents on them," Angela said.

"Actually I noticed there are far fewer reports of crashes here than there were in Dublin. Australians are really law-abiding drivers."

"Well, that's something that's changed for the better then," Angela huffed. "And they have built a few more skyscrapers, I see."

The CBD was much bolder and more impressive than the skyline Angela had left in the seventies. Although she wasn't keen to admit it, the city looked well with perfectly manicured esplanades and beautifully designed architecture.

"Have you seen Julia. Mum?"

"Just at the funeral. Oh, Ruth, it was terrible – I never remember one like it. Everyone was so bewildered at how someone as steady and reliable as Craig could do such a thing – it really didn't make any sense."

"I've been wondering how or why he did it, and I can't understand."

Angela nodded. "And poor Odette will never know, I'm sure. His brother is a lovely chap and he carried his coffin with such decorum and compassion. There wasn't a dry eye in the house when the kids got up and put his photo on the coffin."

"It sends shivers down your spine. Have you any other news from home?"

Angela had to think. "Kevin and Orla have packed up and left for Canada with God knows how many other Irish tradesmen and engineers."

"How's Dad?"

"Ah, you know your father – he just potters. I'm glad that he didn't come out here to be honest – it means that we'll have a better chance to do what we want."

Ruth was happy with this golden opportunity to see her mother on Australian soil.

If Julia was here she would be itching to ask about Peppermint Grove. Ruth wondered if and when would be a good time to bring up the subject. She could always take a drive through the suburb and see her mother's reaction. But then again she didn't want to run into Brian either. He hadn't called today so far but she had a feeling that he wasn't going to leave her alone until she heard him out properly – and facing the truth was something that Ruth had always found difficult to do.

Angela unpacked her luggage in the spare room while her daughter made them a cold salad for their supper.

Ruth uncorked a bottle of dry white wine and poured some sparkling water into two glasses.

When Angela returned to the kitchen she was carrying packets of fig-roll biscuits and a twelve-pack of King crisps.

"I thought you'd like these, Ruth – I know they're your favourites."

"Thanks, Mum – that's really good of you. I do miss my King crisps. But, you know, the food is really good over here and portions are massive in all the restaurants."

"I'm glad to hear that because it was bloody awful when I lived here. Subiaco has come on in leaps and bounds and I see there are more public-transport options than in my day. Do you know we had no streetlights?"

"I'm sure that you'll see lots of changes. Is there anything in particular that you want to do or see while you're here?"

Angela shook her head. "No, my love – I came here to see you and we can do whatever you like. Sure, I can always meet you for lunch and do a bit of shopping and that."

"Of course – and take in some sun – I've a lovely back garden – come out and see."

Ruth opened the back door. The two stepped out onto the sun-drenched decking. A wave of warm air flowed past them as they took in the view. In the distance a crow cawed from the top of a tree.

"Those bloody crows – I never heard such an awful noise in my life from any animal." Angela scowled.

"I thought it was a baby crying the first morning after I got here."

"So did I – you don't appreciate the little things about home until you leave it."

"The birds don't bother me, Mum – it's really nice living here – I love my job and the sunshine is great. It's just people that you miss when you live abroad."

"And then again it's nice to be away from other sorts of people," Angela said with a nod of her head.

"Work is great – I've never enjoyed a job so much. You see, you never worked while you were here."

Angela winced. "I did so work – I took a part-time job when Kevin started school."

"Really? I never knew that – I thought you were always saying that Dad went out too much when you lived here and you were alone in the house."

"He was always out but I took the job to get a few extra bob – your father wouldn't join the union so he didn't get the top rate of pay and he would never have made enough, for all the hours that he put in. I was working in a restaurant . . . waitressing for a while . . ."

"Where? Is the restaurant still going?"

"Oh, I wouldn't know." Angela hesitated. She was becoming more uncomfortable as she spoke about her employment. "Let's go back inside to the cool. I see you have a nice bottle of wine waiting for us."

Ruth wouldn't push it tonight but she was keen to find out all abut her mother's time in Perth and she had three weeks to do so.

Chapter Fifty-one

Angela woke to the cawing of the crow. The room was stuffy and she felt around to turn on the air-con. She had slept right through the night. Silence rang through the house as she went out into the hall. She called Ruth's name but there was no reply.

A note on the kitchen table was scribbled roughly, using a pencil and the back of a torn envelope.

I've gone to work mum. Will ring you at twelve to see if you want to come into town to meet me. xx Ruth

Angela looked at her watch. She had forgotten to change it to Australian time. She realised that it was almost twelve o'clock already. She had slept like the dead and was grateful for the rest although she knew that jet lag was likely to hit in a few hours. There was time for a bowl of cereal at least and a shower before her daughter rang. It was peaceful and soothing in the bungalow although she didn't want to be on her own for long.

Ruth called on the dot of twelve o'clock.

"Will I come to meet you?" she asked.

"Don't go out of your way, love – I'm fine with my own company and happy to take it easy today."

"Well, I could continue working until three thirty and then come home for the day. I came into work early – I did this while Julia was here and it worked well."

"That sounds good, love. I would like to just sit in the shade for a while – is there a supermarket near?"

"Coles is only two blocks away. But let me know what you want and I can get it on my way home."

"It's okay, love – I might go for a wander."

"I've left a key on the hall table. See you soon, Mum."

Ruth hung up and went straight back to her emails. Her eyes were focused on the computer screen when she heard Helenka laugh and say that she would get Ruth.

Ruth looked up and, standing there beside Helenka, was Brian. She started to shake – her eyes widely focused now on his tall dark figure as he walked over to where she was working. It was clever of him to come to her work – she wouldn't make a scene in front of her workmates and she damned him for the move. He looked wildly attractive and she hated and loved him at the same time.

"How you going?" he said with a big beaming smile.

Her heart melted. She couldn't move.

"I-I-I'm fine, thank you."

"I was hoping that you'd lost your phone – haven't had a text from you for a while."

Ruth was going a bright crimson and Kai was peeping over the top of his computer to hear the exchange.

"I, eh – actually, can we go outside to the corridor for a moment?" She stood up briskly and ushered Brian out of the office.

When they got outside Ruth frowned crossly at him but words failed her. She had to hand it to Brian – he was persistent.

"I was hoping that you would take the hint."

"I think you owe it to me to hear me out!"

Ruth was incensed with his forthright arrogance.

"I owe it to you!" she said, a bit too loudly for her own liking as Helenka walked out into the corridor.

Helenka smiled awkwardly at the two as she waited for the lift to arrive. "Em, why don't you guys try the conference room?" she suggested. "I'm sure it's empty."

Ruth wished that she had thought of that two minutes before but she wasn't sure that she wanted to be in a room on her own with Brian either.

"Right . . . it's just over there." She indicated that Brian should take the lead.

He opened the door and Ruth followed him in. They were on the thirty-first floor with a stunning view of the rambling green shoreline and river below. She walked over to the window and looked out.

Brian went over beside her. "I'm sorry, Ruth. I shouldn't have lied to you – it was unforgiveable – but I was torn when you said that you wouldn't give a married man a chance. I wanted to get to know you better and hoped that you would mellow when you got to know me. Something special happens when I am with you. You did read my texts?"

Ruth nodded. "Yes, I did read them – but you don't understand."

"Understand what?"

"I wanted to meet someone with a clean slate," she sighed. She had nothing to lose by telling him the truth – it was hypocritical but he had to know the reason why she needed to be with a single guy. "You see, I was in a relationship for ten years with a guy in Dublin before I came over here."

Brian felt a stone land on his dreams. Was she about to swear undying love for someone else?

"And the facts are this." She turned away from the beautiful view to face him. "He was married. Not when we met but he was engaged and he went through with his wedding – I've been the other woman for ten years. I thought when I met you that you were single. I wanted to be with someone who hadn't been married to someone else."

It was Brian's turn to be surprised. "That sounds tough, Ruth – but we don't get to our thirties without some baggage – none of us do. And are you going to let the past get in the way of our future?"

His eyes were wide and Ruth wanted to melt into them. He was easily the most handsome man that she had ever been with.

There was so much about him that she liked so why did she find it so hard to forgive him?

"Will you hear me out?" he asked.

Ruth nodded and they went over to the conference table and sat down beside each other.

"I was married for five years. Jessica is an interior designer. We met doing a job in Dalkeith – it was a very big rebuild. We fell in love but the honeymoon period didn't last long – she was more keen to have her Big Day than focus on the relationship. We were swept along by friends and my mother was so keen to have grandchildren I think she would have liked to see me married at eighteen. But she never got to see them. Anyway we were only married two years when the holes started to show. Jessica didn't really want to have kids at all and I had a niggling feeling in my gut all along, telling me that something was wrong. Then one day she arrived home with her ex-boyfriend who showed up from Sydney – he just happened to be in Perth and had phoned her mother and got her number. For the next two years he came and visited every couple of months. It was very unsettling for our marriage. He was a surfer and didn't believe in the corporate world of jobs and finance – instead he bummed his way around Australia begging from family and friends. I quickly realised that we had become one of his pit-stops as he cruised from beach to beach. But it was more than that for Jessica. She fell in love with him again and they had an affair."

Ruth was entranced. She wanted to hear every detail so remained silent.

"I walked in from work one day and the two of them were 'at it' on the kitchen table. It was like something from a soap. I couldn't go back with her after that and she agreed to separate but property has gone through the roof for the last couple of years and every time we find somewhere to move the price keeps going up – our house has gone up too but we each want to buy something nice and it's more difficult to do it now."

"Why don't you rent while you wait?"

Brian shrugged. "I'm an architect so I like to own my home.

The house is really big – you should come up and see it. I've told Jessica about you – she won't mind – we are civil at this stage. We've put in our divorce papers and are just waiting to hear from the courts. It was a big mistake – what's it they call them now – starter marriages or something? So you see, you are getting a guy who has been broken in if you take me back."

Ruth did feel like she had been unfair – he had a very plausible way of explaining his predicament.

"If you do decide that you don't want to see me again then I'll take it like a man but I needed you to hear me out."

Ruth found it difficult to answer him properly. She wasn't a vestal virgin herself and now that he had explained himself perhaps her attitude had been over the top.

"My mum has arrived in Perth so I am going to be busy with her – can I digest what you said and maybe we can talk again in a couple of days?"

Brian nodded. He was relieved to have got so much off his chest. Ruth was the first girl that he had been truly interested in since he had split from his wife.

"Will you let me meet your mum?"

Ruth had to think that one through. "Give me a day or two, please, Brian. She only arrived last night."

"Of course." He stood up and she followed his lead. He opened his arms. "Any chance of a hug?"

Ruth nodded. She put her head on his shoulder and breathed in the fresh scent from his crisp white shirt.

"I'm going to Peppy Grove now for the rest of the day – maybe you can call around with your mum some day – I'll be there all week. It might help jog her memory?"

Ruth pulled away from his strong hold and smiled. "Maybe I will."

"And then I can take her out and try and impress her?"

Ruth smiled. "Okay maybe." She was warming to the idea.

When he was gone she felt sad and wanted to run after him but she had to be strong and this was a different sort of relationship to the one that she'd had with Ian. She wanted it to be right. But now she was so happy inside because the days that she had spent away from Brian had been more miserable than any she had suffered while in her relationship with Ian.

Ruth returned home to Subiaco some time around three o'clock.

"I'm home, Mum – where are you?"

"I'm in the garden!"

Ruth went into the kitchen and out the back door.

Angela looked up from her book. She was sitting under the shade of a eucalyptus tree. "I've been like a big lump of jelly for the last hour – this must be how it feels to be one of those moonwalkers. I didn't get to Coles. I was at the front door and I couldn't find a key."

"I left it on the hall table."

"Yes, but there were a few of them and I couldn't get any to turn in the lock and I was afraid to risk it – just as well really because I'm still so wobbly."

"Well, take your time – tomorrow you'll see a big difference."

"Oh, I'm sure."

"Is there anywhere that you would like to go now?"

"I wouldn't mind a little trip to the beach – maybe just sit on the sand?"

"Sure – I'll bring the Esky and some cold wine. We can get fish and chips and watch the sunset."

"That sounds nice – we used to do that with Kevin."

"You and Daddy?"

Angela laughed. "Eh, no – as I said before your father was always working. Me and Myra Jones from Cardiff. She was a great friend and companion and she had a little girl called Sian who used to play with Kevin. It's hard to believe how long ago that was!"

"Alright then, do you want to go now or wait until nearer teatime?"

"Whenever you think, Ruth – don't worry about me and time – I'm so all over the place you could give me some breakfast and my body wouldn't be any the wiser. I don't know where I am at all."

"Okay then, I'll have a quick shower and we can go to Cottesloe."

"Lovely," Angela said, turning back to her book.

While Ruth was foaming her skin with soap, her head filled with thoughts of her meeting with Brian earlier. She couldn't let him slip away now. He was so gorgeous – she couldn't blame him from hiding a disastrous marriage from her until he was sure that they were going somewhere. She believed him utterly. He was so different to Ian and she had to remember that all men would not lie and hurt her like he had. Brian deserved a second chance. She might even mention him to her mother – she would see how the trip to Cottesloe went. She rinsed off and put on a pair of shorts and a fresh T-shirt.

Angela was standing ready for action when Ruth went out to the garden.

"Okay, are we off?" she asked.

"Yes, I'll just get the Esky and some water for the car journey."

Ruth got some things together and the two went out to her little Jeep.

"Oh, I love these great big high-up Golfs."

Ruth chuckled. "It's a Toyota, Mum – it's called a Rav 4."

"It's like a blown-up Golf."

Ruth had to laugh. "So let's go!"

They drove down Railway Road as she had done with Brian not so long ago. She was tempted to swing onto Stirling Highway and take the scenic drive through Peppermint Grove but her mother might suspect something if she didn't take the direct route. Although the chances were that the roads had changed a lot over thirty years.

"I took Julia to see Peppermint Grove when she was here. The houses are fabulous – was it like that in your day?"

Angela's ears did prick up when she heard the mention of Peppermint Grove.

"Oh there!" she sighed. "Yes, it was the place where the wealthy and powerful lived – there and Dalkeith. I'm sure it still is."

"Actually you won't believe this but we bumped into a friend of Julia's from years ago – Richard Clery – and he lives there now."

"I think I remember Julia going out with that chap – he had piranha fish or something like that – very strange."

"Yes, and a motorbike – well, he is married to an Italian woman and lives in Peppermint Grove."

"He's done well for himself then – there were the lucky ones, I suppose, but most of us worked hard and saw little reward. You had to be *in the know*!"

Ruth took a right off Curtin Avenue and onto Eric Street – she could see the sea in the distance almost immediately.

"Do you think Dad regrets going home?"

"Oh, he did for a little while but you know he is a home-bird really and there were plenty of times – especially in the last few years – that he said he is glad that he did come back."

"You mean 'we' came back surely?"

Angela swallowed hard. "I came home a few months before he did because I was pregnant with you."

"Why did he stay on – was it to do with his work?"

Angela hesitated. "Work? Oh yes, that's what it was – his work delayed him." She turned her head and looked out the window, lost in her thoughts. She had played those few months back in her head during the plane journey, over and over – she didn't want to tell her daughter the truth. She was concerned that she wouldn't understand.

They parked at the beach and decided to walk along the sand. It was blissfully warm with the temperature just over thirty-two degrees and coming into the nicest part of the day.

"I was only here for the first time a couple of weeks ago actually. I went for dinner in the Tearooms."

"Oh, Myra and I used to dream of eating in there – but we had to make do with our homemade sandwiches." She chuckled.

"You never spoke of Myra before – have you kept in touch with her?"

Angela shook her head. "After I left Australia I was so happy to be home that I wanted to focus all my time and thoughts on Dublin. It wasn't like nowadays where you can just Skype someone for free. It took up to three weeks to get a letter – airmail was more than a week. And the telephone line would be so crackly and it was just too expensive."

"That must have been hard with Dad still here. He wasn't with you when I was born then?"

"Well, in any case men were never allowed into the theatre in those days and it was just as well sometimes."

"I think if I was having a child I'd want my husband to be there."

"Well, things were different in those days," Angela said curtly. "Things weren't great with your father and me for a number of reasons. I had been very lonely, you must remember. All sorts of things happened and well . . . let's just say they worked themselves out, thank God!"

Ruth was very curious – these were all new revelations. She would love to know more and she had plenty of time to draw it out from her mother.

"Who did you say you went to the Tearooms with?" Angela asked.

"A guy called Brian – Julia and I met him and his friends on Rottnest Island. We then met back here – I've seen him a couple of times."

It was Angela's greatest fear that her daughter would fall in love with an Australian and stay. It was the first thought that sprang to mind when Ruth had said that she was going to Perth in the first place.

"And is it serious?"

"No, Mum – I don't know him very well – we've just had a couple of dates."

"I'd like to meet him," Angela said forcefully.

Ruth hadn't expected such a strong reaction. "Why?"

"I want to make sure that he's good to you, Ruth."

"Ah, Mum – it's only been a few dates. But he would like to meet you too so I guess that you will."

Now Angela was surprised. She would have thought a man would shriek at the thought of meeting his girlfriend's mother so soon. She had to be careful not to be prejudiced. Not all Australian men were like Charlie Walters and she didn't want her daughter to know the real reason why she had left Australia.

Chapter Fifty-two

Michael got the DART from Howth Station to Tara Street. He enjoyed taking in the new architecture along the River Liffey – Dublin had come a long way. His walk finished at Julia's office – but she wasn't in work yet.

Gillian was thrilled to meet Julia's brother and gushed with pleasure as he spoke. He was attractive and she always fancied guys with receding hairlines.

"She should be here any minute – can I get you a coffee?" she gushed.

Michael nodded his head in appreciation. Gillian was a pleasant girl and he wondered why Julia had been so dismissive when she mentioned her before.

"That would be lovely, thanks."

"Milk?" she asked.

"Just black, please."

"I'm so pleased to meet you at last, Michael. Julia has told me so much about you – how do you feel now that you are home for good?"

"I'm very glad I've made the move – just hope that I get the job now."

"It's been difficult times – we've had to be very creative to survive. Julia is a great boss though – I've learned so much working for her."

"Glad to hear it."

With that the pounding of footsteps could be heard coming into the office. Michael and Gillian turned around.

"Morning, Gillian," said Julia. "Oh hi, Michael, I didn't realise you'd be in so early."

"It's really the afternoon for my body clock." He grinned. "Can I help you with anything?"

"Actually, now that you ask I could do with a hand with the figures for this month – I'm so behind and I have to send them in to the cruise company. Gillian, would you mind dropping the paperwork into my office. I think they were in yesterday's post and I didn't file it away before leaving."

"Of course," Gillian said with a beaming smile aimed at Michael.

When the office door was closed and brother and sister were sitting at the desk, Julia was happier than she had been for a long time.

"So are you ready for the interview tomorrow?"

Michael grimaced. "I'm nervous now – it was impetuous of me to throw in the towel the way I did but I really think I made the right move. I just hope I feel that way if I don't get the job."

Julia felt for her brother. "Well, you know, if you don't get it you can always come and work with me – it might be a nice change. Odette was considering coming in a few days to work with me at one point."

"Maybe she'll need to work even more now – now that she is on her own?"

Julia had thought about that too – she was concerned about how her sister was going to manage.

"What if the insurance won't pay?" she asked.

"I don't know how that works, Ju."

"I'm sure she wants to stay in her house – it's the other investments that she needs to offload."

"Well, now that I'm home I'm keen to help her sort things out

– no point having a brother who's a financial consultant without getting him to help."

"I told Odette that we would be out to her house for lunch – we should be finished up here by then."

Michael nodded – it sounded good.

Gillian watched through the window of Julia's office door. She was so jealous of her boss. Michael was her brother, of course, but it was obvious he adored her. She wondered if Julia realised how lucky she was and how much men were drawn to her? After the other night it was apparent that Dylan was a lost cause but Michael might be an easier fish to catch.

Lydia looked at her watch – it was eleven o'clock and she wanted to see Julia again. Her head was so full of wild thoughts she couldn't work and she'd had a difficult evening pondering over their chat in the Bailey pub. Julia was the rock of sense that kept her on the straight and narrow. She would wander up to Grafton Street and just pop into her office on the off-chance that she was there. She pulled on her light jacket and stepped out into the sunshine. It was a beautiful mild day for March.

Gillian was at the reception desk, waiting with a smile. When she saw that it was Lydia she rang through to Julia's office.

"It's Lydia for you, Julia," she said.

Julia turned and looked at Michael in a state of panic. Darn her! Why hadn't she rung first? She didn't want to see Michael upset so early on his arrival and especially with his big interview the next day.

"You'd better send her in," she said reluctantly.

Gillian went back to her work, oblivious of the situation that was about to unfold.

Lydia stopped dead at the door. She looked at Michael first and then at Julia.

"Oh, I'm so sorry, am I disturbing you?"

"Lydia!" Michael was astonished to see his old love.

Julia looked first at Michael and then at Lydia. She jumped to her feet and rushed over to her dumbstruck friend.

"Lydia – Michael was helping me do some figures before I present them to a company tomorrow – how are you?"

Lydia couldn't speak.

"Hello, Lydia," Michael said politely.

"Hi," she winced. "Sorry, Julia, I should have called. Maybe I'll come back another time."

"We're going to Malahide after we finish here so I can't do lunch today," Julia said, taking Lydia gently by the arm, ushering her out of the office and closing the door behind them.

"I'm sorry, Lydia – you didn't need to see him at the moment."

Lydia's eyes filled up. "I'm a mess, Julia – I can't seem to get through to Peter at all – he's just continued to brush it all under the carpet and carry on as if the other night never happened."

Gillian had her head behind the computer screen on her desk but all the time her ears were sharply pricked to pick up any information worth knowing.

"And the last person you need to see right now is my brother."

"Oh Julia, it always unsettles me when I see him. You know it's always been this way – and I can't cope with the rejection from Peter at the same time."

Gillian was putting two and two together and getting a perfect four.

"I'm sorry but we have to go to Malahide – can I call you later?" Julia suggested.

Lydia nodded. "Thanks, Julia, you're such a great friend."

Lydia almost tripped over on the way out and Julia looked over at Gillian who had obviously been listening to every word. Gillian's head ducked behind the screen again and Julia returned to her office.

"What's wrong with Lydia?" Michael was visibly shaken but Julia wasn't keen to start a full-blown conversation about her friend right now. "I can't believe I've seen her!"

"Nothing's wrong – she didn't know you were going to be here. Look, maybe we'll just finish up and go visit Odette now?"

"God, she looked gorgeous!" Michael shook his head.

"Michael, I'm sorry that you had to see her but I can't talk to you about her – she spoke to me in confidence."

"Fuck me – I think I'm too old for bombshells, Julia."

Julia actually felt bad for her brother in light of the entire Lydia saga.

"Look, I'm sorry to change the subject but we have to move – let's go and see Odette and maybe you can come and help me tomorrow?"

"Sure – I can finish this in the morning – my interview will be over by eleven."

Julia sighed. "That would be a great help, thanks – it's nice actually, having you here."

"This is a lovely set-up that you have, Ju, and your figures are coming in good. Glad to see someone doing well in the recession."

"It's a lot of hard work but it seems to be paying off."

Julia handed Michael his coat and breezed by Gillian. "I'll be back at about four if anyone is looking for me!"

As they walked out to the car Michael had to pry more. "So please, Ju – tell me – what's up with Lydia?"

"I said – I can't say."

"Did Perfect Peter not propose then?"

Julia knew that her brother was going to drag it out of her at one stage or another so it was probably better to get it over with.

"She's gutted because he has said that he doesn't want to rush into marriage."

Michael's eyes brightened. "Ah, so there's hope for me yet!"

Julia frowned at him. "Just concentrate on one thing at a time – and take my advice – leave her alone, okay!"

"Hey, did she propose then on the 29th? I was thinking about it during the flight. I put up a request for proposals on Facebook but didn't get a comment!"

Julia laughed. "If I tell, you must promise not to say anything to Lydia, okay?"

"Cross my heart!" he said making a Boy Scout's pledge with his fingers.

"Okay, she brought it up and, well, let's just say it didn't appeal to him. He doesn't want to get engaged."

Michael laughed out loud.

Julia thumped him in the arm. "You are too cruel."

"I'm sorry, Ju, but it was a crazy idea – and he said no – well, it's funny."

"I can't believe you're so heartless, Michael."

"I'm not – I mean, I really do feel for her but you know she could have had me!"

"I know that you're irresistible but she wants Perfect – I mean Peter."

Michael laughed even more. "You know, I think she's falling off that pedestal I had her on!"

Julia frowned. "If you're telling me now that you don't like her because she might be available again, I swear, Michael, you will rot in hell!"

Michael shook his head. "Ah, don't be so serious, Ju! Actually, I was thinking I might ask Gillian on a date."

Julia frowned harder. "I don't want you seeing her – there's something freaky about her – she's a good worker and all that but there are times when I think she is a bit psycho about men – she seems to have the hots for Dylan anyway. Besides, you need to concentrate on getting that job tomorrow!"

The pair drove to Malahide, discussing tactics and interview techniques, so Michael didn't have a chance to consider how he would feel on seeing his bereft sister.

Dylan was on his way out the door as they parked in the drive.

"Hi, Michael, good to see you again – I hear you're back for good?"

Michael held out his hand and shook Dylan's.

"Yes, back for good – hope to get working now. How is she doing?"

Dylan smiled. "Good form today – she's looking forward to seeing you. She wasn't great last night – sure she wasn't, Julia?"

Julia shook her head. "I was glad that you were here, Dylan. Why don't you go on in, Michael, so you can be with her on your own."

Michael nodded and went inside.

Dylan turned to Julia. "So how are you doing?"

"I'm fine – I was just in work. Actually Gillian has been great, keeping the show on the road for me."

Dylan hesitated. "Eh, that's good. She comes across as a bit crazy but I think her heart must be in the right place!"

Julia was puzzled at this reaction – why had he asked Gillian out again then? But certainly 'crazy' was a good word to describe her. Or maybe 'desperate' would be a better one. She wanted to hook a good catch and seemed to think that Julia was the supplier of eligible men – Julia's own fault admittedly. Well, she would do her very best to steer her brother and anyone else away.

Dylan was smart – a really clued-in guy. Whatever Gillian was, she had certainly helped Julia to figure out in her own head what she thought of Dylan. She was becoming more fond of him every time she saw him since Craig's terrible passing and she didn't want Gillian or anyone else getting close to him – but now it looked like she had left it too late because in one month he would be gone for a year around the world. It was terrible timing and her own fault.

Chapter Fifty-three

Ruth received a text from Brian before she woke up the next morning.

I couldn't sleep all night. Call me please ?

Ruth was keen to hear his voice. She looked at her watch. It was only seven. She could hear her mother snoring in the room next door.

She dialled but didn't have to wait long.

"Ruth – g'day. How are you going?"

"Good, thanks – my mum and I went out to Cott beach last night and got fish and chips."

"It must be nice to see her."

"Yeah, it is – how's the house coming on?"

"The walls are up and the roof is going on next week. That Arthurs chap is causing us a bit of grief though – seems to be having cash-flow probs! It's going to be a beauty. You should come and see it."

Ruth needed to think about that carefully. "Eh, I'm not sure my mother is ready for that."

"Why don't I just drive by later and we can maybe go to Fraser's for dinner? My treat."

"Where's that?"

"It's the place in King's Park where we parked last time."

"I remember. Will we have to book?"

"Leave it with me. Call by – I'll be at the site all day."

"I've got to go to work now but I suppose we could go to dinner if you like – is that place very expensive?"

"Don't worry about the price – I said it's my treat."

Ruth was grateful for his gesture and she was delighted that he was keen to impress her mother by choosing such a classy restaurant. "Okay then, if you insist."

"Fine – I'll call by at seven, okay?"

"See you at seven."

Ruth was feeling nervous already. She wasn't sure how her mother would behave – she had always been acrimonious towards Australian men. Maybe she could sway her opinion. And if anyone could suss a person out it would be Angela Travers. She had nothing to lose and they were going to have a nice meal regardless.

Her mother stirred and got out of her bed. She went to the bathroom, giving Ruth just enough time to think about what she was going to say.

Angela came into Ruth's room and smiled when she saw her daughter lying on the bed.

"Good morning, love – I slept like a log – I guess that's partly the jet lag! But it's been very difficult to sleep with your father this last year or two. He's always moaning in the middle of the night with his arthritis and he doesn't realise that he wakes me up!"

"Why don't you get two single beds and put them together? That way you each have your own space and are still beside each other."

"Now that's not a bad idea, Ruth – I'll say it to your father when I get home. It's great to have the bed to myself."

"Can I get you some breakfast?"

"Not at all – I can help myself – you have to go out to work."

"I'm putting the kettle on anyway."

"I'll make us scrambled eggs on toast – how does that sound? And you can get ready for work."

"Okay – thanks, Mum – it's so great having you here."

Angela was feeling more comfortable the longer she was in the country – time must indeed be the greatest healer of all. She set about whisking the eggs and was busy over the stove when Ruth came into the kitchen.

"Mum – Brian was wondering if we would join him for dinner this evening?"

"Brian – oh, your boyfriend?"

"Well, it's early days – he's still just a friend."

"I'd better meet him then," Angela said with a smile. "I just want you to be happy, love."

The clock approached seven and Ruth's stomach started to flit. She had chosen to wear a blue dress and her strappy silver sandals. Her mother was composed at the kitchen table – sipping a cup of tea and looking serene in a rose-printed fabric sundress.

Brian was at the front door at seven o'clock sharp and wearing what Ruth now considered his trademark white shirt. She loved how it contrasted with his tan.

Pride swept over her as she introduced her mother to the man with the dark good looks.

"Mum, this is Brian. Brian – my mum, Angela."

Angela's first impressions of her daughter's attractive friend brought a smile to her face.

"Very pleased to meet you," she said, holding out her hand.

"Good to meet you," he smiled.

The three got into his Jeep and drove the short trip to Fraser's Restaurant.

Ruth had fond memories of the wonderful picnic she had shared with Brian not too long before. How they had walked through the manicured pathway paved with beautiful palms and the lights of the skyscrapers had started to turn on one by one as the sun dipped lower in the sky.

"My, look at the Anzac memorial!" Angela declared. "You know, I always think of my friend Myra's Anzac biscuits when I hear that word."

"I bought Anzac biscuits when I was in Coles not so long ago," said Ruth. "They are gorgeous – although I did squash them up a bit by mistake!" She grinned over at Brian.

"Well, you never tasted anything like Myra's. Full of oats and she used to use honey as well as syrup – lovely!"

"My mum used to make Anzac bickies too," said Brian. "I'd take them to school when I was a kid and swap them for choccy when I could."

The three entered the spacious foyer of Fraser's which was built in the round so that the full expanse of the bay could be enjoyed by its patrons. The windows were tall and wherever you sat you could be assured of a good view from your seat. The maitre d' showed them over to a window seat and they took a menu each to peruse the selection.

"Yum – I'll have the steak, I think," Ruth said.

"It's really good here. Do you see anything that you like, Angela?" asked Brian.

"Oh well, there's so much choice I don't know where to start. Maybe I'll have the chicken."

Angela was impressed with Brian and she liked his relaxed easy manner. But she would reserve her judgement on him until she had spoken to him some more.

Angela was laughing heartily by the time dessert was served.

"I used to do the late shift when your father came in from work," she said, nodding towards Ruth. "We'd scrape up the leftovers and bring them home – Kevin loved the chocolate gateaux that we served and sometimes he'd have it for breakfast – of course he wouldn't remember that now."

"I'm surprised that you never told me any of this before," Ruth said with her chin resting on her palm.

"I suppose I swept any memories of my time in Australia under the carpet – I wasn't all that keen to remember some of it. But we did have good fun with the other waitresses. Alan Bond – you know, the businessman – came into the restaurant a couple of times but none of us knew that he was going to be such an important figure in Perth. He was very definitely a player."

"I bet you could tell a story or two alright, Angela. And who owned the restaurant?"

Brian wondered if he might have some memories of it.

"It was owned by Charles Walters – he was a really wealthy man and this restaurant was only a folly – he made his money from shipping," Angela said in a very matter-of-fact manner.

Ruth's ears pricked up at the mention of Charles Walters' name. So it was a business letter after all – written to her boss. But, why on earth keep a letter for all those years? Like a treasured keepsake next to her diaries?

"He was good to his staff as a rule but only ever came in as a guest," Angela went on. "He was never involved in the running of the place."

Brian was putting two and two together and was obviously about to launch into the fact that he was working on his house. But Ruth kicked under the table to silence him.

"Tell us more about him, Mum."

"Oh, I didn't know much about him – but he did tell me about his history – he had come from very humble beginnings. His father was English and one of a twin – they played truant often around the streets of Perth at the end of the nineteenth century and they were sent to borstal."

"Borstal?" Ruth quizzed.

"Yes, an industrial school – like the one in Artane or Letterfrack at home. God-awful places, by all accounts."

"Like the boys' reformatory on Rottnest Island?" Ruth asked.

"That was the place – they used to send boys there – I think it was a prison for Aborigines as well. Terrible thing to do to young lads – it sounded like Alcatraz to me when I first heard about it back then."

Ruth was stunned. A link between this Charles Walters and Rottnest!

"Well, Charles credited his success to the fact that his father threatened him with borstal if he didn't work hard at school and get himself a respectable profession," Angela went on. "Apparently Charles's uncle died in a freak accident while he was at the reformatory on Rottnest – I suppose it could have been a good beating or something that did it. Anyway I am sure they don't keep records of that sort of thing – no more than they recorded half the deaths in the Irish industrial schools."

"That's amazing," Brian said. "I've always been fascinated by Rottnest and it is a strangely haunted place."

Ruth was silenced by the story. Could she have been prompted to delve further into this mystery by the ghost of Charles Walters' uncle? She'd had such a strange experience there.

"How old was the boy when he died?" Brian asked.

"Oh, I don't know that sort of detail – I just know that when Charles's father returned to the mainland he was tormented and driven to become a financially successful man so that his son would never be sent to such a place."

Ruth was beyond curious now – she was desperate to know why her mother was writing to her boss. How was everything so connected? The fact that she met Brian at Peppermint Grove and then again on Rottnest – it was like they were meant to be there at exactly the same time. And then the letter . . . what was in it and why was her mother telling her all of these facts about her time in Perth now? When for years she had brooded over diaries and letters and kept all her thoughts to herself?

Angela looked at Ruth. "I suppose being here has me thinking about all the things that happened. Charles was a good man – a product of hard work and dedication. His father's time spent in the reformatory would have done him good. It's a pity the same can't be said for all his family."

Ruth's ears pricked up – was Angela going to elaborate even more?

"So," Angela continued, "Ruth tells me that you are an architect, Brian – do you enjoy it?"

Brian was also curious to know more about Charles Walters but Angela had obviously said enough for one night.

"I love my job – I've a partner who is boss of the building side of the business and we generally go around doing rebuilds and large extensions. Mostly on homes – we don't do commercial as a rule."

"Lovely – I suppose you are busy with the building going on at the moment?"

Brian nodded. "Yes, work is good. We are doing a rebuild at the moment in Peppermint Grove and it's coming on well."

Ruth kicked him again under the table. She wanted the evening to end on a good note. Her mother had divulged enough for one night. It was a huge revelation and she wanted to draw her mother's story out slowly and gently.

Chapter Fifty-four

"He's a very nice chap." Angela said the next morning as she shared toast and coffee with her daughter over breakfast.

"I'm glad you like him – he's full of interesting stories about life and he has a really spiritual perspective on everything – I've never met anyone like him."

"He's certainly not a typical Australian man. But then again most Australians are only a couple of generations away from being Irish, English or Italian – especially on this side of the country."

It was true – and Brian was keen to find out more about his Irish heritage. It was a wonderful coincidence that her mother's letter had led her to him but also ironic that she possibly would have met him regardless as they both ended up on Rottnest at exactly the same time. She considered telling her mother the fact that she had seen the letter but instead decided to wait.

"What are your plans for today, Ruth?"

"I thought we might go out to Fremantle this evening – there's a place called Little Creature's Brewery that Brian said was very nice."

"A brewery? I'm not sure I would like that."

"They do amazing pizzas though and you do like them, don't you?"

"Yes, I do – I like Fremantle too. That's the town that Alan Bond transformed – he hosted the America's Cup out of there in the eighties – I remember chuckling to myself when I heard about him and all those highflyers. I was flabbergasted to hear he went bust in the nineties."

"We could pop by and Brian can show you the house that he's working on if you like?"

"I don't mind. I think I'll come into town and do a bit of shopping today while you're at work."

"That's a good idea – we can meet for lunch so."

Angela stood up. "Well, I'd better have my shower and get ready to face the heat of the day."

"Great – we can go in about twenty minutes if that's okay with you."

Angela went into the bathroom and Ruth decided to see if Julia was online. She wanted to tell her what she had found out the night before.

It was eleven thirty in the evening but Julia's Skype was online so Ruth called.

"Hello, Ruth?" Julia was wearing her pyjamas and sitting up in bed.

"Hi, Julia – I'm just giving you a buzz before I go in to work. How are things there?"

"Oh, Ruth, it's just been manic here. Michael is home and has an interview in the morning. Mum is up in Gerry's but will be back tomorrow. Poor Odette has good and bad days. It turns out Gillian was stalking Dylan who really is a gem and I've been so wrong about him and now he's announced that he plans to go around the world for a year. He's lovely and I'll miss him when it comes to looking after Odette – he's so good to her and the kids. How are things with you?"

"Well, I've been wrong about Brian – you were right that I should give him a chance to explain – in fact, he came into my work and made me listen to his side of the story. And he has even taken me and Mum out for dinner."

"Oh wow! That's amazing! He seems to be really interested, Ruth."

"And it gets better – Mum really likes him and she opened up for the first time about Charles Walters – it turns out that he was her boss. She says he was really nice but he sounds like he was old – about Horatio's age if he was still alive. But Brian said that he died not long after his son, didn't he?"

"I wonder what the son was like? He's the one that you need to quiz Angela about."

"Yeah, I think so – but wait for it – remember that freaky experience I had on Rottnest?"

"Yeah?"

"Well, this man Charles Walters had an uncle who died when he was sent to the reformatory there as a boy!"

"That's spooky – I wonder how he died."

"No idea but Mum might know more than she is saying. I feel so connected to this story for some reason."

"Ruth, you have to ask her straight out." Julia was clapping her hands with excitement. "This is a brill story – oh, Angela should write a book about it all!"

"I was thinking of bringing her out to Peppermint Grove later on our way to Fremantle."

"Do, Ruth, and tell me what happens tomorrow."

"I will – and keep me posted on the Dylan saga!"

"Of course – and I knew there was something I was forgetting to tell you – Lydia proposed to her policeman and it turns out that he doesn't want to get married – he just wants to live with her until they get to know each other better. And she was selling her apartment and everything – I swear some men just take the biscuit!"

"Wow, you are busy in Dublin! Look, we'll talk tomorrow – sleep well."

"Have a good day and give my love to Angela."

Ruth was brimming over with excitement. She was getting closer to her mother by the minute and she hoped that visiting Peppermint Grove would bring her some peace.

Angela had a short rest when she got back to the house after shopping. It had been a lovely day wandering around all the new shops that weren't there in the seventies. At this rate Ruth would be home soon. When she'd met her daughter for lunch the two had chatted with a closeness that Angela had never enjoyed before. Maybe coming to Australia was the move that they both had needed.

For Angela it was wonderful to enjoy her daughter's company without her husband's presence. He had always been protective of his relationship with his daughter and Angela was well aware why. But this was a good place to tell Ruth the truth. There had never been a good time and for many years Angela had considered never telling her at all but now that she was here she had a duty to come clean.

When Angela returned to Dublin, at least Ruth would have the comfort of Brian who was a good man. It was strange for Angela and eerie in many ways – her greatest fear was in some way a prophetic feeling that she had harboured deep inside. She had always known that Ruth would end up back here one way or another and it was better that it was this way than any other.

Suddenly she heard the front door bang.

"Mum, I'm back!"

Angela went out to the hall and gave her daughter a kiss on the cheek. "I'm not long in ahead of you.

"I'm roasting – let me have a shower and then we might pop in to see Brian on the way to Fremantle."

Angela was pleased by the idea. She had loved Fremantle – the hippy market was where she had picked up some of her nicest clothes. She thought that she still had a kaftan somewhere in the attic that she had kept from those days in the sun.

Ruth didn't take long and it was only five o'clock when they set off down Railway Road.

She expected to see a reaction from her mother and was pleased at the relaxed nonchalant way that she looked at the houses as they raced by.

"Are we in Peppermint Grove yet?"

"Yes, we are just there now."

"I was only here a couple of times. Myra was very strange about coming into posh areas. The view is beautiful from here though, isn't it?"

Ruth agreed and drove on. She turned up a side street and the road sign Peppermint Grove Road flashed at the side of the kerb. Ruth glanced at her mother and saw her wince upon seeing the words.

"Does that say Peppermint Grove Road?"

"Yes," Ruth said, trying desperately to sound casual. "This is where Brian is working. He's still here – he texted me just before we left."

Ruth watched as her mother craned her neck to see the house numbers. She passed Number 14 then 11 then 7 and as they pulled up at Number 5 Angela froze.

"Are you okay, Mum?"

"Yes, yes, I'm fine – I think I'll stay here."

Angela looked as if she had seen a ghost. Ruth felt very cruel for not telling the truth to her mother now. She should have warned her where they were going.

But Brian was already at the gate, standing next to the Number 5 on the pillar. The house had come on leaps and bounds and Ruth hardly recognised the place from the empty plot that had been there when she first visited with Julia a month before.

Brian walked over to the car and leaned his head down to the level of the side window.

"G'day, ladies. Nice of you to drop by. Do you want to see the house now, Ruth?"

Angela was fanning herself with a leaflet that she had found in the pocket of the door.

"Angela, would you like to pop in and see my design?"

"It's very hot," she said shaking her head. "I'd much rather stay here."

Brian looked at Ruth as she got out of the car.

"Are you sure, Mum?"

Angela nodded vehemently. "Quite sure. Now you two go ahead and leave me with the air-conditioning on."

"Okay, we won't be long," said Brian. "They're finishing up for today."

Ruth followed Brian up the drive.

"I feel terrible – she's obviously upset. I didn't warn her."

Brian was concerned for her mother too. "Maybe say something later. I won't come with you to Fremantle – she probably needs to speak with you alone. The Walters family are all gone – that nephew doesn't seem concerned about the finer details of the house. I have a gut feeling that he's developing it for resale."

They wandered into the new house which was taking shape beautifully. Brian really was a very talented architect. It was modern and spacious and had a good feel about it.

"I'm impressed. You've done so much in such a short time."

"We have to be quick – there's another job waiting for us in Mosman Park soon as we finish here. Thanks for calling by, Ruth – it's just a shame your mum didn't come in."

"I know but thanks anyway, Brian. I'll call you later and see what she says. It's all very weird – especially when she spoke about the reformatory. I feel this story isn't over yet."

Brian nodded as he walked her back down the drive.

"Catch you later," he said.

He gave her a warm kiss hard on the lips that sent a thrill through her spine. It would have to keep her going until she saw him again. For now she had a more pressing job at hand and she had to be very careful that she did it without upsetting her mother.

Angela was silent for the entire car journey and as they turned on to Mews Road and off the Esplanade she let out a loud sigh.

Ruth parked at the Little Creatures Brewery which was a hive of energy and activity with flashing lights and jazzy new-age music greeting all patrons as they passed through the doors. The symbol of a Cupid drinking a pint of beer was painted boldly under the eaves and popped up on the menu and along the walls. It had the strangest atmosphere – almost church-like with high ceilings, white pillar candles dotted along the bar and long rows of tables. There was an outdoor option but 'The Doctor' was sweeping in through the back door and they decided to stay inside. They took a booth so they could have some privacy.

"Sorry, Mum, I didn't expect it to be so noisy."

To Ruth's surprise her mother shrugged and said that she liked it. The kitchen was open-plan and behind it the huge silver drums used for holding the freshly brewed beer glistened like giant trophies.

They scanned the large card menu and Ruth felt bad for doing what she had done. Her mother's silence spoke a multitude. Did she suspect that Ruth knew possibly more about the Walters family than she would like her to know?

"Is everything okay, Mum?"

"Of course – I said I liked it here."

"No, I mean . . . you've been very quiet since we left Brian."

Angela put down the card and looked her daughter straight in the eyes.

"Did you know where you were bringing me tonight?"

"Here?"

"No, not here!" Angela said crossly. "What is Brian's business with Number 5?"

"He's doing the building work for a man named Arthurs."

"But why that house and how did you really meet Brian?"

It was Ruth's turn to come clean – she couldn't expect her mother to tell the truth if she didn't come clean first.

"Okay, Mum . . ."

Just then a waitress came over to take their order. They chose a pizza each and a salad to share before getting their privacy back.

"I have a confession to make," said Ruth. "Before I left I went up to the attic to store some bits and pieces and I came across a box and a letter that was addressed to Charles Walters at Number 5, Peppermint Grove Road. I remembered that you mentioned Peppermint Grove and I wanted to know more, so when Julia came over here we searched the house out and that's where we met Brian. I was curious to know who Charles Walters was and why you never posted the letter. But now that I know he was your boss – it was probably just some work stuff and, well, I let my imagination get the better of me."

Angela was white in the face now. This was not the way that she had planned on telling her daughter this news. She pondered if this was the right place but with so much noise and so many people there probably wasn't any better.

"And what did you think?"

"Honestly?"

Angela nodded.

Ruth continued. "We thought that maybe this man was someone that you had an affair with or something like that."

Angela laughed. "Do I strike you as the type?"

Ruth was now mortified. She wanted to tell her mother about her own infidelity with Ian but couldn't bring herself to do it.

"I'm only messing with you, love," Angela said gently. "No, I didn't have an affair while I was here. You see, the reason I left Australia was because your father let me down. Something terrible happened to me while I was working in the restaurant. I told you already that Charles Walters was a good man and that was true but he had a son who wasn't. Charlie was a silver-spoon kid. He drove a Mustang convertible and flaunted his cash about town. He had any girl that he wanted. He used to come into the restaurant and demand the best table. He never paid and always felt up the waitresses while his girlfriend was in the bathroom. Sometimes he would come in on his own and he was always very drunk before leaving."

Ruth was agog. She hung on her mother's every word. Something told her inside that what she was about to hear was not something that her mother would necessarily have ever told her if she hadn't come to Australia.

"One night he hung around until after closing. He particularly liked me because of my red hair. He followed me out to the back kitchen and small staff room that was just for the waitresses. He got it into his head that I was teasing him and I assured him that I was a married woman. He said that he didn't mind." Angela stopped to take a deep breath. "Anyway this night he grabbed me and told me that if I screamed he would kill me. He had a knife in his hand and was getting some sort of twisted pleasure from threatening me. He forced himself upon me and, well, I don't need to tell you I was scared and I let him have his way." Angela's eyes filled up as she continued with the story. "I was a broken woman after that – I went home and your father was in the pub. Myra helped me to have a bath and she gave me a shot of brandy. I was vomiting and terrified. When your father got home he didn't understand. He had drink taken and blamed me for having sex with another man. He was more hurt at that thought than anything I had been put through. It was horrific and I wrote to Mr Walters telling him that I wasn't going back to my job. His son must have told him what happened because he came around to my house full of apologies and offering me money not to charge him. I wasn't interested in anything like that – I was unhappy with your father at this stage and his drinking and I knew the only way I could recover would be if I got home to Dublin. Myra helped me to organise it and that's what I did."

Ruth was horrified to the core. "But did you not press charges?"

"I knew there was no guarantee that the police would believe me – we are talking about rich and powerful people – it was a different time. But Charles Walters knew what his son was like and he was sick of him."

Angela paused. She wasn't sure if she was ready for the next piece that she had to tell.

"So I went home and had you and your father still couldn't cope with the fact that I had been with another man."

Ruth banged the table. She was so angry with her father. How could he be so spineless! "I don't understand why Dad let you down this way – why didn't he support you?"

Angela shook her head. "You have to understand it was a different time – he genuinely thought that I must have led the young Charlie Walters on. But his father knew just what his son was like."

Suddenly a dreadful thought struck Ruth. Her eyes widened as the penny dropped.

"Mum – the baby you had – that was me – was that from the . . .?" She couldn't bring herself to say it.

Angela's lips tightened. It was a good time to tell her. She hadn't had sexual relations with her husband for three months before the rape – there was no doubt in the world that her daughter's father was Charlie Walters. A nod was enough to speak a multitude.

Ruth gasped. The man who she always thought was her father was not.

"And Charlie Walters is dead?" She remembered what Brian had told her about the son – killed in a car accident.

Angela nodded again. "Charles wrote to me after I got back to Dublin. He told me that his son had been killed in a car accident – I wasn't surprised as he was always racing around town and was a heavy drinker. That was when he told me about his humble beginnings and how sorry he was that he had let his family down. There was nobody left for him to leave his fortune to. I cried when I read the old man's words. He was broken and had lost everything and he desperately wanted to see you – his grandchild. He wanted some connection with the next generation. I couldn't do it though – I didn't want him or his money and I couldn't allow them to enter our family. Kevin needed his father so much when we returned – he had developed an Australian accent and it wasn't easy for a child to be different in seventies Ireland. I begged your father to come home and when he saw you he found it difficult at first to hold you but you were the only girl . . . and with the years we never mentioned the differences. It was easy – you are the picture of me."

"And what about Dad – how long did he stay on?"

"For six months but that only helped him to make up his mind to come home. He was hurt and I was hurt and in our roundabout way we found each other again. We are still together so there must have been something pulling at us both."

Ruth was trembling at this stage.

Just then the waitress arrived and put their food down on the table. "Enjoy!" she said and left.

"I wish I had a stiff drink now!" Ruth said. "I need one after that."

Anglea put her hand out and rested it on her daughter's. "I'm sorry that I had to tell you in this way. There was never a proper time or place to do it – when you were in school you were too young – in college you were under too much pressure and then for the last couple of years I felt like I was losing you or something."

Ruth understood what her mother was saying – all the years she had spent with Ian she had lost herself. There had been enough revelations tonight, however, without bringing him into the conversation.

"I don't know what to say, Mum. And that letter in the attic – what is in it? Why didn't you post it to Charles Walters?"

"He had offered me money and all sorts, as I said, when he came to my house begging me not to charge his son – and later he contacted me again and said he wanted to help provide for his grandchild and be able to see the child. But all I was interested in at that point was to get back home and have you born there. Then, when your father returned to Dublin I didn't want to have any contact with the Walters in case it would jeopardise our marriage. When I finally got around to answering Charles, I heard from Myra that he had died – a year to the day after his son. Some said it was a broken heart but it was a heart attack. I don't know what happened to the wife."

"Emily," Ruth prompted.

"Yes, that was her name – how did you know?"

"She died only recently – Brian was asking around. A nephew inherited the house and she had lived alone for years. Oh my God – that would make her my granny!"

Angela gently pinched her daughter's hand. "No, they are not family – none of them – you are a Travers and we are your family."

Ruth realised that Angela had dealt with the trauma in her own way many years ago and had come to terms with it to a great extent – until recent events had stirred it all up again. Now it was her own turn to deal with it.

Her mind was racing – this meant that she was really half-Australian and that the house in Peppermint Grove was her ancestral home. In a funny way it might just be the key to her future – a future with the man rebuilding it.

Chapter Fifty-five

Michael was high on adrenalin as he walked out of the interview. He had done his very best. But then it began to perturb him that he had spent so much of the time talking. While he was in full flight he felt that he was giving the interview panel what they wanted to hear. But with each step he took along Custom House Quay doubt began to seep in. He was strolling through the middle of the Famine memorial statues when panic hit. The panel had never said if or when they would call him for a second interview or let him know if he had the job. He stopped to look at the gaunt sculpted figures and scrawny mongrel at the back of the pack and winced – a stark reminder of the Irish Holocaust. How many of those poor souls boarded 'coffin ships' to be part of the famous Irish Diaspora? What if he didn't get this job – or one of any worth? Would he have to set off on his travels again? After all, he was forty now and there were thousands of younger graduates with masters and doctorates knocking around that would do the job for half what he expected to be paid.

He continued walking until he came to Butt Bridge and crossed over in the direction of College Green – he had promised Julia that he would go straight to her after the interview.

Julia made Michael a cup of coffee and shut the door of her

office hard. She didn't want Gillian listening in on their conversation.

"Go through it again with me. Why do you think it was such a disaster?"

Michael shook his head. "It's been five years since I've had an interview and I'd hardly call the one that I had for the job in Singapore an interview – they headhunted me. I rambled on too much, Ju – I was like the Duracell Bunny."

"It's natural to feel that way after an interview – don't worry about it. Did you make massive mistakes?"

Michael gasped. "That's just it. I can't think of anything that I said that was of any merit. I was good about blowing my own trumpet alright but one of the panel was just staring at me – she never even asked one question but she was writing it all down like an android of some sort."

Julia didn't know what to say to help. "Come on, let's get out of here and go for a walk on Grafton Street – do you want to go to Bewleys?"

Michael nodded.

All the while they walked he talked and rolled his eyes and shook his head.

Julia stopped when they came to the top of the street.

"Hang on – what's the worse that can happen?"

Michael frowned. "I won't get the job – isn't it obvious?"

"We don't know that yet and if you don't there are other jobs in Ireland. It's not like you're going to starve – you could rent out the apartment and live with us for a while?"

"Granddad and I would end up in the pub every night if I moved in! No, I need my own space. I'm not like you, Ju – I've lived on my own too long."

"Well, here's another idea – I wasn't joking when I said you could work for me – I need someone to share the responsibility and you are perfect – it might be nice for you to get involved in the marketing and other areas – not always doing figures – what do you say?"

Michael looked at her. "Thanks, Ju – I don't want to seem ungrateful or anything but I would need a good salary."

"We could look at share options – I might like to split the company up a bit and we would be running it together? I'm thirty-five this year and don't want to be a career woman all my life – watching those around me this last few months has made me assess just what the hell I am doing with my life!"

They walked on.

"It's a nice suggestion, Ju, but let's just wait and see – I get the feeling that you're only trying to make me feel better."

Julia shook her head. "No, Michael, I have selfish motives of my own here. I am too caught up in the business and I need to diversify – your timing is perfect. Just think about it, please?"

Michael nodded his head although he was convinced that she was only trying to make him feel better after his lousy interview.

Dylan was on his way into Odette's house and he smiled when he saw Julia's car there. He hoped that she hadn't forgotten about the upcoming St Patrick's Day parade. If only there was some way that he could have got on friendly terms before now! But it was really too late – he would be gone in two weeks and she was now busy with her brother and the rest of her family. It was blatantly clear that Gillian had tried to trap him when she asked him to meet her. She said she wanted to discuss the pressures that Julia was under but as they chatted he could see that she wasn't concerned for her boss at all. She had even tried to make a pass at him and in a way he felt sorry for the silly girl.

Julia answered the door as Odette was in the kitchen serving dinner for the children.

"Hi, Dylan – Odette was hoping that you were coming for dinner tonight – she has prepared a lasagne for us all."

"Sounds delicious – when you live on your own anything you don't have to make yourself is good."

"Believe me, when you live with your family anything you don't have to cook is good," she said with a smile.

The warmth that she greeted him with made Dylan relax. He hadn't been putting his foot in his mouth with Julia recently – maybe the entire family had just become more considerate of each other in light of what they had all been through.

"Hi, Dylan," Odette said happily. "I made us all a big dinner. The kids have no school tomorrow so the long weekend has begun."

"I'd like to take them to the pictures tomorrow afternoon if that's okay with you, Odette?" Dylan said.

Odette nodded. "That would be great, thanks – I want to do a spring clean. The weather has been so lovely I want to make the place nice."

Julia and Dylan were pleased to hear the positive tone in Odette's voice.

"I'll be in work tomorrow but I could meet you after the movies if you like?" Julia suggested to Dylan.

"Great – I'm going to take them out to the Brass Monkey in Howth – you know they love to see the seals and if the weather is anything like today it will be lovely."

"We can all go?" Julia said, looking at Odette.

"Well, if you don't mind, I've had an offer from my neighbour to go to a fundraiser – a kind of girlie day out in aid of the lifeboat. I might just go along if I feel up to it."

"That's a great idea," Julia nodded. "Okay, Dylan, let's book that and I'll see you after work."

It was a strange set-up but Odette was getting much-needed support and Julia wanted to help in the same way that Dylan did. The fact that she was warming to his company was just a consequence of that – but a nice one!

Peter came through the door of his apartment and slouched straight onto the couch. It had been a rough day and he had seen some things that he would have been much happier not to have seen.

Lydia stepped out of the bedroom on hearing him enter.

"Hi, Peter – you're home late?"

He shook his head. "I've had the most horrendous day, Lydia – I can't talk about it."

Lydia did want to talk – she wanted to talk about everything between them. She wasn't happy just pottering along. She had thought that Peter was a fast mover and wanted to be settled like her. Instead he had just been perfect at enticing a woman enough to think that she had a guy who was ready to commit. But the fact was that he wasn't the commitment type or else he would have married his previous girlfriend. Julia had warned her about men like this before but Lydia had never suspected for an instant that Peter was one of them. She could see herself in five years' time still living in his apartment and no change in their status. She wasn't desperate to have a big white wedding but she wanted kids – and soon.

"Peter, I think we need to talk about things – I can't go on like nothing has happened for us. I laid my cards on the table and we need to see where we are going."

Peter turned on the TV. The news was on.

The headlines showed that there had been a rise in sex offenders and the treatment centres were brimming over.

Peter waved the remote control at the TV. "Do you see what's out there, Lydia – the scum that I have to pick up and prosecute – the things that are happening to young men and women and children all over the city."

"I just want to talk about our future."

Peter looked at her with the severe wildness that she had seen in his eyes the night that they had spent together in the Unicorn. "What is the future going to be like – will Dublin be the sort of place to bring up children?"

"We can move if you like – down to Waterford – where your parents are."

Peter hissed. "I live with horror everyday, Lydia – I know that you want to paint a pretty little world around you but I just want to live for now and enjoy what I have – what we have. Why are you so determined to ruin it? Jesus, we are only six months together! Most women wouldn't put this sort of pressure on until they were six years going out."

Then Lydia realised that she had to be strong and do something about her situation immediately. She was lucky that she saw it clearly now before she fell any further.

"I don't think you have any intention of taking our relationship to the next stage."

"It's getting less likely now, isn't it?" he said wryly.

"I th-th-think I should move out." Her voice trembled. Her stomach was flipping.

He just looked up at her and raised his eyebrows but showed no real emotion.

"I'm going," she said.

She took her coat and bag and slammed the door behind her and he didn't try to stop her.

Chapter Fifty-six

The next morning Ruth rang Brian. She wanted to make sense of all of the information that Angela had told her the night before. When she heard his voice at the end of the line she felt relief.

"G'day, Ruth – what did you think of Little Creatures?"

"Well, I certainly won't forget that place in a hurry – Brian, my mum told me the most unbelievable story – I'm finding it difficult to digest the news. When can I see you?"

"I'll meet you after work. Come to Peppy Grove."

Ruth sighed. How ironic – that house was where her father had lived. But he was a brute and it made her feel bad about herself.

"Okay – I'll clock off early and call by about two."

"Ruth, are you okay?"

"I'm a bit shook but I don't want to talk about it over the phone. I'll see you about two o'clock."

"See you then." He wanted to say 'I miss you' but didn't want to sound soppy. He couldn't wait to see her.

When she hung up she was tempted to call Julia but she heard her mother stir – she would try to call when she got into work.

Ruth parked outside Number 5. She would have loved to see the old house – maybe Brian still had a photograph. Her mind raced. The owner was her cousin in some way – albeit very distant.

Julia hadn't been on Skype so Ruth figured that she might have stayed over in Odette's and had her phone offline. Either way the news could wait. She needed to digest what her mother had told her the night before. Anyway she was keen to see what Brian thought of her news.

Brian was around the back and Ruth asked one of the builders to tell him that she was here. When he came around he could see that she was shaken by something. He planted a kiss on her lips and hugged her tightly.

Ruth was so happy to see him. Her view on the world was completely different after last night – she wanted to tell him at once what she had learned.

"Fancy going for a cappuccino – there's a little place on the river?" he suggested.

"That sounds perfect."

"We can walk to it if you like."

They began to stroll in the warm sunshine past the Yacht Club and the serpentine bay.

Ruth launched into her tale straightaway, hurriedly getting it off her chest.

"It's crazy but my father isn't who I thought. My mother was raped by Charles Walters' son who died in the car accident – it turns out that he is my biological father."

Brian stopped dead and turned to her, his eyes wide. "Your father?"

Ruth nodded – she was shaking now.

"Charles Walters, the father, wanted to make amends and offered money and said he wanted to see his grandchild. But my mother wanted nothing to do with him."

Ruth looked up at Brian and he hugged her tightly. It helped sharing her distress with him.

"It must have been so difficult for her," he said. He put his arm around her shoulders and helped her to walk on.

Ruth's eyes welled. It was incredibly difficult to accept what she had learned. These characters that had been associated with the house were blood relatives.

"Yes, I-I-I – eh, I just realised that Emily was my grandmother and she spent all those years on her own in the house with no family. It must have been terribly lonely and all the while I suppose she knew that I existed on the other side of the world."

Brian was shaking his head in disbelief. "That's a crazy story. You know, I don't have much to do with the Arthurs chap but it strikes me that you are the real heir to Number 5."

Ruth stopped still in her tracks.

"What do you mean?"

"Well, from what I gather they had to give it to this nephew – grand-nephew, mind! Because he was next of kin. The old lady didn't leave a will . . . wait, I have the name of the solicitor – I might do a bit of detective work!"

"Brian!" Ruth warned. "What are you up to?"

"I'm not sure about the law – let me look into it but from what you say you are the closest living relative to Emily Walters."

If it was true it would be amazing but Ruth was concerned. "I don't want to upset the past – I mean, things should be just left the way they are."

Brian shook his head. "I believe your ancestors are trying to get through to you – why else did you have those strange feelings on Rottnest? It's all a bit too spooky. And this house is your destiny . . ."

Ruth blinked back the tears. It had been a remarkable few days. She was disturbed about her mother's revelation but she was so happy to have Brian back in her life that it counterbalanced her distress. Besides, she felt that things were unfolding around her beyond her control. The universe had stepped in and all she had to do was let her future happen.

"Brian – I know that you are trying to help but I don't want to have anything to do with that family – I mean, after what happened to my mother . . ."

Brian paused. "I'm sorry, Ruth – I'm being insensitive – of course I wouldn't dream of interfering. You know what is best."

He stopped walking and hugged her tightly.

"I just want to be at peace with this huge news. I haven't spoken to my father yet!"

"Of course – and I am here for you – you know that?"

Ruth looked up into his clear blue eyes and melted as he leaned forward and kissed her the way that she loved to be kissed.

Chapter Fifty-seven

Michael got an email to thank him for coming to the interview but the position had been filled. He was gutted beyond words. He went into the kitchen where Horatio sat sipping a mug of tea.

"I didn't get the job, Granddad."

Horatio looked up at his grandson. "What's for ya won't go by ya, son! If you didn't get it there's a reason."

Michael wished his grandfather was right but he was feeling very dejected right now.

Julia walked into the kitchen behind him.

"Morning, everyone!" she breezed. "I see Mum came back late last night – is she up yet?"

"I haven't seen her but I heard her car drive in at all hours," Horatio said. "Michael has a bit of unfortunate news but I told him it could be a blessing!"

Julia looked at her brother. "The job? Did you hear?"

He nodded. "I didn't get it – I got a generic email. I swear, I leave everything in Singapore to come home for this and all I get is a generic email!"

Julia patted her brother on his back. "It's okay – Granddad is right – there are lots of other opportunities and you did say that you would like a change or a challenge."

"But I need to earn money too!"

"Well, as I told you, I need help. I've been relying on Gillian too much and I really need a stand-in that I can trust."

"But I don't know the business," Michael said defensively.

"Michael, you have been in business for years! It won't take you long to figure it out. You can come into work with me today."

Michael groaned.

"That's a great idea!" Horatio agreed.

Carol stepped into the kitchen as he spoke. "Morning – what's a great idea?"

"Oh hi, Mum," Julia said with a smile. "Michael is going to come and work with me – I'm about to take on some more products – I need help."

Carol hugged her son warmly. "It's so good to have you home, love."

"It's good to be home, Mum – and you've been having a good time from what I hear?"

Carol blushed. "Don't mind these two. But tell me, did you not go for that job?"

"Eh, don't mention the war, Carol!" Horatio butted in.

"Okay – I won't!" Carol said. "Well, to change the subject, I had a lovely time with Gerry and if it's okay with everyone he's coming down this weekend."

"I'll be back in the apartment by then!" Michael said quickly.

"I'll probably be staying with Odette anyway," Julia piped up. "It's Paddy's weekend and I'm going to the parade with Dylan and the kids."

Horatio chuckled. "Are you now?" He winked at his granddaughter.

"Granddad!" Julia berated. "We are taking the kids out to give Odette a break."

"Whatever you say," the old man grinned.

Gillian greeted Michael at the reception. She was determined to meet a man and Michael would be just perfect – Dylan was obviously besotted with Julia and she couldn't be wasting any more time on him.

"Oh, Michael, lovely to see you again!" she beamed.

"Hi – Gillian, isn't it?" Michael smiled.

She nodded her head like the dogs who sit in the back of car windows.

"Gillian, Michael is going to be working with us now," Julia said.

"Oh really – great news!" Gillian blushed. "If there is anything I can do to help, please let me know."

"I'll be straight on to you, Gillian!"

Gillian giggled at the double entendre and Julia wanted to be sick.

"Come on, Michael – no slacking now!" she said, ushering her brother into the office where she shut the door and hissed, "Michael, Gillian is insatiable – don't tempt her – I don't want her for a sister-in-law!"

"Uh – I could do worse – she seems nice."

"I'm seriously having my doubts – I think she's attracted to any man with a pulse."

Michael titled his head. "That does wonders for my ego, sis!"

"I'm not worried about your ego! Now sit down and let me show you the accounts – I want to introduce you to the cruise company this afternoon – cruises are going to be a major product this season."

Michael covered so much ground so quickly that Julia was confident she had made a great decision. He was pouring out new ideas and they were working like a finely oiled machine in unison.

The hands turned on the clock on the wall and both were surprised when they saw that it was already three o'clock.

"I'll send one of the girls out to get us a sandwich for now – we've worked through lunch!" said Julia. "And I have to pop out and meet Lydia in a while. She wants to speak to me about something."

Michael raised his head on hearing his old love's name. "Leave me here and I'll finish off."

"Are you sure? That would be a great help. She sounds upset."

Michael raised an eyebrow. "There's hope for me yet then?"

"Don't hold your breath," she sighed.

"Okay, talk later, and if I'm still here when you're finished maybe you can drop me home?"

"I'll be right back as I have to be in Howth by six!"

Julia said her goodbyes to Gillian and rushed out to Wicklow Street where she had agreed to meet Lydia for a quick coffee at the Butler's chocolate café.

Lydia was sitting up at a high stool devouring a chocolate truffle when Julia came into the shop.

"Sorry I'm a bit late – I've got a new employee."

"It's okay – I got started," Lydia said, giving her friend a peck on the cheek. "Thanks for coming to meet me at such short notice. I need to thrash my thoughts out with someone and I trust your opinion more than anyone."

"I'm honoured – that you chose me to talk to." Julia smiled gently. "You are a good friend, Lydia, and deserve to be happy. So is it Peter?"

Lydia nodded. "Oh Julia – I think I dived in too quickly – I seriously think that he has no intention of ever getting married. It's like he loves being in a stable relationship with just a certain amount of commitment and he goes there really quickly with his girlfriends and then just strings them on for years."

"There are guys like that . . . I did say so before . . ." Julia hated it when she was right.

"I told him that I'm moving out!"

Julia could see the pain in her friend's eyes. She put her hand out to console her. "Are you okay?"

"My heart was hoping that he wanted the same as me but my gut was saying something else. My head said get out now before I get hurt!"

Julia nodded. "But maybe you can just enjoy what you have?"

"Does any woman just want that?"

Julia shrugged. Commitment was definitely not on her priority list. But most of her friends had different needs.

Lydia sighed. "I'm going around to collect my things this evening – I'm lucky that I didn't sell my apartment! Maybe I should just take a break from men!"

Julia raised her eyebrows. "I think you're right to trust your gut but don't shut yourself off from love."

"You know me too well! I haven't the nerve to tell my mother – she thinks he's the best thing since sliced bread."

Julia did know her friend and she was sure that she would do the right thing.

"I'm there for you if you need me."

"I know that. I just needed to say it to someone and you are the person that I trust the most. Thanks, Ju. So who's your new employee then?"

"Don't laugh but I think it's going to work out really well – it's Michael."

"Your brother?" Lydia asked in amazement.

"Yes – he came home for an interview and didn't get the job."

"Is he really home for good?"

"Oh God, yeah – he was becoming one of those miserable homesick Irishmen crying into his pint. He's been up in the Abbey Tavern every evening with Granddad since he got back and he's happy out."

Lydia smiled. "He's not the settling down type either."

"All he's talked about for months is settling down. I seriously think that he will settle for the first girl he meets that will have him."

Lydia laughed. "I feel I've been very harsh with him."

"Don't feel bad – he's his own worst enemy."

"Maybe I'll give him a second chance then?" Lydia joked.

Julia warned. "Give him time to prove himself."

"I'm only joking – I'm going to give myself some time before I jump into another relationship. But, tell me – are you really meeting Dylan at six? I was stunned when I read your text."

"I, eh, yeah – funny but we've been hitting if off rather well and he's a great support to Odette and the kids – we're both trying to help ease things for her."

Lydia couldn't wipe the grin off her face.

"What's that face for?" Julia asked defensively.

"I always knew you would cave in eventually."

"What?"

"Oh nothing." Lydia stood up. "I'd better let you go. I'll keep you posted on my decision."

Julia stood up and kissed her friend on the cheek. "I have saved so many calories! I forgot to order a coffee and chocolate – I'll have to meet you more often!"

Lydia walked away with the elegance of a swan and Julia wished that her friend would find happiness soon.

Michael heard a little tapping noise on the door.

"Yes – come in!"

Gillian peeked her head around the door and batted her lashes.

"Hello – I was wondering if you would like a coffee or anything? You've been working very hard."

"Oh, a coffee would be lovely – thanks, Gillian."

"How do you like it?"

Michael was so tempted to say 'with you on top' but refrained. "Eh, black, please – no sugar."

Gillian trotted out in the new shoes that she had bought which were five inches high and desperately uncomfortable. They were a vain attempt to help her feel as tall and elegant as Julia but had only succeeded in giving her blisters.

When she returned she placed the cup on the table in front of Michael, making sure that she was revealing some cleavage. Her bra had successfully pushed up her small bosoms to make two plump appealing curves.

"Thank you for making me feel so welcome." He grinned.

"Oh, I could make you very welcome . . ." She had said the words before she realised and stopped.

Michael laughed. "Could you now?"

It was all the encouragement that she needed. A pent-up impulse took over and she sat herself up on the desk, looking Michael right in the eyes all the time. She lunged forward and smacked her lips on his.

He was too startled to move but the next voice he heard was his sister's and she was not happy.

"*What's going on here?*"

Gillian jumped down off the desk and started to button up the shirt that she had opened before delivering the coffee.

"Ju – we were just having a coffee."

"Is that what you call it now?" Julia couldn't believe her eyes and she was feeling very disconcerted by the scene.

Gillian wanted the floor to open up. "I'll just go out to the bed – I mean *desk* – and tidy up – eh, goodbye, Michael, Julia."

A mortified Gillian closed the door behind her.

Michael had a wild cheeky grin on his face and Julia wanted to hit him.

"Your first day in the office and I can't trust you! I'm a stupid fool to think that you have changed. I was even telling Lydia that you'd changed but you haven't at all."

Michael got up from his chair and went over to his sister.

"Ju, I'm sorry, I swear I was just sitting here and she made a lunge at me – you can see I was just sitting at the desk."

"But I bet you led her on!"

"I swear, Ju – it was just friendly office banter. Please, I've had a great afternoon – I do want to work here."

Julia didn't know what to believe. She looked at her watch – she had forty-five minutes to get to Howth.

"Just pack up here, will you," she said sternly. "I'm in a rush."

Chapter Fifty-eight

Angela was quiet when Ruth got home from her chat with Brian. She had sat in the sun for most of the day and was scribbling on a notepad.

"Hi, love, how was your day?"

"Fine, thanks, Mum. In fact, it was a bit strange – I can't stop thinking about what you told me. You know I met Brian – I hope you don't mind but I had to tell him."

Angela nodded. There had been a tremendous lift of the burden from her shoulders since she had spilled her soul the night before.

"You have to do what is best with the knowledge now – I'm sorry that I never told you before but I hope you believe me when I say the timing had to be right and it is now."

"I do, Mum – I wouldn't have understood if you had told me in Dublin."

"And I'll have to tell your father – I think that's why he didn't come out here, to be honest. He has been dreading the day that you would know the truth. I think we should ring him and tell him that everything is going so well."

"I've been thinking about him – it's important that he hears how much I love him. Do you mind if I make that call now?"

"I think that would be a good idea," Angela agreed.

Ruth lifted her phone and dialled the number in Sutton. It was early morning in Dublin but she knew that her father would be up.

"Dad?"

"Ruth, how are you getting on – is your mother there with you?"

"Yes, she is – we are having a lovely time. How is Dublin?"

"Not too bad today – it's been very mild."

"Mum is finding her way around – she says Perth's changed a lot."

"I'd say it has. Is it very hot? Although I suppose you have air-conditioning now?"

"Yes, it's roasting." She paused. "Dad, there's something I need to tell you. Mum's been chatting with me about the things that happened before you left Australia." She looked over at her mother who was biting her lip nervously.

There was silence at the other end of the line, until he said, "Oh really?"

"Dad – I know the truth and I want you to know that I love you – you are my dad – that is the way it's always going to be."

A sob came down the line. It was difficult for Fred to deal with this now – on his own and so far away from his daughter and wife.

"Angela had said that she might tell you when she was out there. It doesn't change a thing, Ruth. You are my little girl – and I know I don't say it often enough but I love you."

Ruth felt a lump in her throat. "I love you so much, Dad. I'll be home for Christmas, I promise, and I'll ring you often."

"I know that – now put your mother on."

Ruth handed her mother the phone.

Angela was shaking as she took the receiver. "Thanks, love."

Ruth left her parents alone to speak to each other in privacy and went into her bedroom to change out of her work clothes. Her laptop was open on her dressing table and she went over to check for messages on Skype. There was a chat message from Julia. She was asking her to pick up the painting that she had bought in Fremantle prison and completely forgot about with the trauma at home. Ruth decided to Skype her quickly.

"How are you, Julia – I've been needing to speak with you – we're finding out amazing things here."

"Oh really, I can't wait to hear! Sorry for the late notice about the painting – I only remembered it today."

"I can drop out there now. Mum and I need to go for a walk so we can go there – that's where we were last night when she told me about my father."

"What about him?"

"Julia, I hope that you're sitting down for this. My father was the son of Charles Walters who owned Number 5."

"*What?* I don't believe it! Angela had an affair?"

"No, she was working for the family in a restaurant. It was awful, Julia. She was raped – and I am the product of it. I've been trying to get my head around it all day."

Julia was stunned.

"Oh my God – I don't know what to say – are you okay?"

"Kind of, in a crazy way – I mean, it's too weird – it probably hasn't sunk in properly."

"Oh, Ruth, I wish I were with you! Look, ring me if you're upset at any time – won't you?"

"Yeah, but I think it was better hearing this while I'm in Australia – I think I would have been distraught if she had told me back in Dublin but here it feels like I am where I am meant to be."

"You are half-Australian – oh my goodness! We needn't have got you that work permit after all! Oh, I'm sorry, Ruth – I don't mean to be flippant – I'm just shocked."

"Hang on – I'm not sure if that would be true – I mean, I know my father's name is on my birth cert so I probably wouldn't be entitled."

"That's crazy news – so the man who owned Peppermint Grove . . ."

"Was my grandfather!"

"Well, that's fate if ever I heard it!"

"That's what Brian said."

"How are things going there?"

"Fantastic – I really like him, Julia. Thanks – none of this would have been sorted if it wasn't for you."

"I'm sure it would have but I hope that I didn't make things worse. Poor Angela – it must have been awful for her, carrying this information around for so long."

"I've been thinking that too. But she feels better now that it's all in the open. I've talked to my dad too and he is so relieved. Listen, I have to go here – I'll get that painting for you."

"Thanks, I owe you – just hang on to it for me."

"No worries!"

"Hey, Ruth, you're even sounding like a real Aussie now! Love you – miss you."

"Me too – bye, Julia."

Ruth smiled as she switched off her laptop. It felt so much better now that the truth was out in the open. She would get the painting for Julia and stroll around Fremantle with her mother. She had an ocean of possibilities ahead of her.

"It's a lovely painting, isn't it?" Ruth said to Angela as they drove back from their brief visit to Fremantle Prison.

"I was never fond of Aboriginal art but that picture is very relaxing or something – I don't know what it is."

"It's the symmetry. It's the way that all the parts are equally balanced. I can see why that appealed to Julia."

"Brian will know whether it's good art or not."

"Yes, he might even know what it means. He said he might call by later if we were home early – is that okay with you?"

"Of course – I'm tired anyway and going to have an early night – I was jotting down my thoughts today while you were at work. You know, talking with you has sorted out a lot of things that were crowding my head for years. Thank you, love, for taking it so well."

Ruth didn't know what to say. She didn't have a choice in the matter and she felt sad for her mother. She also felt sad for her father – she loved him dearly and nothing would change that.

They arrived home to find Brian sitting in his Jeep outside the house. He jumped out immediately and came to meet them.

Ruth took out the painting from the boot and showed it to him.

"Nice work – it reminds me of the 'Country' landscapes that the Abos make in the desert. Huge aerial murals made from stone and sand, giving a kind of maplike bird's-eye view of the desert landscape. They are telling a story about dreaming – and usually planned out perfectly like this painting. This guy is a mathematician of some sort."

"I was wondering what you'd think of it." She smiled at him. "I'm really glad you like it. I do."

Angela headed to bed very soon – making her apologies, saying she was really tired. Ruth was taking a beer and a box of wine from the fridge when Brian went over to her and wrapped his arms around her waist.

"So how have you been? I've got something I thought you'd like to see."

Ruth giggled. Closing the fridge door, she turned around and gave him a playful smoochy kiss. "You always have something I'd like to see!"

"Hey there – you Irishwomen are minxes – I'm trying to be nice!" He grinned as he took something out of his breast pocket.

It was a photograph of a Federation house with a pretty green door and climbing pink clematis flowers around the frame. A bunch of lavender sat to the left of the door and a big brass Number 5 hinted to Ruth that this was the Walters home.

"My goodness! Where did you get this?"

"It was in a pile of old photos that the Arthurs chap had. I rooted it out today. We used it in the planning-permission documentation."

Ruth was agog. "Wow – I don't know what to say."

"Don't say anything," Brian held her firmly. "I had a word with our company solicitor today and enquired what Arthurs is doing with the new house. As I suspected, he has no big interest in it – he just sees it as a chance to make some cash. He's only been on the site once!"

Ruth shook her head, puzzled. "So?"

"It's just a notion I have – I'd say he's going to sell it as quickly as possible – it would be a very good investment."

"You're not suggesting *I* buy it?"

Brian shrugged – it wasn't his initial idea but he wanted to hear her opinion. "I thought you might be interested . . ."

Ruth sighed. "Brian, I'm only on a work permit here – I'm not sure how long I'm going to stay in this country. Yes, it's a stunning house and in the most beautiful part of the city and if I was staying it would be a fabulous place to live. But I've no collateral – not even in Dublin. I'd be lucky to afford a one-bed apartment anywhere in this city."

Brian was deflated by her response and her mention of leaving Australia. Maybe he was speaking out of turn – it was early days in their relationship and he didn't want to come on too heavy – not after their recent bust-up. But, the truth was, he had put some of his best ideas into the design of the house and had grown to love it. An offer had been put in earlier for his house in Karrinyup and it was a good time for him to move on to a place of his own. At least now he knew that Ruth really liked it – if she had an issue with the owners or found it creepy she would have said.

Chapter Fifty-nine

Julia checked that her make-up was smooth and fresh before stepping out of the car on the West Pier. Dylan's Mercedes was parked outside the Brass Monkey restaurant and she felt a strange thrill as she went through the door.

Charlotte spotted her first and jumped down from her seat and rushed over to her aunt.

"Juju – I've been waiting for you! Uncle Dylan and Jamie were bold. They said that there's a monkey in the kitchen and if I don't eat my dinner he will come out and scare me."

Julia lifted her niece into her arms. "Don't mind them – they are very bold. There's no monkey in the kitchen or the restaurant would be closed down."

"Huh?" the beleaguered six-year-old looked at her with wide eyes.

"It's an adult rule – no monkeys in kitchens! So nothing to worry about. Anyway you will love your dinner so much that you will just gobble it all up!"

Dylan stood up as Julia came over.

"We've just arrived. You missed a great movie – didn't she, Jamie?"

"Sure did, Julia – we needed you to stop Charlotte from

complaining – she was scared of the bad guys!" He shook his head in disgust.

The waitress brought down a menu and the four chatted about the movie and what they were going to eat.

Julia felt as though she was enveloped in a warm cloak of love and security that was as infectious as her niece's and nephew's laughter.

Dylan made a paper hat out of his napkin and placed it on his head to the children's delight and Julia got a clear glimpse of how it would be to have a family and a man of her own.

After they ate copious amounts of chips and ice cream the kids insisted that they weren't ready to go home until they had fed the seals. In their role as aunt and uncle, Julia and Dylan felt compelled to take them out to the harbour wall with some scraps left over from the fishmonger's a few doors up from the restaurant.

Jamie threw in a fishtail and the seals dived quickly to catch it before the seagulls got there first.

"This has been a lovely end to what was a crazy day!" Julia assured Dylan.

"We've had a great time at the flicks and now this – I love being eight!" he grinned. "So what made your day crazy?"

"Oh, it was nothing really – but actually you might have some insight for me – what do you *really* make of Gillian?"

"Eh – I think she's a nice girl but she's a bit odd."

"Thanks but I think I am beginning to realise that – she made a massive pass at Michael today and it was only the second time that she met him. And they were both working!"

Dylan threw his head back, laughing. "I think she's man-hungry alright and she completely misinterpreted my friendship. She was cute enough to get me to meet her last week though by feigning concern for you."

She got him to meet her! Julia tried to disguise her relief. "Concern for me? Why ever would she feel that?"

Dylan shrugged. "She said that you had a lot on your plate after Craig's death – but I think she was just keen to get me on her own. You did encourage her friendship, you know – you did try to get her out and about if I remember?"

Julia closed her eyes. It was true and she had only herself to blame for crossing the boundaries between boss and employee. She had to stop meddling with other people's lives and then not expect them to do the same in return.

"I'm sorry about that, Dylan. I'm going to have to be clearer with her in future."

"It looks like she has her sights on Michael now, though!"

That was true. Maybe Michael deserved to have a Gillian in his life. But he was her brother after all and she would sit him down and have a straight chat with him.

"Thanks for telling me, Dylan. I think it's best if I set my boundaries straight – you are right."

Dylan took Jamie and Charlotte by the hands. "Right, guys, are we ready to go home? We've a busy day tomorrow."

Julia walked along at their side. She had a lot to look forward to before Dylan went away. There was the Parade and then a Mother's Day dinner in her house and Gerry was coming too.

"So how did your dinner go with Dylan?" Horatio asked.

Julia tried to hide the wide grin on her face but realised that there was no point – her grandfather knew her too well.

"It was fine!"

Horatio chuckled under his breath. "It was only a matter of time. So when are you seeing him again?"

"Seeing who?"

"Don't mess with your grandfather, Julia – I'm too old for that!"

"We're taking the children to the zoo if you must know over the weekend."

"Ah – they're a grand excuse, those lovely children! And tell me now, is Dylan still going on that trip around the world?"

"Of course he is – in two weeks' time. Don't go making assumptions – okay?"

"Alright but I'll be interested to know if there's any news," he said with an exaggerated wink.

"So, where is Mum?"

"She's playing bridge with Treasa – although when Gerry gets down here it might curtail her gallivanting!"

Julia kissed her grandfather on the head. "I'm off to bed now – night-night!"

"Goodnight, Julia – it's a grand day altogether – but do you think Paola might be interested in a sort of spring/autumn relationship?"

"Goodnight, Granddad!" Julia giggled as she went out the kitchen door.

She was almost ready for sleep when her phone bleeped with a message from her friend in Fáilte Ireland.

Hi Julia 2 spare tickets for grandstand @ St Patricks Day Parade – interested?

Julia was about to reply and then had an idea – she had promised that she wouldn't meddle in people's lives any more. She was going to stay clear of all forms of matchmaking. But this could be her swansong – her very last little bit of interference done with the best possible intention.

She typed in a message: Would you like to go to the Parade next week – I have seats for the grandstand love Ju xx

She sent the message to two people who were very dear to her. Everyone deserved to be happy.

Chapter Sixty

Angela was waiting for Ruth to get home from work. Brian had insisted that he wanted to take her out before she returned to Dublin. It had been an adventure beyond her wildest dreams and she had found a peace that she never imagined possible by revisiting her past. She had been tinkering with her thoughts and jotting down ideas while Ruth was at work and now felt ready to start that novel she had always dreamed of writing. She certainly had plenty to write about. And the irony and coincidences would make a great plot.

Brian had announced the night before that he had made an offer on Number 5 and it had been accepted – he had offset it against all the work that they had done. Building costs had soared and the Arthurs chap was keen to offload the house – he had bitten off more than he could chew.

The front door slammed shut and Ruth breezed into the kitchen where her mother sat at the table.

"Phew, it's hot out there – hotter than usual for March – so they tell me in work!"

"It is and you're so lucky to have air-conditioning. We had to rely on The Doctor in the old days!"

Ruth giggled. She felt so at home here.

"Thanks for coming, Mum, and I hope you feel better going back after all that has been said."

"Oh, I do, love. You have no idea how much better and I'm looking forward to seeing your father."

"I'd love to see him soon – maybe he will come out?"

"I doubt we'd ever get him back to Dublin if he came out here again," Angela chuckled. "Has Brian any more news on the house?"

"His solicitor is working on the contract – I find it all a bit weird but it is Brian's creation and in a funny sort of way he has healed the land by putting his beautiful building on the site."

Angela nodded. "I think I know what you mean."

"Oh, I spoke to Julia earlier and she told me to keep that lovely painting that she bought in the prison – she said that in hindsight it would be better suited in my home in Australia."

"That's nice of her. Dear Julia – and all that her poor family have been through . . . you know, it's a funny old world, love, and the older you get the stranger it all becomes. But the thing is we are all connected no matter how near or far we are from the ones that we love."

There was a resignation in her mother's tone that resonated in Ruth. Did she know something that she wasn't saying? Or was it just feminine intuition?

If her relationship with Brian continued on its current course she wouldn't be going back to Dublin – only for family visits or holidays. And in a way it was what her mother had feared most when she told her about her departure before Christmas. But as Brian had said – it was her fate!

Michael was happy to go along to the Parade, providing the seats were as good as Julia had assured him that they would be. But he hadn't expected to see Lydia sitting right beside him.

"Michael?" she cried in disbelief.

"I thought Julia was going to be here!" he said with the same amount of discomfort.

"I think we've been set up!" she gasped.

Michael nodded and pointed to a corner of the stand at least twenty rows away where Julia was sitting next to Dylan and their niece and nephew, oblivious to the tension and surprise down at their level.

"So – do you mind if I sit here – or would you rather I go somewhere else?"

"I don't mind where you sit!" Lydia replied defensively.

Tension hung between them for the first five minutes of the parade. Lydia texted several times but for once Julia had her phone on silent.

Michael reached into his pocket for his flask of whiskey that he used to bring to rugby matches in Lansdowne Road. He took off the cap and offered it to Lydia.

She looked down at it and decided that it might help her through the next couple of hours – it would steady her nerves at least.

"Thanks," she replied and took a swig. It was sharp on her tongue but warmed her.

Michael took it back and drank without wiping first – he dreamed of the lovely lips that had recently touched the rim.

"I think Julia had the best intentions – I promise I didn't know that she was doing this," he said.

Lydia nodded. She was used to her friend's antics and she believed him.

"It's okay . . ."

"But if she'd told me she was doing it I'd have been delighted," he added with a cheeky grin.

Lydia couldn't help but smile. There was something of the lovable rogue about Michael that she couldn't resist. "Give me another drink of that whiskey, Michael – it's warming me up!"

Michael felt a thrill that sent his heart soaring. Thank you, Julia, he said silently. You really are the best sister a fella could hope for.

It was to be a Mother's Day like no other. Carol was anxious and excited at once. She longed to tell her family the good news and yet she was dreading getting a negative response. She still felt like a bold child bringing Gerry to her bedroom at night.

Now her children were downstairs waiting and she knew that Julia had put a lot of work into this dinner for her. She was fortunate indeed.

Michael was first to appear, beaming with contentment now that he was settled back into his apartment.

Odette arrived next and the children ran into the house ahead of their mother, still gushing with the great sights they had seen the day before at the parade – the famous first kiss of their aunt and uncle undoubtedly the highlight for Charlotte who took great relish in describing it in detail to anyone that would listen.

Then Julia who was accompanied by Dylan.

"And where did you spend last night?" Horatio asked his granddaughter, giving Dylan a knowing wink.

There was enough embarrassment going around for an army, let alone one family.

After they had tucked into the beautifully carved duck with gratin potatoes and roasted vegetables. Carol did something unusual. She stood up to thank her family for making Mother's Day so special.

"I don't want today to go without saying how proud I am of my children and especially my daughter Odette – who is the best and most inspiring mother that I know."

Odette felt a lump in her throat. It had been lovely eating dinner together but this was the first time that they had all gathered like they used to and, she was painfully aware of Craig's absence throughout. She hoped that with time she would be able to cope with situations like this and not be dragged back to the abyss. But this was a happy day and she was feeling buoyed up by the positive vibes around her.

"There is someone else who has joined our family since Christmas and I know that he appreciates how welcome you have all made him feel. We know this is a bit soon but we haven't got time on our side – so I have something to tell you now. Gerry and I want to set up home together."

The room was filled with a stunned silence and Carol threw a pleading look at Julia.

"Congratulations, Mum and Gerry!" Julia said as she raised her glass of Cabernet Sauvignon in a toast. "To Carol and Gerry!"

The rest all raised their glasses and loudly echoed "To Carol and Gerry!"

"Right," Julia continued. "While you are all still receptive, I have a bit of news – we all know that Dylan is going to travel around the world for a year . . . well, he has asked me to join him when he visits Australia in July so . . . I've said yes! We're going to spend six weeks going around the country, ending with a visit to Ruth"

Everyone hollered and the children danced around the table, showing their excitement at all the news.

It was Michael's turn next.

"While you are all spouting out your news, I've agreed to work for Julia – I should be well settled by the time she goes away. . . . and there is another little development . . . I'm not too sure how it's going to go yet but Lydia has agreed to go on a date with me!"

Dylan looked at Julia and she shrugged her shoulders. "I had to save him from the wrath of Gillian, didn't I?" she whispered naughtily.

Horatio couldn't be left out – he had to have the last word. He was loving every moment as he watched his family around the table. He stood up and cleared his throat, then lifted his glass of Guinness.

"You'll be glad to hear that I have decided not to emigrate to Brazil and although I don't have a special announcement about the lovely Paola and myself it is wonderful to see my family so happy around me . . . and I've said it before but I'll say it again – good news or a good woman is a bit like the Number 31 bus – none for ages and then three come along together!"

Epilogue

Six months later

At 5 Peppermint Grove Road, Peppermint Grove,
Perth, Western Australia

"He still looks good, Ruth, doesn't he?" Julia said, nodding over at the handsome Richie as he helped Brian turn the steaks on the barbie. "I find it hard to believe that he's your neighbour!"

"I can't get my head around any of this," Ruth agreed. "To think that a year ago I was still dating that ass Ian!"

Julia giggled. "Isn't it amazing what time can do?"

"Speaking of time, there's something I have to tell you – well, you know the way I'm meant to be coming home for Christmas?"

"Yes," Julia didn't like the sound of this or where it was leading.

"Well, I may not be able – we'll have to see how it goes."

"What are you talking about?" Julia had a hunch and she knew her friend well enough not to beat around the bush.

"I may not be able to travel – I'm pregnant."

Julia gasped – she had suspected it. "Oh my God – that's terrific news!"

She hugged her friend tightly and caught Brian looking over from the barbeque. Dylan had joined the men now with fresh refills of beer.

"That is the best news I've ever heard," Julia said. She was so warm inside. "But how far along are you? Surely not long?"

Ruth shook her head. "No, only eight weeks – but you see the reason it will be best not to travel is because I'm having twins!"

A shiver ran up Julia's spine. "I was about to ask if there were twins in your family but I've just remembered the story of Charles' father."

Ruth nodded. "It is fate, isn't it?"

"It is certainly fate that you have ended up living in this house. Brian is so proud of you – he can't wait to get you up the aisle, I bet!"

"And what about Dylan – he's been watching you like a cat watching a mouse since you guys landed in Perth."

"Good – I love Dylan. We've had the most amazing holiday. I'll miss him so much when I go back to Dublin – I'm hoping he will shorten his travels and come home soon."

"So it's going well then?"

"I couldn't ask for more and you know this is as much commitment as I can handle so who knows someday . . . He's already proved what a great father he could be with his niece and nephew and, you know, now that Michael is handling the business so well I can see myself happily working part-time."

"Wow – that's a big change, Ju – I never ever thought I'd hear you say something like that."

Julia was beaming. "I think we've both come a long way."

"To the other side of the world!" Ruth giggled.

"It's a small world really and you will never be far away." Julia's eyes welled up.

"Two little flights – that's all that's between us and we can Skype every day!"

Ruth nodded. "Come inside and see where we have decided to hang the painting."

Julia followed her friend into a small room that wasn't yet painted.

"This is going to be the study and we both agreed that we'll hang it here. Brian will have all his astronomy books on this wall and I'll have my maps and travel stuff along here. We want to set it up as a good room for chatting and Skyping."

"I love it and that's the perfect space for the picture. I'm so glad you kept it – it's nice to know that something I liked and picked out is on your wall. You know, I think that you are probably right with all of those gut feelings and intuitions that you have. It's like I bought the painting for you to hang in this room."

Ruth had to agree. "I'll miss you, Ju, when you go back!"

"I'll miss you too, Ruth, but I couldn't have lost you to a nicer guy or a better place. Peppermint Grove is your true home and now it will be a second home for me and maybe someday my family!"

The two friends looked at each other. They were friends for life and it didn't matter where they lived – they would never be far from each other's hearts.

If you enjoyed
5 Peppermint Grove by Michelle Jackson
why not try
4 a.m. in Las Vegas also published by Poolbeg?
Here's a sneak preview of Chapter One

MICHELLE JACKSON

4 a.m.
in
Las Vegas

POOLBEG

*The Great Spirit is in all things: he is in the air we breathe.
The Great Spirit is our father, but the earth is our mother.
She nourishes us; that which we put into the ground
she returns to us.*

~ *Big Thunder (Bedagi)*, WABANAKI ALGONQUIN ~

Prologue

Viva Las Vegas Wedding Chapel

October 31st

Vicky jumped out of the Cadillac and slammed the door shut. She gasped for air, trembling as the adrenalin rushed through her.

"Wait for me," John called as he catapulted out of the car and followed her through the doorway of the wedding chapel.

Vicky pushed past the man standing inside the door – knocking over his television camera. Dry ice rose from the floor, tinted lilac by the flashing spotlights. Candlelight illuminated the dark walls and the strains of a church organ playing a macabre melody filled the air. Large cobwebs draped down from the rafters and hung over the aisles – Vicky pushed them out of her way to get to the bizarre altar. Standing in the middle was a gentleman wearing a black suit and top hat, his fangs exposed as his mouth opened in shock at the intruders. On his left was a young man with a pallid face and blood dripping down his chin. To his right stood the bride, wearing a long green satin dress and black shawl.

Vicky tripped over a tombstone in her anxiety to reach her daughter. Hysterically she waved her arms in the air and screamed.

"Tina, what do you think you're doing?"

The organ started up with the Dead March as two trapeze vampires glided through the air over their heads.

"I'm getting married," Tina replied. Her voice trembled – this wasn't the way she had planned it.

Vicky shook her head in disbelief. "Tell me this is some kind of joke – you can't honestly be getting married!"

Tina moved in by her groom's side and he put his arm protectively around her.

"This is my wife," the boy said brazenly. "And we *are* married!"

"Tina Hughes, come with me now!" Vicky roared.

"Her name is Tina Haycock now," the young man said coolly. "And she's going with me!"

They had started to walk away when Dracula called them back.

"Hey, kids – you gotta sign the register."

"We'll do that outside," the groom said and continued to walk, with his arm wrapped around his wife's shoulders.

John put his arm around Vicky who was shaking so hard she wasn't conscious of the tears dripping down her cheeks.

"It's okay – calm down. At least we know she's safe and nothing has happened to her," he said gently.

Dracula approached Vicky respectfully.

"I'm sorry, ma'am, but you'll have to leave – there's another wedding in two minutes."

As the strains of Aerosmith's rock classic "Love Bites" filled the chapel, Vicky and John walked back down the aisle.

"We're all done here!" the cameraman said to his assistant and they gathered up their equipment and left through the side door.

"What's going on?" Vicky said in dismay. "Why the TV crew?"

The camera crew had come to film the spectacle, *Fox News* emblazoned across their equipment. Vicky would only have to look at the TV later to see the evidence that the wedding had taken place.

"Let's go back to the hotel," John said gently. "Connie will help sort this mess out."

Vicky could hardly speak with shock. "Tina's eighteen – there's nothing I can do about this."

"She probably got carried away. Don't worry!"

But John knew that she was right – an eighteen-year-old was perfectly within her rights to get married, but now he was going to have to cope with this mess on top of everything else that had happened over the last few days in Las Vegas.

Chapter 1

*You can't wake a person who is
pretending to be asleep.*

~ NAVAJO PROVERB ~

Connie Haycock flicked open her diary – it was that crazy time
of year again. Halloween in Las Vegas meant even more
weddings than usual. So many people chose to blend their big
day with a stay in the city of excess and fun that she loved so
much.

She was a Californian girl who had run away at a time when
she felt there was no hope. Fourteen years ago, with a Chrysler
Estate and two snotty-nosed little boys in the back, she had
checked into a motel room off The Strip and spent her first night
in the city that she now called home – relieved to be away from
the sham of a marriage she had endured for six years, but
frightened about how she would survive in this new city of neon.

She had come a long way from those early days of working
on the blackjack tables in the Golden Nugget to the point where
she was one of the most successful wedding planners in Las
Vegas. She lived in a smart bungalow in the suburb of
Summerlin and last year had a pool installed in her garden. Her
life had blossomed in a way she could never have dreamed

before leaving California. Her eldest son, Troy, was now at the Arizona State University on a football scholarship and doing exceptionally well. Unfortunately, she still worried abut her moody and mixed-up son Kyle – he had always been a sensitive child. So different from his brother who seemed to love life with the same passion as his mother.

Yes, Connie had a lot to be thankful for. She loved her role as wedding planner – such a pity that she never seemed to meet anyone to marry herself.

She looked through the diary. Yes, she had everything covered up to Sunday 31st – which was Halloween of course – and knew that all arrangements made would go ahead and work like clockwork as usual. Connie's organisational skills were honed to perfection at this point in her career and all her support systems had been tried and tested over the years.

She checked to see what she had in store for the following week. First up was that Irish couple.

Tuesday November 2nd
at 2.30pm

Marriage of Vicky Hughes and Frank Proctor
Witnesses and guests: Tina Hughes and John Proctor

Reception at the Bellagio Hotel

Wedding chapel to be arranged on arrival in Vegas.

At Heathrow Airport Vicky and Tina Hughes were running frantically to the boarding gate. It was a long way from Terminal 1, where they had arrived from Dublin. They had ten more minutes to get to Terminal 5 where a shiny British Airways 777 was waiting to take them to McCarran International Airport, Las Vegas.

Finally reaching Gate 35, the two sat down in relief and waited to be called to board.

Vicky was fearful, and disappointed that her fiancé wasn't with them – she wasn't a good traveller and she'd have liked the security of his presence.

"I really hope Frank gets away tomorrow," she said, her emerald eyes peeking out widely through the attractive new fringe she'd had cut into the soft brunette curls that fell to her shoulders. "I didn't want to do all of the planning on my own!"

"You're not on your own," Tina assured her. "I'm here."

Vicky reached out and gave her daughter's hand a squeeze. Her words of comfort were sweet but unrealistic. Tina was more likely to be a liability than an asset. And Vicky knew that the minute her fiancé landed in Las Vegas, Tina's hackles would rise and it would be eggshells all the way after that. Vicky wished she could soothe her daughter's worries and concerns. She wished she was a bigger part of her life.

Tina turned on her iPod and Vicky looked at her in dismay. So much for company and support! Tina seldom communicated with her any more – she was always tweeting or Facebooking or listening to her iPod. Any technical device was more appealing than having an actual conversation with her mother. Vicky felt as though she had failed her, spending too many hours working since her husband, David, had left and earning as much as she could so that her daughter could have everything that her friends had. Maybe, if she had spent more time with her, she wouldn't be the way she was now. Always sombre and solemn in black – with tattoos and piercings which made her appear fierce and unlike the lovely little girl she used to be when her daddy was around.

Vicky went out of her mind when Tina got her first tattoo. It was a source of constant anxiety for her. She had to tell someone because her ex-husband wasn't interested in hearing about his daughter and it was during a conversation about Tina with her boss, Frank, that a relationship between them had started to develop. Frank was so sympathetic and understanding – their initial little chats after work turned into drinks in the Residency Club and quickly became dinner at least twice a week. It was such a delight to be with a man who could support her emotionally. So unlike her ex-husband.

Vicky had met David in her first year of commercial college. He was a student in the neighbouring Dublin Institute of Technology – studying architecture. They had been inseparable all the way through their college years, then she got a job as a secretary and married at twenty-one. Vicky never dreamed that there would ever be another man for her but, after twelve years of what she thought was a very happy and successful marriage, David announced one day out of the blue that he was leaving her. She was stunned beyond belief and fell into a deep depression that lasted for three years. Meanwhile, he was riding high on the Celtic Tiger property boom and quickly filled her shoes with a younger blonde woman who since had produced twin boys.

Vicky felt terribly for Tina who was marginalised by her father in favour of his new family. She blamed the birth of the twins for Tina's transformation into a Goth. It happened within days of their birth and Tina was still rebelling.

Frank Proctor shook hands with the bank manager and pulled his navy-blue linen jacket on over his pinstriped shirt. It had been a tense meeting, and warm and sticky in the office of the Bank of Ireland. Frank had a lot of pressures weighing down on him today – he was wondering if he was doing the right thing at all. Business wasn't good and hadn't been for some time and this wedding was enough to bring his blood pressure to boiling point.

He walked out onto Baggot Street and hurried down to the premises of his most popular restaurant. He had been in the business so long he couldn't remember a time when he wasn't involved in catering. As a teenager he used to wait on tables and dream of owning his own place. He was fortunate to get the position of commis chef in the King Sitric restaurant in Howth and that set him up with the know-how to move in the right circles when the time came to open his own place. The boom had given him the opportunity to expand and develop at a rate he had never dreamed he could. He had mixed with property developers and bankers who were only too keen to steer him into all sorts of schemes and investments that were now coming back to haunt him. If only he had concentrated on the restaurant business and kept away from property speculation! But everyone was doing it during the noughties and you didn't have anything to talk about if you weren't involved in it too. Now, pushing forty-two, he was in a mess and not just financially!

He came to the door of his restaurant and went inside, only to be greeted by the sight of his brother on the way out.

"Hey, John. What's up?"

"You said to be here an hour ago – I got tired of waiting. You asked me to get the rings – remember?"

Frank ran his fingers through his black mane which curled slightly at the ends where it reached the collar of his shirt. "Sorry, John – I forgot!" He didn't want to trouble John with his worries.

John Proctor shrugged and shook his dark-brown hair that also was longer than the norm for men. He was a ruggedly handsome man who fitted his 6 foot 3 inch frame squarely – the type who commanded a natural respect from other men. He was used to his brother's unreliable ways and this latest offence was merely one in a long list over the years.

"I've got to go home and pack – unless you've also forgotten that you're going to Las Vegas tomorrow?"

Frank shook his head. "No, of course not – I'll see you at the airport at eleven – okay?"

"I'll be there," John said.

John brushed past his brother, walked out onto Baggot Street and headed in the direction of Stephen's Green and his apartment. John had bought it the previous year on the advice of his older brother. Frank had been desperate to offload properties to increase his cash flow and John had a stash of cash in the bank from the previous two years' heavy gigging around the globe. Frank assured him that he was getting a bargain. Now he was really pleased that he had a place of his own and the views down the quays and over the River Liffey were spectacular.

John was happy with his decision to settle back in Ireland. He had lived a Bohemian life in his twenties, playing in all sorts of bands and shows. There was nothing to hold him in Ireland: his father was dead and he had an awkward relationship with his mother. Frank was always the golden boy in his mother's eyes and John felt that it gave him free rein to go off and pursue the life of a musician, whereas if he had been his mother's pet she would have wanted him to go into a solid reliable profession. Sometimes he felt that Frank had got the short straw, for all that favouritism came with a price. John couldn't remember his father. Frank had been six when he died and could still recall snippets of him but John was only three and couldn't honestly say that he remembered anything about him. Kieran Proctor was a merchant seaman who drank his way through his days on shore and offered little support or comfort to his poor wife. Bernadette Proctor scrubbed floors and took any job that she could get to put her boys through school and give them a good start. When Frank was set up as a chef she was happy enough to let John leave school early to pursue whatever career took his fancy, and if that was the life of a wandering musician she didn't care. As long as she had Frank to fuss over and make Sunday lunch for, then her life was fulfilled.

Now John was enjoying a less nomadic lifestyle, largely based in Dublin, but he still wasn't interested in putting down roots. He was a free spirit and wasn't in any rush to get married – if he ever would. He had moved in with a Japanese girl in Amsterdam when he was twenty-five and that had lasted three years. So far that was the longest he had spent in any relationship with the opposite sex. He usually spent months contentedly without any steady female company, usually while on tour, and then would fall into meeting someone when the mood took him. No, he wasn't in any rush to settle into a life of responsibility. He went with the flow and did whatever felt right at that time and this was how he intended to continue for the foreseeable future.

The British Airways aircraft rumbled down the runway and rose up and into the air.

Vicky leaned over and whispered in her daughter's ear, "Isn't it lovely, Tina?"

The teenager shrugged. They were sitting in spacious reclining seats – an upgrade from economy that Frank had insisted upon, which was going to make their ten-hour-plus journey really comfortable.

Vicky savoured the little luxuries she had come to experience since Frank and she became a couple. Her daughter didn't seem to have the same appreciation of her future stepfather. Even the World Traveller Class seats and extra pampering couldn't raise a smile on her daughter's face.

Tina had cried for hours and insisted on spending the weekend with her father in Limerick when she heard the news of her mother's forthcoming nuptials – but her father's new partner Maria was even less appealing than Frank. At least Frank flashed his cash regularly and she took it from him without batting an eye.

Vicky couldn't understand why Tina wasn't thrilled at the prospect of having a man about the house again. Vicky had her own demons from her childhood which brought her pain. Her own father had died when she was only seven years of age. It was no wonder that her relationship with her own mother was so intense and in its final years so strained. She wished that her mother had told her more about her father, but she had felt that it was okay to brush aside an entire part of the family's history, leaving Vicky always longing to find out what her life would have been like if he had lived longer. Maybe then she would have had brothers and sisters and Tina would have more cousins and extended family. It was one of the reasons why she was so keen to begin again with Frank.

Frank went over to the till and had a look to see the takings. He was lucky that the turnover hadn't dropped too badly – he would be in the soup without the cash flow from the business. Twenty apartments and houses around the city had his name on them and half were without tenants – the other half brought in well below what was needed to pay the mortgages. He had kept this mounting debt secret from his fiancée. He didn't think that Vicky would be able to cope with the weight of his worries. He would be on the plane with her now only for the meeting demanded by his bank manager – the same man who had encouraged him to borrow cash so liberally a few years back.

He hadn't wanted to travel to Las Vegas to get married – it had been Vicky's idea, but when he realised that by doing so he would be able to save on the expense of the occasion, he changed his mind. Two weeks was too long to be spending away from the business at this crucial point but she had managed to convince him to stay long enough to have their honeymoon as well when it occurred to him that, if he was lucky, the trip to Vegas could solve all his problems in one swoop.

Then there was the matter of his mother's absence from the occasion – at first Frank thought she would be so dreadfully hurt that he would have to insist on getting married in Ireland, but he was surprised when she took the practical stand and encouraged him to save his money. He wondered if she had an idea that something was amiss with her once-affluent son's finances. She was no fool when it came to money. Besides, it was on her insistence that Frank had hotly pursued a wife and Vicky was there in his restaurant working as the temporary maitre d' at the right time. Frank realised that part of the reason his mother wanted him to get married so badly was her desire for grandchildren. And Vicky was so feminine and gentle with her pretty little-girl-lost appeal that he had no need to look any further.

The pressures were mounting so heavily on Frank that his temples were aching. He went over to the bar and poured himself a quick brandy. There was so much to do before the next day.

If you enjoyed this chapter from
4 a.m. in Las Vegas by Michelle Jackson,
why not order the full book online
@ www.poolbeg.com

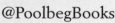